Shadow Lives

Michael Evans

First published 2022
by Rowanvale Books Ltd
The Gate
Keppoch Street
Roath
Cardiff
CF24 3JW
www.rowanvalebooks.com

A CIP catalogue record for this book is available from the British
Library.
Paperback ISBN: 978-1-914422-08-9

Chapter One

The Day Life Changed

Monday 1st July

The biker, dressed in black leather and a dark grey helmet, waited round the corner on a single yellow line. He was perfectly still, though the 650cc BMW engine was running. Pedestrians walked past him without looking. Behind him, traffic on the Embankment heading for Parliament Square was building up. It was 8:12 a.m.

Five minutes went by. The biker glanced into his right wing mirror and spotted a Jaguar saloon turning from the Embankment into the road. He checked the registration and tightened his lips. As the Jaguar passed him, he turned his head slightly. One passenger, sitting on the right-hand side at the back, reading *The Times*. Female, smartly dressed, auburn hair. She was focused on the newspaper and was not aware of the biker. Her driver did glance at him but was unbothered. His mind was elsewhere— already at his favourite café, where he'd be going for breakfast once his passenger was delivered.

The biker moved off slowly and followed the Jaguar as it turned left. The street was almost empty of people. One woman was walking a dog on the opposite pavement. No other cars. The Jaguar slowed down by a large building, waiting for garage doors to slide up. As the driver began to turn left down the slope into the underground car park at Thames House, headquarters of the security service MI5, the biker accelerated.

The woman in the back of the car briefly lifted her eyes from the newspaper and saw the rapidly approaching motorbike. Her mouth opened. But at that moment, the black-leathered biker, now armed with a modified Glock 19 pistol in his right hand, fired four .50-calibre rounds, each travelling towards the intended target at 1,400 feet per second. The first was blunted by the bulletproof glass, transforming the window into a kaleidoscope of shattered lines and circles. The woman's face disappeared from view behind the rippling mess of glass. The next three rounds penetrated the smashed window with explosive force.

The Jaguar driver slammed his foot on the accelerator, and the garage doors closed behind him. As the biker sped away, he heard a screech of brakes and a crash from behind the garage doors.

Three seconds passed. The biker turned left at the end and then right, swerving recklessly across the Embankment traffic lanes, heading west. He drove through a red light and crossed Vauxhall Bridge, now travelling at sixty miles per hour. Staff in offices on the south side of the bridge, overlooking the Thames at 85 Vauxhall Cross, home of MI5's sister agency, the secret intelligence service, MI6, were too busy on their computers to notice.

The biker sped through red lights a second time. He heard the first police siren but it wasn't close.

***

The woman passenger in the government Jaguar lay on the back seat, her face and hair covered in blood. The driver was badly concussed and his right leg was broken. He couldn't turn his head to see whether his passenger was alive. The car was filled with smoke.

A tumult of MI5 security guards came rushing into the garage, guns raised. They wrenched open the front and passenger doors, but before handling the driver and passenger, they checked everywhere inside the car, looking for any sign of an explosive device. MI5's emergency alert alarm pulsated throughout the building.

***

Rollie Gibson's mobile phone rang at 9:05 a.m. Number 10 ringing.

"Colonel Gibson. You're needed here as soon as," the caller said without introducing himself. "COBRA at nine thirty."

Colonel Rollie Gibson, an impressive-looking man with a shaved head and prominent cheekbones that made his navy blue eyes appear more pronounced, strode to his office. He grabbed his laptop, a black contacts book with an elastic band wrapped round it to keep the middle pages from falling out, and a notebook. He shoved them into his backpack. His custom-built racing bike, designed to his specifications by a small Oxford family firm, was leaning against the wall in the hall. A green and black helmet hung from the handlebars. He opened the front door of his apartment block in Westminster, picked up the ultra-light bike and carried it down the steps to the road. He was at the security gates in front of Downing Street in three minutes. He showed his pass to the policemen on duty and was waved in.

***

The black-leathered biker had driven fifty-five miles along country roads in Kent and Sussex before stopping outside a mobile home park located in an old chalk quarry, about two miles from the coast. He parked the bike at the back of a small mobile home in a bad state of repair. Inside, he took out his phone and made a call.

"Nul," he said in a low voice.

Then he removed his helmet and went to the bathroom. He, too, had a shaved head, but there was nothing impressive about his looks. His face was unshaven, his nose was blunted and his eyes were an unremarkable light brown. He had thin lips and a small chin. The one feature that stood out was the shape of his face, which was almost perfectly round. It was the sort of face that might have looked more appropriate on a short, stocky body, perhaps a little overweight. But the biker, now ready to relax after the completion of his mission, was skinny. Narrow shoulders, thin chest, about five foot ten. You'd never have guessed he was a former corporal in the Royal Logistic Corps.

***

Around the oak table in the basement of the Cabinet Office in Whitehall, nine men and three women had assembled for an emergency COBRA meeting. Prime Minister Jonathan Ford, who had been in the job for only ten months, had entered the room last. He was a tall man with thinning hair, which seemed to bother him; he was always trying to coax the strands into some form of order. Unlike his predecessor in Number 10, he liked to be smart at all times. He was never seen without a formal tie and wore a middle-range expensive suit, always navy blue.

He had a fairly brusque approach to leadership. He always said he welcomed different views from his cabinet but generally made it clear his way would be the chosen path. He had a reasonable majority in the House of Commons, nearly sixty, and often reminded his ministers of their obligation to remain loyal both to their party mandate and to him as their prime minister. He had chaired COBRA meetings before but not for a security emergency such as this. He was aware that the other attendees at the COBRA meeting would be looking to him to be decisive and reassuring.

When he entered the room, everyone stood up, as the cabinet secretary had discreetly informed them to do. Ford liked his ministers and advisers to acknowledge him as the leader and considered standing up when he entered a room a necessary mark of respect.

He thanked them and sat down in the slightly larger middle chair. Foreign Secretary Elizabeth Gantry, only five foot five but with aristocratic poise, sat to his left, and Home Secretary Lawrence Fenwick, a young politician with well-cared-for good looks and a burning ambition to be prime minister, was on his right.

The anomaly at the table was Colonel Rollie Gibson. He represented no department. Nor did he represent any of the armed forces. The Chief of the Defence Staff and Director Special Forces were present, but neither of them had any warmth or enthusiasm for the colonel sitting quietly at the end of the table.

The prime minister opened the proceedings.

"I will leave Commander Brooks to brief on the details, but this morning an assassination attempt was made on the life of Geraldine Hammer, MI5's director of counter-espionage," he said, looking around the table.

Harry Brooks, commander of the Metropolitan Police Counter Terrorism Command, nodded slightly.

"She is injured but miraculously survived," Ford said.

"We know very little at this stage," the prime minister went on. "But it is the opinion of the DG that this was not necessarily a one-off incident. There could be more targets. We don't know who is behind the attack or who the next victim might be, but JTAC is now reviewing threat levels. I anticipate the level will remain at 'severe', unless we get specific intelligence of another planned attack."

Ford glanced at the director-general of MI5, George Trench, an imposing man with thick eyebrows and the darkest of brown eyes. Trench had spoken to the head of the Joint Terrorism Analysis Centre a few minutes earlier, and he nodded, although a final decision had yet to be made. JTAC was housed in the same building as MI5 headquarters and led by a senior member of his staff.

There was a brief pause. Major-General Thomas Lockridge, Director Special Forces, immaculately attired in a tailored charcoal grey suit and yellow-striped tie, looked down the table at Rollie Gibson, but his face remained expressionless. Colonel Gibson knew what the glance meant. He and General Lockridge were well acquainted but they didn't get on—for good reason.

The prime minister asked Commander Brooks to take over. A tall, slim man with questioning eyes and slightly hunched shoulders, Brooks provided the COBRA members with the barest of additional detail of the shooting incident at the rear entrance of Thames House.

"There were four shots. Fortunately, Dr Hammer had looked up and spotted the approaching gunman before he fired his first shot. She ducked right down. It saved her life. The gunman was moving fast but managed to shoot pretty accurately. He was no amateur. He was waiting for her, so he knew she was coming. There is absolutely no question in my mind that the gunman was specifically targeting Geraldine Hammer."

The second person to glance in Colonel Gibson's direction was the foreign secretary. Elizabeth Gantry momentarily tightened her lips but quickly looked away again. She knew the prime minister trusted Gibson, probably more than anyone else in the room. But she, like General Lockridge, privately disapproved of his presence at the COBRA meeting, even though he was a Foreign Office asset. He was her responsibility.

Colonel Rollie Gibson—fifteen years as an officer in the Parachute Regiment, three years with the Special Reconnaissance Regiment and six years with the SAS—was the commander of the Foreign Office's unofficial "Shadow Force", a small quasi-mercenary group of ex-military, created to provide an alternative option for the prime minister in circumstances where neither the SAS nor other sections of the armed forces were deemed appropriate or lawful.

Aged forty-seven, unmarried, supremely fit and a veteran of five wars, Colonel Gibson, MC, DSO, had resigned his commission in the army to pursue a new career in the civilian world. His talents, and his contacts book of equally experienced ex-military men and women, had remained in high demand.

General Lockridge, in command of one of the world's most feared and respected special forces organisations, resented his former colleague. He considered him an unwelcome rival.

After Commander Brooks had spoken, Ford asked George Trench for his views.

"It's not the sort of terrorism we've got used to," he said, keeping his eyes on the prime minister. "I doubt there's a Middle East connection. Why would they target Geraldine? The usual suspects wouldn't know her name."

"Russian?" Rollie Gibson suggested at the end of the table.

Trench glared at him. "No evidence, not yet."

"But could there be a Russian connection?" Ford asked.

"We're checking everything," Trench said.

"It was definitely a professional hit," Commander Brooks interrupted.

"Sounds Russian," Colonel Gibson muttered.

Everyone except the prime minister gave him an exasperated look.

"Thank you, DG," Ford said. "C? Any input?"

Sir Edward Farthing, chief of MI6, spoke so quietly the other COBRA attendees all had to lean forward to hear him. Sir Edward, known like all his predecessors as C, had thick, sandy-coloured hair and a slightly flushed face which could have suggested overenthusiasm for fine wines. But he was a disciplined man with a long career in MI6, broken only for a two-year period as a counter-espionage adviser at the Home Office. His flushed face was due to windswept walks in his beloved Norfolk, where his family home sat perched on a hill a few hundred yards from the sea.

"Early days," he said, "but Gibson is right, this could be another Russian job. Our head of station in Moscow has been warning for weeks of a new Russian intelligence unit, set up for overseas hits. Even more dedicated and ruthless than the GRU assassination unit we have all come to know."

His remark caused such a stir around the room that Ford had to call them all to order.

"I've not seen any CXs about this new unit," he queried, flicking back a strand of hair which had fallen on his forehead.

When he became prime minister, he had told Elizabeth Gantry that he expected MI6 to be more forthcoming about early signs of new threat developments in their classified CX reports. It rankled to know he'd been left out of the loop again.

"No, Prime Minister, we were holding back for a general Whitehall circulation until we gathered more hard evidence," Sir Edward said.

"I need hardly remind you, C, that after Skripal we need to know everything and anything about Russian GRU intelligence activities."

GRU, Russia's military intelligence service, was regarded as the number one threat in the espionage business, with a long record of assassinations. The Novichok poisoning attack on Sergei Skripal and his daughter Yulia in Salisbury in 2018 had become a benchmark for Russian espionage outrages that had followed elsewhere in the world.

Vladimir Putin had made it clear that traitors to the Russian motherland would be tracked down and punished. Skripal, a former colonel in GRU, had worked as a double agent for MI6 and was caught. He was sentenced to thirteen years for high treason in August 2006. His luck changed when, in a Cold War-style spy swap, he and three other Russian nationals convicted of espionage were freed in 2010 in exchange for ten Russian agents arrested in the United States. Skripal and his daughter flew out of Moscow and set up home in the Wiltshire town. But his betrayal was never forgiven by Putin's Kremlin. A roving GRU espionage and assassination squad called Unit 29155 had been dispatched to Salisbury to take revenge on their former colleague.

"So you think there's another hit squad doing the rounds?" Ford asked.

"It's possible," Sir Edward said, even more quietly.

"Does this unit have a name?" Elizabeth Gantry asked. She had also been taken aback by the MI6 chief's revelation.

"Unit Zero, we believe."

"Right," Ford said, "I want the works on this unit, and I want you all back here tomorrow, nine a.m. C, can you stay behind a moment?"

The COBRA members walked out in grim silence, leaving the chief of the Secret Intelligence Service to his bollocking.

Chapter Two
The Second Attempt

Back at his flat, Rollie Gibson summoned his team.

Always ready for action at forty-five minutes' notice, the five members of his elite squad were sitting in his small Westminster flat by 11 a.m.

The first to arrive was Seamus Murphy, ex-sergeant in the SAS who had also served a two-year secondment with the Army's Special Reconnaissance Regiment, a unique covert surveillance unit formed for Northern Ireland missions during the war with the Provisional IRA. It had remained operational after the Troubles were over and was used in other theatres of conflict. Seamus was slightly scruffy and had grey eyes that never seemed to blink. At thirty-nine, he was of average height, tough, wiry and always cool. Nothing fazed him.

George Walker followed him into the flat. A retired Parachute Regiment veteran, also a sergeant, he looked like a professional boxer, with a squashed nose and a large, protruding chin. But it was rugby, not boxing which had reshaped his face. He had played as a prop for the army team for five years. Like every member of Shadow Force, George had served so many tours in Iraq and Afghanistan, as well as Sierra Leone and Kosovo that he had lost count. He was forty-five.

Major Tim Plews was the next to arrive. A former SAS squadron commander, he had been attached to MI6 for three years and was the quietest member of the group. He had been commissioned into the Parachute Regiment but had transferred to the

Intelligence Corps after three years with the SAS. It was an unusually varied career, which was why MI6 had marked him out for undercover intelligence work. He had been given a roving role and had served as an MI6 officer in the Baltics. Forty-two and always well-groomed, he wasn't sociable but not unfriendly. He preferred to get on with the job without resorting to banter, unlike so many of his army peers.

Former Corporal Rose "Plucky" Wentworth arrived soon after Tim. She, too, possessed a variety of talents. Once one of the top communications specialists with the Royal Corps of Signals, she had also served with the Special Reconnaissance Regiment and knew Seamus well. They'd struck up a firm friendship working together on covert missions. Rose was thirty-seven and not fussed about how she looked, but she was naturally pretty with short, dark-brown, curly hair. Despite her fierce loyalty to the army, she had ended her military career in a state of total exhaustion. She was happy to be back, albeit in a paramilitary, non-official role.

Last to arrive, with apologies, was Sam Cook, a mountain of a man who had served as a bodyguard for a former Director Special Forces for four years. Aged forty-six, he'd had a long career in the SAS and had been one of the regiment's ablest non-commissioned officers, a sergeant with a legendary reputation. He spoke fluent Russian. Sam's presence in every room and every group was overwhelming because of his size. Perhaps to counter his physical impact, he invariably had a grin on his face. He was easy company and almost instantly likeable.

"We're on standby, no orders as yet," Gibson told his team.

His elite group, codenamed Pedestal but known in the top hierarchy of government by its nickname, Shadow Force, had last been used in the Democratic

Republic of Congo, when a thirty-year-old Welsh missionary had been kidnapped by the fearsome Lord's Resistance Army, led by Joseph Kony, one of the world's most dangerous individuals. An SAS unit had been sent to rescue the hapless missionary but failed to find any trace of him. They had a firefight with a Lord's Resistance Army patrol but returned to their headquarters in Hereford without completing their mission.

Following a desperate appeal by the Welshman to the British government in a propaganda video distributed by Kony's gangsters, Foreign Secretary Elizabeth Gantry had reluctantly contacted Colonel Gibson. Shadow Force, so named because it didn't officially exist, left for the Congo and after three weeks in some of the most hostile jungles in Africa, found the kidnapped missionary alive in a cellar in a large house on the outskirts of Kampala, capital of Uganda. The reputation of Shadow Force within the small circle of people who knew of its existence soared. Every national newspaper in the UK reported that the Welsh missionary had been rescued by the SAS.

Shadow Force had been set up by a previous incumbent at the Foreign Office. They were an alternative option to the SAS or SBS, the Special Boat Service. While the SAS and SBS also operated in secrecy, the government was accountable to parliament for their actions. Shadow Force was accountable to no one, except themselves. If something went wrong, especially if it involved fatalities or injuries, neither the foreign secretary nor the defence secretary was held responsible. If a successful mission became public knowledge, ministers were not slow at hinting that the "Who Dares Wins" boys from Hereford were behind it. The SAS received all the glory even if it was not involved.

Shadow Force was considered a key element of Britain's security options because of the increasing threats posed by Russia and China. After the coronavirus pandemic of 2020 and its lingering dangers in 2021, there had been a government review of all security and intelligence. Both Russia and China had exploited the pandemic with a mass dissemination of fake stories about the inability of the West to cope with the economic and social impact of the virus. Cyber attacks had risen sharply.

Moscow, under a leader granted the right to stay in office until 2036, now posed the gravest threat. GRU, the Russian military intelligence agency, had been highly active since the pandemic, with suspected assassinations in the Netherlands and Belgium.

Moscow had made a number of warnings about counter-espionage actions to be taken against Russian "diplomats" stationed in Europe. The prime minister at the time had wanted Shadow Force to be permanently on alert but to remain covered by the highest secrecy classification. When Jonathan Ford was elected and was informed of the special unit, he accepted the justification for it and made sure his choice of foreign secretary felt the same way. Elizabeth Gantry gave the prime minister the support he was seeking, but privately feared that government use of a secret unofficial unit was riddled with political risks.

The news of the attempted assassination of MI5's director of counter-espionage had not yet broken. An early edition of the *London Evening Standard* included a report of a shooting in Westminster but there was no confirmation from Scotland Yard. An elderly woman who had been walking her dog close by the alleged scene of the shooting was quoted as saying she had heard a car backfiring, but confessed she had witnessed nothing dramatic; she said she was partially deaf and had forgotten to put on her glasses before leaving her flat.

Home Secretary Lawrence Fenwick, who generally despised the press and avoided speaking to reporters unless he was forced to do so by Downing Street, had spoken to the Metropolitan Police Commissioner Dame Mary Abelard about imposing a news blackout. But Dame Mary, who was a stickler for doing what was right and always spoke in formal, precise terms, had advised against such a move. It would never last, she argued. The name of the gunman's target, however, could be kept secret because her role at MI5 was covered by the government's D-Notice Committee guidelines, which provided advice to newspaper editors and broadcasters on issues of national security. Naming members of the intelligence services, apart from the heads of each, was taboo. Dame Mary, backed up by the Home Office permanent secretary, won the day. A statement had to be made.

***

The black-leathered biker was sitting in his rented mobile home. There had still been no reports of a shooting in London. When news did break, on Sky TV, he leant forward towards the small screen in front of him. The presenter announced "breaking news" and gave a dramatic account of multiple shots being fired from a motorbike at a car near Thames House. The report was short on detail, but the presenter made much of the fact that Thames House was the HQ of MI5 and suggested that the shooting was connected in some way to the agency. No information had been given about the identity of the victim, the presenter said.

Sky's crime correspondent, Sandy Hall, was asked what extra information he could provide. The biker's face twitched slightly.

"According to police sources, the victim of the shooting was injured but survived the attack," Hall said. "The victim has been taken to University College Hospital. Officials there have refused to give any bulletin on the seriousness of the injuries. At this stage we don't know even know if it's a man or woman. But it's a fact that a lot of senior members of MI5 are women."

The biker stood up. He muttered something under his breath and left the mobile home, carrying his helmet. He started his motorbike, turned right out of the quarry and accelerated fast back in the direction of London.

The police were already building up a picture of the gunman. Debriefed in her private room at University College Hospital, Geraldine Hammer had recalled a surprising amount of detail. With just a glance at the approaching motorbike, she had known instinctively that he was coming after her. She described the motorbike. She told two Scotland Yard officers sitting beside her bed that the roar of the bike indicated at least a 500cc engine. The gunman had been all in black, except for his dark grey helmet, she said. She assumed the outfit was leather. He looked around five foot eight, slimly built. The gun, she said, could have been a Glock.

The most crucial piece of intelligence was the registration. Even as she'd cowered under the showering glass, she had lifted her head to peer at the fleeing motorbike through the shattered glass on the driver's side. She saw a B, a D, and one, possibly two, 3s.

Every police force in the Thames Valley area, and in Sussex, Kent and Surrey, had been alerted and warned that the bike would be heading out of London. But by the time the alert was made, more than an hour and a half had gone by since the shooting. By then, the biker was already settled into the mobile home in the abandoned quarry in Sussex, the bike hidden from view from the road leading to Seaford to the east and Newhaven to the west. Half an hour later, he was back on the road heading for London.

The biker passed numerous police cars moving fast, with their sirens wailing, on the opposite side of the road. He wondered if they were looking for his BMW motorbike. He never made the mistake of underestimating the police, but he had confidence in his ability to evade them. He was also fairly sure that the driver of the government Jaguar would have been too occupied to make a note of his registration, and the woman in the back would have been too shocked or too injured to have noticed anything that could be useful to the police.

***

Geraldine Hammer was tired. Doctors had removed all the glass in her face and head, but she was covered in cuts, some of them deep. She had been given eight stitches and her face was a mess, but her injuries were mostly superficial. The bulletproof window and armoured plating in the door had saved her life. She wanted to leave the hospital straightaway, but both the doctors and her boss, George Trench, were adamant that she needed to rest, at least for a few hours.

She lay back and considered the implications of the attempt on her life. She had already suffered one trauma in her life. Her marriage had broken up after nineteen years. She had married Paul Blake, an academic, at twenty-seven, and at first, her work had not interfered too much with their life together. But after their children, Janie and William, had been born, she'd moved to counter-terrorism. It was three years of intense, high-pressure activity, and she'd seen little of her husband or her children. Weekends were rarely spared. The marriage hadn't survived.

Now forty-eight, she had a job she loved. She had joined MI5 after reading philosophy, politics and economics at Girton College, Cambridge, and had served in counter-espionage during her early career. As director of the branch, she had immense responsibilities, particularly with Russian spying and Moscow-inspired sabotage activities on a scale not seen since the Cold War. She trusted her deputy, also a woman, but she wanted to get back to the office to help in the search for her attacker and pursue every piece of intelligence that might point to a wider security threat.

At Cambridge, Geraldine had flirted with the idea of going into politics. She had always been a confident speaker and had quickly impressed her tutors with her well-argued essays. She was a star undergraduate and worked harder than most of her year. But in the second year at Girton, two events took place which led to her changing her mind about politics. She fell in love with an undergraduate from Corpus Christi College, and soon after, she joined the Labour Party, persuaded by her boyfriend that socialism was the only way forward. But she quickly became disillusioned with the hard-left socialist voices of those who attended the meetings. The undergraduate she had fallen for was among the most radical. While she'd initially enjoyed the chance to enter the debates, she found the atmosphere and the unswerving loyalty to the socialist cause too harsh. It affected her relationship.

When they'd met, it had been a classic beating-heart moment. He was called John George, studying history, a six-foot-three rower with floppy blond hair and a slim physique. She couldn't stop herself from planning a future with this man. She was intoxicated. But the political meetings began to get in the way. Her main PPE tutor had warned her that her previously unblemished academic record was beginning to slip. He said he had seen it too often: distractions, whether from relationships or from other college activities, undermining a good degree. Geraldine had been marked down as a potential First-Class degree undergraduate. Her growing antipathy for the political meetings and the rows it caused with her good-looking boyfriend brought the matter to a head. He broke it off before she had a chance to explain the way she was feeling. She still loved him, but his personality had changed, from carefree and open-minded to fanatical.

The ending of the relationship had been hard for Geraldine. It was the first time she had wanted to commit herself fully to a man. She was twenty-two, and the physical experience of loving someone totally had so absorbed her life that everything else—including her driving ambition to get a First—had been pushed to one side. She never told her parents. They had assumed from her academic achievements throughout her schooldays that she would excel at Cambridge and complete the three years with a First. It took a few weeks, but finally, she decided she couldn't let herself or her parents down by ending up with a Second or Third.

She duly won a First with distinction and resolved to apply for a fast-track entry into the Civil Service. She proceeded swiftly through the interviews, but—on a day she would always remember—she was told that a government official had requested to see her, and she was asked to attend the appointment at a government building next to Admiralty Arch. The official she met was a man in his forties who started the interview by praising her for her academic qualifications and asking why she wanted to join the Civil Service.

She replied by telling him of her abandoned notion of becoming a politician and her growing realisation that she wanted a public service role where she might have influence without having to stand on a soapbox and shout. The official was amused. He said he had a job in mind which might suit her talents. Government work, slightly different from what she may have had in mind but definitely discreet. Geraldine expressed interest and asked which government department he was referring to. He replied that all would come clear but first she would need to go through certain procedures to ensure she was suitable. The procedures, he said, would take some time. He encouraged her to accept what he said would be an opportunity to do valuable and stimulating government work.

Her future employers only confirmed she had been tapped to join the security service, MI5, after her initial interview sessions were completed. When she passed the first stage, she was told she would have to undergo a lengthy security-vetting period. She was asked not to talk about her new job to anyone. If pressed by friends or family, she was advised she could make a general reference to the Ministry of Defence or the Home Office, or just say she was joining the Civil Service.

Geraldine never really had to be told she was going to work for MI5. She had suspected it from the moment the official began interviewing her in the building next to Admiralty Arch. It had taken her by surprise because she hadn't considered at any time applying for a job with the security and intelligence services. But more than surprised, she'd felt excited.

Now, here she was, lying in a hospital bed. It was the first time in her career that her life had been put in grave danger, and she was angry.

She knew Harry Brooks would be leading the investigation, but he was a straightforward policeman who had been promoted to head Scotland Yard's Counter-Terrorism Command, much to the surprise of some of his senior colleagues. Geraldine liked him and they worked well together, but she had always felt he had shortcomings. As she'd told Grace Redmayne, her deputy, he lacked imagination.

She had asked to be kept informed of any developments. Every police patrol within a hundred miles of London would be looking for a motorbike with a black-leathered rider heading out of the capital.

Geraldine closed her eyes and imagined her would-be assassin. What would he be doing? Where would he be going? Would he have stopped off anywhere? And most importantly, would he have heard the news on Sky, and now every news bulletin on radio and television, that the target of the shooting had survived and was receiving treatment at University College Hospital? She cursed Sky for breaking the news. Surely those facts should have been covered by a D-Notice? Someone in the Met Police had given away this precious information to Sky's crime correspondent without thinking of the potential consequences.

She opened her eyes and grabbed her phone, wincing in pain at the sudden movement.

"Harry, it's Geraldine. What if the gunman is heading back to London?" she asked her police colleague.

"Surely—" Harry Brooks spluttered.

"If he picked up on the news, he could try again," she replied, interrupting him.

"Jesus, I guess," he said.

She rang home and spoke to her children, who had been taken out of school in order to come and visit her. She reassured them that she was recovering well and asked to speak to the au pair.

"Marie, don't bring the children today. I'll ring you when it's a better time, ok?"

Twenty minutes later, Commander Brooks rang back. "Geraldine, the hospital's surrounded. Armed cops everywhere. Two outside your room. Give them a wave. I hope you're wrong, but we're ready if the bastard has a second go."

***

At Thames House, a small team of analysts was trawling through the security service's database of known and suspected international terrorists and state-sponsored killers. Russian connections were top of the list. Under the watchful eye of Grace Redmayne, a serious-looking thirty-eight-year-old woman with thick-lens spectacles, the team had been working at full stretch ever since the shooting at the rear of their building.

Redmayne's secret weapon was the brilliant Jasper Cornfield, only twenty-nine, a graduate of Balliol College, Oxford. He had a mass of black hair which usually flopped over his piercing blue eyes. He had only been with MI5 for four years, after a brief period in publishing, but his intellect and encyclopaedic mind had proved invaluable when hunting for terrorist or espionage suspects.

The Met came up with fifty-four names of motorbike owners with registration plates that included B, D and 3. All the names were put through MI5's database. Only one name came up.

Joseph Paine. A former corporal in the Royal Logistic Corps. Aged thirty-two. One incident in which he had been photographed shouting at a rally outside a mosque in Birmingham and talking animatedly to a Muslim cleric known to espouse dangerously radical views. In the photo, Paine had a long beard. He wasn't suspected of planning anything linked to terrorism, but his army background and apparent familiarity with the cleric, who had been on MI5's database for four years, were considered justification for adding his name to the "persons of interest" section.

Corporal Paine had been discharged from the army after getting into a fight with three other soldiers, one of whom was seriously injured. A check on his internet habits had uncovered an interest in Islamic activities, especially in Afghanistan. He had been in the database for fourteen months, although no recent activities had been logged. Paine owned a BMW motorbike, registration BFD 331.

"Got him," Jasper Cornfield told Grace.

At that moment there was an alert from GCHQ, the government communications headquarters outside Cheltenham in Gloucestershire. The briefest of suspicious phone calls had been picked up by the signals intelligence centre at around 9:25 a.m. The call was from somewhere in East Sussex to an unidentified line in Moscow. Only one word had been spoken.

"Nul."

***

Paine was in Streatham, southeast London, outside a row of lock-up garages. There was no one around. He opened the one on the far right and pushed his BMW bike into the darkness. Five minutes later, he emerged wearing a dark green anorak, jeans, heavy boots and a grey woollen hat, pulled over his ears. He was carrying a large backpack. He was clean-shaven, his round face pink from the rapid about-turn journey back into London.

**

"Nul is Russian for zero," the prime minister was told after he had been informed of the GCHQ snippet of signals intelligence.

"So, if that's our man, Gibson was right."

Ford told his private office to get Sir Edward Farthing on the phone.

Chapter Three
Shadow Force Steps In

Joseph Paine stood absolutely still but his eyes were constantly moving, scanning his surroundings. Round the corner from where he was standing was University College Hospital. One of the busiest hospitals in London. He had seen half a dozen police cars around the front entrance. Someone smart had figured out he might be back in London. His second attempt at killing his target was going to be more challenging. But he would find a way.

Despite his military training, he was nervous. The message he had received two weeks earlier had been brutally clear: the woman was to be eliminated. The repercussions of failure would be terminal.

Paine had been a hired assassin since leaving the army. Although he had served in the Royal Logistic Corps as a mechanic, he had always enjoyed guns and excelled on the firing ranges. He became one of the best shots in the corps. He had successfully carried out one mission, fatally shooting a low-level gangster involved in a family dispute in south London. But this assignment was different. He had been contacted by a courier who had handed him an envelope containing £5,000 in £50 notes. There was also a photograph of a woman, slightly blurred; a name, a date, a car registration, a grid reference, and a time. Whoever had contracted him had done his homework.

A subsequent couriered envelope contained a small piece of paper with a phone number and the briefest of instructions, written in capital letters: RING NUL WHEN MISSION COMPLETE. An additional £5,000 would then be paid.

Paine was in a dilemma. He didn't know how badly the woman had been injured. The bulletproof glass had resisted the full force of the first round but she could have been covered in deadly splinters from subsequent rounds. Jagged shards of glass could have resulted in serious injuries to the face and head. Either way, she would need to stay in hospital for some time. But what if the doctors, on police advice, decided to move her to another hospital? He needed to act fast.

He had returned to London after a speedy one-hour drive up the M23. The woman would only have been in the hospital for a maximum of two and a half hours. Chances were good that she would still be there, receiving treatment.

Paine moved away from the shop doorway where he had been standing and stepped off the pavement. Euston Road, a few yards away to his right, was busy with traffic.

A black Land Rover Discovery with tinted windows screeched to a halt, nearly hitting him. As he hastily retreated back to the pavement, a huge man dressed in a dark blue roll-necked sweater opened the rear passenger door. The man grabbed Paine round the neck and forced him into the car. The Land Rover accelerated away so fast the tyres squealed for more than ten seconds.

There were a lot of people in the side road, all potential witnesses to the violent kidnap. But when subsequently interviewed by the police, they gave varying accounts. One couple insisted the kidnapped man was black. Another witness, a middle-aged man with glasses, said he thought it was just an accident; he hadn't spotted anyone climbing out of the Land Rover. None of them could remember the registration.

Corporal Joseph Paine was in a state of total shock. He could hardly breathe; the huge man sitting next to him still had his massive left forearm around his neck. There were two other people in the car. The driver was a woman and the passenger next to her was a scruffy bloke with a baseball cap round the wrong way. He didn't turn round once.

Paine gripped the forearm around his neck and tried to ease it away from his Adam's apple. But he achieved nothing. The huge man maintained the hold as Paine struggled, choked gasps coming from his mouth. No one in the car seemed to care.

The driver slowed down and joined the traffic on Euston Road, heading for the Westway. After ten minutes, when Paine's face began to turn purple, the mountain of a man relaxed and let his arm fall loosely on the corporal's shoulder.

Paine coughed and spluttered. He took huge breaths, convulsing in coughing fits as his lungs took in the air. The scruffy man in the front still didn't look round. No one spoke.

"Who the fuck are you?" Paine shouted after his chest had stopped heaving.

He got no reply.

"What the fuck's going on?" Paine looked at the mountain man next to him and peered at the driver in the mirror. She kept her eyes firmly on the road ahead.

"Where are you taking me? Where the fuck are you taking me?" Paine tried again.

Still no response.

He tried to move away from the giant body next to him, but suddenly the arm around his shoulders returned to the neck hold. Not as tight as before, but clearly a warning. Paine slumped in the seat and stopped talking.

"Bastards," he muttered. Quietly this time.

The big man gave him a menacing stare.

There was silence for a few minutes.

Then Paine said, "I would have succeeded the second time."

That made Seamus Murphy in the front passenger seat grin from ear to ear. Even the driver, who had been focused solely on weaving through the traffic, gave a hint of a smile. Rose "Plucky" Wentworth rarely showed emotion. Her military career had put lines on her forehead and made her forget what it was like to laugh and joke. She had been called "Plucky" ever since she removed a bag containing a bomb from outside the gates of a Protestant primary school in Belfast, placed it in a heavy-duty wheeled dustbin and pushed it calmly to dead ground behind a disused factory. The bomb never went off.

"You didn't give me a chance," Paine said.

"Shut your mouth," Sam Cook, the third member of the group, said without looking at the passenger next to him.

Shadow Force had been called in as soon as the alert had gone out that the gunman could be heading back to London. Rollie Gibson had received the call from a senior Foreign Office official called Jim Petherwick, director-general of defence and intelligence. He was the main point man with MI6 and GCHQ, both of which were part of the foreign secretary's political remit. Petherwick, a humourless fifty-seven-year-old who had served as ambassador in Kabul, Islamabad and Belarus, was the only official at the Foreign Office designated to have contact with the commander of Shadow Force. The foreign secretary herself had neither reason nor desire to dirty her fingers by personally communicating with Colonel Gibson and his team.

Elizabeth Gantry had been informed by the prime minister's private office that there was a special opportunity for Gibson's team to operate separately from the Metropolitan Police in the hunt for Geraldine Hammer's would-be assassin. Petherwick had put Gibson on red alert and informed him that the gunman, now identified as Corporal Joseph Paine, was suspected to be on his way back to London for a second attempt at killing Dr Hammer.

"Colonel, we need this gunman, and I don't mean in the custody of the Met," Petherwick had said.

Nothing would appear in writing. Nothing on officially-headed notepaper. This was to be an extra-judicial mission to grab the gunman. The details were left to Gibson.

He had alerted Sam Cook, Rose Wentworth and Seamus Murphy and relayed everything that was known about Corporal Joseph Paine, including photos of him with and without a beard.

"Find him and bring him to the farm," Gibson had told them.

***

At midnight, Geraldine was taken by ambulance from a side entrance at the hospital and driven to Thames House on Millbank. She had insisted that she be taken to MI5 headquarters. There was no time to recuperate at home. She had to join the teams trying to uncover the apparent link between the gunman and Russia.

Geraldine thought of her children. Janie, eleven, and William, eight, spent more time with Marie, the au pair, than with their mother. She worked long hours and would often disappear for several days without explanation. They saw their father most weekends.

For Geraldine, having children made her feel constantly guilty. She wanted to be with them, but her job always took preference. Since separating from her husband, followed by divorce, she had found little time for socialising. She had met one man, but the liaison had been only brief, for reasons she wished to forget. She had made an extraordinarily uncharacteristic misjudgment. Since then she had been ultra-cautious about meeting anyone new. It made her life less complicated. After a few months, she no longer missed the intimacy of having a man in her bed. She enjoyed sleeping alone.

***

Sam Cook stood towering over Joseph Paine. The former corporal turned contract assassin was strapped to a chair with layers of duct tape.

They were in a basement of an Edwardian farmhouse outside Oxford. The whole Shadow Force team had assembled at the house, which they used for training, planning and emergencies. Most of the land had been sold off, but Colonel Gibson and his colleagues still had about three acres, a number of barns and sheds and an underground storage site. They had to be cautious about training, wary of alerting the local police. As an organisation that did not officially exist, the last thing they wanted was an inquisitive policeman arriving at the farm.

Gibson was upstairs in a room he called his study. It consisted of a desk, one swing chair and a telephone. Rose and Seamus were resting in the backroom downstairs.

Sam was joined by Tim Plews and George Walker.

Tim and Gibson went back a long way. Gibson had won promotion more rapidly, but Tim had been an exceptional SAS squadron commander, serving in Iraq and Afghanistan. Like so many of his special forces comrades, he was slim and devoted to supreme fitness. His one eccentricity was that he never sported a beard nor allowed his hair to grow long. Most of the men under his command had adopted beards and long hair, especially in Afghanistan. But, while he never disapproved, he preferred to be clean-shaven. As an officer commanding G Squadron, his smooth face and carefully combed hair had stood out when in the company of his men, who looked scruffy and wild, more in keeping with the stereotypical image of a British special forces commando.

Tim had been seconded to MI6 after showing particular skills in interrogating captured Taliban and al-Qaeda fighters in Afghanistan. He had found it difficult to adapt after the army but was eventually won over by the quality of the professional intelligence officers with whom he had daily contact. In his army career, he had served alongside a number of MI6 officers in the field, principally in Afghanistan but also in Iraq, and had been impressed by their courage and tenacity.

The SAS, SBS and MI6 had developed a formidable working relationship in war zones. In the Iraq War in 2003, MI6 officers, backed by special forces, had gone covertly into Basra in the south to investigate whether the citizens were ready to help British forces liberate the city from Saddam Hussein's elite Fedayeen paramilitary force. Tim had been there, a junior officer in D Squadron SAS. The intelligence brought out of the city helped the commander of Britain's 1st Armoured Division outwit the Iraqi militia and occupy Basra in force. It was a model that had been tested on numerous occasions since the Iraq War. Tim had played his part in making the joint operations with MI6 work effectively.

He had been tapped by Gibson to join Shadow Force after he resigned his commission. Although he had misgivings about the existence of such an organisation, he had been intrigued, and Gibson had been persuasive. Tim and Gibson were from the same mould. They had both married in their mid-twenties but neither marriage lasted. There were no children. Now Tim shared his bed with a series of contrasting girlfriends, but not his life. His life was the army, even after he had been seconded to

MI6. Whenever he felt a woman was beginning to harbour emotions towards him, he would move on to the next one. He enjoyed women's company but he knew that at any time he could be whisked off on an overseas mission at short notice. Personal emotions got in the way.

By contrast, George Walker, former sergeant in the 1st Battalion Parachute Regiment, was a family man. He had a wife he adored and four children, three boys and a girl. He had never applied for special forces, partly because he couldn't imagine leaving his beloved Parachute Regiment. He had served all over the world and seen combat in Iraq and Afghanistan. At one point he had been seconded to the US Army in Kuwait, acting in a liaison role. He had hated it. The food was good but there was too much of it—every day three huge meals. He'd had to work harder and harder to stay fit.

After retiring from the army at the age of forty-four, following more than twenty years in the service, he had suffered intense withdrawal symptoms, almost a clinical state. His wife, Suzanne, had become worried and contacted the regimental association. It was through the association that his name had come up when Gibson was drawing up a potential list of individuals for Shadow Force.

Sergeant Walker had been feared and loved in equal measure in the Parachute Regiment. Both Gibson and George had served in the Parachute Regiment, but Gibson had been in the 2nd Battalion, George in the 1st Battalion, and their paths had seldom crossed, except on one short but highly successful operation in West Africa.

Gibson had rung George and arranged to meet him at his flat in Westminster. It didn't take George long to throw in his lot with Gibson's maverick group, although he was concerned that Suzanne would be furious with him. How would he explain what his new role involved? She had always supported him when he was in the army, putting up with his long periods away from her and the family. When he'd retired, he had promised her that sort of life was over. He would be the man at home from now on. But he had felt restless after just four weeks of retirement and gone hunting for jobs. Gibson had made his move at the right time.

It was not surprising that Joseph Paine was petrified of Sam Cook. Sam was six foot eight and weighed 280 pounds.

He was the sort of character who was irreplaceable in whichever army unit he had served, with an infectious sense of humour. For reasons that no one among his friends understood, he had never married. Whenever his friends tried to set him up with a woman, he laughed but seldom went along with it. He wasn't shy but in many ways he was an intensely private man. Some of his friends wondered if his sheer size had made him wary of going out with women.

He had served in Iraq and Afghanistan with the SAS and had been the largest soldier in the elite regiment by at least five inches and fifty pounds. He was also one of the most decorated members of the regiment. Often special forces personnel didn't receive medals for acts of gallantry because with their extraordinary training and skills they were expected to perform in the most courageous and daring fashion every time they went on covert missions. But Sam had always gone beyond even what was expected of a soldier of his experience. He had been awarded the Conspicuous Gallantry Cross after leading an operation to rescue a British aid worker held by the Taliban in northern Helmand. Under continuous attack by insurgents armed with rocket-propelled grenades, machine guns and AK-47 Kalashnikov rifles, he had slung the aid worker over his shoulder, firing his M16 carbine as he zigzagged to cover.

Sam had finished his career in the army by being selected personally by one of Major-General Thomas Lockridge's predecessors as Director Special Forces to be his principal bodyguard and military adviser. While to some of his comrades it seemed a step down in seniority, Sam had relished the opportunity to serve with a commander he admired and to advise on the most secret and covert missions around the world.

Tim approached Paine, who appeared resigned to a painful end. Paine was still under the impression that his captors had been sent to punish him for failing to kill the woman target. George stood with his back to the door as if on guard, although Paine was going nowhere.

"So, Corporal, how are you feeling?" Tim asked in a soft voice.

Paine glanced at him, surprised by the question. "Wonderful, what d'you think?"

"Why are you here? Have you worked it out yet?"

"Eh? I told your mates in the car, I would have got her the second time."

"What are you talking about?"

"That woman. She was lucky first time. I had it sorted."

"Do you know who she is?"

"Fucking spy!"

"So, what's that to you?" Tim asked, moving closer to Paine.

"Nothing, doesn't matter who she is." Paine looked down and tried to wriggle his legs, but the plastic tape was too tight around his knees and calves.

"So, who hired you?" Tim put his face six inches from Paine's.

Paine looked up and flinched.

"I said, who hired you?" Tim asked again.

"What's going on?" Paine muttered to himself.

Sam took four steps towards him, and Paine visibly shuddered.

"My colleague here wants your answers even more than I do," Tim said.

"Who the fuck are you?" Paine was clearly confused.

"Never mind who we are. Just give me answers and I'll keep my colleague off you," Tim replied.

Paine said nothing.

Sam took one step closer and then walked round behind the chair. He put his huge right forearm around Paine's neck and squeezed until Paine's face turned red and his eyes bulged.

"Ok, that's enough," Tim said.

Sam released his hold. Paine's chest heaved as he tried to get his breath back.

"Bastards," he whispered.

"So, let's try again. Who hired you?" Tim asked, still in a soft voice.

Something changed in Paine's face. Like his brain had started to work.

"You're not from them?" he asked.

"Them?"

Paine shook his head. Suddenly he relaxed. "I get it."

"Get what?"

"You're cops?"

Tim didn't respond.

"Where am I? This is no police station," Paine said.

"Time to talk," Tim said.

"Or what?"

"Or my colleague behind you will finish what he's desperate to finish," Tim said.

"You can't do that. I have rights," Paine replied without much conviction.

Sam laughed.

"We want your cooperation," Tim said. "In return, we might come up with some sort of deal for you."

Paine said nothing.

"Tell us everything about your contract. Who, when, why, how did they contact you?"

Paine turned his head briefly to look at Sam. "Don't know what you mean."

"One more chance and then I'm leaving you in the hands of my friend here," Tim said, tone still soft.

After a long moment of silence, Tim swivelled round and went to the door. As he grabbed the handle, there was a spluttering noise from Paine.

"Sorry? Did you say something?" Tim asked as he opened the door.

"I don't know anything," Paine muttered with his eyes down.

Sam grabbed him around the neck and didn't let go for two minutes. When he released the grip, Paine gasped for air and spat on the floor.

"It was some bloke on a scooter," he said, still choking.

"Tell me more," Tim said.

"He just turned up with an envelope."

"And?"

"I don't know who it was from."

"That's rubbish—how did they know about you?"

"I have an advert."

"Where and what does it say?"

"In the *Standard*. It says 'ex-soldier seeks work', with a phone number."

"That's it?"

"Yeah, that's it."

"And then you get contacted. Who by?"

"Some bloke said he had a job for me."

"Was this your first job?"

"No."

"How many before this?"

"Just one."

"Who was the bloke?" Tim stepped closer to Paine and glanced at Sam.

"I don't know. Just a bloke."

"Did he have an accent?"

"What, like Birmingham, you mean?"

"No, like foreign, I mean."

"Yeah, I suppose."

Something changed in Paine's demeanour, as if he had decided cooperation was his best option after all. Over the next half an hour, Tim—with help from Sam's threatening presence—persuaded Paine to give a more detailed account of how he had been hired to kill Geraldine Hammer.

Three months earlier, Paine had received a brief phone call from a man with a heavy accent, possibly Russian, who asked about his background, although he appeared to already know all about him. The man said he had a job for him but would carry out a full check on him first. Paine said he didn't know what that meant—he didn't exactly have references for the line of work he was in. A month later he got another call from the same bloke, who just said something would be arriving by courier in the next few days.

"And you rang this same bloke after your failed hit?" Tim asked.

Paine looked surprised. "Phone call?"

"Yes, earlier today," Tim said. "We have your phone, remember."

Paine's shoulders dropped. He said nothing.

"Answer me please," Tim said.

"Yeah, I did."

"Who was it?"

"No idea."

"Do you know where you were phoning to?"

"No."

"It was Moscow."

Paine looked startled. "It was long distance, that's all I know."

"And what did you say in this call?" Tim asked.

"Some silly word. You've got my phone, so you must already know."

"And the word?"

"Nul," Paine said.

"And did you get a response?"

"No."

Tim stepped away and called Sam over to where George was standing.

"I doubt we're going to get anything more from him at the moment," he whispered. "He was contracted and it was all done at arm's length. Pretty professional. You stay and I'll go chat to Gibson. You've got his phone. If it rings, you know what to do, right? Let's let him stew for a bit."

Sam and George nodded.

***

Gibson listened without interruption as Tim recounted what he had learned. He had taped everything.

"I've got to attend COBRA tomorrow," Gibson said. "We'll keep Paine here. If his phone rings, let me know soonest."

"We can't hang on to him for long. The Met will go spare," Tim said.

"Let them," Gibson said. "It's the PM's decision, not ours."

He left in the Land Rover for London.

Chapter Four
A Visitor Arrives

Tuesday 2nd July

COBRA reassembled at 9:30 a.m.

Rollie Gibson had already spoken to the prime minister. He told him everything about the snatch near University College Hospital and the interrogation of Joseph Paine. Jonathan Ford told Gibson to keep quiet about Paine. He said it was going to be tricky with the Met, and with the home secretary, who would be opposed to the extra-judicial operation. Elizabeth Gantry, he said, had been squared. She would stay silent. For the moment. Ford's plan was to let the security and intelligence services carry the meeting with the information about the Moscow connection. Gibson's role was to remain totally secret. George Trench had also been sworn to secrecy about the capture of Joseph Paine. But he would have to mention Paine because too many people at MI5 and at the Met's counter-terrorism command already knew about his involvement in the assassination attempt on Geraldine Hammer.

"Well," Ford said as everyone sat down, "we have moving developments. I'll ask the DG to bring us up to date, but first of all, I hardly need point out that this is a very grave situation. We can't have any further statements to the press at this stage. It's being broadcast as an Islamic hit, and that's fine. We make no comment. Let the press speculate. No mention ever of Geraldine Hammer. So, DG, bring everyone up to date."

George Trench cleared his throat. "This is a Russian hit, as far as we can tell," he said. "Cheltenham picked up a one-word phone call made from East Sussex to Moscow. We know who made the call. Joseph Paine, a former corporal in the Royal Logistic Corps and the owner of the motorbike involved. He's, er, still at large. No obvious connection between Paine and the Russians."

Trench didn't seem as self-assured as usual. Commander Brooks sat back in his chair with a mild raising of his eyebrows.

"The word was nul," Trench went on. "Too big a coincidence to ignore. C's reference to Unit Zero yesterday. Nul means zero. Pretty careless of the Russians in my view, but after the swaggering behaviour of the two GRU agents in Salisbury in 2018, perhaps no great surprise. Moscow will deny everything, as they always do. As the PM says, we need to keep this tight. We don't want Moscow to know what we know. Not at this stage while we gather more intelligence."

Trench looked around the table. Sir Edward Farthing seemed uncomfortable.

Jonathan Ford, flicking three strands of hair off his forehead, asked. "You have any thoughts, C?"

The chief of the Secret Intelligence Service leaned forward with his elbows on the table.

"Seems out of character," he said. "The Salisbury Novichok incident was pure GRU. No one else involved. No direct connection to the Russian embassy here either."

He stayed silent for a few seconds.

"This man Paine," he continued, "was contracted. GRU always does its own dirty business, so that's out of the ordinary. It may be that Unit Zero, if it exists, is doing things differently, and that makes it more difficult for us. Perhaps they learned a lesson from Salisbury."

Harry Brooks jumped in. "I agree. Contract kills are messy. Uncontrollable. I can't believe GRU or this Unit Zero would leave everything to an outsider like Paine. But if they did, and this is a new development, there may well be a GRU agent or agents in this country right now assessing what went wrong."

"Perhaps," said Ford, "this was a trial run. Just to see whether it worked."

"So if there are GRU agents here now, we could have further hits," Metropolitan Police Commissioner Dame Mary Abelard said, speaking for the first time. She was one of only two people at the COBRA meeting in uniform.

The other one, Major-General Thomas Lockridge, Director Special Forces, said, "Prime Minister, if that's the case, I should bring a squadron down to London to be ready."

He glanced at Gibson, who remained expressionless.

"Perhaps not yet, General. I don't want word of an SAS unit in town to get around," Ford replied.

The general looked put out. He was astonished that the prime minister appeared to be suggesting there could be a leak. Again, he looked at Gibson at the end of the table. The same expressionless face. Something is going on, Lockridge thought.

"Elizabeth, what's your reading of this?" Ford asked, turning to the foreign secretary on his left.

"Ever since Salisbury, relations with Moscow have hit rock bottom," she answered. "Putin doesn't seem interested in repairing whatever relationship we have left. All the communications we get from the embassy in Moscow warn of an increasingly aggressive stance by the Kremlin."

She shifted in her seat. "There is every possibility that this aggression could increasingly be turned towards us. We've already seen hits elsewhere in

Europe where governments have been tough on Moscow. We are an obvious target for the Kremlin, partly because of our efforts to counter Russian espionage here in London. That could mean more outrages on our streets. I fear we are entering a dangerous period. The political signs are looking very bad, and with Putin, that means he could use the intelligence services to demonstrate his apparent scorn for us."

"Why would Moscow pick on Dr Hammer, if it really is the Russians behind this shooting?" Ford asked.

"Targeting someone in our agencies would send a message loud and clear that they have names and routines and can attack at will," Lawrence Fenwick, the home secretary, said.

Fenwick was young for a home secretary. Only thirty-nine, educated at the London School of Economics with a First in social anthropology, he had been Jonathan Ford's parliamentary private secretary when Ford was education secretary. He was always going to be on the fast track to the cabinet.

"So," Ford said, "all efforts to be concentrated on Russia. If it's a new GRU unit, we need to find out who may be the key players and put out a twenty-four-hour watch for any of them entering the UK. As has been said, agents may already be here."

"The Border Force is already alerted," Fenwick said. "But whether it's a new Russian unit or the same old GRU we know well, they won't be coming in under their real names, of course."

"Unless this new unit, if it exists, is filled with non-military unknowns, it will consist of highly experienced military intelligence officers, probably of senior rank," Sir Edward Farthing said. "We are delving into all known or suspected GRU members."

"Right," Ford said. "Let's report back tomorrow, same time."

***

A tall, square-jawed man in a dark suit, white shirt but no tie, carrying an expensive leather suitcase, stood in the queue for a taxi at Heathrow's Terminal 2, just arrived on a Swissair flight from Geneva. Unlike everyone else in the queue, he was not on the phone. He only had ten minutes to wait before he was in a taxi.

"Royal Garden Hotel, Kensington," he said to the taxi driver.

"Very nice," the driver replied. "Staying long?"

No reply.

The driver glanced in his mirror and saw his passenger was staring out of the window. The rest of the journey was in silence.

After checking in, the man strode out of the hotel and headed for the Côte brasserie halfway down Kensington Court, a narrow lane not far from his hotel. He asked for a table in the window and sat down. He ordered minute steak with French fries and a coffee.

He spotted the woman halfway through his meal. She was sitting alone at a table outside, smoking a cigarette. She looked to be in her early thirties—long, thick blonde hair, legs that stretched out beyond the table. She had a soft, attractive face with minimal makeup. She had an empty coffee cup in front of her.

The recently arrived Swissair passenger finished his meal, paid the bill and walked out.

"Excuse me, I wonder if you could help me?" he asked, standing beside the table where the woman was just stubbing out her cigarette.

She looked up with a quizzical expression.

"I'm really sorry to bother you," the man said.

She raised her eyebrows but said nothing.

"I've only just arrived in London and would love to visit the Portrait Gallery. Do you happen to know if it's as good as it's supposed to be?" he asked.

He had a trace of an accent but it was difficult to pinpoint. He wasn't good-looking, but he had a solid face and short, well-groomed hair. Late forties, with a well-muscled chest that pressed hard against the white shirt.

The woman noticeably eyed him up and down.

"Haven't been for ages, I'm afraid," she said.

"Ah, that's a pity," he replied, giving her the briefest of smiles.

Silence for a few seconds as the woman looked away.

"You wouldn't perhaps like to join me to reacquaint yourself?" he asked.

The woman slowly looked back in his direction. Her eyes were green with flecks of grey. He noticed the cream blouse under her yellow jacket swaying slightly as she shifted in her seat.

"I'm afraid—" she began.

"No, please, don't worry," he interrupted. "It was just a thought. A nice thought. Nice for me that is." He smiled again. "By the way, I'm Jean-Paul."

She smiled for the first time. "Are you French? You don't sound French."

"No, but my mother always loved the French," he said with a grin. "I'm half Dutch, a quarter Swiss and the rest is sort of Eastern European."

"Ha, very contemporary," she replied.

"And you?"

"I'm English, Scottish and Cornish."

"Cornish?"

"Redruth."

He looked bemused. She didn't help him out.

"If I order a coffee, can I sit here?"

She gave him another quizzical look.

"Ok," she replied. "Rebecca." And waved him to sit.

He caught a waiter's eye and asked for a double espresso. He glanced at her cup.

"No, thank you," Rebecca said.

She put away her cigarettes. "So, what is a Dutch Swiss Eastern European doing in London?"

He laughed. "I'm setting up a business and looking for somewhere to live for a few months. What does an English Scottish Cornish Rebecca do?"

"I paint."

"Really?"

"Really."

"Portraits?" he asked, and laughed again.

"No. Sorry. Modern stuff."

"I'd love to..." He trailed off.

Rebecca raised her eyebrows. Again.

"Sorry, I didn't mean..." he said quickly.

She smiled. "Well," she said, "it's been... nice. I have to go."

She stood up. At least five foot ten, he thought, as he also got up.

"Er, it's Jean-Paul van Dijk," he said, holding out his hand.

"Very Dutch," she replied. "And French-Swiss of course. Rebecca Strong."

They shook hands.

"Sorry, very conventional," he said, reaching into his jacket pocket. "This is my card. Perhaps...?"

"I don't do cards," she said. Then wrote her mobile phone number on a crumpled white paper napkin.

"Much better than a business card," he said with a grin.

She glanced at his card.

"So, Mr van Dijk, enjoy your stay in London and good luck with the, er, business."

She wandered off down Kensington Court and didn't look back.

Jean-Paul van Dijk sat down again and watched her reach the end of the lane and turn left into Kensington High Street. He took his phone out of his jacket pocket.

Chapter Five
Geraldine Hammer's Evening of Regret

George and Sam both jumped when the phone rang. They were in a different room in the farmhouse, with a table and four chairs, a sofa and a window overlooking the fields at the back of the building. Paine was on the sofa, his legs still bound in grey tape but his hands free.

George handed him the phone vibrating on the table. The mobile was attached to a recording device.

"Answer it," George said. "Give anything away and you're finished. Understand?"

Paine nodded meekly.

"Hello," he said into the phone, clearing his throat as he spoke.

There was no reply from the caller.

"Hello," Paine repeated. "Who's that?"

"You sound unwell, Mr Paine," the caller said.

"Who's that?" Paine asked again.

"Are you alone?" the caller asked.

"Er, yes, of course, but who am I talking to?"

"You're lying. Goodbye, Mr Paine."

The caller rang off.

Sam replayed the tape.

"Is the voice familiar?" Sam asked Paine.

"No."

"Nothing like the other voice?"

"You heard it," Paine replied. "No foreign accent, not like the other calls."

Suddenly, the phone rang again. Sam grabbed it and handed it to Paine.

"Tell your friends, there's more to come," the caller said.

"What friends?" Paine asked.

But the line went dead.

George and Sam exchanged a look.

"I'll stay here. You better go and brief the others," George said to Sam.

Sam joined Tim, Seamus and Rose in the kitchen. Tim rang Gibson, who was driving back from London.

"Two calls," he said. "How long will you be?"

"Twenty minutes," Gibson replied. "Anything interesting?"

"Yes."

***

Geraldine Hammer was back in the office, looking as if she had spent ten rounds in a boxing ring. She was staggered to be told about Paine's abduction, but George Trench, while also concerned about the legality of the Gibson operation, told her the circumstances were unique. The phone call was a direct threat to the country's national security. Unconventional methods were perhaps needed, he said.

"It's down to Number 10," Trench said.

"Never mind that Paine tried to kill me," Geraldine said with a shrug. "We've got him. He should be charged and be done with it, but..."

"Geraldine, you're right of course," Trench replied. "But the Russia thing is now a major challenge. With the police being kept in the dark, it's up to us to find whoever is now in the UK and unravel whatever he is planning to do."

Geraldine looked out of the window. They were sitting in the DG's office overlooking the Thames. She could see the elaborately designed MI6 headquarters at Vauxhall Cross on the other side of the river and wondered what her sister-service colleagues were thinking at that moment.

"The key thing," she said, "is why me? Paine called me a spy. How did he know that? Who told him? Why is GRU after me especially? Ok, so I ran the op to clear out GRU from London. But how would they know that? It's not like my appointment was announced in the *London Gazette*."

Trench stood up. "I have to go to Number 10, but try and come up with some answers," he said. "I know you've listened to the tape, but have another go. Could there be something you've missed? It's old-school thinking, but is there anything about that voice that sets off even the remotest memory? We'll talk later."

They left the room together. Geraldine went back to her office and called in Grace Redmayne and Jasper Cornfield. She had previously briefed them about Paine being held by Gibson's team.

The three of them sat and listened to the taped telephone call between Paine and the unknown caller.

Geraldine asked Jasper Cornfield what the tape was telling them.

"First of all," he said, "there's a slight trace of an accent. Not obvious. Just the way he says the word 'friends'. We expect him to be Russian but if we heard the voice in different circumstances—just a voice without any prior knowledge or expectation—would we say, 'Ah, that's Russian'?"

"I don't think so," said Grace. "Geraldine?"

"Not specifically," Geraldine replied. "What else?"

"Bare minimum of words," Jasper went on. "He was ringing not to impart information but to receive it. He will have read in the papers that you survived and wanted to gauge from Paine's replies what may or may not have happened subsequently."

"Agreed," said Geraldine.

"So, what did he get?" Jasper mused. "Paine cleared his throat when he said hello. Sign of nervousness. That would have alerted our caller straightaway. Why did he ask if Paine was feeling well? I believe to throw him off course. An unexpected question. And Paine didn't reply, he just asked again who the caller was."

Jasper looked at Geraldine and Grace to see if they wanted to add anything. They said nothing.

"Then the question, 'are you alone?'" Jasper continued. "Paine's reply was a giveaway. Saying 'of course' meant the opposite. Why didn't he reply 'yes I am' or just 'yes'? The words 'of course' were hurried to try and reassure the caller that he was on his own, and why wouldn't he be?"

Geraldine chipped in. "Why wasn't Paine schooled into giving certain answers?" she asked rhetorically. "It wasn't handled well. If the caller was a Russian intelligence officer, he would know what to ask and what to listen out for. He got everything he needed. Smart."

"'You're lying, Mr Paine,'" Jasper quoted. "That was intended to let Paine and whoever was holding him know that he knew what was going on. I doubt if Gibson's lot had provided a script it would have helped. The caller was too clever. His first call gave us nothing except an understanding that he is a professional. Do you think the 'Mr Paine' bit has any significance?"

Geraldine thought for a moment.

"It's a very English thing to say," she said finally.

"Why would he do that?" Grace asked.

"I'm not sure," Jasper said, "but here's a theory. First of all, the caller is telling Paine that he knows his name. Obvious, but that's important because if he hadn't mentioned Paine at all there would have been no direct link between the caller and Paine, no acknowledgement, if you like, that the caller knew he was phoning the right number and that he had the right number to call. In other words, he had

Paine's number because that was the deal between contractor and contracted. An established mobile phone number to ring."

"Go on," Geraldine said.

"If Paine had carried out a successful hit, the caller wouldn't have called," Jasper said. "There wouldn't have been any reason to call. In fact, just the opposite. It would have been too dangerous to phone after a successful assassination. If he's the boss then he would have stayed right out of it. The second payment would have been made by a courier and that would have been that."

"And the 'Mr Paine'?" Grace asked.

"I think the caller did that deliberately," Jasper said. "It's not a Russian thing but it could be a Russian taking on the persona of an Englishman. In other words, I'm here in England and I'm speaking like a polite Englishman."

Jasper looked at both women, expecting to be met with shaking heads.

"Very good, Jasper," Geraldine said instead. "I think you're right, and if you *are* right, the boss, as you put it, is here. And that's as good as confirmed by his second call, which was just a straight challenge to all of us. 'More to come'. And with Paine out of the running, perhaps the boss himself will do the next one. So we may have in our midst a senior, highly professional Russian assassin plotting another hit."

"And my guess," Grace said, "is that whoever it is, his target will be someone from our agency or someone from across the river. The hit against you, Geraldine, is the clearest sign. We have a war on our hands."

***

On her own after Jasper and Grace had left, Geraldine began thinking back to Operation Foxtrot.

It had been launched a year ago. The objective was to expose every member of GRU working undercover in London and elsewhere in the UK and make a good case to the Foreign Office to expel them as persona non grata.

MI5's watcher teams had been deployed on the biggest counter-espionage surveillance operation for decades. It was such a demanding operation that the number of men and women available for counter-terrorist surveillance missions, following suspected jihadist militants, had to be reduced to a minimum. It was a calculated risk, which the DG had approved but only for a couple of months.

The effort paid off. Seven GRU spies working as "illegals", living in Britain as "bona fide businessmen" with false names and passports, were exposed. Some were caught trying to set up meetings with employees of Ministry of Defence contractors. One Russian spy was filmed attempting to blackmail a woman who worked as the personal assistant to the managing director of a major defence company. She was having an affair with her married boss.

The suspected GRU intelligence officers working as "diplomats" at the Russian embassy had been easier to track. Most of them had history and were well documented.

Five GRU "diplomats" and the seven illegals were duly expelled from Britain and Geraldine was praised for the month-long operation. Russia retaliated with the expulsion of five members of the British embassy in Moscow including the defence and air attaches and a communications specialist. Seven British businessmen working for international firms in Moscow were also expelled.

What was significant, however, was the language used by the Kremlin spokesman. He warned the British government that the expulsion of five "innocent" Russian diplomats and the seven "businessmen" was viewed as an affront to the good name of the Russian motherland, and the tit-for-tat removal of five British diplomats and seven businessmen would not be the end of the story.

Geraldine now realised that had been a complacent conclusion. A serious misjudgment by the Foreign Office and MI6. That warning from Moscow had been the first signal of a plot to kill her. It was a sobering thought.

As she thought back to Operation Foxtrot, something else came into Geraldine's mind. About three months after the GRU expulsions, there had been a strange incident outside her house in Kennington, south London. She was always wary when returning home, going through the discipline of checking around her as she approached the steps leading up to the yellow front door of her terraced house. She'd noticed a man sitting in a black Mercedes and heard the sound of an engine turning over but not sparking. The car was just ahead of her, three houses down from her three-storey Edwardian home. The Mercedes engine had continued to misfire. It was around 7 p.m. and still light.

As she passed the car and glanced in, she saw a large man looking angry. He wound his window down.

"Excuse me," he said, climbing out. "This is really embarrassing. I have an expensive car here and it won't work. I've also left my phone in the office. Is there any chance I could possibly ask you to make a call for me to the garage who rented me this rubbish?"

He spoke quickly and had a broad smile on his face. Geraldine was instantly suspicious and said nothing for a moment.

"I'm so sorry," the man said. "I didn't mean to startle you. And don't worry, I'll ask someone else."

Geraldine had hesitated. The man standing in front of her was dressed expensively: a dark blue suit and white shirt with a modest blue-and-green striped tie. Not the sort of man who would leave his phone behind in the office, she thought. His face was pleasant without being good-looking. His eyes were the most impressive feature, a stunning light blue. He sounded European, not English.

The man started to climb back into the car.

"Ok," Geraldine replied at last.

He swivelled round. "Are you sure? I really would appreciate it."

Geraldine felt into her handbag and drew out a BlackBerry.

"Goodness," the man said with a laugh. "I haven't seen one of those for years."

"I like them," Geraldine said without smiling. It was her private phone.

There was an awkward moment when he had put his hand forward to take the phone and she hung on to it.

"Sorry," he said. "I just thought it would be easier."

"You tell me the number and I'll ring," Geraldine said.

He took a business card from his jacket pocket and handed it to her. It was a car hire company based in neighbouring Southwark. Mercedes Rentals. She rang the number, then gave her phone to the man after hearing the ringing tone.

"Hello," he said. "This is Lucas Meyer. The Merc's not firing. Can you please come and get it?"

He looked at Geraldine and shrugged.

"What's the name of this street?" he asked her.

"Gladstone Street," she replied.

"Ha, after the... er... prime minister, right?"

"I suppose," she replied.

"Yeah, Gladstone Street," he said into the phone.

"Halfway down. I can't stay. I'll pick up a new car tomorrow."

Lucas Meyer gave the phone back to Geraldine.

"I can't tell you how grateful I am," he told her.

"No problem. Good luck with the car."

He'd smiled and reached forward to shake her hand. It was a firm grip, and with his light blue eyes looking directly into hers, she felt suddenly awakened. It was not something she welcomed or wanted. But she almost shivered. She smiled and turned away. She knew he was watching her but didn't glance back as she climbed the four steps to her door and went inside.

After the unexpected exchange near her house, she had mulled over what had happened. She tried to bury the weird sensation she had felt. Lucas Meyer? He spoke with near impeccable English, but she knew he wasn't. Danish, perhaps? Certainly charming and polite. Nothing to get suspicious about, she decided—although, why was he parked in her street? Where had he gone after parking before returning to find a malfunctioning engine? In her job asking such questions was unavoidable, but for a reason she couldn't explain, she wanted it to be just a coincidence. His car wasn't working and she happened to be passing by. And he had left his phone in the office. What office?

She had shaken her head as if to stop the questions.

It was just over a week later, on a Saturday, that her BlackBerry rang. She had been sitting at home after supper with the kids. It was her turn to have the children.

"Hello," she said.

"Hello, it's Lucas Meyer here, I'm just ringing to thank you for your kindness the other day. A real Samaritan."

Geraldine's heart lurched. She was just about to ask him how he had her number when he provided the answer.

"I hope you don't mind me phoning," he said. "I got the number from the rental company."

Geraldine stood up from the sofa and went hastily into the hall, away from her children.

"Er, there was no need to call," she said. "I prefer my phone to be private, so..."

"Of course, quite right, I understand. It's a bit forward of me. Sorry." He sounded contrite but didn't ring off. Nor did she.

"Well... So I see your car was removed all right," she said finally.

"Yes, I got a new one and it works," Meyer replied.

There were a few seconds of silence.

"I was wondering if, hm, perhaps... I know nothing about you, of course, and you're probably married and everything, so I shouldn't even ask," he said.

She didn't reply. Her heart was thumping beneath her pink T-shirt.

"But just in case you're not," Meyer continued, "I have a couple of tickets for the Royal Opera House next Saturday and thought, who do I know who I would like to spend an evening at the opera with?" He left the implied question unanswered.

"Very kind, but..." Geraldine started to say, but the whole of her body was now alive with expectation. She found it difficult to sound casual.

"You don't like opera?"

"Actually, I do."

"So... it wouldn't be an evening not to look forward to," he said.

The words sounded a little odd, but Geraldine was fighting with herself and missed the strange double negative.

"I really don't do this sort of thing, I'm afraid," she said.

"I don't mean to make you feel uncomfortable," Meyer persisted. "I don't even know your name, but what I do know is that an evening at the Royal Opera House would be delightful. I love opera."

Geraldine still hesitated. She should have said no and rung off.

"I'm sure it would," she said very quietly.

"Does that mean you might?" Meyer asked.

A long silence. Geraldine could hear her children calling from the sitting room.

"Maybe," she said.

"Wonderful," Meyer said. "I'll check with you during the week, if that's all right. If you can't come, I can still go on my own."

"Ok," Geraldine said, frowning as she realised how tempted she was.

"Annabel? Suzanne? Annie? Alexandra?" Meyer asked and laughed.

"Jane," Geraldine replied and rang off.

The following Saturday, Lucas Meyer had turned up in a taxi and rung her doorbell.

Geraldine was still upstairs. She had decided against a long dress and was wearing a three-quarter-length dark blue skirt, a fitted white jacket, a soft emerald-green blouse and multi-coloured scarf. She was a good-looking woman. High cheekbones, hazel eyes and auburn hair, cut mid-length. She was only five foot five but she always stood tall, her head and shoulders held back.

She took one last look in the mirror and pressed her lips together, tasting the bright pink lipstick. She felt nervous, and her whole body twitched when she heard the doorbell going. What she was doing was against her normal instincts. She knew she was taking a risk. A date with a stranger she knew nothing about breached every training guideline in the book.

However, since the break-up of her marriage, she had felt strangely vulnerable. She had lost confidence in herself. It didn't affect her work—she remained, as always, a dedicated professional—but Grace had noticed a change. Grace knew the marriage's failure had hit Geraldine hard. She offered sympathy and comfort, but Geraldine kept her private life private.

Now, after more than three years without any physical relationship, the sudden appearance of Lucas Meyer had knocked Geraldine off course. Against all her professional instincts, she'd felt she needed to take the risk. It was time.

Geraldine walked down the stairs and went to open the door. Her children were with their father for the weekend.

Meyer was in a dinner jacket with a maroon velvet bowtie. He'd had a haircut.

He smiled. "Wow," he said. "You look great."

"Thank you," she replied.

Throughout Beethoven's *Fidelio*—not her favourite opera—Geraldine was aware of the strength and physicality of the man sitting next to her. Her mind drifted to what might happen when the opera was finished. She resolved that however charming he might be in trying to persuade her to spend more time with him that evening, she would explain that she needed sleep and would grab a taxi home.

As the opera approached its end, she felt her heart pumping. She had caught him glancing at her several times, and at one point her arm had brushed against his. She had forgotten what it was like to be physically attracted to a man. It made her feel uncomfortable but curious.

When the chorus and stars had finished their bows, they both stood up without saying anything. Meyer took her elbow to guide her out of the Royal Opera House. She shivered, and he noticed.

"Jane," he said quietly, "I hope you won't think me presumptuous, but you must be hungry. I certainly am. I've arranged for some food to be delivered to my flat near Blackfriars Bridge, and afterwards, I'll get you a taxi home. What do you think?"

Geraldine had attempted to come out with her planned response, but she found herself saying, "Well, I do need to get home, but a bite to eat would be nice."

Meyer walked to the taxi queue, once again taking her elbow.

He lived in a fifty-storey luxury apartment complex in Bankside, near the bridge, with panoramic views of London across the river. Seventh floor. As the lift climbed, Geraldine and Meyer eyed each other. She looked at her watch. It was 10:30 p.m. She was ready for bed—*her* bed at home in Kennington.

"Please take a seat by the window," Meyer said as they entered the flat. "Champagne?"

Geraldine walked towards the view. "Thank you," she said without turning round.

She didn't sit but looked out at the lights of London.

"Fabulous, isn't it?" Meyer said as he came up close behind her.

She swivelled round and took the glass of champagne.

"Lucas." She spoke his name for the first time. "I have to—"

He leant forward and kissed her.

She was so shocked and at the same time so intoxicated she grabbed his right shoulder to steady herself. He moved up closer to her and took her in his arms and kissed her again.

"Have a sip of champagne," he whispered.

She did as she was told and watched him as he drank most of his glass. They put their glasses down on the table next to them. He picked her up, his hands under her arms, and carried her through to a huge bedroom with the biggest double bed she had ever seen. She made no move to stop him. When they were naked, she didn't look at him, keeping her eyes closed.

Meyer had been tender and gentle at first, but once they lay on the bed, he rose above her and his whole manner changed. He was overwhelmingly forceful. She gasped. It was the most overpowering physical sensation she had ever experienced. It was consensual, but she had not agreed to this sort of all-enveloping male domination. She felt subjugated. Instantly, whatever sexual attraction she had felt towards him vanished. He took his time, seemingly oblivious of her lack of involvement, and then rolled off her body. She had experienced nothing but pain and shock.

Geraldine got off the bed swiftly.

He watched her, lying naked on top of the bed.

"I'm sorry, Jane," he said, his arms behind his head. He didn't seem sorry. "I thought..."

Geraldine was dressed. "Thank you for the opera," she said.

Meyer got up and walked towards her.

Geraldine put her left hand up and shook her head. He stopped momentarily and she turned to open the door.

"Can I get you a taxi?" he asked.

"No... thank you," she replied and walked to the lifts.

She'd had nothing to eat all evening but was no longer hungry. She felt angry, disillusioned, abused and betrayed.

Chapter Six
A Moment of Freedom for Joseph Paine

Wednesday 3rd July

Jonathan Ford waited while everyone took their seats in the Cabinet Office briefing room.

"You have all received the CX about Unit Zero," he said. "C, give us a rundown."

Sir Edward Farthing looked down at the document his staff had circulated to named members of the cabinet and the most senior officials at the Foreign Office, Home Office, Ministry of Defence and Treasury. General Lockridge, Harry Brooks, Dame Mary and Colonel Gibson had also received copies.

"Our man in Moscow has done a good job," Sir Edward began. "We know more about Unit Zero now. To summarise: after Salisbury and the outrageous cavalier actions by the GRU agents of Unit 29155, there seems to have been a rethink in the Kremlin."

He looked at the prime minister. Ford nodded impatiently.

"Out of this rethinking came this new unit, Unit Zero," Sir Edward said. "Our guys in Moscow have delved as deep as they can, and their conclusion is that Unit Zero is exclusively a GRU Spetsnaz operation. But instead of it coming under the sole authority of the GRU leadership, which would be the normal case, it is a separate unit, selected and run by the Kremlin, with the GRU leadership subordinated. This is unusual. But what we have are veteran combat special forces soldiers ultra-loyal to Putin with service in Ukraine, Syria and Libya. Dedicated professionals with the sort of discipline absent in some of the ranks in Russia's military intelligence."

"The CX makes no mention of a possible leader," Ford said.

"No, Prime Minister, we don't have a handle on that at the moment," Sir Edward replied. "We're going through the files on all senior officers of Spetsnaz that we know of who played a role in Ukraine, Syria and/or Libya."

"So, no names at all of anyone in this Russian hit squad?" Lawrence Fenwick asked.

"Not yet," Sir Edward replied. "But by cross-referencing with intelligence we have of those particular military operations, we might be able to make an educated guess."

Jeremy Blunt, defence secretary, a politician with a reputation for impatience and bad temper, exploded. "We can't base our strategy for dealing with this threat on the basis of an educated guess."

"Thank you, Jeremy," Ford chipped in quickly. "I'm sure C is aware of that."

Ignoring the intervention by the defence secretary, Sir Edward said, "By that, I meant we could at least draw up a list of potential Unit Zero members and have their photos, if available, put out to all airports. Hopefully, I'll have such a list within the week."

"In a week!" Blunt blurted out. "By then we could have another hit in London and still be none the wiser who the hell we are dealing with."

Harry Brooks sympathised with Sir Edward. Politicians always wanted instant results.

"For the Met, we'd appreciate any names, C, whenever you get them," he said, being careful not to look in the defence secretary's direction. "This is terrorism pure and simple, whether it's Kremlin-inspired or not, and we'll need all the help we can get to catch these individuals."

"That," said Ford, "is the most important point made this morning. The first priority of course is to stop another assassination attempt, but absolutely crucial this time is to catch and arrest any Russians responsible for the attack on Dr Hammer before they leave the UK, if they are still here plotting further attacks. We can't have another Salisbury. The Met did wonders in identifying the Russian agents responsible for the Skripal hit, but they skipped the country too quickly. They will never end up in a British court, and Moscow can go on for ever denying any involvement. This time, we need arrests here in our country, Russians we can charge and bring to court."

Everyone around the room nodded in agreement.

The Metropolitan Police Commissioner, who had only been in the job for six months, cleared her throat and said, "Prime Minister, we're clearly in a grave situation. My concern is the safety of the public. If we have some Russian assassin in our midst hunting down his next target, both my officers and the general public are in danger. All the senior members of MI5 are going to need protection. Especially Dr Hammer, who must surely still be at risk."

Fenwick agreed. "The Mayor of London has already been on the phone demanding maximum police coverage."

"Commissioner, I'll leave that in your capable hands," the prime minister said. "Meanwhile, we need your list of potential suspects as fast as possible, C. The defence secretary is right; we can't wait. And what are we going to do about all the media speculation? I want that sorted out quickly. Stamp down on some of the more hysterical stories."

Sandy Hall, the Sky News crime correspondent, had been leading the field. He'd been the first to speculate that Russia might be behind the attack on the unnamed MI5 officer. There had been mass coverage in all the newspapers of past Russian assassination plots; Sergei Skripal and his daughter Yulia in 2018 and Alexander Litvinenko in 2006. Scotland Yard had been ordered to make no comment, other than to say that an investigation was still underway and no suspects had been arrested.

"We're getting pestered a hundred times a day," Harry Brooks said. "I think it's time to put out the name of our chief suspect to the media. That will keep them busy for a few days and may help us catch this Joseph Paine. There has been no sighting of him. And his bike has vanished, too. Once we get him, the press will focus on him."

Ford spoke quietly. "Let's leave it one more day, Commander, then, I agree, we should broadcast his name."

Rollie Gibson, sitting in his usual place at the end of the table, looked up, but his face gave nothing away. George Trench also showed not a flicker of reaction.

The prime minister brought the meeting to an end. As everyone stood up, Ford looked at Gibson and gestured to him with the simultaneous raising of his eyebrows and chin. Gibson left the room with the others but returned after a couple of minutes.

"Colonel, come up with a plan, please," Ford said. "I don't need to know or want to know, but tomorrow morning at this time I will need to give Commander Brooks the authority to release Corporal Paine's name."

Gibson nodded and left the room.

***

Midnight.

Joseph Paine had only slept for an hour, but he woke with a start. His room was small, just a bed and a wooden kitchen chair. There were bars on the window and he knew the door was locked and one of his interrogators would be sitting outside. But he climbed out of bed and walked slowly, almost on tiptoes, towards the door. He tried the doorknob. It turned easily. His heart jumped. He turned the knob all the way round. It was open. He drew the door back very slowly and peeped through the crack. No one there.

He closed the door and walked back to the bed. He was only wearing pants. His clothes were sitting in a pile in one corner. He dressed quickly.

There wasn't a sound in the house. He opened the door gingerly, expecting to be grabbed. But there was no one. This time, he did tiptoe. Down the corridor. He was on the ground floor. In the dark, he could see a room to the right and then the front door. Every instinct warned him it was a trap. Any moment those huge arms would be round his neck.

He stood still and waited, but the house remained silent.

Very slowly, like a blind man finding his way in an unfamiliar environment, he approached the front door. It was unlocked. His first thought was to burst through it and run. But he was a trained soldier. He needed to take advantage of the new situation. One or more of his captors could be upstairs asleep. But if there was no one outside his room and the front door was unlocked, that seemed unlikely. He was alone. They had abandoned him. Why, he had no idea, but he could worry about that later.

He turned round and tried the door of the room now to his left. It opened. His eyes had adjusted to the dark, and he saw he was standing in a large kitchen with a huge Welsh dresser to the right. He pulled out one of the top drawers. It was filled with cutlery and mats. Another drawer contained condiments. He opened the larger door beneath the drawers. Several shelves, empty except for a plastic, lidded box pushed to the back. Paine brought it out and put it on the long farmhouse-style table. He lifted the lid. Inside was his Glock. His mouth opened in astonishment. He picked it up and checked the safety mechanisms. There were still eleven rounds left in the fifteen-round magazine. He shoved the Glock down the front of his trousers.

The plastic box contained something else. A bunch of keys, including one marked "BMW". His keys. He put them in his trouser pocket.

The fridge had cheese, ham slices, bread, butter, a carton of orange juice. Paine looked back at the door of the kitchen. Nothing. He made two sandwiches and drank from the carton. Still not a sound from the rest of the house.

He removed a sharp vegetable knife from the cutlery drawer, returned to the front door and left the house. It was 12:20 a.m.

As he walked across the fields in front of the house, he kept looking behind him. But there was no sign of anyone following him. He had no idea where he was but headed in the direction of lights in the distance.

It took him forty minutes to reach the village of Old Marston. He still wasn't sure what county he was in. There was no one around. Most of the houses were dark, just the occasional bedroom light still on. Paine took the knife from his pocket and approached a Ford Fiesta parked outside a house made out of Cotswold stone. He looked around and down the street, then slid the knife between the door and the doorframe until he felt the bolt move back.

His luck was in. He found a screwdriver in the glove compartment and worked it into the ignition. The engine fired. He checked the petrol gauge. It was half full.

Eighty yards away, Rose, dressed in black, standing behind an oak tree, whispered into her phone, "Ford Fiesta, red, LB08 7QE. Wait two, pick me up opposite 12 Mortimer Drive."

Seamus, waiting in a dark blue Mini Cooper with the engine running, responded. "Roger that."

Paine set off down Mortimer Drive. It took him a few minutes to discover where he was. The first sign he saw was for the A40 to London. Perfect. He glanced in the wing mirror. Nothing to concern him. He joined the A40 and for the first time since he had been seized off the street, he relaxed.

Seamus kept well back although there were plenty of cars on the road to give him adequate cover. He and Rose were not talking. They had a job to do. Compared with their past experience of following IRA gunmen in South Armagh as members of the army's Special Reconnaissance Regiment, this was a routine surveillance mission. Paine had taken the bait and was heading for London as expected. So far he had adopted none of the counter-surveillance techniques used as a matter of course by the IRA.

It was 2:40 a.m. by the time Paine arrived in Streatham. He parked the car in a side street behind St Peter's Church in the Charwood district. Then he walked towards Leigham Court Road and the lock-up garages where he had hidden his BMW bike. He turned only once to look behind him and spotted a couple staggering drunkenly along the pavement on the other side of the road, about a hundred yards back. He hesitated, but when they fell against a shop window and started kissing, he turned round and headed for garage number seven.

Rose extracted herself from Seamus's embrace and rang 999 on a burner phone.

"Police," she said.

Two seconds later, she was put through to the police switchboard.

"Yes, quick quick. There's a man with a gun. Just going into a lock-up. Number 7, Leigham Court Road, Streatham." She rang off.

Rose and Seamus sat in the Cooper within range of the garages. Paine had yet to emerge. He had closed the door behind him and there was a light on.

A police van with lights flashing arrived within three minutes. Half a dozen cops armed with MP5 Heckler & Koch carbines jumped out and took up positions around the number 7 garage.

"Armed police!" one of them shouted. "Come out with your hands in the air. If you have a weapon, leave it there."

Paine was dumbstruck. He had changed into his bike gear and was at the point of raising the door of the garage. He stood still.

"Come out now!" the voice shouted.

"Bastards," Paine muttered. What the hell was going on?

His Glock was now tucked inside his leather jacket. No point, he thought. He emptied the magazine and hid the rounds in the left-hand corner of the garage, where there was already a pile of bricks and old carrier bags. He buried the pistol.

He removed his helmet and put it on the seat of the bike. Then he bent down to lift up the metal door. He raised his hands.

"Get down, get down!" the nearest police officer shouted. "Full length, on your stomach. Hands where we can see them."

The former corporal of the Royal Logistic Corps did as he was ordered.

Seamus had kept the engine running. Neither he nor Rose said anything. The job was done.

Chapter Seven
Sandy Hall Gets a Breakthrough

Thursday 4ᵗʰ July

News of the arrest came too late for the daily papers. But the BBC Radio *Today* programme had the story at the top of the list on the 7 a.m. news. Sky News pipped the BBC with a short item at 6.30 a.m. Sandy Hall was not yet in the office and missed the breaking news. Scotland Yard had put out a brief bulletin.

"In the early hours of today, an armed response unit arrested a man in Streatham, south London as part of the ongoing investigation into the shooting incident in central London on Monday the first of July. The suspect is being held for questioning."

The suspect was not identified. Reporters ringing the Met's Press Bureau for further details were fobbed off with "no comment".

Sandy was on his way into the Sky News office in Isleworth, west London. He was in the back of a minicab when his mobile phone rang.

"Hello," he said. "Sandy Hall."

A voice he didn't recognise asked if he was covering the story of the arrest.

Sandy told the caller he was Sky's crime correspondent. So, yes, he was doing the story.

"He's a former soldier," the caller said.

"Sorry?"

"He's an ex-soldier."

"How do you know?" Sandy asked, immediately sceptical.

"Corporal Joseph Paine."

"Sorry, what name?"

"Paine, p-a-i-n-e."

"Who is this?"

"Royal Logistic Corps."

"Sorry?"

"He served with the Royal Logistic Corps. A good shot. If you're not interested, I'll go elsewhere."

The caller rang off.

Ever since he had been crime correspondent, Sandy had been good at wooing contacts in the Met. He was well liked at Scotland Yard. Occasionally he had received anonymous tips, and he knew they were probably cops. Not all of them bore fruit, but he had learned never to dismiss tip-offs. There were enough cops with grudges or with an oversized sense of their importance who enjoyed ringing reporters to reveal titbits that should have stayed confidential. It was a game.

His personal contacts were different. He could ring them for guidance and sometimes received information that helped him develop the bare bones of a story into something that would hit the headlines.

However, anonymous tips were the most exciting, especially when they proved to be accurate. Sandy's instinct, as the minicab drew up outside the Sky News headquarters, was that this anonymous caller with the low voice had given him a vital piece of information. Not a nutter but an insider. He would tell his news desk nothing until he had checked it out with his Met contacts. It was a golden rule for him. If he told the news desk prematurely what he was working on, they would start writing the headline for the next bulletin before he had even written a word.

Sandy was a reporter with little life outside his job. He lived alone in a flat in Brentford, west London. With so many experienced crime correspondents working for the nationals, every day was a competitive challenge. He could get any breaking news on his patch on air within minutes, giving him an advantage over the printed media. He enjoyed that edge. He still had to worry about his counterparts on the other television channels, but none of them had managed to oust him from the top slot as the recognised crime correspondent who was generally first with the news.

Sandy, thirty-seven, good-looking by most standards, had unfashionably long hair and had been tempted to tie the wavy locks in a ponytail. But as a reporter expected to be in front of the camera several times a day, he knew that would be frowned on. In fact, banned. He also worried that a ponytail might be associated, wrongly in his view, with being either eccentric or gay. He was neither.

He rang a detective inspector with the Met's Counter-Terrorism Command.

"Rick, it's Sandy," he said, leaning forward to open a notebook on his desk.

"Hi, Sandy, what's up?"

"I have a name. The bloke arrested this morning. Just wondered if I could put it by you?"

"Can't do that. Sorry, Sandy. It's too early. The guys are still at the lock-up."

"Lock-up? You mean in Streatham?"

"Shit, yeah, but I didn't say that."

"Ok, but what if I say the name and you don't reply but I can then feel I'm not way off?"

Silence for a few seconds.

"Go on then," the detective inspector said.

"Ex-Corporal Joseph Paine?"

Silence the other end.

"See you around, Sandy," the detective inspector said and called off.

"Jesus," Sandy said.

He googled Corporal Joseph Paine, Royal Logistic Corps and came up with bits and pieces. Served with his unit in Afghanistan. Won top marksman award four years ago. Left the army under a cloud. An assault charge. No picture available. When Sandy checked Facebook there were plenty of Joseph Paines but none that matched what he knew of the man arrested at a lock-up in Streatham. What was in the lock-up? The motorbike, obviously. But why would a former corporal in the Royal Logistic Corps, not the most glamorous of army units, be involved in the attempted murder of someone in MI5? No Russian connection there, surely? Unless he'd been contracted.

Sandy sat back and summed up in his head what he had so far. It wasn't much, but it was a lot more than he had two hours ago. What could he go with? Could he name the corporal as the Met's suspect? Or just run a story saying the suspect was believed to be a former soldier. That was the safe option. If he named Paine, the Met's Press Bureau would be furious. Not that it was his job to keep the Press Bureau happy. But Sandy had to work with the police and the Press Bureau every day, and he had to find the right balance between breaking great stories while making sure he didn't get blacklisted by Scotland Yard. Accuracy was the key. If a story was right, there was no justification for blacklisting him. Wild, inaccurate stories were what really angered the police hierarchy. So should he just ring the bureau, tell them what he had and ask for a reaction? At least he would be giving them notice that Sky might be broadcasting the name of the suspect.

It was close to 8:45 a.m. He had only minutes to make up his mind. He decided to go for the soft option for the 9 a.m. bulletin. No name but definitely a former soldier of the Royal Logistic Corps as the suspect, as well as armed police at a lock-up in Streatham. It was enough for the moment, and he would be ahead of the field, which was where he liked to be.

Following the Sky News report, every other TV station and all the national newspapers rushed to update their stories. The Press Bureau refused to confirm Sandy's story on the record. But off the record, they said the information was not inaccurate. Sandy rang the bureau after his story had run and told them he had a name, but he was informed that any identification of the suspect would be prejudicial to the police investigation.

It was tricky. Sandy knew that the sharpest reporters in rival organisations would be ringing their contacts in the police and military to try and get the name. He couldn't let them scoop him when he had the name in his notebook. His own news desk was also pushing for him to come up with a name.

His phone rang.

"Hello," he said, a bit impatiently.

"You haven't given the name."

It was the same caller.

"How can I be sure it's the right name?" Sandy asked.

"It is. Joseph Paine is being questioned at Paddington Green police station."

"Anything else?"

"They found a Glock pistol in the lock-up, and eleven rounds in a pile of rubbish. It's the same gun used in the shooting at the back of Thames House."

Sandy was writing furiously.

"I won't be phoning again," the caller said, and rang off.

Sandy rang his contact in Counter-Terrorism Command.

"Rick, it's Sandy. I'm really sorry to ring again but I've got some information which I need to check out. Can I just say what I've got and you can help or not?"

"Be quick, I've got a meeting in two minutes," the detective inspector replied.

"Joseph Paine is being held at Paddington Green. The police who arrested him found a Glock and eleven rounds. The gun is linked to the shooting behind Thames House."

"Bloody hell! You'll be crucified if you broadcast all that," his contact said.

"But is it true?"

"Got to go."

"Rick?"

"Sounds ok."

The phone went dead.

Sandy told the news desk what he had. He was ordered to run it past the lawyers once he had written the script.

***

Shortly after 10 a.m., following Sandy's updated report that included the name of the suspect, Gibson's phone rang.

"It's rolling," Seamus said.

"So I see," Gibson replied. "Did he ask you anything?"

"No, except who I was."

"Well, it should do the trick. They'll be running lots of hares for a bit. It might bring out our Russian friend. Who knows. Still waiting for some names from Six."

Sir Edward Farthing had so far failed to report back to COBRA with a list of potential suspects. But Gibson hoped for something by the end of the day.

***

In jeans and a loose white shirt, Rebecca Strong was painting at home in her flat, a one-bedroom apartment on the top floor of a Victorian townhouse on St Lukes Road, Notting Hill. She rented the flat, which was decently furnished. She painted for the commercial market: big impressive colourful abstracts, favoured by companies that liked to adorn their foyers with artistic works.

Her phone rang.

"Hello, it's Rebecca," she said.

"Hello, Rebecca. It's Jean-Paul. Remember me?"

"Hey."

"Are you painting or...?"

"Painting."

"Any room for an admirer?"

"Admirer of my paintings?"

Jean-Paul van Dijk laughed. "Well, of course."

Rebecca didn't say anything.

"So, what do you say?" Jean-Paul asked.

"Aren't you supposed to be busy setting up a company or something?"

"Still working on it, but I'm free this afternoon."

"Well, Mr Dutchman, I had planned an afternoon of painting," Rebecca said.

"Perhaps tea?"

"Very English. Tea at four, if you have to."

She gave him her address.

"Sounds posh," he said.

"Not really. I only rent."

"Tea at four. Look forward to it."

Two hours later, he was ringing the bell for her flat at the apartment block front door. It was buzzed open. He climbed the stairs to the top floor. She was waiting for him with the door open.

"Hello again," he said.

"Come in. Ignore the mess."

He walked into a spacious living area. Rebecca's easel and paint pots were in the corner by the window. Her picture was a mass of yellow shapes and what looked like running water.

Jean-Paul took a good look at it. "Hm, certainly hits you."

"Is that a compliment?" Rebecca asked, looking at him quizzically, just as she had done at the brasserie in Kensington High Street.

"I'm no expert, but yes," he replied.

"Do you always wear a suit, Mr Dutchman?"

Jean-Paul smiled at her. "I guess I could take off my jacket; it is quite warm."

She watched as he removed his dark blue suit jacket and laid it carefully over the back of one of the two armchairs in the room. His white shirt was so tight-fitting she could see the firm outline of his chest. She was attracted to him but was wary.

"Tea?" she asked.

"Actually, I don't like tea," he said.

He got another quizzical look.

"So you're here under false pretences," she said.

He grinned. "Perhaps coffee?"

Rebecca went into her small kitchen. He followed and came up close behind her.

"Not so fast, Mr Dutchman," Rebecca said, half turning round.

He hesitated.

"This is a picture-viewing visit and tea—well, coffee," she said.

"Of course," he said and backed off.

He stayed for a quarter of an hour. They chatted and got on well. She liked his pale blue eyes. He made no further moves. Eventually, she looked at her watch, and he stood up.

"Thank you for allowing me to see your paintings and for the coffee, of course," he said and walked to the door. "Can I ring you?" he asked.

"You can always try," she said.

He reached forward to kiss her on the lips, but she turned her head away and the kiss landed on her right cheek.

"Goodbye, Mr Dutchman," she said.

He gave her a long look. No smile.

***

A CX intelligence report from MI6 arrived on the prime minister's desk at 5 p.m. Restricted circulation and headed "Unit Zero".

Moscow head of station, July 4.

Unit Zero formed a year ago. Specific missions: assassination, sabotage. Elite membership, Spetsnaz. Nothing in the Russian press, no hint of it in the military journals. Estimated half a dozen assigned to the unit.

Names: only four so far but passed on with a degree of confidence—Major Dimitri Andreyev, Lieutenant-Colonel Mikhail Gerasimov, Captain Leonid Kuznetsov, Colonel Alexie Goncharov. Military careers attached. Photos of Kuznetsov and Goncharov. Who is in charge? This is speculation based on well-sourced intel. No confirmation. But one ex-Spetsnaz officer who used to work in the presidential executive office with unidentified duties has the right credentials for running a unit like this. He has not been seen for months. He is Major-General Maksim Popov.

Chapter Eight
Unit Zero Unveiled

Friday 5th July

On the fourth floor of Thames House, Geraldine Hammer sat at the head of the table in the conference room. Around the table were Grace Redmayne; Jasper Cornfield; Frederick "Freddie" Stigby, Russian expert from MI6; and Major John Fisk from the Ministry of Defence. Harry Brook's representative from the Met's Counter-Terrorism Command was due later.

Geraldine opened the proceedings. "Freddie, perhaps you could give us your views on the four names, and—most important—what you know about Major-General Maksim Popov."

Freddie Stigby, fluent Russian speaker, three years in Moscow, still only thirty-five but regarded as the best Russia man at MI6, nodded at Geraldine.

"I know about the four. They all served together in Crimea in the Special Operations Forces section of Spetsnaz. They were sent on day one of the annexation of Crimea in 2014. I tracked them there throughout the operation. When they returned to Moscow they vanished for some months. They were of course more junior in rank then. I spotted two of them a few months back in satellite photos serving in Syria at the Russian base in Latakia province."

"And Popov?" Geraldine asked.

"He's a bit of an enigma," Stigby replied. "Intensely secret. We don't have a photo of him. He may have been part of Putin's private staff but he was never seen in public with him. The only open reference to him was in 2020 when *Krasnaya Zvezda* had a small item saying he had been promoted from lieutenant-colonel to colonel. But the spelling was different. It was Maxim Popov."

He fell silent for a few seconds, as if gathering his thoughts.

"There was definitely a Popov in Putin's presidential executive office up until a year or so ago, but neither we nor the Americans, as far as I know, could pin him down. In other words, exactly who he was, his background, his past links to Putin or any confirmed biographical details are a bit sketchy."

"Is there anything that will help us if he comes to the UK or indeed if he is here already?" Geraldine asked.

"No, I'm sorry," Stigby replied. "Just supposition. As major-general, if that is his rank, he would normally be in his early fifties but could be younger."

"From past experience," said Major John Fisk, who had spent three years with the MoD's defence intelligence staff and was also a Russian speaker, "none of these Russians will come here in disguise. They are who they are. In other words, they will look like military. Short haircuts, good physique."

"Except they won't be here under their real names," Jasper Cornfield said.

"No," Major Fisk and Freddie Stigby said at the same time.

Geraldine was about to speak when the door opened. It was Detective Chief Inspector Joe Macmillan from the Met's Counter-Terrorism Command.

"Sorry I'm late," he said.

"Any news, Joe?" Geraldine asked.

"Well, a bit strange. Joseph Paine is claiming he had already been arrested a few days ago and set free, or as he put it, allowed to escape."

Geraldine and Grace Redmayne tried to look as surprised as everyone else in the room.

"Exactly what has he said?" Geraldine asked.

"Well, he says on the day of the shooting he was back in London and got grabbed by a bloke with huge arms and hustled into the back of a Land Rover, or what he thought was a Land Rover, and taken off for interrogation in some farmhouse. He said there was a woman in the car, driving, and another bloke. Harry's going ballistic, thinks he might be telling the truth, but he's getting no help from anywhere."

DCI Macmillan looked around the table with his eyebrows raised.

"Thank you, Joe. We'll leave that side of things to Harry," Geraldine said. "Right now we have to concentrate on the Russians, where they may strike next—if there is to be a next."

Freddie Stigby said, "My opinion is that Moscow is not going to send a whole team here. Salisbury was a shambles, and by the way, unsuccessful, apart from that poor woman who died.

"I believe they might only trust the next stage of whatever it is we're facing in the hands of their most experienced man. On that basis, if we start looking for the four suspects referred to by my colleagues in Moscow, we will be wasting our time. I reckon our man is that major-general, Maksim Popov."

He continued: "If it really is true that Operation Foxtrot is the motivation for the attack on Geraldine and for what may come in the future, the Kremlin will want someone of supreme ability and loyalty to deliver the message that the expulsion of Russian diplomats has not been forgotten and will never be forgiven. In my opinion, Popov is in our midst."

Geraldine gestured to Grace and Jasper. "We all came to the same conclusion, Freddie. I think you're right. That doesn't mean we should eliminate the four you have provided for us. They must be at the top of the watch list for every police officer just in case. But the focus for us must be on Popov. When will he make his next move? Where might he be staying? For Salisbury they booked a two-star hotel in East London. Would a man like Popov go for a better hotel, three or four stars? If so, where, and would it necessarily be in London?"

John Fisk looked worried. "Just one point," he said. "Are we sure Moscow would send a major-general to do a job like this? Isn't that a bit senior for an operational role?"

Geraldine turned to Freddie Stigby.

"Well it is unusual, I agree," he said. "But our head of station is convinced this time the Kremlin will have turned to their top man. His high rank doesn't mean he's a desk man. It's not like the old Soviet days when generals tended to get fat and lazy. Moscow central won't stand for that. The Kremlin demands fitness at all levels and all ages. No spreading waistlines. So this General Popov is likely to be a tough guy with a mass of combat experience behind him."

"Ok," said Geraldine. "I hardly need say, but we need a photograph urgently. I can't believe he has never appeared at some function and had his photograph taken in a group. Please tell Moscow that's the priority. Without it we're operating in the dark."

***

Jean-Paul van Dijk left his hotel and caught a taxi to Euston. He was dressed in dark blue jeans, a navy blue fleece and a white T-shirt. He bought a first-class return ticket to Birmingham and spent the day in the city. He met no one but walked around, taking the occasional photograph. He was back in his hotel in High Street Kensington by 9 p.m.

***

Sandy Hall had been running with the Joseph Paine story all day, although he had been unable to glean any extra detail. He filled his reporting with speculation about why a former corporal in the Royal Logistic Corps was allegedly behind an assassination attempt on a senior security official.

He still had no idea who the victim of the shooting was. He had someone he could ring at MI5. Not a press officer—MI5 didn't have a press office—but for a few selected journalists, generally one for each of the serious newspapers and the four main television stations—BBC, ITV, Channel Four and Sky—there was a name and a phone number to ring to receive guidance on an unattributable basis.

However, all his approaches to his contact at MI5 had drawn a blank. No comment, no guidance, nothing to move Sandy in one direction or another. The contact referred all questions to the Press Bureau. The bureau was also being unhelpful.

Sandy got a breakthrough after lunch.

He rang his contact at Counter-Terrorism Command.

"Rick, hi, it's Sandy, are you busy?"

"Always," the detective inspector replied.

"Apologies. But I just wondered whether she is involved in the investigation?"

"Who?"

"The woman who was shot." Sandy held his breath.

"Yes, of course," Rick replied.

"Why, of course, sorry…"

"Well, it's her neck of the woods, isn't it?"

"Counter-terrorism?"

Silence the other end.

"Not counter-terrorism?" Sandy tried again.

"No," his contact replied. "The other one."

"Counter-espionage?"

"If you say so."

"But, I'm right?"

"Makes sense. Got to go, Sandy."

"Rick, sorry, one more question?"

"Ok."

"So that makes it definitely a Russian hit? Paine is the contract man? Is she the top of the department, the director of counter-espionage?"

"That's three questions."

"Only need one answer for the lot," Sandy said, his heart beating fast.

"Sounds good to me," Rick replied. The phone died.

Sandy didn't know who the director of counter-espionage was at MI5. But even if he did, he wouldn't be allowed to make it public.

If he went ahead and reported what his contact had told him, would he be in trouble? Would his contact at MI5 refuse to deal with him in the future? Could he put at risk his relationship with the Press Bureau? He sat at his desk and thought through all the possible consequences. It was just too good a story. If he wasn't mentioning the name of the woman, what did it matter? The would-be assassin presumably knew who she was, or at least, the Russians behind the shooting knew who she was. That in itself was a fascinating piece of information, and he'd got it all through deduction alone. Of course, the Russians knew she was MI5's director of counter-espionage. Why would they order a hit if they didn't know exactly who she was?

But why her? And how did they know her name when he didn't? The answer to the first question came to him quite quickly. Operation Foxtrot. The government's campaign against the Russian intelligence services, particularly GRU, in the years after the Salisbury poisoning. He remembered his contact at MI5 had freely told him the codename for the operation—in fact, had taken some delight in telling him. Operation Foxtrot had been hailed by the government as a success, and the Home Office had praised both MI5 and the Met Police for their combined operation.

So, Sandy thought, the female director of counter-espionage at MI5 had been marked out for assassination for leading the operation against London-based Russian spies. Assuming, that is, she was in the job at the time of Operation Foxtrot. He needed to check that.

Sandy rang MI5.

"David, it's Sandy Hall."

"Yes, Sandy?"

"Just one quick question for guidance. Would I be right in saying that the woman in the shooting incident on Monday was the same person in charge of Operation Foxtrot?"

"Sandy, I just can't help I'm afraid."

"But would I be wrong if I said that?"

"That's kind of the same question."

"Well, would it be ok to say there is believed to be a connection between the shooting and Operation Foxtrot?"

"That would be a matter for you," the MI5 man replied.

"But would you never talk to me again if I reported that?" Sandy asked, laughing nervously.

"I'm sure we will continue to be able to do business with you, Sandy. Does that help?"

"Thank you. Brilliant."

Sandy decided to go as far as he could—further, in fact, than he had mentioned to his MI5 contact. His report on Sky said the victim of the shooting was now known to have been the director of counter-espionage and that the woman had masterminded Operation Foxtrot. He said it looked like a revenge attack and speculated that more hits could be on the way. He then quoted a Tory MP who fancied himself a security expert. The MP said it was vital for the government to make a statement to parliament about the danger to London posed by Russian assassins.

***

Geraldine Hammer's life had changed. She now drove to work accompanied by two armed police officers. An unmarked police car with two more armed officers sat all day outside her home in Kennington. For the time being, while the threat level for her personally was raised to maximum red alert, her two children had been sent to stay with their father. Every member of MI5's counter-espionage department had been ordered to remain vigilant and to travel to work by different routes every day, but it had been assessed that Geraldine was the main target and the only one needing round-the-clock armed protection.

Her father had been a senior civil servant, ending his career as an adviser on Northern Ireland in Number 10. Before that, he'd worked closely with MI5 on countering Provisional IRA and Loyalist terrorism before the Good Friday Agreement was signed in 1998, bringing the Troubles to a close after thirty years. During one stage of his career, he and his family had to live with a police sentry box at the front gate. Geraldine was only young then and had thought the security precautions were over the top, especially when she was taken to the local park with her mother and father, escorted by two police officers armed with Heckler & Koch semi-automatic submachine guns.

Now she accepted the need for protection. It was still not something she welcomed.

She was on the point of leaving her office in Thames House when her phone rang. It was George Trench.

"Geraldine, I've just had a call from Number 10," he said. "The PM's taking a personal interest in your safety. He wants you to have someone inside your house overnight."

"What! That's not necessary. I've got the guys outside. I'll be fine."

"It's what he wants. To be absolutely sure. Someone from Rollie Gibson's team."

"But the Met will go mad. It's their job, not some jumped-up secret force from the Foreign Office."

"Well, I agree, but the PM insists. I spoke to Gibson. He's sending over his guy Sam Cook. He'll meet you here in twenty minutes. Outside at the back. He'll have his own car."

"It's like a bloody circus," Geraldine said.

"Just go with it. Once we get the details of this Popov fellow, we'll be on better ground. At least we will know who we're looking for," the MI5 chief said.

"Ha, let's hope so."

Chapter Nine
A Breakthrough at Last

Sunday 7ᵗʰ July

Shortly after 10 p.m. the MI6 head of station in Moscow sent an urgent top-secret communication to London. A photograph of Major-General Maksim Popov had been found. It was several years old, from when Popov was a lieutenant-colonel. His name appeared in a caption under a photograph of a group of Russian military officers in Krasnoyarsk in Siberia. The photograph, a little obscured, was on the Facebook page of the mayor of Krasnoyarsk.

Blown up and cleaned up, the image was adequate. Popov's picture was circulated to MI5, the Metropolitan Police, the Border Force, and copies were passed to the prime minister, selected cabinet colleagues, Colonel Gibson and the SAS headquarters in Hereford.

The CX intelligence report included a caption attached to the photograph:

"Major-General Maksim Popov is 49. Just over 6ft tall, pale skin, broad face, bushy eyebrows. Thought to be fluent in English. Still no sign of him in Moscow."

Geraldine Hammer was in the first-floor sitting room of her house in Gladstone Street, Kennington when she received the secure email. The room was decorated to suit a relaxed, calming mood. The walls were painted in a soft yellow and the curtains were a similar colour with a light blue flower-patterned effect. The room was modern and expensively furnished but without branding it as an up-to-date fashion statement. It was a timeless example of good taste. The only thing in the room which seemed out of place was the large mirror above the fireplace. It was elaborately framed with gold-coloured serpents and dragons. The mirror had hung in her parents' house in Tunbridge Wells throughout her childhood. It was gaudy but her mother said it was a family heirloom, bought by her grandmother. It was passed to Geraldine on her fortieth birthday, and she loved it. Her father had always hated it.

Geraldine looked at the emailed photograph closely and found herself breathing a sigh of relief.

Ever since MI6 had identified Major-General Maksim Popov as the likely selected assassin to carry out the Kremlin's revenge plots against London, she had been harbouring a secret fear.

She had never lost the niggling anxiety that her encounter with Lucas Meyer had been staged. She had told no one about the man who had asked to use her phone and a week later taken her to the Royal Opera House. That whole evening was something she wanted to push out of her mind. But as the search for the Russian connection to the shooting on the first of July absorbed everyone's attention in her department and at the Met's Counter-Terrorism Command, she had the image of Lucas Meyer in her head. She should have taken Grace Redmayne into her confidence, but for some reason she held back. She had made two discreet inquiries. She checked on the car-leasing company Lucas claimed to have used. It existed and had done so for eight years. Then she made inquiries about the apartment at One Blackfriars. A Mr L. Meyer had taken out a one-year rental. Still, she worried.

But the photograph of Maksim Popov looked nothing like Lucas Meyer.

Geraldine had been a professional intelligence officer long enough to know that she should never take anything for granted. No intelligence picture should ever be constructed to fit a preconceived idea or conviction. There were too often surprises in the intelligence world. Her father had taught her that even before she joined MI5 as a graduate trainee.

The photo of Maksim Popov gave her at least some confidence that the Russian military officer deemed by her MI6 colleagues to be the Kremlin's chief assassin and probably behind the attempt on her life was not Lucas Meyer; and that Lucas Meyer was neither Russian nor a member of GRU, let alone Unit Zero, but was an unfortunate part of her life, briefly, and nothing more.

She still shuddered when she remembered the moment when he had picked her up and carried her to his luxury bedroom. At the time she had felt intoxicated with desire and a yearning to make love and feel once again the intimate physical togetherness of joining with a man. Her marriage to Paul had been perfectly happy and the intimacy they'd shared had been passionate and absorbing for many years, but the birth of their two children and the ever-increasing pressures of their respective jobs changed that relationship. They rarely talked about it. But the intimacy vanished. Paul had never insisted on trying to revive what they'd had before. Indeed, he'd seemed to accept their lack of physical closeness with relief. Geraldine worked longer hours than he did as an academic. He spent more time at home with Janie and William and resented her when she returned home late and exhausted.

It had taken them another two years to realise that separation was the only answer. Paul told her when they agreed to divorce that being married to a senior MI5 officer could have been exciting and fun but in reality, he had increasingly become isolated from her and knew he could never be part of her world. His lawyer claimed irreconcilable differences and Geraldine put up no defence, other than to fight for custody of her children. An amicable arrangement was agreed.

Geraldine's whole body had been stirred when she first stood naked in front of Lucas Meyer. It was why she had closed her eyes. She could hardly believe in those first few seconds that another man actually found her attractive and wanted to be intimate with her. She longed for it. But as Lucas came towards her, she had in her mind the night of her first love-making with Paul. He had been tender and gentle. They were in love.

Lucas was so totally different that her nostalgic thoughts were shattered immediately. It was not just the power of the naked man on top of her. The sheer brutal force made her feel instantly vulnerable. She was lying naked with a stranger. After such a long time of sleeping in a bed alone, all she experienced was fear.

Afterwards, she blamed herself. She hated Lucas Meyer for what he had done to her—but it was her fault. She had gone to his apartment for food and drink, knowing what he had in mind. She'd known, but she went along with it. It shocked her that she had taken such a risk.

She had no reason to expect ever to hear from Lucas Meyer again. He had made no attempt to get in touch with her, either to apologise or to try and make amends. She knew almost nothing about him. Whether he was still in London or whether his permanent residence was elsewhere in Europe. She was reluctant to seek help in tracking him down for fear of raising awkward questions. She had contacts in the Home Office but she couldn't even begin to imagine how she'd explain this to them. A personal unofficial request from MI5's director of counter-espionage would have caused alarm bells, not just at the Home Office but inevitably, eventually, at Thames House. She couldn't risk it, even though it would have been comforting for her to know that Lucas Meyer was a legitimate businessman who had returned to his home city of, say, Copenhagen.

Geraldine left the sitting room and went downstairs to the kitchen. Sam Cook was sitting at the table. He jumped up.

"Sam, for goodness' sake, stop being so gentlemanly," Geraldine said with a smile. "I've just received some developing news. With any luck, if I have anything to do with it, you'll be able to go back to your wife soon. I won't need you to stand guard over me."

Geraldine liked Sam. His huge size had been more than reassuring, but she had also enjoyed his company in the brief moments when they'd had time to chat. The only other member of the Shadow Force team she'd met was Colonel Rollie Gibson, who she'd seen on a couple of occasions during previous security crisis occasions but they'd never had cause to work together. If Sam Cook was typical of the type of person recruited to Gibson's unit, she felt she had been too quick to judge them when she'd dismissed the Foreign Office's unofficial "hit squad" as jumped-up. Nevertheless, she disapproved of the whole concept.

She worried, too, about what was going to happen with Joseph Paine. Stamping national security on the case as justification for ignoring the police and turning to Gibson's team was never going to impress a judge, and certainly wouldn't help to get her would-be assassin convicted and sent to prison for life. In her view, it was a huge error of judgment on the part of the prime minister with potential damaging legal and political consequences.

She didn't tell Sam the news about Major-General Maksim Popov. She would leave that to others.

She couldn't imagine how Popov or indeed anyone in the Kremlin would know where she lived. It was one of the reasons she had argued to herself against Lucas Meyer being a Russian agent.

The police guard and the addition of Sam had been an unnecessary precaution, she thought. But she had gone along with it, first because she had no choice and second because of that secret doubt about Lucas Meyer. That doubt had been lifted with the arrival in her email account of the picture and description of Maksim Popov. She shrugged away the thought that Lucas Meyer, physically, looked more like the stereotypical Russian agent than Maksim Popov.

"I've had no orders yet about leaving here," Sam said, "so I'm afraid you're stuck with me for the moment. And by the way, I don't have a wife."

Geraldine laughed. "Well, Sam, it has been a pleasure. I'm very happy and relieved that you've not had anything to do other than lose sleep, for which I apologise."

"No problem," he said.

Geraldine went to the fridge, took out a bottle of white wine and handed him a glass from the cupboard.

"I have to go back upstairs to do some work," she said, filling both glasses. "But cheers, and thanks."

***

The prime minister had a telephone call with Lawrence Fenwick at 11 p.m. They discussed whether to put out a nationwide alert, to include the media, about the potential threat posed by the Russian agent now identified by MI6. Fenwick strongly advised against it. It would lead, he said, to multiple calls from every crank and well-meaning citizen. The police would be overwhelmed having to check out every claimed sighting of the Russian. The threat and the identity of the suspected Russian assassin should be kept strictly within the law enforcement and security community, the home secretary said.

Jonathan Ford agreed. But he was worried about leaks, particularly from the Home Office. He ordered Fenwick to reveal the name of the Russian general only to the smallest possible circle of officials at the Home Office.

Ford then rang Elizabeth Gantry and gave her the same message. On the whole, the Foreign Office seemed to leak less than the Home Office. But her assurance that the name would remain a secret as far as her department was concerned did little to relieve his concerns that the latest development might be leaked.

His last call before turning in was to Rollie Gibson.

"Colonel, I will need your services," he said.

"Of course, Prime Minister," Gibson replied. He was in his Westminster flat and had been studying the photograph of Major-General Maksim Popov.

"What's your feeling about this Russian?" Ford asked.

"He may not be here yet," Gibson replied. "He could be waiting for his moment."

"But surely that's a risk. After the failed shooting, wouldn't he have been here already or at least flown here soon after, like the same day?"

"I assume checks are being done on all passengers arriving in the UK since the shooting?"

"Of course," Ford replied abruptly. "But that'll take time. We only got the picture ninety minutes ago. Nothing so far."

"The phone call to Paine was from someone in the UK, but it may have just been an intermediary," Gibson said. "There's no way of knowing whether it was Popov himself. If it was, then the question is answered: he's here now and preparing for his next move. Or if it was an intermediary, Popov is biding his time. He won't fly in from Moscow, and he'll be using a false passport."

"Trench and Farthing are both convinced the man is already here, Colonel, and I'm going to go along with their instinct."

Gibson kept quiet.

"I want you to set up a base in central London, somewhere nondescript," Ford said. "Hereford is constantly pressing me to authorise one of their squads to form up at Chelsea barracks. I may still do that, but a leak from the Ministry of Defence about the SAS on the way, and the Opposition will be screaming cover-up."

"I'll start on it tomorrow, Prime Minister," Gibson said.

"No, Colonel, I want it now. I want you and your team ready to go from midnight," Ford said.

"Yes, Prime Minister."

Chapter Ten
Murder Most Foul Followed by Play

Monday 8th July, 2:30 a.m.

The two police officers sitting in their car outside Geraldine Hammer's house had been on duty for five hours. It was the worst sort of job, and now the inevitable tiredness had begun to affect both of them. It was summer but the night was cool. The engine was running to keep them warm. They hadn't spoken for ten minutes or so. The inside of the car was steamed up.

Another ten minutes went by. Suddenly there was a knock on the window on the passenger side. The officer sitting in the front turned to his colleague in the driver's seat and raised his eyebrows. The driver lowered the window. A large man was standing on the pavement with a balaclava covering his face. The man leaned in with a gun in his hand and shot both police officers in the head. No silencer. The shots shattered the silence of Gladstone Street.

Sam was still inside Geraldine's house. Gibson had rung him to tell him of the prime minister's order but told Sam to stay where he was for the time being, while Gibson and the rest of Shadow Force settled down in a rented flat above a shop near the Oval cricket ground. A promise of a down payment of a thousand pounds and a vague reference to a "police surveillance matter" had persuaded the shop owner to meet Gibson around midnight and hand over the keys to the flat. Tim, George, Seamus and Rose arrived soon afterwards.

At the sound of gunshots, Sam leapt up from his makeshift bed in the kitchen and peered through the curtains. A man was standing next to the unmarked police car. Then ran off. Sam nearly tripped over the mat at the entrance to the kitchen as he rushed to the front door, unlocked it and hurtled down the steps. The police officers were dead, blood down their faces and staring eyes. Sam started running down the street but stopped at the end of Geraldine's road. There was no sign of the gunman, and he had abandoned his prime duty, which was to protect Geraldine. He ran back to her house, ringing 999 and then Gibson as he stumbled up the steps.

Sam had been out of the house for no more than four minutes.

The gunman had not gone far. He had hidden the other side of a four-by-four Nissan parked directly behind the unmarked police car. After Sam dashed up the street, he moved swiftly to Geraldine's front door and inserted a knife in the lock. The door opened. He took the stairs two steps at a time and ran to the room where he could hear a woman's urgent voice on the phone. Geraldine, in pink bra and pants, was talking to the Met Police emergency line when the gunman burst in with his pistol outstretched pointing at her chest. She dropped the phone and tried to cover herself. The gunman hesitated.

Sam came into the room like a charging rhinoceros and hurled himself at the gunman, pinning him down on the bed. Geraldine cried out and leapt from her bed as the two men struggled. Sam was much bigger, but the gunman was skilled. He brought the gun round in a twisting movement and struck Sam on the side of the head. Sam briefly released his hold around the gunman's neck but then attempted to pile his huge fist into the man's throat. The gunman broke away and took only a glancing blow to his head. His face was still hidden behind the balaclava.

Police sirens were approaching. The gunman swung the pistol through the air and crashed it into Sam's face. Sam threw his head back, and in that moment the gunman pushed him away and launched himself off the bed. Without looking at Geraldine, who was cowering by the window, he ran from the room, down the stairs and headed for the back of the house.

Geraldine heard the door leading to her garden splinter open. There was a curse in a foreign language. Two minutes later, her bedroom was filled with armed police officers, followed soon after by Gibson.

The gunman sprinted through Geraldine's small, paved garden, leapt over the fence and ran down an alley leading to the back of a school. He clambered over the perimeter fence and headed for the front gate. He jumped over the gate into Lambeth Road. The sound of police sirens filled the air.

A white van with fresh food supplies written on the side turned into the road from St George's Circus, eighty yards away. The gunman stood in the middle of the road with his gun pointing at the windscreen. The van skewed to a stop. The gunman opened the passenger door and climbed in.

"Do what I want and you'll deliver your fresh food," he said, waving the gun in the driver's face. "Turn round and make for Blackfriars Bridge. Head north. Keep to the speed limit."

The driver was so shocked he obeyed automatically, doing a three-point turn and driving back to St George's Circus before going up the A201 to cross the Thames at Blackfriars Bridge. He glanced at the man next to him and wondered how he would describe him to the police, if he survived. The balaclava completely covered his face and head, but he was a big man. He spoke with a slight trace of a foreign accent. Calm, not panicking. Dressed in a black tracksuit.

"You've got satnav. Keep north. Head for Kentish Town," his passenger said.

"My delivery's in south London, opposite direction," the driver said.

The gunman looked at him but said nothing.

After thirty-five minutes, the white van reached Kentish Town. They hadn't spoken again.

"Tufnell Park," the gunman said.

"What?"

"Drop me off at Tufnell Park."

"Whereabouts?"

"When I tell you."

Seven minutes later, the gunman shouted, "Stop."

The driver braked and parked outside a row of shops.

"Give me your phone," the gunman said.

The driver handed over his mobile, his heart beating as he kept his eyes on the gun.

"Get the hell out of here," the gunman said, and opened the door. He slammed it shut and banged it with his fist. The driver accelerated away, still going north.

There was no one around to witness what had happened. The gunman ran down a side street filled with parked cars. He selected a maroon Vauxhall Viva, broke in, played around with the ignition and started up the engine. Then he removed his balaclava and replaced it with a cap from the pocket of his tracksuit top and wrapped a scarf around his neck. He knew there would be cameras watching. He waited ten minutes with the engine running while he checked Google Maps on his phone. He plotted a complex route south, using side streets as much as possible, and then moved off slowly, heading south-west.

***

Back at Geraldine's house, there was still bedlam. She had put on a silk dressing gown. Sam was talking to Gibson. He had a large cut on his face but refused to be taken to hospital. The police had cordoned off the whole street. Commander Harry Brooks had arrived five minutes earlier and taken charge. Forensic teams were examining the police car with the two dead bodies. Every police officer at the scene, including Harry Brooks, looked stunned. It was now 3:30 a.m.

A London-wide operation was launched to catch the gunman on camera. But even though the city was awash with CCTV networks, it was not an instant process. If he had a vehicle parked for his escape, though, he would be spotted eventually, especially if he was going fast. There were no witness reports. It was the wrong time of night for observant pedestrians or drivers. No reports of a stolen or hijacked vehicle. The gunman had vanished.

Geraldine and Sam had given as much detail as they could about the armed intruder and police killer. Tall, probably six foot, broad shoulders, solid body, physically strong, fought like a veteran scrapper. He had said nothing except some indecipherable curse, or what they assumed was a curse. Definitely foreign. Popov? Could it have been Maksim Popov? Geraldine and Sam had no idea.

"We'll get him," Harry said. "Two dead cops. We'll definitely get him. CCTV will deliver. There's no way he can just disappear without wheels. We'll get an image before the night's over."

"He must have had an escape plan," Gibson said. "He shot the two officers and then waited. He knew there would be more security inside the house and deliberately drew them out. Well, Sam in this case. Sorry, Sam, but you did what he wanted you to do."

Sam nodded.

"But why didn't he shoot me, why did he hesitate?" Geraldine asked.

"That's a mystery," Brooks said. "He came here to finish off the job. Can you think of anything? Anything you said or did to make him hesitate?"

Geraldine's heart missed a beat.

"I said nothing," she said. "It was all so quick."

Gibson asked, "What were you doing when he pointed the gun?"

Geraldine thought for a few seconds, her heart still thumping against her chest.

"I was in my bra and pants. I think I tried to cover myself with my hands," she said. "Like I was trying to protect myself. Stupid, but..."

"Forgive me, but perhaps he liked what he saw," Gibson said.

Geraldine stared at him.

Brooks interrupted. "Geraldine, you've faced enough already. We'll leave you and we can talk more tomorrow."

"I'm sorry, I didn't mean to be disrespectful," Gibson said.

"No, Colonel, it was a good question. It was the right question," she replied.

"If it's true then it saved your life," Gibson said quietly.

"And Sam. Sam saved my life."

"Yes, of course."

***

10 a.m.

Jean-Paul van Dijk was having a long shower and thinking of Rebecca Strong. Once dried and dressed, he rang her.

"It's Jean-Paul," he said.

"Well, hello," Rebecca replied.

"I have a relatively free day today. I wondered if you might like to come and have lunch with me here at my hotel," he asked.

"No business today, eh?"

"No so much."

"I'll check my diary."

"Busier than me, obviously."

"An artist's work is never done."

"Ha."

"Looks like I might be free," she said.

"Great. How about you come here to the Royal Garden Hotel at, say, twelve thirty, or shall I come and pick you up?"

"Send a limo," she said.

"A limo?"

"A long one."

"I could send a taxi."

"Not very impressive, Mr Dutchman."

"I'm sorry, what do you want exactly?" He sounded a little confused.

"Relax, it's called British sarcasm."

"Ah, right, I see."

This time he sounded relieved.

"I'll see you at twelve thirty," she said. "I'm a grown-up, I can make my own way."

She rang off. He looked at the phone briefly and smiled. Then he turned on the TV. Sky News.

There was only one story: the overnight fatal shooting of two police officers. Sky's crime correspondent, Sandy Hall, looking somewhat dishevelled, was standing outside Scotland Yard. As he was speaking, he regularly pointed behind him to remind viewers where he was. He summarised what he had learnt from his police sources:

"A gunman wearing a balaclava shot the two officers at close range and then ran off. Armed police arrived on the scene in minutes, but the gunman had vanished. The Met Police are not saying why the two police officers were sitting in a car at two thirty in the morning in Gladstone Street, Kennington. There is speculation that the officers were guarding a house, but the Met Police are refusing to give further details. Several ministers and MPs are known to live in Kennington because of its easy access to Westminster. The police declined to say whether the shooting had any connection with the attempted assassination of MI5's director of counter-espionage a week ago."

Sandy went on to remind viewers that the director of counter-espionage was a woman, that she had been injured but had recovered and had been targeted, according to his sources, because she had masterminded Operation Foxtrot a year ago, aimed at expelling members of the GRU military intelligence agency from Britain. A full-scale hunt was on in London, he said, to find the gunman, who was believed to be still in the capital.

Jean-Paul van Dijk was about to switch off the TV when the crime correspondent appeared to receive something in his earpiece. He said there was breaking news.

"We've just heard that the driver of a van has come forward to the police to say he was hijacked by a gunman in south London and forced at gunpoint to drive north. The driver was on his way to deliver fresh food to a store in Stockwell when the gunman stopped him. The driver is still being questioned because when they searched his van they found no food in the back. He appears to have delivered the food before contacting the police. Vital hours were lost."

At 12:40 p.m., Jean-Paul was waiting for Rebecca in the foyer. She was late. He spotted her walking up the steps of the hotel. She was wearing a flowing green dress with a yellow belt.

He kissed her on each cheek, with one hand on her shoulder and the other on her left side. He felt the shape of her breast and removed his hand, but not immediately. She gave him that now familiar quizzical look but said nothing.

He guided her into the restaurant.

"Well," he said. "It's wonderful to see you. I'm glad you could make time for me in your crowded diary."

They sat down at a table by the window.

"Could just squeeze you in," she said, brushing her long blonde hair out of her eyes.

He smiled. "So you have to rush off after lunch?"

"Depends," she said.

"On what?"

"On whether I have to rush off."

He frowned slightly but then grinned. "It's like a code?"

"Only if you're a spy. Are you a spy?"

"Yes," he said.

"Oh good. Who for?"

"For Holland, of course."

"Very good, Mr Dutchman, you're catching on fast."

They chose their food and he ordered champagne.

Rebecca mentioned the news and asked if he had heard about the shooting. He nodded.

"No city is safe these days," he said.

"Not even in Holland?"

"Not even in Holland."

They fell silent and ate their food. The bottle of champagne soon emptied.

"Rebecca, I'm afraid I need to go to my room," he said suddenly. "Do *you* need to go to my room?"

Rebecca wiped her mouth with her napkin and stood up.

In the lift up to the sixth floor, they stood apart but their eyes were locked. They walked quickly to Room 607. Once inside, they grabbed each other. She removed his jacket and unbuttoned his shirt. He undid her belt and lifted the dress over her head. He stood back to take a look. She was wearing a large yellow-flowered bra with a deep, bursting cleavage and matching panties which clung to her hips. He stripped.

"Bloody hell," Rebecca said, staring at him.

He stepped forward as she undid her bra. He began to push her backwards towards the bed but she turned him round and he fell onto his back. She swung his legs round and leapt on top of him before sitting up. He stayed quiet.

"Just lie back and think of Holland," she said, her hair almost covering her face. She took charge.

"Well, well, Mr Dutchman," she said into his chest when they were finished. His chest was so firm and shaped it was like lying on metal plates.

His eyes were closed. She raised herself on one elbow and examined him from top to bottom. His chest was rigidly muscled. She could see the muscles in his stomach. His arms and legs were powerful. If he was a businessman, he was a fanatical weight trainer. If he wasn't a businessman, what was he? She had known him for only a short time but he had revealed almost nothing about himself. All that lineage banter she treated with suspicion. But he had behaved in her flat.

Yet there was something almost unreal about him. As if he had planned everything. The chance encounter at her favourite brasserie, the chat-up lines, the interest in her painting. Was he just playing the male game to get her into bed, or was there something else behind it all?

She had willingly gone along with it. It had been exciting. She had wanted excitement. But as she examined his body, Rebecca felt a tiny tremor of doubt. He was too good to be true. His charm was too obvious. She didn't think it came naturally to him.

She fell back on the bed and closed her eyes, and was soon lightly asleep.

Jean-Paul's phone pinged. He reached for it and read the text. Rebecca appeared to be asleep. He moved off the bed and went for a shower.

Rebecca opened her eyes and saw for the first time that he had a long dagger tattoo on the back of his left leg.

Chapter Eleven

Sandy Gets Another Scoop but Fears for His Story

Monday 8th July, 11 a.m.

Sandy had been standing outside the taped-off area at the end of Gladstone Street with his cameraman for a couple of hours, along with a crowd of other reporters, television crews and curious onlookers—a typical reporters' vigil. It was a warm day, but everyone, including Sandy, had come in thick anoraks. It often got cold waiting for something to happen.

Reporters with nothing to do but stare beyond a cordoned-off area started complaining very quickly, and in the cold, the whingeing was always worse. All the reporters had been demanding a briefing from the senior officer present but to no avail.

Every report referred to the constant flow of light-blue-overalled forensic police officers going in and out of one particular house. The house with a yellow front door. Like the other reporters, Sandy had checked the electoral register to see who was living at number 16, but no names were listed. It didn't surprise him. If it was a government minister or even an MP, they wouldn't want their London address to be so easily accessible.

One reporter, from the *Daily Star,* said he had heard the Home Secretary lived there. But Sandy knew where Lawrence Fenwick lived in London, and it wasn't number 16 Gladstone Street. He kept that information to himself.

Sandy's instinct was that the house now at the centre of police activity was the home of MI5's director of counter-espionage. There was only one person who might confirm that for him, but Sandy was worried he was pushing his luck with his best contact in Counter-Terrorism Command. The detective inspector had always been an exceptional source, but Sandy knew that with this story the Met and the government would be ultra-sensitive about leaks. His contact might be suspected and investigated. He couldn't risk that. Even if he got confirmation, he wouldn't be able to publicise the fact that MI5's top counter-espionage official lived in Gladstone Street, SE1. Anything revealing a senior MI5 officer's identity or address or family details was prohibited under the MoD's D-Notice system. But if he was right, it meant that a Russian intelligence unit or someone acting unofficially for the Kremlin or even a rogue agent was trying to finish off what ex-Corporal Joseph Paine had started. This was so huge that he didn't see how the D-Notice system could prevent him from telling the public what was going on.

The local police commander walked up to the throng of reporters standing behind the taped barrier, but all he had to say was that there would be no statement of any kind while further investigations continued. Sandy and others shouted questions, but he just turned away and walked back down Gladstone Street.

Sandy rang his news desk to say he was coming back to the office. It took him twenty minutes to get a taxi.

Back at his desk, he thought for a few minutes about his best strategy. He had to ring his contact; there was no other option.

The phone rang for a long time before it was picked up.

"Rick, it's Sandy," he said quietly.

"Jesus, you're going to get me into trouble," the detective inspector replied. "Questions are already being asked."

"Rick, I'm so sorry, I don't want to cause you any trouble."

"But..."

"But I've been down at you-know-where this morning and no one is saying anything."

"Hardly surprising."

"I assume she is no longer there?" Sandy held his breath.

"Sounds like a cunning question."

"No, I was just thinking after what happened there that she would be moved elsewhere?"

"Well, wouldn't you want to move somewhere safer?"

"Of course, absolutely," Sandy said, desperately thinking of the best way to get the answer he needed without being blatant. "You mean after it being the second attempt on her life?" he asked, holding his breath for the second time.

This was a pure guess on Sandy's part. The story was about the killing of two police officers. But had something else happened? Had the gunman gained entry to the house and threatened the head of MI5's counter-espionage department? If so, it was an even bigger story.

"Quite," Rick replied.

"I assume she did survive... again?"

"Yes."

"But terrible about the two officers guarding her home."

"Yes."

"How the hell did the gunman know where she lived?"

"Above my pay grade. Got to go." He rang off.

Sandy sat back. Now what? He had to write it. He went to see the news editor and told him what Rick had. The news editor exploded.

"My God, get it out fast," he said.

"But you realise this could bring the police and MoD and everyone down on to us like a ton of—"

"Damn them all. They're covering this up. The public needs to know. Our public needs to know!" the news editor shouted. "Write it as strong as you can and let the legal boys sort it out."

Sandy went back to his desk and wrote what he thought was a pretty good script. He wrote it straight. The drama was in the words; he didn't need to sensationalise. He decided against ringing the Press Bureau but wondered if he should warn his MI5 contact. He rang Thames House.

"Is David there? It's Sandy Hall."

The phone had been answered by a woman.

"He's tied up at the moment," she said. "Can I tell him what it's about?"

"The shooting."

"I don't think he's saying anything on that but I'll let him know you called."

"Thank you. Tell him I have a story which will be running within the hour."

Sandy rang off.

Ten minutes later his phone rang.

"Sandy, it's David. How can I help?"

"David, thanks for coming back to me. I'm running a story saying the two police officers shot dead were guarding the house of the same MI5 official who was shot at on July first," Sandy said.

"Have you had that confirmed by Press Bureau?"

"No, but..."

"I think you should tell Press Bureau," David replied quietly.

"So you're not commenting at all?"

"I'm not saying anything. I'm not confirming or denying, but I really advise you to speak to Press Bureau."

"Ok, thanks."

Sandy knew Dave's guidance was more warning than advice. He told the news editor, who agreed he should ring the Met.

He rang the Press Bureau and told them briefly what he was about to report. The spokesman refused to comment.

He finished writing his story. The phone rang.

"Is that Sandy Hall?"

It was a posh voice.

"Yes," Sandy replied, looking at his watch. He was due on air in fifteen minutes.

"It's Rear Admiral John Cartwright at the MoD."

"Oh yeah?" Sandy said, not registering who his caller was.

"D-Notice Committee."

"Ah," Sandy said, and his heart thumped. His story was about to be binned.

"It has come to my attention that you have a story that might breach national security guidelines as set down for all editors. You know the system."

"Well, I'm about to run a new story about the killing of the two police officers," Sandy replied cautiously.

The admiral who held the post of secretary of the D-Notice Committee had retired from the Royal Navy. His job was to be knowledgeable about the difference between a good story that might be embarrassing to the government and something that genuinely might damage Britain's national security interests. He had only been in the post for a year and had yet to get to know all the reporters writing about defence, security and crime, but he had a good rapport with all the security and intelligence services and kept abreast of likely sensitive areas. As secretary, he was also well acquainted with the D-Notice Committee members, who were editors from selected national and provincial newspapers as well as television and radio broadcasters.

The Sky News editor was on the committee. None of the media members were enthusiastic about the MoD D-Notice system. However, real problems rarely arose. In any event, the rear admiral had little real power and authority. He was there to offer guidance and to be persuasive if he could. The slapping of a D-Notice on a newspaper was the boldest move he could make, but even that was not like an injunction. It was a reminder, not a writ.

"So," said Admiral Cartwright from his tiny office in the MoD main building in Whitehall, "are you going to name the individual who is at the centre of this unfortunate incident?"

"No," replied Sandy.

"You have already written about this particular individual in relation to the first shooting incident on July first," the admiral said. "You're now, I'm informed, going to link the two incidents to the same individual?"

Sandy wondered who had rung the admiral: Press Bureau or MI5?

"Yes," he replied. There was no point in denying it.

"But you're still not going to name this person?"

"No, I'm not."

"Well, that's good," the admiral said. "And what about the address? Are you going to identify the full address of this person?"

Sandy hesitated. "Everyone knows the shooting of the two police officers took place in Gladstone Street, Kennington."

"Indeed. But you're linking the two shooting incidents with the same individual and revealing this person's address, which could be compromising, security-wise," the admiral persisted.

"What if I left out the number of the house and just said a house in Gladstone Street?" Sandy asked, looking again at his watch and realising he was running out of time.

There was a pause, and then: "I think that would be acceptable."

"So, no problem with me going ahead then?" Sandy asked, surprised.

"On the basis we have just agreed, I'm quite happy," the admiral said.

"Thank you."

"Thank you for being so understanding."

When the phone clicked, Sandy looked amazed. The admiral had been perfectly nice and accommodating. Sandy had assumed the worst. He picked up his script and ran to the studio. He had three minutes.

***

Geraldine Hammer had been moved to a safe house not far from the Houses of Parliament while the police continued to examine every room in her home. Sam had wanted to stay with her, but Gibson said the Met would provide all the necessary protection from now on. Sam was needed back with the team.

The prime minister told Gibson that Shadow Force had to remain out of the limelight at all costs. Sam's presence in Geraldine's house had been fortuitous, but Ford didn't want Gibson and his team to do anything that might draw unwelcome publicity. Hereford had also finally been authorised to send a counter-terrorism squadron to Chelsea Barracks, and they were on their way.

However, Ford still wanted Shadow Force to be fully alert. The suspected Russian agent, Major-General Maksim Popov, had murdered two police officers and there was no way he was going to evade capture, whether it was by the police, SAS or Shadow Force, the prime minister had told Gibson. Assuming the Russian was still in London or at least in the UK, there was every possibility he had other targets in mind, he said.

**

GCHQ, the Government Communications Headquarters, was by statute employed to monitor and intercept electronic signals from overseas that could have a malevolent intent towards the UK's security and economic wellbeing. Coming under the auspices of the Foreign Office, its principal mission was to focus, in alliance with the global-reach US National Security Agency, on communications of all kinds from hostile or potentially hostile parts of the world. But GCHQ was also legally authorised to assist in the prevention and detection of serious crime.

The director of GCHQ, a former senior MoD civil servant, received an order from the Foreign Office to focus some of their vast eavesdropping capacity on the whole of Greater London to try and pick up any sign of the evasive Russian agent.

Eavesdropping within the UK on a large scale was a sensitive issue after the revelations by Edward Snowden of wholesale snooping by the NSA in the US. However, in such an emergency, Jonathan Ford decided it was justified, for a short period, for British citizens' right to privacy to be set aside for the safety of the nation as a whole.

***

The hunt for the killer of the two police officers was getting nowhere. The media knew nothing about the added drama inside number 16 Gladstone Street. The police had taken the driver of the white van along the same route he had driven with the gunman in the passenger seat. Every camera on the way had been checked, but there was no image of the gunman that gave any hint of what he looked like. The balaclava was the perfect disguise. When the van came to an abrupt halt in Tuffnell Park, cameras on both sides of the road showed the gunman leap out with the gun still in his hand and run down a side street. Despite the mass CCTV coverage in London, the gunman vanished. There were no cameras in that particular street. But where did he go? Another camera would surely pick him up. Every car that appeared on screen was peered at by the experts, image frozen. Even at that time of the morning, there had been plenty of traffic. Especially white vans and lorries engaged in their night-time deliveries.

There was no image of a maroon Vauxhall Viva driven by a man with a cap and a scarf round his neck.

The cameras, however, did manage to follow the fresh-food delivery van as the driver drove fast south, reaching his destination at a supermarket in Stockwell. He unloaded pallets of food, taking around twenty minutes. It was only then that a 999 call was made to inform the police that a gunman had hijacked his vehicle and forced him at gunpoint to drive north. The driver claimed his life had been threatened and that he was scared. He also said the gunman had taken his phone and he'd had no way of ringing the police.

When he was asked why he hadn't stopped at a phone kiosk to ring 999, the driver said he didn't think public phones worked anymore. The police officers who questioned him said it was obvious he had decided to make his delivery before doing his duty and contacting the police. The driver said he had been through a terrifying experience and it wasn't right to accuse him of anything. There was a discussion about charging him with failing to report a crime, but he was released.

A maroon Vauxhall Viva was later caught on camera driving round the back of Harrods, but the face of the driver was obscured by a thick scarf. It was several hours before the car was reported stolen. By then, both the car and the driver had disappeared.

Chapter Twelve

Shadow Force Wonders if Geraldine Hammer Is Hiding Something

Monday 8th July, 7 p.m.

Rollie Gibson had his team around him. The flat had only two bedrooms, but they had arranged for extra mattresses to be delivered. Tim joked that it was like the Mafia "going to the mattresses". Gibson said there would be little chance of a cook-up Mafia-style.

"I want to go through everything we've got so far," Gibson said.

Sam, Tim, George, Seamus and Rose were sitting on uncomfortable kitchen chairs. Sam was the only one who had seen real action so far in their secret mission. Apart from the seizing of Joseph Paine and his subsequent interrogation, it had been relatively quiet for a team more used to intensive, often violent, activity.

George, in particular, felt frustrated. He had told his wife he would be away for an indefinite period. It had only been for a week so far but he was on edge. He had always hated the waiting when he was in the Parachute Regiment. Crazy action for a short period and then waiting around for the next move. There had been no crazy action for him with this current mission.

Seamus and Rose had had their fun following Paine to the garage in south London, and Tim seemed unconcerned about the lack of action. Seamus and Rose were an amusing pair. They seemed to enjoy each other's company and worked well together, chatting and laughing. George missed his wife and kids.

George didn't know Tim that well. He was less companionable than Seamus and Rose, and George wondered whether it was the officer thing. Tim and Gibson were the officers and the rest of the team was made up of non-commissioned officers, three sergeants and a corporal. But it had never been a problem for George throughout his career. He had been lucky, with good officers in command of his battalion. Officers who recognised and appreciated that it was the sergeants in the battalion who made it work while the man in charge set the example and moral compass for the unit as a whole. It wasn't always the case with army battalions.

George knew that Tim had been an inspiring SAS squadron commander, and that was good enough for him. If he was less outwardly friendly than the other members of Shadow Force, so be it.

Gibson was different because he was a full colonel. He needed to be apart. Not aloof, but separate. He was in charge and was respected by all of them.

George and Gibson had served in different battalions in the Paras. But on one occasion, in 2000, George had been assigned to Gibson's battalion when he was the commanding officer. A company strength of about 120 Paras had been deployed to Freetown, capital of Sierra Leone. The country had been relatively stable since the civil war after more than ten years of brutal insurrection. But a new crisis had erupted.

Britain had historically close ties to Sierra Leone. When the president sought help from the UK government to guard his palace in Freetown after days of violent protests in the capital stirred up by an Islamic militant group calling itself the United

Revolutionaries, British troops were offered. Gibson's mission, codenamed Operation Gabriel, lasted four weeks. Based on intelligence provided by the Sierra Leonean security service, MI6 and the CIA, Gibson's Paras carried out a ruthless search-and-capture mission, seizing the known leaders of the United Revolutionaries off the streets. George had been Gibson's most experienced non-commissioned officer, and Gibson put him in charge of the snatch squads. Forty-five militants were detained and handed over to the Sierra Leonean authorities, and the violent protests abruptly stopped. For George, it was one of the best tours of his career: short, successful and filled with action. He realised how much he still needed the adrenaline of military action.

Tim was also thinking about the last week. The interrogation of Joseph Paine had produced very little. Paine was clearly just a small cog in a much bigger, dangerous organisation. He had only the tiniest amount of information in his head. But the phone call set-up had been worthwhile. From the content of the two calls to Paine's phone, Shadow Force knew that they were dealing with an aggressive, professional, arrogant Russian unit. Beyond that, Tim had become convinced very quickly that Paine was not going to provide the sort of intelligence which Gibson, and ultimately the prime minister, had hoped to glean to justify the involvement of Shadow Force. Tim, as the main interrogator in the team, felt he had played only a minor role so far. But he was happy to wait.

Tim was essentially a loner, even though he had spent all his military life working as part of close-knit units. It was the reason he had never married. He could not imagine living in a permanent home with a wife and children. When he wanted a woman, he never had difficulty finding someone who was attracted to him.

He liked working with Gibson, who seemed to him to be a similar character.

While Seamus and Rose noticeably enjoyed each other's comradeship, they were loners at heart. It came from relying for so long on their own individual skills. In combat environments, they frequently needed to depend on other members of their unit to complete a mission, yet they always knew that in the end they had to be strong and determined enough as individuals to survive and win. After years of combat and undercover surveillance operations in their individual army careers, each member of Shadow Force had built up an iron inner strength. They all also shared one common golden rule: never underestimate the enemy.

Rose, like Tim, had no time or desire for a permanent relationship. She'd had several lovers but never gave herself fully to any of them. She was always wary of too much attachment. She had found it impossible to trust anyone outside her immediate military circle. And yet, there was never any question of forming a sexual relationship with anyone within that circle. Her job was everything to her. Both her parents had died when she was in her late teens. She had a one-bedroom flat in Hackney but she had never regarded it as her home. When she was involved in army undercover missions, she had sometimes spent months without returning there. Now, she looked at her boss and wondered whether their current mission was going anywhere.

Gibson was also worried that the mission on this occasion was too imprecise. What exactly was their role? The prime minister had insisted on having Shadow Force involved—the first time the unit had been tasked to carry out a mission in the UK. It was a highly suspect decision. They were attached to the Foreign Office, not the Home Office, and already the former Parachute Regiment colonel had sensed the resentment among the senior hierarchy of the Metropolitan Police, as well as the outright opposition from the Director Special Forces Major-General Thomas Lockridge.

The Joseph Paine issue was another concern. He knew that Paine could not identify any member of Shadow Force, but if his lawyer could find proof that it was not the police but some unofficial Foreign Office unit that had grabbed his client off the streets and taken him for interrogation at a remote farmhouse in Oxfordshire, it would lead to an outcry against the government, and in particular against the prime minister. Shadow Force would be exposed. That could lead to Paine's acquittal. But Jonathan Ford had been adamant: he wanted Gibson's unit on standby for whatever happened next.

The problem for Gibson was that whatever did happen next, the police would be in the lead and wouldn't want some freelance unit getting in the way. Gibson had already detected Harry Brooks' annoyance at his presence in Geraldine's house after the gunman had fled. And that was despite the heroic attempt by Sam to detain the gunman.

He would never reveal to anyone his hidden demons, but Gibson was consumed by the fear of failure. He needed to succeed in every mission to prove to himself and to the members of his unit that he was the best. His rivalry with the Director Special Forces was all about demonstrating that he was the better commanding officer. But with this operation, it was going to be difficult to prove anything. In fact, there was a serious possibility that he and Shadow Force might have no further role to play.

Gibson was determined that this would not be the case. Nothing else in his life gave him the sort of personal satisfaction he felt when a mission achieved its aim. His marriage had broken up because he never gave his wife enough time to make the relationship work. He was totally committed to his professional life, but after his divorce he was wary of commitment in his personal life. Now, at the age of forty-seven, he had given up any thought of meeting a woman he might wish to live with on a permanent basis.

As the leader of a special quasi-military unit, he had never found the need to discuss personal matters with his team. But as he looked around at each member of Shadow Force, he knew that at least two others shared the same wariness about settling down with one partner. He didn't know much about Seamus's private life, but he knew he had been married in his twenties and divorced after five or so years. The job, he assumed, was to blame. Three of them were divorced. It was a sad reflection of the high-pressure careers they had chosen.

"There is one aspect of this business that worries me," Gibson said finally.

They all looked alert.

"Six is convinced it has nailed the Russian agent, this Maksim Popov. But the danger is, if they're wrong, we're all chasing after a Russian assassin who might well be sitting at home, unaware that he is the most wanted man in the UK."

"Why the doubt?" Tim asked.

"Sam's description for a start. It didn't quite seem to fit the physical description Six gave us. Sam, tell us again."

"A big guy, plenty of muscle on him," Sam said. "But the height was about right. He knew what the hell he was doing, that's for sure. Big, but lithe at the same time, if you know what I mean."

"There was no suggestion in Six's description that Popov was a big man," Gibson said. "Tall, but not big."

He continued: "My other concern is why he didn't shoot Geraldine Hammer. He came back into the house for one purpose only and that was to kill her. In my book, it makes absolutely no sense that he hesitated, even for a second. Anyone got any ideas? Rose?"

"Not really," she said. "Unless he knew her from some previous occasion."

Gibson looked at her curiously. "Go on."

"Well, I'm just thinking aloud," she said. "He bursts into the room with his gun, instantly targeting her, and she's cowering in her underwear, trying to protect her modesty."

"As I told you, I made a remark about that at the time. But that was just suggesting he liked what he saw," Gibson said.

"Yes, but what if he liked what he saw because he had seen her before?"

"But that makes no sense," Sam said. "She would have said something. She gave no hint that she had any suspicions about who he was. Other than possibly Maksim Popov, of course."

"I was just surmising," Rose said.

"Tim, George, Seamus, what do you think?" Gibson asked.

"I go along with Plucky," Seamus said. "Maybe he was momentarily fazed by her fancy underwear because it reminded him of something in the past." He grinned.

Tim shook his head. "He may have liked what he saw. But this is a full-time Russian hoodlum. He wouldn't be sentimental about anything, let alone a woman's near-naked body, would he? There must have been some other reason. Perhaps for the briefest of seconds, he needed to make sure she was the right woman."

George agreed. "Can't see a guy like this going all coy over a woman in her whatsits."

Gibson thought for a moment. "He knew he had very little time to act. He had to shoot and leave, and he must have taken into account the likelihood that the bloke who charged out of the house after him would soon charge back in again. In my view there is still a question to be asked. Why did he hesitate? Rose could be right."

"If I am right—and I'm only sort of guessing at possible reasons—then obviously she didn't recognise him," Rose said. "His face was covered. But if she had some instinct that he was someone she had met before, she would have said so. It would be her duty to say so, right?"

Gibson nodded. "Her reaction to my comment about him liking what he had seen was a little strange. I apologised for the remark but she quickly reassured me that it was the right question to ask. At the time I thought she was just being kind to me because Harry Brooks looked as if he was going to explode."

"She needs to be questioned more closely," Rose said.

"But that's a matter for the police, not us," Gibson said. "We're not involved in this as an add-on to the police. We have to keep separate. Downing Street is adamant about that. We got involved with Paine because we were told to. But that could all go wrong if his lawyer turns up anything embarrassing about our involvement in his detention."

"I doubt the police will ask the question," Seamus said. "It means no one will unless we do."

"No," Gibson said. "We stay out of this. Geraldine Hammer is now out of our hands. It's up to the police."

Both Rose and Seamus shook their heads but kept quiet.

***

GCHQ had been on high alert for anything that could be linked to the security crisis in London. No communications between Moscow and London had indicated anything either suspicious or interesting enough to follow up.

There had been one text with a curious message, but it had been sent from Geneva, not Moscow. It was sent to a phone in West London which had subsequently gone off-line.

The text said simply: "*Tovar dostavlen.*"

Order delivered.

Chapter Thirteen
Jean-Paul Picks up a Package

Tuesday 9th July

Sandy was up early. His mind was filled with all the questions that remained unanswered about the assassination attempt on MI5's counter-espionage chief, the double fatal shooting outside her house in SE1 and the likelihood that a Russian gunman was still roaming the streets of London. It was Sandy's biggest story since he joined Sky five years ago. He had the right contacts in the best places, but it had been hard work to move the story on.

The police, it was clear, were struggling with their investigation. Sandy wondered whether they had any idea who the Russian assassin might be. If only he could get the name of the suspect, it would project the story to another level. Sitting in the kitchen of his one-bedroom flat in Brentford, West London, Sandy thought he might try his MI5 contact, although he doubted he would be able or willing to help him.

Sandy had moved into the flat in John Busch House, a modern apartment block in London Road, the previous year. There was a large living area, but he had found little time to make it feel homely. He planned most weekends to go out and buy a new sofa and armchairs, but work invariably got in the way. The location was not glamorous, but it was only a short taxi ride to his office in Isleworth.

He was in the office by 8 a.m. The news editor was already sitting at his desk, surrounded by television sets. He was busy putting together the news list for the morning editorial conference. He waved Sandy over.

"What you got?" he asked.

"Nothing at present, but I'm trying to find out if the police have a named suspect."

"Fine," the news editor said, "but keep pushing about Gladstone Street. I want to know everything that happened inside this woman's house. Did she have armed police inside as well as outside? If so, what were they doing when their colleagues were being shot? If not, why not?"

Sandy sighed. The news editor was right to ask the questions, but it was easy for him, sitting at a desk. He had been asking himself the same questions ever since the double shooting. But the incident was being treated with such sensitivity by the police and MI5 that Sandy, like the rest of his rival reporters, was getting the bare minimum of information.

Sandy had moved to Sky from Fleet Street. He had been taken on at the *Daily Mirror* after five years on a regional paper in Yorkshire. The *Mirror* had taught him everything he needed to know about writing concisely, working to impossible deadlines and building up a contacts book. He had proved his worth as a reporter but knew he had to keep ahead of the game.

He rang his MI5 contact.

"David, it's Sandy."

"What can I do for you, Sandy?"

"I wondered if you and the Met have a particular individual in mind for the shootings? A suspect?" Sandy asked, expecting a no-comment reply.

"There's very little I can say," his contact said, somewhat obscurely.

"But you can say something?"

"Well, obviously we have been trawling through the likely candidates."

"And with any conclusion?"

"Not as such."

"What does that mean?"

"Well, you can imagine the organisation we are looking at most closely."

"Yes, the GRU."

"Exactly. But not necessarily only the GRU."

"You mean the SVR?"

"Well, we look at all the different organisations, including their foreign intelligence service."

"Could there be a new unit, something you have not known about before?" Sandy persisted.

"It's a possibility."

"So, that is something you are looking at?"

"As I said, we're looking at all possibilities."

They were going round in circles.

"But is the new unit possibility looking more likely than, say, that GRU unit responsible for the Skripal poisoning?"

"It's up there."

"You mean it's top of the list of suspects?"

"We don't know yet."

"But this is what you're thinking right now?"

"I think that would be accurate."

Sandy had known his MI5 contact, David, for two years. He had become accustomed to these roundabout conversations and knew when he was being told something interesting without it being baldly stated as a fact. There were few facts in this game; it was surmising and steering and careful choice of words.

"But not GRU at all?"

"I didn't say that."

"So it could have GRU members but is not a GRU operation as such?"

"Something like that."

"GRU and others? What about Spetsnaz?"

"Spetsnaz is GRU," David replied unhelpfully.

"Ok, but if it turns out that this is a new unit not coming under the command of the GRU or the Russian General Staff, is there a chief suspect leading this unit?"

"I can't give you his name, I'm afraid."

"So can I get this clear: you believe or suspect that Moscow has formed a new assassination unit that is linked to the GRU but is taking its orders from higher up, and you have the name of the Russian who runs it?"

"This is all surmising on your part."

"But my surmising is going along the right lines?"

"I think that would be fair."

"If you do have a name of the leader of this new unit, are you suggesting he might be personally involved in the shootings in London, or is he just masterminding in Moscow?"

"We don't know for sure. It's possible."

"It's possible he is personally involved? In other words, he could be here in London right now?"

"It's always possible. Sandy, I have to go—I have a meeting in two minutes."

"Ok, thanks, David. Very helpful."

"On the usual basis of course."

"Of course."

Nothing could be attributed to MI5 directly. "Security sources" was a favourite for reporters, although even that could sometimes be frowned on by MI5. "Whitehall sources" was another favourite, but news editors often baulked at that, saying it was too vague and general and could mean anything. Sandy's news editor always crossed out "Whitehall sources" if he wrote it in his script.

"Our viewers want to know where you are getting your stories from. Whitehall sources could be anyone from a permanent under-secretary to the MoD tea lady," he liked saying.

Sandy decided against ringing the Press Bureau. He already had what he needed to run a story. He told the news editor, wrote his piece, and within fifteen minutes was facing a camera with a red *Breaking News* strapline running at the bottom of the TV screen.

He had no name, but his story about the head of a new Russian assassination unit on the loose in London was instantly followed up by the BBC and all the national newspapers. It looked to Sandy as if none of his rivals had bothered to check with MI5 or the Met. They just ran his story, but in their own words. He didn't mind; it was an acknowledgement by his fellow reporters that he had good contacts and that the story was accurate. Most of his rivals had the decency to mention the Sky report, but one or two tabloids ran the same story but claimed to have their own "security sources". Sandy somehow doubted that.

When Sandy ran a big story based on sources, he always worried that it might have repercussions. His sources might ring to complain that he had gone too far or that he had put information into the wrong context or, worst of all, that he had breached the trust that was so vital when reporters deal with sensitive contacts.

Had he gone too far this time? Sandy waited for his phone to ring, expecting David to object to some aspect of his story. But an hour went by. No complaints. Sandy was relieved, and relaxed.

Then his phone rang.

It was the switchboard. The operator told Sandy someone called Ed Claridge was asking to speak to him. Should he put him through? Sandy said yes.

"Is that Sandy Hall?" his caller asked.

"Yes. Mr Claridge?"

"Ed Claridge, yes. I've been following your reports."

Sandy waited.

"I'm a solicitor acting for Corporal Joseph Paine."

Sandy sat up and grabbed a biro.

"I wondered if it might be possible to meet," the solicitor said.

"Of course," Sandy said immediately. "Is there something particular you want to talk about?"

"My client is making certain allegations."

"Like what?"

"I'm afraid I can't talk about that on the phone but would be happy to do so when we meet. Although it's a little irregular," Mr Claridge said.

"That's fine," Sandy said.

"And it must be off the record."

"Oh, well, ok."

"I'm taking a risk here," Mr Claridge said. "Can I trust you to keep things confidential?"

Sandy's heart fell. Off the record was one thing, confidential was another. Was he going to be told something he could never use, or could he use it but without attributing it to the solicitor?

"Let's meet and then we can sort out the ground rules," he said.

"But you agree off the record, no quotes from me?"

"Absolutely," a relieved Sandy replied.

They arranged to meet the next day for a coffee in Paternoster Square in front of St Paul's Cathedral. They swapped mobile phone numbers.

***

Jean-Paul van Dijk, dressed casually in jeans, a white shirt and a light jacket, walked down Piccadilly and turned off into St James's Street. He was carrying a large holdall. He stopped at an imposing building on the right-hand side of the road and looked around

133

before pressing the buzzer. The door opened. He handed his passport to the desk security officer, who checked his computer.

"Thank you, Mr van Dijk," he said, pressing a button under the desk which unlocked the heavy doors at the back of the foyer.

Jean-Paul opened the door and went through, down a long corridor, and turned left into a large room filled with safe deposit boxes. He took a key from his jacket pocket and inserted it into a drawer just below eye level. Inside was a large box-shaped parcel wrapped in heavy-duty cardboard. He removed it and put it into the holdall. He then returned to the foyer after locking the safe deposit box.

"Have a nice day," the security officer said as he walked past.

Jean-Paul didn't acknowledge him and left the building.

He rang Rebecca as he was walking down Piccadilly. There was no reply.

He left a message: "Rebecca, it's Jean-Paul. Could you do me a favour? I have a package which contains some sensitive business stuff. I don't want to leave it in my room in the hotel. I don't trust hotels, and anyway I'm checking out in the next day or so. Do you think you might hold on to it for me in your flat? I'd be very grateful. Ring me back."

***

Rebecca heard the voice message as she was painting in her flat. It was very impersonal, she thought. No mention of their last meeting, no hint of affection, no warmth at all. She was surprised at how disappointed she was. If she was honest, she had been longing for him to phone. He was kind of scary, but she didn't mind that. But a message just asking her to turn her flat into a left luggage office was not what she had been hoping for or expecting after their passionate get-together only twenty-four hours earlier.

She listened to the message again. He said he was checking out of his hotel. What did that mean? He was leaving the country? She shook her head. She didn't like being used by anyone, especially by a man.

The phone rang. She didn't answer it.

"Hi Rebecca, it's me again. Sorry about the rather business-like message earlier. I was walking down the street with lots of people around. Amazing to see you yesterday. Can't wait to see you again. Bye."

Rebecca grinned. He was forgiven. But only just.

"Typical man," she muttered.

She rang him back.

"So, Mr Dutchman, are you leaving the country?"

"Ha, well no, not quite," he replied. "It depends on various things."

"Business things?"

"Yes. Well, no, not just business."

"Hm... Am I a various thing?"

"Of course."

"Why *of course*?"

"Well, after yesterday..."

"Oh, that! You probably do that all the time."

"Of course not."

"There you go again."

"I don't follow you."

"Of course, you don't. You see now I'm doing it."

There was silence at the other end.

"Rebecca..."

"Don't worry, Mr Dutchman, I'm just playing."

"Ah, I see. Well, shall we do some playing later? I could bring round the package if you were willing to look after it for me."

"Is the package big?"

"Yes."

"I thought so."

"How do you know?"

"Just bring it round, Mr Dutchman. My double entendres are lost on you."

"Now?"

"Yes, now is good."

They rang off.

Chapter Fourteen
The Police Arrive at the Hotel, Too Late

Tuesday 9th July, 12 p.m.

Harry Brooks rang Geraldine at her office in Thames House.

"Geraldine, how are you doing?" he asked.

"Harry, I'm fine, thanks for asking," she replied, looking at her watch. She had a meeting with the DG in ten minutes.

"I have to ask, do you know anything about this Joseph Paine allegation?"

Geraldine was momentarily fazed by the question. What she knew about Joseph Paine and his abduction was classified information. Classified personally by the prime minister. She couldn't reveal Shadow Force's involvement in Paine's detention. Yet she knew it was wrong. It should have been a police matter. The potential for embarrassment was huge. It was particularly galling for her because Paine had tried to kill her, and if he was acquitted as a result of the unlawful abduction, she would find it difficult to forgive the prime minister or Gibson.

Geraldine replied, "I know what the lawyer is claiming, but I'm assuming Paine has made up this story to try and build a defence."

"So, it's definitely not true? Rollie Gibson and his lot weren't involved?"

"Harry, I was in hospital, if you remember, and wasn't in the loop about what action was being taken," she replied. She was tempted to tell him everything, but it was up to Downing Street to admit what had taken place.

"I have my strong suspicions," Harry said. "The arrest in Streatham sounds to me like a stitch-up. Some woman rings in and voila, Paine is caught. All very convenient."

"Harry, I'm sorry—"

"And why has Gibson been at the COBRA meetings if he wasn't involved in some way? Something smells. I know Lockridge feels the same. He rang me yesterday from Hereford. There's no love lost between those two as you know. But I think he's right to be suspicious. In my view, Shadow Force was set up for all the wrong reasons. It's government playing soldiers."

Geraldine agreed, but she didn't say so.

"If it turns out Paine was grabbed in some Gibson operation and it's made public, all hell's going to let loose," Harry went on. "And I'm not going to let the Met be linked in any way with it. The Commissioner shares the same view. We talked about it this morning. She was all for ringing Number 10 and demanding answers but I persuaded her to hold fire."

"That's probably sensible," Geraldine replied. "Harry, sorry, but I've a meeting with the DG and am late already."

"Ok, Geraldine, stay well." Harry rang off.

***

Jean-Paul van Dijk arrived at Rebecca's flat with the heavily wrapped package under his arm.

"So, you want me to hide it somewhere where no one can find it?" Rebecca asked. "It's spy stuff, right?"

"Just boring business documents," he replied.

"If you say so."

She tried to take it from him but he pulled back.

"Hmm, very touchy," Rebecca said.

"No, really, it's quite heavy. I'll do it," he said quickly.

"Put it in my cupboard in the bedroom."

She led him to the bedroom and opened the wardrobe. He put it down carefully. Her long dresses covered the top of the package.

"Are you staying or is that it?" she asked, looking at him with her familiar quizzical expression.

"I do have another favour to ask," Jean-Paul said.

"You don't have to ask," she replied with a grin.

"No, not that," he said, smiling at her. "Later, if that's all right. No, I was wondering if I might stay here for a bit. I want to check out of the hotel. It's possible I may be called back soon to my head office, and I'd like to spend more time with you."

Rebecca looked surprised. "You want to move in with me? Really? We've only met like three times. You have no idea what I'm like in the mornings."

"I don't mind finding out," he said. "And I'll pay your rent. All of it, for as long as I stay."

"Very romantic."

He looked puzzled.

"So, you're going to pay me for sex, is that it?" she said.

"No, no, that's not what I meant." He reached forward to hold her shoulders. "Nothing like that. I just think it's right for me to pay you for staying here. It could just be a few days or maybe slightly longer. Depends on head office."

"So, it's like a business arrangement?"

"Yes, exactly."

"As I said, very romantic."

"Rebecca, I'm sorry, I'm getting it all wrong."

"I don't have a spare bedroom, but you could sleep on the sofa," Rebecca said.

Jean-Paul was stunned. He had met his match in Rebecca. Her surname, he thought, was more than appropriate. He knew she was baiting him, and he was struggling to find the right words.

"It must be your strange origins," Rebecca said, moving away from him and going back into the living area. "French-Swiss, Dutch, Eastern European. I would have thought the French bit had at least some knowledge of how to treat a woman. It's probably the Eastern European blood that's screwing everything up."

Jean-Paul followed her. "I only mentioned the rent because I thought it would be fair," he said, sounding exasperated.

"I don't want your money, Mr Dutchman," she said, sitting on the sofa.

"Excuse me, that's my bed you're sitting on," he said.

Rebecca stared at him with astonishment, then burst out laughing. "Very funny—and I'm so sorry, do you mind awfully?"

"Not at all." He grinned.

He sat down next to her and kissed her on the lips.

"So, no money, but are you ok me staying here?" he asked.

"Sure."

"Tonight?"

"Tonight's fine."

"On the sofa?"

"We'll see."

***

At 9 p.m. three police cars arrived at the Royal Garden Hotel in Kensington. Six officers, two of them armed with Heckler & Koch submachine guns, entered the hotel and went to the reception desk.

The lead officer, a chief inspector, showed his warrant card and asked to see the manager. People in the foyer stopped to watch.

When the manager arrived, the chief inspector asked him, "Can you take a look at this photo, please. Is this man staying here?"

He handed over the blown-up photograph of Major-General Maksim Popov. The manager looked and shook his head.

"I'm not sure. We get so many people coming in and out," he replied.

"Please show your staff. The bellboy in particular," the police officer said as the rest of his colleagues spread out in the foyer.

The manager called over the uniformed employee working at the porters' desk.

"Take a look please, Mr Goodwood. Do you recognise this man as a resident?"

"Could be Room 607," the bellboy said. "Arrived last week. A big bloke. I don't think he had these eyebrows though."

"Room 607?" the chief inspector asked, turning round and beckoning the armed officers to approach the reception desk.

The police had received information from MI5 that a text in Russian sent from Geneva to someone in West London had been intercepted and tracked to the hotel in Kensington. MI5 had made no mention of GCHQ's involvement.

The manager, who was looking increasingly worried at the presence of armed police officers in his hotel, glanced at the register.

"Mr John Adams," he said. "He checked out earlier this afternoon."

"When did he arrive?" the police officer asked.

"A week ago. Last Tuesday."

The bellboy interrupted. "He had Swissair labels on his suitcase. A fancy leather one."

The chief inspector thanked him and turned back to the manager. "His address please," he said.

The manager glanced down. "It's an address in Geneva," he said. "But he gave us a business card."

"And you have it still?"

"Yes, we keep all business cards for future reference." He opened a drawer under the front desk and found the card. He gave it to the chief inspector.

The officer read out loud: "John Adams, vice president, IT Group Holdings, Head Office, Rue du Rhone, 40 Geneva. London office, 21 Hercules Street, Finsbury Park N7 6AS."

Two of the police officers were ordered to search Room 607. The chief inspector relayed the information about the business address in Finsbury Park to the Met's Counter-Terrorism Command. A maximum alert was ordered and a mobile armed unit was dispatched to Finsbury Park.

The chief inspector asked the manager if he could see the hotel's CCTV recordings for the last week. The bellboy who claimed to have recognised the man in the photograph was told to assist the police.

The police mobile unit arrived at Hercules Street, Finsbury Park nine minutes later. Twelve armed police leapt out of the back of the van and set up positions outside number 21 and across the street. Number 21 didn't look like a business premises. It was a house; the road was residential. Two armed officers went up to the front door and banged their fists on it. They heard movement inside and stepped back. The door opened slowly and a woman's face appeared round the corner. She looked shocked.

"Does a John Adams live or work here?" one of the officers asked her brusquely.

The woman opened the door wider. She looked out and saw the police everywhere.

"Madam?"

She was a woman in her forties. "No," she said. "You must have the wrong house."

"What's your name?"

"Marjorie, Marjorie Potter, as in Harry."

"Your husband's called Harry?"

"No," she said. "I meant as in Harry Potter."

The police officer looked bemused until his colleague tapped him on the elbow and said, "Potter. Harry Potter."

"Mrs Potter," the first police officer said, shrugging his shoulders. "Do you know anyone living in this street called John Adams?"

"No, I don't," she replied. "My next-door neighbour is called John, but not Adams."

The police officers didn't have a search warrant. There hadn't been time. So they couldn't barge in and hunt through all the rooms. But they knew it would be a waste of time. John Adams and IT Group Holdings clearly did not reside at 21 Hercules Street. And the head office was probably not in Geneva. Or anywhere else.

The senior police officer rang in to Counter-Terrorism Command.

"Looks like a blind alley," he said. "Adams or whoever he is has given us the slip."

A phone call was made to the police in Geneva. They checked and confirmed that no such business called IT Group Holdings had a head office in Geneva. They had no record of a John Adams living in the city.

The search of Room 607 at the Royal Garden Hotel had produced almost nothing of interest. A forensic team in blue plastic coveralls took the room apart, and the only thing discovered that was slightly interesting was three long blonde hairs lying almost invisibly on the carpet at one end of the bed. The chambermaid had cleaned the room but the hairs had survived the vacuum cleaner. Further inquiries with the manager elicited the information that John Adams had had lunch with a tall blonde woman the day before.

There were no cameras in the dining room, but the CCTV in the foyer had spotted her entering the hotel and being greeted by Adams. Her face was caught perfectly by the camera, but his was obscured. He was looking down and seemed to be covering the lower part of his face with his hand. The image was poor and certainly didn't clear up the question about the eyebrows.

The waiter who'd served Adams and his blonde companion told the police he had no idea whether the man had bushy eyebrows or not. He was, however, able to describe the woman's face with surprising detail, including the colour of her lipstick and the shape of her nose. He apologised when the police asked him if he had seen the colour of her eyes. He said he wasn't sure but they might have been green. Or maybe grey. And anything notable about John Adams, the police asked?

The waiter replied, "No, not really. Just sort of big."

Chapter Fifteen

Doubts Are Raised About the Russian Suspect

Paternoster Square was bathed in sunshine, as was St Paul's Cathedral at the top of the steps beyond the square. It was 11 a.m., and the square was bustling with people. Sandy arrived on time for his meeting with Ed Claridge. Joseph Paine's solicitor was already sitting at a table outside Paul café. He spotted the reporter, recognising him from his daily television appearances, and waved to him.

Sandy shook his hand and sat down. He ordered a coffee.

"Well, Mr Claridge, tell me what's on your mind. And is it ok if I take notes?" Sandy asked.

"Yes, but only for your use. No attribution, no quotes," the solicitor replied.

"Yes, we agreed that," Sandy reminded him.

"Ok. What I'm going to tell you is what my client claims," Claridge said. "I have had no luck checking it out so far. I have to admit, I am somewhat out of my depth."

"Sounds intriguing," Sandy said.

"Alarming, in my view. In fact, unlawful. Wholly extra-judicial."

"Blimey."

"So, what my client is claiming is that he was grabbed off the streets by some big bloke and bundled into a Land Rover with darkened windows," Claridge said. "There were two others in the van:

a woman driving and another bloke in the front passenger seat. The big guy in the back next to my client wrapped his arm around his neck so he could hardly breathe. Am I going too fast for you?"

"No, it's fine."

"They gave no explanation who they were. My client assumed they had been sent to do him over for failing to complete his contract."

"You mean Paine has admitted the shooting?"

"Not in so many words, and obviously for me to tell you that would be in breach of every rule in the book. I'd lose my job."

"Ok, ok, don't worry. I couldn't report that even if he did admit the crime."

The solicitor nodded and seemed reassured.

"Whether he was involved in the shooting incident or not," he said, "he never for one moment thought they were police. They didn't act like police. He was driven out of London to Oxfordshire to a big house with land—a farmhouse, he thought—where he was tied up and interrogated by a new man. My client said he was cut from a different cloth. Smoother and more in charge. He did the interrogation."

"So, definitely not a police station of any kind?" Sandy asked.

"Absolutely not. My client says they were military, especially the smooth one. Remember, my client was in the army. He knows the type," Claridge said.

"Bloody hell."

"Yeah, bloody hell."

"So, then what happened?"

"I'm not going to go into any detail about the interrogation, other than to say that the big bloke stood behind him and when he failed to cooperate he was given the full treatment, the arm round his neck squeezing the life out of him."

"When did he realise they weren't who he originally thought they were?"

"Well, it became obvious. If they'd been anything to do with his alleged contract, he wouldn't have survived. They would have bumped him off. At least that's what my client said. But apart from the big guy's ill treatment, it became clear to him that he wasn't there to be killed. They just wanted information from him. That's when he became convinced they were military or ex-military."

"Did he tell them what they wanted to know?"

"I can't talk about that."

"Even if it's all off the record?"

"No, 'fraid not. I'm taking a big risk here and I don't want to screw up what could be a pretty good defence if it ever gets to court."

"So, who were these guys? Where do they fit in?"

"I have no idea. All I can tell you is that he woke up around midnight in the room he was locked in and discovered the door was unlocked and the place was empty. They had all gone. He just walked out of the house. No one stopped him."

"What!"

"Yeah, I know it sounds ridiculous. Why go to all the trouble of abducting him and interrogating him in some remote farmhouse and then let him go?"

"But he got arrested, right? At a lock-up in Streatham?"

"He says it was a set-up," Claridge said. "He was inside the lock-up garage and suddenly there were armed police everywhere."

"What was in the garage?"

"I can't tell you that."

"Well, we know what the police have said. They found a motorbike, a gun and rounds of ammunition. Are you saying that was all planted?"

"I'm not saying anything about that. I have to believe my client, and he says he was set up."

"And the military or ex-military guys? Did Paine see them again?"

"No. From then on it was just the police, and he was taken to Paddington police station. Whoever the hell the others were, they had vanished from the scene."

"SAS? Could they have been SAS?" Sandy asked.

"I really have no idea, sorry. But that's why I decided to take this risk on my client's behalf. Perhaps you could make inquiries with your sources."

Sandy felt uncomfortable.

"Look, it's a great story. But I have to be careful," he said. "I can't be seen to be acting on behalf of someone who is accused of trying to kill a senior member of MI5."

"I don't expect you to do that. I just thought that if the authorities have been engaged in some covert operation outside the law, it's something that needs investigating. I'm trying my best but I'm getting nowhere. Just a solid wall of shaking heads."

"Is there anything else you can tell me?" Sandy asked. "Did Paine hear any of the names of those who grabbed him?

"No, I asked him that," Claridge said.

"How did he get from this farm in Oxfordshire to Streatham?" Sandy asked.

"I can't tell you that."

"And where was he grabbed in the first place?"

"I'm afraid I can't comment on that."

"Can you tell me if it was in London at least?"

"Yes, it was in London."

"But you can't say where?"

"No."

Sandy had a sudden thought. If Paine was caught in London, did that mean he never left after carrying out the shooting? If so, where had he gone into hiding? Or did he come back? Perhaps to have another go?

"Do you know what time he was taken?" Sandy asked.

"I do, but I can't tell you that. Sorry."

Sandy picked up his notebook and stood up. He shook the solicitor's hand and accepted a business card.

Claridge said, "If I hear anything that I can pass on to you, I'll let you know. Could you possibly do the same?"

"We'll see what happens," Sandy replied cautiously.

He had his doubts about the whole story. Claridge was just passing on what the former army corporal was saying, but it seemed to Sandy that the solicitor had become convinced of his client's account. As he walked away down towards Fleet Street, Sandy wondered how on earth he was going to check it out. He had his excellent contact in Counter-Terrorism Command, but if he started questioning the way Paine had been arrested, he might get a negative reaction.

It looked like Paine was without question the gunman who tried to kill MI5's director of counter-espionage. The police had recovered the motorbike used in the shooting, and the gun. So it wouldn't go down well with the Met if Sandy started ferreting around about the circumstances that led to his capture. On the other hand, if the government had some secret military or ex-military force roaming the streets, doing what should have been the Met's job, then it was a legitimate line of inquiry.

Sandy thought he might start with the MoD, although he didn't have any special contacts in the defence ministry.

***

A summit had been called in the main conference room of Thames House. Downing Street wanted a full update report on what was now codenamed Operation Buster. Geraldine chaired the meeting.

"Thank you all for coming," she said. "I feel it's fair to say that after nine days we've gathered a lot of information but we've learnt little about our opponent."

Most people around the table either nodded or raised their eyebrows.

"We need to go over what we have, see where it's going, make some decisions," she continued. "Freddie, perhaps you could start by bringing us up to date. I think you have some bad news for us."

Freddie Stigby, MI6's chief expert on Russia, looked like a man with bad news.

"I'm afraid we think we can rule out three of the names we first came up with when this all kicked off," he said. "If you recall, our guys in Moscow listed Major Dimitri Andreyev, Lieutenant-Colonel Mikhail Gerasimov, Captain Leonid Kuznetsov and Colonel Alexie Goncharov as likely or very likely members of Unit Zero. I've only heard this morning that Colonel Goncharov apparently died six months ago. He had been ill. Cancer. We think Major Andreyev and Captain Kuznetsov are currently in Syria. Our cousins over the water have been monitoring known GRU members operating in Syria and sent word that they were spotted there a month ago at the Russian air base at Khmeimim. If they were members of Unit Zero, we don't believe they would be serving there. That just leaves Lieutenant-Colonel Mikhail Gerasimov, and Major-General Maksim Popov of course."

"Are you still sure about Popov? " Geraldine asked, fearing the answer.

"Well, we don't know," Stigby replied. "We still think he's probably our man. But we have no confirmation. If it is him and he's in London then so far he's pretty cute at avoiding all CCTV cameras, according to the Met."

Geraldine turned to Harry Brooks, who had come to the meeting instead of his deputy.

"We've trawled every camera on every street in London," the Met commander said. "We have, as you know, very poor images of the man who hijacked the white van, and the Royal Garden Hotel produced nothing to show whether it's the same man. The best line for us was the blonde, although we've had no luck tracing her. If John Adams turns out to be Maksim Popov, or whatever his name is, then hopefully we'll find him through her. But, as I said, no joy so far."

Jasper Cornfield, his black curly hair flopping over his eyes, raised a finger.

"I don't want to be too negative," he said, "but have we not made too many assumptions? Are we really sure that Popov is the man we're looking for? What evidence do we have that he came here at all? And Unit Zero—does it actually exist? I know our sister agency gave the nod on this new organisation. But if three of the suspected members can now be crossed off, what have we got left? Gerasimov and Popov. Maybe it's Gerasimov who is here, not Popov, or maybe neither of them. Should we look again at Gerasimov?"

"Ok, Jasper, thank you," Geraldine interrupted. "All good questions. Any thoughts?" She lifted her right hand to throw it open to everyone.

Major John Fisk from the MoD was the first to answer. He had studied GRU more than anyone in the room. He had been a member of the defence intelligence staff for eight years and had a reputation for competence and sound judgment.

"I've gone over the photos Six gave us a hundred times," he said. "The trouble is none of them are up to date. For example, Gerasimov as a lieutenant-colonel should be in his late thirties or forties. But the picture shows a man who looks more like in his twenties. He doesn't seem to have the build of the man who fought his way out of Geraldine's house.

But add another ten or twenty years, and he could have bulked up significantly. His face could have changed shape as well. That means it's possible he could have come here to the UK and we've not spotted him because we're looking for a younger guy. I've had my doubts from the beginning about Popov. If he is a major-general, that's too senior to be sent scurrying around Europe on assassination and sabotage missions. It can't be ruled out, but somehow I doubt he is our man."

Geraldine's heart jumped. "Does anyone else feel we're going down the wrong track?" she asked.

"My worry," Harry Brooks chipped in, "is that if we become obsessed with one guy, this Popov fellow, we might be missing out on something that we are currently ignoring because we think we have our man. Take the hotel waiter's account, for example. He was pretty sure that this John Adams was the man in the photo, but even he cast doubt on the size of his eyebrows. I mean, is that what we're really doing? We're looking for a Russian with bushy eyebrows?"

Nobody laughed.

"And we shouldn't regard the waiter as a reliable witness," Harry continued. "He was far more interested in the blonde, down to her painted fingernails."

Geraldine turned to her deputy, Grace Redmayne.

"Ok, let's look at what we do have," Grace said. "The only confirmation, if that's the right word, that Unit Zero exists is that one word picked up by GCHQ. Nul, meaning zero. It could be a coincidence, but it neatly fitted with what we thought we knew about this new unit. For the moment, I don't think we should focus on whether there is a new unit or just another name for an old one. It will matter eventually if we do catch our man and we can draw a link between him directly to the Kremlin."

Grace glanced down at some notes in front of her and then continued: "What is obvious and won't surprise anyone is that this Russian agent or agents are travelling on false passports. If John Adams has anything to do with it at all, it's probably one of many identities. The business card led the police to a dead end. The Russian, if he is Russian, didn't even bother to pick a street in Finsbury Park with lots of businesses. He just picked a street at random. He was playing with us. The same with the address in Geneva—although the choice of Geneva is interesting. It may well be that Unit Zero, if it exists, operates from Geneva. For that reason I think we need to go over once again every passenger who has flown to London from Geneva in the last two weeks. Every airline, despite the hotel bellboy saying Adams had arrived with a suitcase labelled Swissair. We know there was no John Adams on a Swissair flight going back two months."

Harry Brooks looked worried.

"Harry, you have something?" Geraldine asked.

"Not really," he said. "I agree, we'll check the passengers again, although nothing came up when we looked before. I just wanted to make sure that the police are allowed to get on with the job. No interference from elsewhere—and I mean Colonel Gibson's lot. Highly irregular if they have been involved in anything."

"Yes," Geraldine said. "Of course, you are fully in charge."

"That's not what I was asking," Harry said. "I want Gibson and co called off if they are lurking in the background. There's going to be a helluva screw-up if this investigation isn't carried out according to the book."

Geraldine nodded and called the meeting to an end.

Chapter Sixteen

Geraldine Asks Her Deputy to Investigate Lucas Meyer

Thursday 11th July

No John Adams was found travelling from any Swiss airport to Heathrow throughout June and the beginning of July. Every passenger from Switzerland was checked out and their passport photos compared with the photo of Maksim Popov. One or two could have been described as possibles, but when further checks were made they turned out to be bona fide businessmen. Not Russian.

The hotel bellboy was adamant that John Adams had arrived with a Swissair label on his suitcase. Geraldine didn't doubt it, but she had begun to get the measure of this mysterious Russian agent. False trails were being left everywhere. Had he even arrived at Heathrow? Could he have entered the country by some other means and taken a taxi to Heathrow to pretend to be arriving from there? The police had checked with all the London taxis and minicab companies which operated from Heathrow. Eventually, they found a London cab driver who remembered picking up a customer with a leather bag asking to go to the Royal Garden Hotel. He described him only in general terms: big, blue suit, white shirt, short hair. When shown the picture of Maksim Popov, the cab driver gave a nonchalant shrug. "Could be," he said, but, like the bellboy, he couldn't remember such prominent eyebrows.

Geraldine had wrestled with her conscience for days. She had been so relieved when the Popov photograph was shown to her. She felt she had been paranoid about Lucas Meyer, imagining the worst but without any evidence. The Popov photo reassured her. But now, after the previous day's meeting at Thames House, she had begun to have her doubts once again. Could it be that Lucas Meyer was the man they should all be looking for? Was it possible? He fitted the description without looking like Popov. And he certainly didn't have bushy eyebrows.

She sat at her desk, staring at her computer screen. It was time to pass on her fears but without making it official. She couldn't bear the thought of the looks she would get if she announced her liaison with Lucas Meyer as if it was some afterthought. Harry Brooks would be furious. George Trench could take her off the case. It would be humiliating. She still thought she was probably worrying unnecessarily. But she knew she couldn't and shouldn't rule it out. If Lucas Meyer was the Russian assassin and the man in the balaclava who'd stood before her in her bedroom, her career would be over if she told no one about her suspicions. And more importantly, two police officers had been murdered while trying to protect her. She *had* to tell someone.

Every evening in her safe-house flat in Westminster, she had gone over the Lucas Meyer situation again and again. The circumstances of their meeting that first time were highly suspicious. But she had fallen for it. He had been charming and her guard had dropped. She still shuddered at the memory of the evening at the opera and her weakness. She had meant to say no but had gone along with it. She had felt out of control. He had enjoyed conquering her.

Geraldine thought of his body. But she had had her eyes closed when they were naked. She felt his body, the muscled chest and strong legs and arms, and she couldn't forget that moment which instantly changed her desire for him into an overwhelming sense of vulnerability.

Suddenly something did come to mind. After she had got off the bed and put her clothes back on, he had remained lying there, looking untroubled. For a brief second, he had raised himself on one elbow and removed the duvet covering the lower part of his body. It was when he'd offered to get her a taxi. She had glanced at him and, for the first time, she saw his whole body. There was something on one of his legs. She couldn't see it for sure—she only glimpsed it when the duvet fell to one side and he turned towards her—but it could have been a mark of some kind. A dark blue mark. Possibly a tattoo? Running down his left calf.

She rang Grace Redmayne and asked her to come and see her when she was free.

Grace arrived ten minutes later.

"Sit down, Grace, please," Geraldine said. "I have something I want to talk to you about, but confidentially."

Grace looked surprised. "Something personal?" she asked.

"Not exactly. But yes, sort of personal."

"Of course."

They had worked closely together for three years. They liked each other. But there was no social relationship. Grace was younger, and her personal life was a bit of a mystery. She was still single and devoted to her parents. She had an older married sister who was a civil servant at the Treasury and had two children. Grace adored her nephew and niece but never mentioned wanting children of her own. Educated at Roedean girls' private school, set in isolated splendour overlooking the sea outside

Brighton, followed by a scholarship in classics at Oxford, Grace was a serious woman. She spoke of her sister with admiration but had never referred to any relationship with a man, at least not to Geraldine. And not to human resources, who needed to know everything about the staff at Thames House.

"I've been going over everything," Geraldine said. "There is one thing that has been bothering me for some time, but I'm pretty sure it's not relevant."

Grace said nothing.

"About three months after Operation Foxtrot was wrapped up, there was an unexpected... incident outside my house. I was hailed by a man in a car who said it had broken down. He didn't have a mobile, and could he borrow mine to call for help."

"You said no," Grace interrupted.

"Well, actually, no. He was, you know, very pleasant, and for some reason I let him use my phone to ring the rental company. And that was it."

"You never saw him again?"

"Not that day, no," Geraldine replied. "And the car was duly moved. So I thought nothing of it."

"But..."

"But a week later he rang and said he had two tickets for the Royal Opera House and would I like to go with him."

Grace tightened her lips and frowned.

"It was stupid on my part, I admit. But since the break-up of my marriage, there had been, well, nothing. It was tempting. Just a nice evening at the opera. I said yes."

Grace said nothing.

"So we went to the opera. Afterwards, we were both hungry and he invited me back to his flat, where he said he had some food prepared or delivered or something."

"I don't need the details, Geraldine."

"Well, you should know."

Grace looked uncomfortable.

"The point is, it's probably nothing. It was nine months ago. I've never seen him since. I checked him out briefly and it all seemed to be ok. He hasn't tried to get in touch again."

"How would you describe him?" Grace asked.

"Big. He was big," Geraldine replied. She noticeably blushed.

"And his name?"

"Lucas Meyer."

They sat in silence for a few seconds.

"So, what do you want me to do?" Grace asked.

"I want you to discreetly, very discreetly, check out Lucas Meyer. See if that name crops up on any passenger list on airlines flying in from Europe in June/July. You have a good contact in the Met, don't you? Would he help if you concoct some story?"

"He's no fool," Grace said. "He'd smell something was odd."

"Just come up with something to convince him. I'm really sorry to ask you, but it's difficult for me to produce this name now after all this time. You understand, don't you?"

Grace seemed doubtful.

"All I want," Geraldine continued, "is reassurance that I'm blowing this up out of all proportion, and then we can knock this guy's name off the list."

"But he's not on anyone's list," Grace pointed out.

"He's on my list," Geraldine said firmly. "Just see what you can find and let me know. Urgently."

Grace stood up and left the room.

***

Sandy rang the MoD press office and asked to be put through to someone he could talk to about military involvement in the hunt for the Russian assassin. The girl manning the desk phones made no comment other than to say she would put him through to a press officer. It took a few minutes. Sandy expected a no comment.

"Hello. You have a question about...?" It was a male voice this time.

"Er, yes, it's Sandy Hall from Sky News here— I wanted to ask about any military involvement or ex-military involvement in the hunt for the Russian gunman, and in particular relating to the arrest of Joseph Paine."

"What is your question?" the press officer asked.

"Was there any military group of any kind involved in the arrest of former Corporal Joseph Paine?"

"The suspect, if I recall correctly, was arrested by the police."

"So there wasn't any military or ex-military organisation that detained Paine before he was arrested by the police?"

"I don't follow—what do you mean? How can you be arrested before you are arrested?"

Sandy knew he had to tread carefully. It was clear the press officer hadn't a clue what he was referring to. If the solicitor's account was correct, then a press officer in the MoD wouldn't be in the loop. But surely someone in the MoD would be?

"There is a suggestion," Sandy persisted, "that before the police arrested him in Streatham last week, he had been detained and interrogated by some military unit, or ex-military, and held somewhere outside London."

"Who is making this suggestion?"

"I can't say that."

"Well, it's not something I have any knowledge of. As you know, we never make any comment about special forces, if that's what you're implying."

"I'm not implying special forces were used. I was just asking whether there is any truth in the claim that Paine was picked up and questioned before the police became involved in the arrest."

"Sandy, I really don't understand what this is about. You said it was a suggestion and now it's a claim. Which is it?"

"A claim."

"Who by?"

"I can't say."

"Well, the MoD doesn't comment on suggestions or claims. Nor do we comment on hypothetical questions."

Sandy had one more try.

"Would it be possible to pass my question on to someone at a more senior level? Sorry, I don't mean to be rude. But—"

"Well, it's a waste of time."

"But will you?"

"I'll pass it on. Give me your details."

Sandy put the phone down and sat back in his chair, frustrated. Was it really worth pursuing when he had so much to do on the bigger story about the Russian agent? He didn't expect to hear back from the MoD.

But twenty minutes later his phone rang.

"This is James Lewis. I'm the director of strategic communications at the MoD. I understand you have been in touch with the press office."

"Yes. I wanted to know whether—"

"Yes, I know about your question," the MoD man interrupted. "I'm afraid we can't make any comment about the Joseph Paine case. It's all sub judice."

"So you can't say whether there is any truth in this claim? About Paine being taken off the streets and bundled into a Land Rover?"

"You made no mention of that in your call to the press officer. And in any event, as I said, the MoD can make no comment about this case."

"Can anyone comment on it?"

"You could try Number 10."

"Number 10?" Sandy asked, surprised.

"Yes, but I'm sure you will get the same response."

"Ok, thanks."

Sandy rang the press office at Number 10.

"It's Sandy Hall here. Is there someone I can speak to about an allegation relating to the arrest of Joseph Paine?" he asked.

"Please wait a moment," a girl's voice replied.

Exactly the same routine then followed. A wait of a few minutes and then a man's voice.

"Hello, can I help?"

"Who am I speaking to?" Sandy asked.

"Patrick Mickleford."

"Patrick, hi. I wanted to ask about something I've been told. That Joseph Paine was detained and held for questioning by some military group before he was arrested by the police?"

"We don't comment on ongoing police investigations."

"But this was before the police were involved."

"Sandy, the police launched an investigation as soon as the first shooting incident took place. There was no before or after," Patrick Mickleford answered obtusely. "I suggest you raise your questions with them."

"The MoD said I should ring Number 10. Why was that?"

There was a brief silence.

"I can't imagine," the Downing Street press officer replied. "This is a matter for the Metropolitan Police, not Number 10."

"So you're making no comment?"

"Correct," Mickleford said, but then added: "I don't know where you're getting your information from but it all sounds a little fantastical, don't you think?"

"We'll see," Sandy replied and put the phone down.

***

A restricted CX report from MI6 was circulated late afternoon. It said that Major-General Maksim Popov had still not been seen in Moscow or anywhere else in Russia. But Moscow head of station said reliable, or at least longstanding, sources had claimed Popov was abroad and had been overseas for some time on an unidentified mission. There was no confirmation about the existence of a new organisation called Unit Zero. But the same sources had indicated it would be no surprise if the Kremlin had formed a new unit to do the bidding of the president. The president was obsessed with getting revenge for the way London had damaged Russia's ability to maintain an effective spying mission in the UK. Maksim Popov was known to be close to him.

Geraldine read her copy of the report. Nothing in it gave her reassurance about Lucas Meyer, despite the intelligence hinting that Popov might be abroad on some mission. MI6 still seemed fixated on Maksim Popov, and they might be right. He could be the travelling assassin. But she remembered Major Fisk's reservations at the meeting. Would someone as senior as Popov be chosen to carry out a mission which would normally be assigned to an agent lower down the ranks?

Sir Edward Farthing and her boss, George Trench, had lunched that day at the Reform Club, and the message that came back to her was the same as before: Six believed Popov was the man everyone should be looking for. Sometimes, Geraldine thought, the sister agency over the Thames seemed to get tunnel vision. It was almost as if it had to be Popov for the sake of MI6's reputation in Whitehall.

She had heard nothing more from Grace but accepted it would take time to see if a Lucas Meyer had flown to Heathrow or any other airport from Europe over a three-week period. She had no idea whether Meyer had continued living and working in London since she'd seen him nine months earlier. When she made inquiries about One Blackfriars and his rental contract, she had been told he was no longer a resident. There was no forwarding address. That hadn't reassured her either. Of course, businessmen came and went, and he was probably in and out of different countries in Europe—nothing particularly abnormal about that—but in the context of her personal doubts, there seemed to be a pattern. He arrived in her street out of the blue, had dominating sex with her a week later and then vanished out of her life. She was relieved, but was that normal for a man like him? Why hadn't he tried to get in touch? Why had he bothered to chat her up in the first place? Was there another reason, some dark scheme?

The biggest question of all was one she hardly dared consider. Could he have returned after all? Was he the balaclava-wearing gunman in her bedroom? She had been a hopeless witness. It had been such a sudden shock after the shooting outside, and the way the gunman burst into her bedroom was so quick the only thing she'd done instinctively was to try and cover her flimsy bra with her hands. Perhaps she feared being raped more than she feared being shot. She had no way of defending herself against a man determined to kill her. But she could do her damnedest to prevent rape. Then Sam had hurled himself into the room and at the gunman. Could that man have been Lucas Meyer? She had asked herself that question a hundred times.

Grace knocked on her door late afternoon, just as Geraldine was thinking of leaving for the day. Grace didn't sit down, although Geraldine had waved her to a chair.

"Nothing," she said. "No Lucas Meyer anywhere on any flight manifesto in the last three weeks, either coming in or going out."

"And nine months ago?" Geraldine asked.

"No, nothing," Grace replied.

"Did you speak to your friend at the Yard?"

"Yes, in a roundabout way. I told him we had had some tip-off from an unknown informant that a man called Lucas Meyer was somehow wrapped up in the Russian business. I asked him if the name meant anything to him, but he said no."

"Was he suspicious at all?"

"No, why should he be? He did ask if I wanted him to make further checks but I thought that was probably unwise, so I said no thanks."

"Grace, thank you. It hasn't really got us anywhere, but at least we now know for sure a Lucas Meyer hasn't flown into the UK recently," Geraldine said.

"Well, we can't be sure of that, of course," Grace said as she turned to the door.

"How do you mean?"

"If Lucas Meyer is a Russian agent, an assassin, he's going to have multiple identities. You know that. He's Lucas Meyer one day and John Adams another, and who knows what the day after."

Chapter Seventeen
Special Sources and Special Forces

Friday 12th July

Tovar dostavlen. The Russian text saying an order had been delivered was put into an alarming new context by an intelligence source. MI6 head of station in Moscow had revealed that according to a recently recruited agent, a package had been delivered in the diplomatic bag to the Russian embassy in London. The source said it was his understanding that the package contained some form of device.

The source disclosed that the Ninth Directorate of GRU had recently produced a new small, lightweight device modelled on an old naval limpet mine with significant explosive power. The MI6 chief in Moscow had no secondary source to back up the claim.

Jonathan Ford told a COBRA meeting that without proof, there was little the government could do diplomatically.

"The priority is to find this device, if it exists, and we'll deal with Moscow later," Ford said.

MI5 had announced that although the threat level remained at "severe", extra measures were considered necessary. Newspapers, TV and radio stations were demanding to know what was going on.

"Lawrence, put out a brief statement explaining the general nature of the new threat without going into specifics," the prime minister told the home secretary.

Police Commissioner Mary Abelard outlined the additional steps that had been taken. Mobile armed units had been doubled and concrete barriers were at that moment being placed at the front and back of Thames House. Surveillance of the Russian embassy in Kensington had been significantly increased.

The prime minister had also authorised the SAS to join the police efforts to track down the device and the Russian assassin, but not in military fatigues. He didn't want to create panic on the streets.

He had asked Gibson to hold fire for the moment. Shadow Force was principally focused on overseas missions. When in the UK, the team was not armed but could be issued with weapons under extreme circumstances. Ford felt it prudent to restrict the number of officially armed personnel in the capital and didn't want the risk of Shadow Force clashing with the police or the SAS.

Elizabeth Gantry said it was her view that Moscow should be issued with a warning.

"Not an official one through the normal diplomatic channels, but perhaps via some other method, so at least they know that we know or believe we know what they are planning."

"I agree," said Jeremy Blunt, the one member of the cabinet always in favour of instant action. "The bloody Russians think they can get away with anything these days. If Moscow is behind these shootings—which I think we all know is the case—it will be seen as a sign of weakness on our part if we don't issue some formal warning. Who knows, it might even persuade Moscow to recall their agent."

"Recalling their agent is not what I want," the prime minister said. "I want this man caught here in the UK and put on trial. That will do more damage to the Kremlin's reputation and standing than anything else. We have to catch this assassin and put him through the British justice system."

"But even if we do manage to get him," the foreign secretary warned, "Moscow will just claim the whole thing is a show trial."

"Stuff Moscow!" Blunt roared.

Since being appointed defence secretary, he had taken on the persona of an irate retired general from the Home Counties.

"Thank you, Jeremy," Ford said quickly. "I'm sure that reflects most of our feelings. But I'm inclined to stick to our current approach. If we get copper-bottomed intelligence of Russian government participation, then we'll take the matter to the UN Security Council if necessary. But right now we'll leave it to the media to spread the word that the Russians are suspected of being behind the outrages on our streets."

Fenwick pointed out that Moscow had already dismissed the newspaper reports as fake and defamatory.

"Nevertheless," Ford replied, "Moscow is getting the message one way or the other without us having to give an official warning."

"And my suggestion of an informal approach, perhaps through intelligence channels?" Gantry asked again.

"I don't think so, Elizabeth," the prime minister said. "An informal approach would definitely be seen as weakness by Moscow, a sort of special pleading for them to be good citizens. No, I don't think that would work."

The foreign secretary looked a little crestfallen. Ford noticed.

"But we'll keep it as an option," he said.

**

Rebecca had woken up late to discover she was alone in her bed. She had relented over the ambivalent agreement to allow Jean-Paul to stay in her flat but not necessarily in her bed. The first thing he did was place his one piece of luggage in her bedroom cupboard before climbing into bed with her. That night, she'd asked him about the tattoo on his leg.

"Just something I did on the spur of the moment," he had replied.

"Where did you get it done?" Rebecca asked.

"Mosc... Maassluis," he replied, stumbling over his words. "I was born there, a Dutch town."

"Never heard of it," Rebecca said. "So is it Moscluis or Marsluis?"

He spelt out the name.

"Why the dagger?" She pressed him. "You served in the military?"

"No, nothing like that."

Now, alone in her bed, Rebecca wondered why he had seemed confused over the name of the town. For a man who gave the impression of being totally in control of himself, the apparent mix-up over the name of his birthplace didn't make sense.

She wanted to test him again. But he had left. There was no goodbye.

***

Sandy went up to central London. There were more police on the streets and extra armed officers guarding key buildings. He was due to give an update on the extra security measures for the one o'clock news. He had rung his contacts at Counter-Terrorism Command and MI5 but had learned nothing new. He had also rung the Home Office, but the press officer dealing with terrorism and security issues had been less than helpful.

Sandy walked from Parliament Square down Millbank towards MI5 headquarters and spotted a group of dark-blue-overalled men climb out of a police van. As a crime correspondent, he rarely had occasion to deal with the SAS—that was normally left to the defence editor—but to Sandy, the dozen men climbing out of the van were either a specialised police unit or members of the SAS. If it was the SAS, he had a scoop. "Government calls in SAS to protect London" would make a good start to his one o'clock report. He had an hour to chase it up and try and get some form of confirmation, on or off the record.

He rang his contact at the Met. There was no reply, so he tried his mobile.

"Rick, it's Sandy," he said when the detective inspector answered.

"Can't talk now," the detective replied.

"Just very quickly," Sandy said. "Would I be wrong to say that the SAS has been brought in to help the police?"

"Can't say. No comment."

"So, it's not true?"

"Sandy, I can't help on this one. Got to go. Try the MoD or Number 10."

Sandy stood in the street a hundred yards down the road from the impressive front entrance of Thames House and went over in his mind what his contact had told him, or not told him. In the past, his special contact had often hinted at things without actually saying anything concrete. Had he been hinting at something by telling him to ring the MoD or Number 10, or was this just a standard reply to any question from a reporter about the SAS?

He rang the press office at the MoD and asked if the SAS was currently working with the police in London.

"We never comment on special forces," a young-sounding press officer replied.

"I know you don't normally," Sandy said, "but surely on this occasion when London is facing a heightened security threat, it wouldn't be unusual for the SAS to be brought in?"

"We never comment on special forces," came the reply.

Sandy tried once more. "So you can't confirm or deny that the dozen military-looking men in dark blue overalls climbing out of a police van near MI5 just now are army rather than police?"

There was a brief hesitation, then, "I don't know what you have seen or claim to have seen, but we never comment on special forces."

Sandy was getting nowhere. So he rang the press office at Number 10.

"It's Sandy Hall, Sky News. Can I speak to someone about the SAS in London?"

He thought the bold approach might get a different response.

After several minutes of waiting, he was put through to the head of the press office and the prime minister's press secretary.

"What's this all about?" the press secretary asked.

"Hi, I've just seen a dozen SAS soldiers near Thames House and wondered what their role was?" Sandy asked, continuing with his attempt to sound authoritatively knowledgeable.

"Are you an expert on the SAS?"

"No, but—"

"And did they have SAS emblazoned on their dark blue overalls, as you described?"

"No, but—"

"So, how could you tell they were SAS rather than a police unit?"

"Well, it seemed to me they looked military, and London is facing a potentially dangerous security situation, so I thought it made sense to have a Hereford team in. Reassuring for the public, if you like." Sandy was not sounding quite so authoritative.

"You're entitled to your views, and your imagination, Mr Hall, but as I'm sure you know, we never comment on special forces."

"But if they are not special forces, presumably you could just say they are a police squad dressed in blue overalls."

"I could, but that would be a matter for the Press Bureau, not Number 10."

"So, if I speculated that the SAS may have been brought in, would that cause a problem?"

"Nice of you to be so amenable, Mr Hall, but I spot a cunning plan behind your question and I'm not going to rise to it. It's still no comment."

Sandy tried once more. "So, can I say you neither confirm nor deny the presence of the SAS in London?"

"No, you can't. All I have said is no comment. Is there anything else I can help you with?"

"Would it be the same answer if I asked you to reply off the record, strictly unattributable?"

"Absolutely no sourcing to Downing Street?"

"Of course."

"Then, off the record, without any government attribution, it would seem to be prudent to have at our disposal all forms of security apparatus to deal with this current dilemma," the press secretary replied.

"Including the SAS?"

"Including the military, in whatever format might be thought appropriate."

"I'm still not absolutely sure whether I can suggest it's the SAS."

"I admire your integrity, Mr Hall. Some of your colleagues might have run off to report the news by now."

"Ok, thanks, thanks a lot, very helpful," Sandy said, now as sure as he could be that he had sufficient guidance to be able to say that the SAS was in town. It had been a hard grind. Finding the true meaning in Whitehall language was like digging up gold nuggets from historic burial grounds.

But Sandy had another scoop.

Chapter Eighteen
The Unit Zero Agent Disobeys His Orders

Saturday 13th July, 1:30 p.m.

Lieutenant-Colonel Mikhail Gerasimov, alias Lucas Meyer, alias John Adams, alias Jean-Paul van Dijk, was on his way to Birmingham.

Colonel Gerasimov, twenty years a GRU Spetsnaz officer, ruthless killer, lover of women, key member of Unit Zero, Hero of the Russian Federation, was about to engage in an unplanned mission. It was not Moscow approved. Nor had he discussed it with his commanding officer, Major-General Maksim Popov.

It was all because of Geraldine Hammer, or Jane as she had called herself when he first met her nearly a year ago. The contents of the holdall should have been used to target her. But instead, for reasons he was trying to come to terms with, he was planning a totally different mission. He risked incurring the wrath of his superiors in Moscow, but he had finally admitted to himself that he had no wish to blow up the woman he took to the Royal Opera House.

His orders had been to eliminate the director of Britain's counter-espionage agency. Nothing else. That was his task. After the failure of the contracted assassin, the Kremlin, through a committee of GRU generals, had selected him out of the newly formed Unit Zero because of his reputation for ruthlessness, his heroism for the motherland in eastern Ukraine and his record for completing covert missions and evading capture.

His selection of Rebecca Strong to provide safe-house accommodation when the heat was on and a storage place for whatever Moscow had sent him through the diplomatic bag had worked well so far. He was a little wary of her inquisitive nature and British sense of humour, but he liked her and had few concerns that she would jump to any conclusions about who he might be.

Geraldine was a different matter. He had known only the basic facts about her when he started preparing the ground for the first meeting in Gladstone Street. Information obtained by an unnamed officer of the Russian SVR foreign intelligence service based at the embassy in London had provided him with the name of the MI5 counter-espionage director, her address and a photograph. The photo was unexceptional. It had been taken covertly and in poor light. Her face was half-shaded. The collar of her raincoat was turned up. She looked like a spy trying to avoid unwelcome photographers. She had partially succeeded. When Gerasimov first looked at the photo, he wasn't sure whether she was attractive, but he made the assumption that she wouldn't have been promoted to a top job in MI5 if she was good-looking. His experience of Russian intelligence services was that the top jobs went either to men or to women known to have impeccable political connections, but never for their beauty. Lower down the chain there were plenty of attractive female spies. But that was different. Their role included the age-old honeytrap routine, where attraction was a necessary requirement.

Gerasimov, who had a wife and two sons, both of whom were earmarked for the army, was taken aback when he stopped Geraldine in the street to ask for her help. He found her instantly attractive. The soft, wavy auburn hair and hazel eyes were the first things he noticed. She didn't smile when he accosted her from his car. But her caution was understandable. She was trained to be cautious. Just as he was. His only purpose that afternoon had been to check her out, confirm her address and get her mobile phone number. It was not part of the plan to invite her out a week later and take her to his flat. Even when he considered it, after that first meeting, he didn't imagine for a moment that she would agree. The head of MI5 counter-espionage taking such a risk? But he'd been tempted to try his luck, and amazed when she said yes.

He knew from the biographical information supplied to him that she was divorced, that her former husband, Paul Blake, was an academic and they had two young children. He made the phone call suggesting opera more out of curiosity than expectation.

The way the evening had ended had satisfied him for two reasons. It reminded him that any form of romantic attachment was out of the question. He also thought, wrongly as it turned out, that her shock and rejection of his muscular lovemaking that evening would make it easier for him if he were to be personally part of any future attempt to eliminate her. At that stage there had been no decision either by the committee of generals acting on behalf of the Kremlin leadership or by Maksim Popov about whether the elimination would be carried out by Unit Zero itself or by some contracted assassin.

Gerasimov had been honoured to be invited to join Unit Zero. He had served in Donbass, eastern Ukraine, for nine months without returning once to his wife in their Moscow apartment. He had been awarded the Hero of the Russian Federation for singlehandedly driving back a Ukrainian government special forces unit which had tried to penetrate a Russian-occupied training camp. He was given two weeks' home leave and then ordered to present himself at the headquarters of the chief of the

Russian general staff in Znamenka Street in central Moscow. Gerasimov often wondered whether he had been selected for Unit Zero partly because he had the same name as the chief of the general staff, General Valery Gerasimov. But he never met the general. The Russian military intelligence officer who had interviewed him was Major-General Maksim Popov.

As a Spetsnaz officer operating in a war zone, he had learned on numerous occasions that hesitation in combat was fatal. If an opponent hesitated, he was dead. His training had instilled into him the basic rule that even a second was too long to make a decision. A millionth of a second perhaps. A millionth of a second to put pressure on the trigger and fire. The Unit Zero mission was not combat, but the same rule applied. But in that millionth of a second, his instinctive training had failed him. His target was unarmed. She was in her underwear. She looked terrified. In the two seconds of hesitation before Sam Cook bounced into the room, Gerasimov knew he couldn't shoot her either in the face or in the chest. Anywhere else would not have been fatal. The meeting nine months earlier, intended to lay the ground for a future hit, had been a mistake. It had set in concrete his one weakness as a government-hired assassin: he couldn't kill an attractive woman.

That was why he was on his way to Birmingham.

***

The security supervisor at MI5's regional office in Birmingham was supposed to be on maximum alert, constantly checking the CCTV cameras that covered the whole of the outside of the building, back and front. But he had been on duty for four hours and the streets around the regional HQ in Snowhill, Queensway, seemed exceptionally quiet. He was feeling sluggish. He had eaten an oversized sandwich filled with ham and cheese and mayonnaise and needed to relieve himself, and the nearest toilet was a minute away down the corridor. He took one more look at the row of screens in front of him, then got up slowly from his chair and walked to the door. He was away from his desk for ten minutes.

Halfway through his ten-minute break, Mikhail Gerasimov appeared in the street carrying a holdall. He was in dark clothes with a mask covering the lower part of his face. He clambered swiftly over the steel security wall, removed something from the holdall and pressed it against the solid front door, also made of steel. No alarm sounded. The intruder then stood back and lay on the ground. Two seconds later there was a loud explosion. The front door held, but a large, jagged hole appeared in the middle. Gerasimov threw something through the hole and then ran back, over the wall and down the street as another explosion was heard inside the building. Alarms went off, filling the air with a cacophony of noise. Within fifty seconds, police were on the scene—West Midlands central police station was in the same street. Fire engines arrived eight minutes later. No one came out of the MI5 building, and for a few minutes, there was total confusion.

The intruder had disappeared.

The fire brigade battered down the remains of the front door, and smoke belched out into the cool night air. The entrance area was checked for further devices. Only then were the security supervisor and six MI5 officers on the night shift escorted from the building. No one was hurt.

The explosions at MI5's regional office came too late for the national newspapers' morning editions. But Sandy was woken by Sky's night news desk and he was booked on the first train out of Euston for Birmingham, so he could present his first report of the incident from as near to the MI5 building as he could get.

***

Rebecca had received a text from Jean-Paul at 10 p.m. the previous evening. He would not be back until the following day.

She woke up alone in bed at 9 a.m. and turned on the TV. Sky News's crime correspondent was reporting from central Birmingham. There had been another terrorist attack, although, according to the reporter, the police had not confirmed it as a terrorism incident. Sky's cameras had shown a gaping hole in the front door of a building. The damaged door was lying on the ground. Sandy Hall disclosed that it was one of MI5's half dozen regional headquarters. Rebecca smiled. The reporter looked like he had got up in a rush. She liked him.

Rebecca wondered where Jean-Paul was. He had claimed it was just a meeting. She realised, not for the first time, that she knew next to nothing about the man now sharing her flat. Lying in bed, she decided it was time to investigate.

***

Birmingham was in lockdown. The sound of police sirens could be heard throughout the city. Birmingham New Street railway station was filled with police officers carrying out searches of all well-built men passing through to the thirteen platforms. It was 8:30 a.m. The next train to London Euston was 9:10. A long queue had formed as four police officers went through baggage and asked questions.

Halfway down the queue was a tall, heavy-shouldered man dressed in a traditional green and brown tweed suit with highly polished brown shoes. He had a pipe sticking out of his top jacket pocket, and perched low over his forehead was a wool fedora with a leather band around it. Over one shoulder he had a bag with a long strap. He was also wearing spectacles with large, dark-brown frames. He looked like a country gentleman.

"Excuse me, sir, can I check your bag please?" one of the police officers addressed him.

"Of course," Gerasimov replied, and handed it over.

The policeman opened it and looked inside. He saw several folders, a notebook, a phone and a tube of mints.

"Thank you, sir," the policeman said. "Are you travelling to London?"

"Yes."

"Why are you in Birmingham?"

"Just business."

"You live in London?"

"Yes."

"Thank you, sir," the policeman said and moved on to the next man in the queue.

The country gentleman passed through the ticket barrier and waited on the platform for the 9:10 to Euston.

Had the police officer taken more interest in this particular traveller, he might have pondered on a number of factors. He was wearing what looked like a new suit and shoes for his business trip to Birmingham, but he hadn't bothered to shave. There was a dark shadow of bristles on his chin and upper lip. The glasses looked odd, not quite right for the shape of his face. The pipe sticking out of his jacket pocket looked so old school it seemed more like a deliberate prop than evidence of the traveller's smoking habit. Had the policeman sniffed the end of the pipe, there wouldn't have been a trace of tobacco smell. The three folders inside his leather bag were filled with A4 paper, but there was nothing on them. Just sheets of paper.

The train arrived. Gerasimov glanced up the platform at the ticket barrier and climbed on board.

***

Rebecca had been brought up in a seaside town in Sussex. She still had a love for the sea, but after moving from her parents' home in Eastbourne to begin an art degree at Goldsmiths College in southeast London, she had found little time to venture down to the seaside.

After college, she had struggled initially to start her painting career. Her parents had lent her enough money to find a flat to rent. But she was determined to make her own way without relying on anyone else, least of all her parents. She had always been self-motivated and believed in her artistic talents. With no income when she first lived in London in a tiny flat in Peckham, she was forced to find a job. Waitressing in a restaurant that claimed to serve the finest Persian food. She gave in her notice after six months.

She had her first break when she paid to participate in a gallery exhibition in south Wimbledon. She was allowed to hang only two pictures for her £200 fee. One of them was a five-foot by two-foot oil painting consisting of swirling yellows and greens entitled *Happy Memories*. She sold it for £500 and wished she had asked double.

A few months later she sold another large canvas to a company looking for a splash of art for their conference room. She charged £850. The company paid without demur. From then on, she priced her paintings at more than £1,000 and received regular commissions. She moved to the flat in Notting Hill after her bank balance began to look reasonably healthy.

Now thirty-seven, Rebecca had no particular dreams or ambitions other than to paint and remain independent. She'd had a series of boyfriends, some of them allowed into her bed. But she found men could be irritating once they imagined they had succeeded in getting regular sex. After a time, all her boyfriends would do or say something which brought the relationship to a swift end.

Jean-Paul van Dijk had taken her by surprise. For the first time, she had found herself feeling vulnerable. Not to his charms. But to his masculinity. He was a man who knew what he wanted. She was a match for him, and he was a match for her. She enjoyed that. It was exciting.

But here she was, still in bed in her flat, with no clue where this man might be. She didn't want to ring him because she thought it would be a sign of weakness on her part. It was better to remain aloof. He would prefer that, she sensed. When he returned, if he returned, she would be cool, offhand even.

Rebecca got out of bed and went to the cupboard where Jean-Paul had put his smart leather suitcase. It was locked. She picked it up. It wasn't that heavy, even though he hadn't taken anything out to hang up in the cupboard. He seemed to be a one-suit man. Whatever underwear, spare shirts or socks he had were still in the case. No spare shoes. No coat. A toothbrush, razor and shaving cream in the bathroom. That was it. He had used her toothpaste, she noticed. He had left the flat the day before with a holdall, which she assumed had been inside his suitcase. The special package she had theoretically looked after for him was no longer in the flat.

She was glad he hadn't cluttered up her flat with all his belongings. Yet it seemed strange that he had arrived to live in her flat, albeit temporarily, with so little to show for himself. Whatever documents he had, such as his passport, she assumed were either with him or in the suitcase.

"Where's the bloody key?" she said to herself.

Jean-Paul didn't return until 2 p.m. Rebecca was wearing a painting smock over a pink shirt and blue jeans when he opened the door and walked into the small hall.

"Good God, what the hell are you wearing?" she asked.

He grinned.

"Just thought I'd like a change," he said, giving her a kiss on the lips.

She winced as she brushed against his unshaven upper lip and chin.

"Where did you buy that lot, in a theatre accessory shop?"

"So, you don't like it?"

"Well, it's not exactly you, is it?"

"How do you mean?"

"All country style. I don't see you as a country-style person."

"I have a hat too," he said, pulling the fedora from his shoulder bag. He put it on his head.

"I like that," Rebecca said. "But the rest is a bit... old. Are you old?"

Jean-Paul took her arm and guided her into the bedroom.

Chapter Nineteen
Geraldine Targeted by Shadow Force

Saturday 13th July, 5:30 p.m.

The Shadow Force team assembled in the cramped sitting room of the flat in south London. Gibson had just come off the phone after a brief conversation with the prime minister. The Birmingham incident had been a shock. Everyone had been expecting an attack in London, and the location of the MI5 regional office in Birmingham had never been published. No one had even suggested that the Russian agent, assuming it was the same Russian, might travel there to carry out his latest strike. The fact that no member of MI5's staff had been killed or injured was a huge relief. But the sheer audacity of the attack had caught the police and MI5 by surprise.

CCTV cameras had witnessed the whole incident but without providing any physical details of the Russian other than what had now become a familiar refrain. He was big but agile. And, inexplicably, he had vanished. A police helicopter had been sent up to wash the whole area with searchlights, but there was no sign of a large man in dark clothes wearing a mask scurrying through the streets. A hunt involving a hundred police officers and dogs went on for the rest of the day. Every hotel, bed and breakfast and garden shed was searched. But there was no sign of the man. Nor were there any CCTV images of a motorbike or vehicle leaving the scene at speed.

Nothing had emerged from the police checks at New Street. Several large men had been stopped and questioned, and their luggage or briefcases searched. No suspect holdalls were spotted.

Every member of Shadow Force wanted to be more involved.

"Colonel," Rose said. "If you don't mind me saying, this Russian is taking the piss. The police have got nowhere. MI5 also seems strangely mute. And as for MI6, I reckon they've got it all wrong. Popov is either a figment of their imagination or there really is a tall bloke with bushy eyebrows who is a major-general. But he's not in London. No one has spotted a suspect with bushy eyebrows. If you ask me, it's all part of a very clever Kremlin game to steer us off course."

"Anyone else?" Gibson asked.

Seamus, who always seemed to support Rose, said, "The Birmingham fiasco this morning was definitely a piss-take. No real interest, it seems, in killing people, just causing panic and confusion for fun because he knew or thought he knew he could get away with it. And he did. So far. In my view we're missing something. There's something going on that the police are just not taking into account."

"Such as?" Tim asked.

Seamus looked at Rose, who nodded.

He turned back to Tim. "Geraldine Hammer is the key," he said. "She is at the centre of this whole thing. Apart from the Birmingham incident, which is neither here nor there, she has been the target of this Russian plot from the very beginning. Ok, the first shooting is easier to explain: she was in charge of Operation Foxtrot, and the Kremlin decided she should be bumped off. They made a mistake recruiting that idiot Paine for the job, so they sent their top man to finish it off. But he failed. He had her literally in his sights but something stopped him, and I don't mean Sam here."

Sam grinned.

"So, we have to ask again, why?" Rose took over from Seamus.

"We've been through all this," George said.

Rose ignored him. "Colonel, I am convinced that this Russian—Popov or someone else—had met Hammer before. He knew her and she knew him. In those few seconds before Sam burst in, their eyes met. There was some form of acknowledgement between them. I'm sure of it."

Gibson played devil's advocate. "But you weren't there. How could you possibly know that?"

"I don't. Not for sure," Rose replied. "But my gut instinct is that Geraldine Hammer, even though she is the director of counter-espionage at MI5 and has a brilliant reputation as an operational officer, is hiding something. Call it a woman's instinct if you like."

Tim spluttered.

"Tim?" Gibson turned to him with a frown.

"Sorry, that sounded rude, sorry, Rose," Tim said. "But it seems inconceivable to me that someone like Geraldine Hammer with all her experience—and her responsibilities, for God's sake—would keep something from us when she knows that people's lives, actually *her* life, are at stake here."

Gibson replied, "I have to say I initially shared Rose's view. There was something very strange about the bedroom scene, if I can put it like that. But I agree—if she knows something we don't know, she would surely tell us. Well, not us necessarily, but certainly her colleagues at MI5 and through them or her to the Met."

"The point is," Rose said, "if she does know something, she hasn't told anyone because the police are still chasing around for a large man with bushy eyebrows for God's sake. As I have said before, someone needs to ask her straight what she is concealing. The police aren't doing it. Her people aren't doing it. Six is still obsessed with this guy Popov, and as far as I can see we're the only ones raising these questions and yet, according to you, Colonel, we're not allowed to get involved."

Gibson didn't seem to take offence.

"What are you suggesting?" he asked.

"Would there be any way in which you could fix it for us to speak to Hammer?" Rose asked. "I don't mind being the one to ask her the difficult question."

There was a brief silence.

"Tim, what do you think?" Gibson asked.

"I still find it difficult to imagine the head of counter-espionage at Thames House is not playing ball," he said. "But why not, if only to reassure Rose that Hammer is dealing straight on this."

"This is not about me," Rose said angrily. "If there is any chance Hammer is keeping something important to herself, we have to find out. Otherwise, all of us are going to be chasing around after the wrong bloke."

"Ok, ok," Gibson said quickly. "I don't want any falling out here. Rose, I will ask for an interview with Hammer. If it can be arranged, then I want you and Tim to do it."

Rose looked put out. So did Seamus, who wanted to be with her for the questioning. But they kept quiet.

"I'll make the request through Downing Street," Gibson said. "That's more likely to get a result."

***

For the first time in several days, Geraldine had her children with her. She had persuaded the Met to allow her to spend a few hours with Janie and William at her safe house in Lord North Street, a short walk from the House of Commons. The au pair, Marie, brought them in a taxi from their father's home in Highgate. Both children wanted to know why she was living in a strange house. Who was living in their home in Gladstone Street, they asked? Neither of them knew anything about her job or the circumstances that had led to their mother ending up injured in hospital. She had told them she had been involved in a car accident.

Marie had been vetted before she was hired to look after the children, but she too was unaware of the role her employer played. She had been told that Geraldine worked as a civil servant in a sensitive post, and after seeing the reports on television and in the newspapers about an assassination attempt on a woman who was director of counter-espionage at MI5, she had her suspicions. The later report on Sky News that there had been another attempt on the woman's life at her home in Gladstone Street confirmed her fears. She had been reluctant to bring the children away from the safety of their father's house to the place in Westminster, but Geraldine had persuaded her, and the Met had provided her taxi with an escort.

Geraldine was reading to Janie and William when her mobile phone rang. It was George Trench.

"Geraldine, how are you?" the MI5 director-general asked.

"DG, what's up?" She immediately got up from the sofa and moved into the small kitchen, mouthing "work" to her children and Marie.

"Sorry to ring," her boss said. "I've just had an odd call from Number 10."

Geraldine said nothing.

"They want you to have a session with Gibson's lot," he said.

"Gibson? What on earth for?" Geraldine asked.

"I'm not sure. Apparently, they feel there are loose ends that need tying up."

"I've been through everything a hundred times."

"I know."

"And Gibson and co are outsiders. They should have no role to play in this investigation. What the hell's it all about?"

"Geraldine, I'm sorry. I agree with you of course. But Number 10 is adamant."

"Adamant about what exactly?"

"That they send someone to see you to go over the ground again."

"This is highly irregular and unnecessary. I'll talk to Harry Brooks if that's what they want."

"Number 10 has told me to tell you that it has to be Gibson or one of his team. I'm sure there's no problem. Is there? There's nothing you haven't told me?"

"DG, I'm just doing my job as best I can, as always."

"Of course," he said.

"So what happens next?"

"You'll get a phone call. Could even be today."

"But I have my children with me today."

"Well, I'm sure you can arrange a day more convenient for you. But there is one thing."

Geraldine frowned. "What?"

"They don't want to question you at Thames House. They want to come to your house. Well, your present address."

"Again, highly irregular."

"Geraldine, I really wouldn't worry. Sometimes, as you know, you have to play politics, or I have to in my capacity, and if Number 10 is pushing this I don't see we have any alternative."

Janie was crying.

"I have to go," Geraldine said.

***

Sandy was enjoying a day off. The office hadn't phoned for a change and he was indulging in one of his few interests outside work. Music. Specifically, Johnny Cash. He had been a fan since his late teens.

As he listened to his favourite singer, he started thinking about Birmingham, wondering what it was all about. It appeared to have achieved nothing except a damaged front door and embarrassment for MI5's security set-up at its regional headquarters. Perhaps it was intended as a warning. The Russian wanted it to be known that he could carry out attacks with impunity. But, again, what was the point?

The only common denominator with the previous two attacks was the target. MI5. The Russian— or more accurately, the Kremlin—had decided to punish Britain's security service. So far the biggest victims had been two members of the Metropolitan police service, gunned down just because they were protecting MI5's director of counter-espionage.

Not for the first time, Sandy wondered who she was. Not only her name but what sort of person she was. Her age, whether she was married or had children. He knew nothing about her. But under the strict rules governing what he was allowed to report, even if he discovered everything about her, he wouldn't be able to include it. It was understandable but highly frustrating.

The woman, whoever she was, must be living a personal nightmare, knowing she was the target of a Russian assassin. Was she going to work every day, or was she stuck in some MI5 safe house with armed police bodyguards?

Sandy's story about the arrival of the SAS in London had become big news. Neither the MoD nor Downing Street had confirmed his story, but it ran in every newspaper. *The Sun*'s front page headline was the best: "Who Scares Wins". Underneath was written "Russian Assassin in SAS Sights".

He tried to stop thinking of all the angles to the story and closed his eyes, focusing on the deep, sexy voice of Johnny Cash. He felt his phone vibrating in his pocket.

"Hello," he said wearily.

"Sandy, it's Ed Claridge. I'm sorry to phone you on a Saturday."

Sandy inwardly groaned. He had tried to check out the Joseph Paine claim but had received not even a hint that Paine was telling the truth. He hadn't given up, but there were so many more important lines to follow up he hadn't had time to give it his full attention. Now Paine's lawyer obviously wanted to hear what he had found out. On a Saturday.

"Mr Claridge..."

"Ed, please."

"Ed, I haven't anything to tell you yet—"

"No, I wasn't ringing about that," the solicitor interrupted. "I have some interesting information which I thought might help."

"Oh, right."

"I have been informed by the Crown Prosecution Service that the home secretary has applied for a public interest immunity certificate for my client's trial."

"What!"

"They want the whole thing under wraps. Most of the trial will be in camera," the solicitor said.

"But apart from the name of the MI5 woman, surely there isn't a national security issue here?" Sandy asked.

"Not in my opinion, but if Paine's allegation about being grabbed by some paramilitary force and interrogated without any legal support is true, which I believe it is, the government has every reason to keep things secret."

"Bloody hell."

"I shall be fighting the PII," Ed Claridge said. "I've never had one before, but I think it's pretty outrageous. If the government is allowed to get away with covering everything in secrecy, it will make my job impossible."

"Well, that is something I can report if I get it confirmed," Sandy said.

"Would you be able to hint possibly at why the PII has been applied for?"

"I guess I could," Sandy said, but he felt awkward. Knowing what ex-Corporal Paine had done, he didn't want to be seen to be chasing a story that might help him get off a conviction.

"Anyway," Ed Claridge said, "I'll leave it with you. You can't quote me, of course."

"Fine," Sandy said, and called off.

***

Gibson rang Geraldine on her mobile at 6:30 p.m.

"Dr Hammer," he said formally, "I'm sorry to ring you on a Saturday, but—"

"You're the second person to apologise for ringing me on a Saturday," Geraldine said.

"Oh, sorry."

"You want to talk to me."

"Yes, if that's all right. I know it's a little irregular."

"Yes."

"One of my team, Rose Wentworth, has something buzzing in her head and wants to get rid of it."

"Odd."

"Well, yes. She's like that."

"I'm really not sure. It's a waste of time. My time," Geraldine said.

"I'm sorry. Again. But..."

"Yes, I know, Number 10 is on your side."

"It's nothing to do with Number 10. We just wanted to clear something up."

"Colonel, I'm not a fool. I know you approached Number 10 and they backed you up."

"Dr Hammer, you make it sound as if I'm trying to undermine you. I'm not. Absolutely not. But if we could fix a time, it would be fifteen minutes. No more."

"Tomorrow. Here. Twelve o'clock. But you'll have to clear it with my security detail. As you know, I'm not at home. I'll give you a number to ring. It's Sergeant Drake. Fix it with him," Geraldine said and gave him a mobile number for her lead police bodyguard. "I'll tell him you'll be calling in five minutes. It's just this woman Rose Wentworth?"

"Er, no. Major Tim Plews as well, if that's all right."

"I know Tim," she said. "How's Sam, by the way?"

"Sam's good. Thank you."

Geraldine had taken the call in the kitchen while the children were watching the television. Her weekend was ruined. She had planned to be with Janie and William for the whole two days. Now she would have to arrange for Marie to take them out while she had her two visitors from Shadow Force.

And to make matters worse, she knew exactly what Rose was going to ask.

Chapter Twenty

Rose Asks the Question No One Else Has Dared Ask

Sunday 14th July

A CCTV image of the man who'd scaled the steel barrier in front of MI5's regional headquarters in Birmingham had been released to the media. Like all the images of the supposed Russian assassin caught at various moments by the huge network of cameras in London and Birmingham, there was nothing definitive for the police to provide a full and detailed description of the suspect. His face always seemed to be turned away or lowered into his clothing. The earlier pictures of the Russian after he had hijacked the white food van following the fatal shooting in Gladstone Street were the least helpful because of the balaclava. He wasn't wearing the balaclava in Birmingham, but he was wearing a mask. It covered only half his face, but a woollen beanie concealed his hair and half his forehead. However, close examination had revealed one thing which was regarded as a vital piece of information. The Birmingham attacker had bushy eyebrows. Very bushy. Both the police and MI5—and, of course, MI6—agreed that the images taken outside the building in Birmingham backed up the original description of the suspected assassin, Major-General Maksim Popov.

Press Bureau noted the bushy eyebrows in a brief press release circulated on Saturday evening but made no mention of the name of the suspect.

***

"Bushy eyebrows," Rebecca said, lying next to Jean-Paul. They were watching the morning news on TV.

"Hm."

"Not much to go on," Rebecca said. "Police hunting for a man with bushy eyebrows."

"No, I guess not," Jean-Paul replied.

"You don't have bushy eyebrows."

"Nor do you."

They laughed.

They were watching BBC, but Rebecca switched to Sky. Sandy was reporting from outside Scotland Yard.

He was going over the same ground as the BBC, bringing viewers up to date with the Birmingham incident and the release of the CCTV image of the suspect. But then he came up with something different.

"I understand from sources that the Home Office has applied for a public interest immunity certificate for the trial of former Corporal Joseph Paine, who has been charged with the attempted murder of the director of counter-espionage at MI5," he reported. "This certificate, if granted by the court, would mean that key aspects of the trial would be held in camera on the grounds of national security."

He went on. "Neither the Home Office nor Downing Street would say why a public interest immunity certificate has been applied for. However, a spokesman for the Home Office confirmed to me that such a certificate was being considered."

Pointing behind him at the famous revolving New Scotland Yard sign in front of the building, Sandy said, "Corporal Paine, I understand, has made certain allegations about the circumstances of his arrest by the police outside a lock-up garage in Streatham in south London. He is alleging that he was arrested twice. The first time by non-uniformed individuals who may or may not have been military or ex-military, and the second time by armed police. For legal reasons I am unable to speculate on what might be behind this alleged account of Paine's detention. The Home Office spokesman made no comment. The Met, too, had nothing to say."

"What's all that about?" Rebecca asked, sitting up.

Jean-Paul seemed uninterested.

The more she saw of him, the more Rebecca liked the look of Sky's crime correspondent. She reckoned he was about her age. She had noted that he appeared to be well ahead of other media organisations with breaking news about the Russian assassin.

"What's your view of this Russian?" Rebecca asked Jean-Paul.

"I really don't know," he replied. "Do you know he's a Russian?"

"That's what Sky and everyone else is saying."

"You believe them?"

"Well they must be talking to the police, so yes, I believe them."

"They don't seem to be any closer to catching him."

"Ah, but now we know about the bushy eyebrows, his days are numbered," Rebecca laughed.

"Come here," Jean-Paul said, grabbing her shoulders and pulling her towards him. She didn't resist.

***

Sandy suddenly remembered something which had slipped his mind as he rushed from one story to

194

another. The original tip-off about Joseph Paine. He had been phoned by someone who didn't identify himself, revealing that Paine was a former corporal in the Royal Logistic Corps. At the time, Sandy had wondered whether it was a soldier or ex-soldier. Now, he was sure of it. He was also becoming convinced that Paine's claim that he'd been abducted off the streets by a big bloke and then held for interrogation in a farmhouse in Oxfordshire was probably true. Could it have been the SAS? But why? It wasn't the SAS's job to go around taking people off the streets for interrogation. Not in mainland Britain. In the bad old days in Northern Ireland, definitely yes. But not in London. Not when the Met Police were supposed to be in charge.

So, if not the SAS, who? Could there be some unofficial unit contracted by the government to carry out extra-judicial detentions? Sandy thought it unlikely. He had never heard of such an organisation. But then, if it did exist, it would presumably be all hush hush. Sandy didn't want to get Sky's defence editor involved in tracking down a secret ex-military unit. This was his story, and he intended to guard it jealously. She would walk all over it if he told her what Ed Claridge had revealed to him.

He looked through the calls register on his mobile phone and found the day he had been rung by the mysterious anonymous informant. The same number appeared twice. He rang, but it was a discontinued line. Whoever had rung him had thought it through carefully. Definitely military, Sandy decided.

***

Rose and Tim arrived by taxi outside the house in Lord North Street five minutes before the agreed noon appointment with Geraldine. An armed police officer examined their IDs and opened the front door. Another police officer, standing in the hall, beckoned them forward, patted them down to make sure they had no weapons, and told them to follow him upstairs. Geraldine stood up from the sofa in the sitting room and shook their hands.

"Hello, Tim," she said. "We haven't come across each other for a bit."

Tim had left MI6 when Gibson invited him to join Shadow Force, but he had become acquainted with Geraldine during a number of joint MI5/MI6 operations.

The police officer left the room and closed the door.

"So," Geraldine said, looking in Rose's direction, "what can I do for you?"

She glanced at her watch.

Rose had asked Tim if she could start the questions, and he had agreed.

"I'll get straight to the point," she said, sitting upright in an armchair across from Geraldine. "We think there's something missing in this whole Russian saga."

"Missing? Meaning what?" Geraldine asked.

"Forgive me, but our instinct—well, my instinct— is that you and the Russian may have met before."

Geraldine knew it was coming. So she didn't react.

"What makes you say that?" she asked.

"It's the only explanation for his failure to shoot you as soon as he entered your bedroom," Rose said.

"What are you implying?"

"To put it bluntly," Rose said, "I think he recognised you."

Geraldine shook her head. "Ms Wentworth, I don't think there is any doubt whatsoever that the Russian knew exactly who I was. Why else would he be standing in my bedroom with a gun in his hand?"

Rose faltered. She realised she had made a mistake. She had wanted to approach her real question in a roundabout way, but now she just looked foolish.

Tim intervened. "Geraldine, sorry, of course, that has to be the case. He was there for one reason only, and that was to finish off what was started by Joseph Paine. No one doubts that."

Rose looked furious. Geraldine caught her eye briefly but turned her attention to Tim.

"So what's the issue here?" she asked.

"Well," Tim continued, ignoring Rose's glare, "the issue is why the Russian failed to shoot as soon as he entered the room. You were the intended target; he had literally a few seconds, as it turned out, to do the deed and run. Why didn't he shoot?"

"Everyone has asked that question," Geraldine replied. "Your man Gibson suggested in a somewhat sexist manner that the Russian liked what he saw and as a result hesitated."

"I don't agree," Rose blurted out.

"You mean he didn't like what he saw?" Geraldine asked with a slight smile.

"No, of course not. I'm sure..." Rose stopped, realising she was about to say something gratuitously complimentary.

Tim intervened again. "Geraldine, we'd just like to know your view."

"Well, I don't know, but–"

Rose stood up. Geraldine looked at her, surprised. Tim was, too.

"We're just beating about the bush here," Rose said. "I know it may sound impertinent, Dr Hammer, but I have to ask because no one else seems interested in asking."

At last, Geraldine thought. *Here it comes.*

Rose remained standing. "Is there a chance that you instinctively knew who the man standing in front of you was? Not this so-called Maksim Popov, but somebody else, someone you had met and knew. Quite well. Have you met someone whom you may have had doubts about, a man with the same physique as the gunman in your bedroom?"

There was total silence. Now she had asked the question, Rose's heart was beating furiously. Tim looked as if he was going to intervene again but said nothing, waiting for Geraldine to reply.

"What is instinct and what is fact are two very different things," Geraldine said finally.

"Yes, but—" Rose started.

"Let me finish," Geraldine said.

Rose sat down.

"What I am about to say has already been discussed fully with my colleagues. So I don't want you to go away with the impression that I have kept quiet about something important. Important for the police investigation."

Both Rose and Tim nodded.

"As I explained to my colleagues at Thames House," Geraldine continued, "I met a man in rather odd circumstances some months ago. Not a Russian but not English either. European. I helped him out briefly when his car broke down near where I live. He acquired my phone number and subsequently rang me to invite me to the opera. I accepted and we spent an evening together. I have not seen him since."

Rose was about to speak but received a warning look from Tim.

"Afterwards, realising that our meeting like that was a little strange, I checked him out and he seemed kosher. I had no reason to suspect that he was anything other than what he claimed to be."

"Which was what?" Rose asked.

"A successful businessman of some sort. He had a luxury apartment with a proper tenancy," Geraldine replied and then bit her tongue.

Rose pounced. "So, you saw his apartment?"

"Yes, I saw his apartment."

"Can I be very rude and ask: if he invited you to his apartment and the evening went well, did you wonder why he just vanished after that? In other words, why didn't you see him again?"

"That's a personal matter which has no bearing on this at all," Geraldine replied.

"Rose, I think—" Tim began but Rose pressed on.

"But, forgive me. I'm a woman. I get invited to the opera and back to his apartment for drinks or whatever, and when it's all over I go away thinking to myself, what next? It's natural. Unless something has gone seriously wrong or I decided I don't like him after all."

Geraldine looked uncomfortable for the first time. "As I said, it's a personal matter and not one I'm prepared to go into."

"But, whatever happened," Rose persisted, "did it make you more suspicious about this man, and was it that suspicion that came into your mind when you were confronted by the gunman in your bedroom?"

Geraldine now looked shocked. It was the question she had been dreading. Even Grace Redmayne, the only colleague in whom she had confided, had not asked that.

"Yes," she said after a few seconds. "It crossed my mind then and since."

Tim and Rose exchanged glances.

"And what about now?" Tim asked. "Do you think there would be any mileage in checking out this guy further?"

"We've already done it at Thames House," she replied.

"What, the full works?" Rose asked. "So the police know about it, right?"

"Er, no," Geraldine said. "As I said, it was all rather personal, and when we checked him out there was nothing in the system to show this man had flown into the UK from Europe or anywhere else in recent weeks. And his description as provided by Six didn't match up."

"So, did you check if he is still living in the same apartment here in London?" Tim asked.

"I did, and he's not," she replied.

"Where is he living?" Rose asked.

"I have no idea."

"And he hasn't been in touch once since?" Rose again.

"No."

"You don't find that strange?"

"No."

"So, he vanished out of your life, left his luxury apartment in London, and there is no evidence that he flew into the UK in recent weeks," Tim said. "Is there evidence that he flew out of the UK some time after he met you?"

"No."

"Don't you find that strange?" Rose asked.

"Possibly."

"Does it worry you in the context of what is going on right now?" Rose asked.

"A little," Geraldine replied. "But none of the checks produced anything."

Rose looked at Tim in astonishment.

"What was this man's name?" she asked Geraldine.

"Lucas Meyer."

Chapter Twenty-One
Four Russian Generals Turn the Screw

Sunday 14th July

"I'm not clear why you haven't told the police about your suspicions," Tim said.

"As I said, it was a personal matter and I thought, hoped, that I was over-dramatising the whole thing," Geraldine replied. "I didn't want the police all over the country chasing after an innocent man, especially when Six was adamant that the suspect was someone totally different."

"But you're not sure this Lucas Meyer is innocent?" Rose asked.

"I don't know what he is. But I don't think he's the Russian agent behind the attempt on my life and the shooting of the two police officers, or the gunman in my bedroom. If I thought any differently, based on hard facts rather than some female intuition, then I would have spread the word."

"So, you admit you do have female intuition about this Meyer?" Rose asked.

Geraldine sighed. "In my profession, intuition doesn't go very far. We have to base decisions and judgements on credible intelligence. I don't have credible or even half-credible intelligence about Lucas Meyer to make him a suspect in this Russia affair."

"But based on what you do know about him—or actually what you don't know about him," Rose said, "he should surely be looked at as a possible suspect, or at least someone of interest for the police to investigate?"

"Well, we did look at him at Thames House and came up with nothing," Geraldine said.

"Forgive me," Tim said, "but it sounds like your investigation might have been a little cursory. So you checked out passenger lists on flights. But in my opinion, if you had found a Lucas Meyer on any flights, that would have been more reassuring than suspicious.

"Even if it wasn't his real name," Tim continued, "at least he was travelling on a flight with a passport in that name and we could check back. But you say no one called Lucas Meyer was on any flight into or out of the UK. This means either he came and left by some other means or he flew in under another name. If the latter, then he is definitely to be regarded as a suspect. I assume you agree with that?"

Geraldine nodded. "Yes, of course."

"So the other thing is to go through every passport picture of male passengers travelling to the UK from Europe over a period of time and see if your Lucas Meyer features," Tim said.

"He's not my Lucas Meyer," Geraldine replied icily.

"Ok," said Tim, "but surely that is what has to be done. You haven't done that?"

"There simply hasn't been time, and I don't want people to be sent on a wild goose chase just because I had a tiny worry about a man who met me near my home and took me to the opera," Geraldine said. She knew she sounded unconvincing.

"A tiny worry?" Rose said. "If I was in your position, a tiny worry would worry me a lot."

Geraldine ignored her.

"Presumably you gave a full description of this man to your colleagues at Thames House?" Tim asked.

"Well, in general terms yes," she replied.

"But you went to his apartment," Rose said. "I'm assuming, rightly or wrongly—and forgive me if I'm jumping to conclusions—that you are in a unique position to give a pretty good description of Lucas Meyer?"

Geraldine noticeably went red in both cheeks.

"You have a way with words, Miss Wentworth," she said.

"I'm just looking at it from a practical point of view," Rose said, untroubled by Geraldine's obvious embarrassment. "All we know so far about this Russian suspect is that he is tall and large and has bushy eyebrows. Does Lucas Meyer share these particular physical attributes?"

"Yes and no," Geraldine said. "No bushy eyebrows."

"Anything else we should know?" Rose asked.

Tim squirmed in his armchair. His colleague was asking the sort of questions one might throw at a suspect in a murder case, not the director of counter-espionage at MI5.

"Anything obviously different about him?" Rose kept at it.

"In what way?" Geraldine asked, looking at Tim, perhaps for help. Tim offered nothing back.

"Moles, tattoos, scars, lumps, bumps, anything unusual?"

Geraldine shook her head in apparent amazement at the question. "I met him for one evening, I have nothing I can add."

"So you didn't...?" Even Rose hesitated to ask the most personal question.

Geraldine waited, and when Rose didn't complete the sentence, she said nothing.

To Rose's surprise, Tim took up her question.

"Geraldine, we're not trying to pry into private matters, but if there is any continuing suspicion about Lucas Meyer in your mind, any distinguishable features would be very helpful.

"The CCTV cameras in London and Birmingham," he said, "have revealed nothing of note to help the police build up a picture of the suspect, apart from his physical size. Except in the case of the Birmingham incident, we have bushy eyebrows. So let's say that was Maksim Popov. Then we have John Adams, the mysterious man who stayed at the Royal Garden Hotel and had dinner and other activities with a tall blonde. We know Adams has a full face with a squarish jaw but no real detail. But no bushy eyebrows. He has dark hair, cut short. That's about it. Now we have Lucas Meyer. You say he is tall and big build but, again, normal eyebrows."

Tim stopped for a moment to make sure Geraldine was following what he was building up to.

"So, for a start, would you say Lucas Meyer had a full face with a squarish jaw?" he asked.

"Yes, I suppose so," Geraldine said.

"And dark hair, cut short?"

"Yes."

"So what we have are two men. Let's put Maksim Popov to one side for the moment. We have two men of the same build, with squarish faces and with dark hair cut short. Theoretically, we could say that John Adams and Lucas Meyer might be the same person. Theoretically, if you look at the common physical factors?"

"Theoretically," Geraldine said.

"Then you add Maksim Popov," Tim went on. "He is tall but, according to MI6's description, not as big as both John Adams and Lucas Meyer appear to be. In fact, a lot slimmer. But then their description was based on a photograph taken quite some time ago. And, of course, there's the bushy eyebrows. Neither Adams nor Meyer have bushy eyebrows. Popov does, or so Six tells us.

"We don't know, nobody knows, whether John Adams and Lucas Meyer are the same person or two totally different people, in London for different reasons and having come from different places." Tim was thinking aloud. "But what we can deduce is that if Meyer and Adams are one and the same person, then he is a highly suspect individual who is hiding his true identity for no good reason. They share one other thing in common. Both have disappeared. You haven't seen or heard from Meyer since you met him, and after Adams booked out of the Royal Garden Hotel, he, too, vanished."

He summed up: "Again, if Adams and Meyer are the same man and he is still in this country, he will be under another name by now. This is all supposition but worth considering. Do you agree, Geraldine?"

"It's an argument you can make, I guess," she replied reluctantly.

"So with this supposition in mind, is there anything you can remember, anything at all, which might add some small detail to the general description we now have for Meyer and Adams, whether they are the same person or not?"

Geraldine really didn't want to play Tim's game. The whole interrogation—that's what it had felt like— was becoming embarrassing and intrusive.

"Nothing that would help you or anyone else pinpoint something that has not already been spotted in the CCTV images," she replied.

Rose had one more question. "But, Dr Hammer, the whole point of this meeting is that your Lucas Meyer—sorry, Lucas Meyer, has never been spotted as you say by a CCTV camera. No one knew about Lucas Meyer until you produced the name. We have images of a John Adams and, maybe, of Maksim Popov. But Meyer is a new ingredient. He will have walked past a thousand CCTV cameras with impunity because no one has been looking for him. I can't believe there isn't something about Meyer which you noticed and which only you can reveal. There isn't going to be a CCTV picture to help us."

Geraldine stayed silent for a full three minutes. No one else spoke.

"It's possible," she said eventually, "that he has a tattoo on his left calf."

Tim and Rose gaped at her.

"What sort of tattoo?" Rose asked.

"I didn't see. I didn't look." Geraldine's cheeks went red again.

"But not 'I love Mum' or 'ring-a-ring o' roses'?" Rose queried.

"No, something straight. I don't know what, but no words. Maybe a knife or dagger or something."

"Thank you, Geraldine. Sorry again for the somewhat personal questions," Tim said, standing up. "If you are happy, I think we should get an artist's impression done. Then it can be compared with the one drawn by a police artist of John Adams. You'll have seen it, it's not very good—the hotel waiter was hopeless."

Geraldine nodded. She said she would arrange for an artist's impression to be drawn up and would ask her deputy to fix it.

Tim and Rose shook her hand and left.

***

Moscow

In the bowels of the Aquarium, headquarters of GRU, four men sat around an oak table. They were all in their sixties and each was wearing the uniform of a three-star Russian general. Their large military hats hung in a row next to each other on the coat rack behind them. They were discussing nothing in particular and appeared to be waiting for someone because they kept looking at the door. After five minutes, a tall man also in uniform walked in and nodded to the four men seated at the table, one of whom waved him to a chair.

The nine-storey building, which looked like it needed a thorough makeover, was at Khodynka airfield outside Moscow. The tall man had entered via a narrow lane behind the neighbouring Institute for Cosmic Biology. He had an appointment with four superiors at 8 p.m.

"Tovarishch, welcome," one of the three-star generals said, addressing the new arrival. "Perhaps you could bring us up to date with events in London first, and then we have new orders for you from the president."

The tall man cleared his throat. "Well, as you know, stage one of the mission did not work out as planned, although the British government will have got the message, I believe."

"And the second attempt?" one of the other three-star generals asked.

"I've had no satisfactory explanation," the visitor replied. "The opportunity was clearly there but it was missed. Our man had the target in front of him but either failed to carry it through or the weapon jammed. Communications are being kept to the barest minimum for obvious reasons, so I have very little I can add to what we know or don't know of the circumstances that led to the second failure."

The same general, whose face remained impassive, asked a second question. "And the third attempt?"

The visitor replied. "This is even more difficult to understand. The instructions could not have been clearer. Two shootings had failed, so the third attempt had to succeed."

"But the orders were disobeyed," the general said, his face still as solid as rock.

"Yes. He was supplied with the relevant piece of kit but instead of targeting the same individual, as he was ordered to do, he took it upon himself to carry out an attack miles from London and achieved nothing apart from a hole in a door."

"Remind me about the door. Why this door?" The same general again.

"General, it was the front door of the British security service's office in the city of Birmingham."

"And was the target for this whole mission sitting inside the building at the time?" The voice was dangerously icy.

"No, I believe not."

"So, am I right in saying that our agent in London, trusted beyond trust to target one particular individual, decided instead to blow a hole in a door?"

"General, yes, it would seem so."

"Would it be too much to ask what your view is on this outrageous example of insubordination?" The general with all the questions was being left to lead the prosecution.

"I am both astonished and bewildered and, yes, angry," the tall man replied. "But because of the sensitivity of the mission, there is no one I can call on in London to get to him and demand an explanation. Or, indeed, to take over the mission and send him home."

"Is our man having sex with the target?" It was the turn of another of the generals.

"He carried out a full background check, of course, some months ago, as you would expect," the visitor replied. "He has never let us down before, and I assumed he had done his homework."

"You haven't answered my question," the general persisted.

"General, I have no idea whether his research included getting to know his target in that sort of way," the visitor replied carefully. "But he has his methods, which I have not found fault with in the past."

"Perhaps," the same general said, "he couldn't shoot her because he had enjoyed the sex too much. Do you think that is possible?"

"It cannot be ruled out, but I really don't believe that would be the case. To my knowledge he has never shown any sign of being either romantic or compassionate or hesitant about anything. He is a professional."

"But not this time," the first general said.

"No."

"He has failed to carry out the mission, he has disobeyed his orders, he has made a laughing stock of us, and he must be punished."

"Yes, General."

"Your career is at stake, not just his."

"I understand."

"There is one final chance for your man to get it right."

The visitor waited.

"The president wants—demands—something spectacular," the general said. "After the failures and the ridiculous door-blowing incident, he says our agent has to come up with something that will make the British government rock. Whatever it is, it has to be big. Do we make ourselves clear?"

"Yes, General."

"Provide whatever he needs but with this message: if he fails, we will hunt him down and end his miserable existence."

"Yes, General."

"Now leave us."

The visitor stood up and walked towards the door.

"By the way, how is your wife?" the general with the impassive face asked.

"She is well, General, thank you."

Major-General Maksim Popov then turned and left the room.

Chapter Twenty-Two
The Safe Deposit Man Has a Tale to Tell

Monday 22nd July

Mikhail Gerasimov took a taxi to Piccadilly and asked to be dropped outside the Ritz Hotel. He waited on the pavement by the hotel and glanced at his watch. It was 10:30 a.m. At 10:35 a.m. there was a ping on his phone. He looked at the text message, and his expression changed. Anyone watching would have described it as a scowl. He then walked off quickly and headed for St James's Street.

***

Harry Brooks and Geraldine Hammer learnt of the news later in the afternoon. GCHQ had picked up another text message in Russian. It said: "*Yeshche odin shans.*" One more chance.

The new Russian text message had been pinpointed to a phone in the Piccadilly area. But the signal had lasted only a few seconds before vanishing.

A COBRA meeting was called for 5 p.m. Gibson was included.

Jonathan Ford made a brief opening remark.

"The text message we have intercepted," he said, "is a warning to the Russian agent, Maksim Popov or whoever. So there is likely to be another attack. And imminent. JTAC has raised the threat level to critical. Commissioner?"

Mary Abelard leaned forward. "The secretary of state for defence has authorised the deployment of troops to guard all government and other sensitive buildings." She nodded in the direction of Jeremy Blunt. "There will be four hundred more armed police officers on the streets," she added.

"Just in London?" Home Secretary Lawrence Fenwick asked.

"The tone of the text and the implication of the words we believe indicates that the message is a direct reference to Geraldine Hammer," George Trench said. "There have been two attempts on her life. Both failed. So this will be the third attempt."

"And what about Birmingham?" Fenwick asked.

"It's our belief," Trench said, "that the Birmingham incident was a one-off. Not part of the Russian mission, if you like to call it that. Geraldine has clearly been selected as the target on two occasions. The Birmingham incident makes no sense to us. It's an anomaly. We have yet to come to a firm conclusion, but it may have been intended merely as a diversion of some sort."

"The critical threat level obviously covers the whole country," continued Trench, "but it's our assessment that the real threat is here in London."

The prime minister turned to the chief of MI6. "C, from what the DG is saying, the threat is not so much in London but wherever Dr Hammer is. Have you any reason to believe or suspect that the Russian agent might have a wider remit? Birmingham may have been an aberration, but it did demonstrate that he is prepared to travel outside London. Could there be something more comprehensive, more strategic in Moscow's thinking? Not just Dr Hammer, but something bigger?"

"It's possible," Sir Edward replied. "But I agree with Trench's assessment. 'One more chance' implies one more attempt to eliminate Geraldine Hammer. Nothing sent from our station in Moscow has indicated that the Kremlin might wish to cause even more widespread damage to our relations by targeting the government as a whole. This is about revenge, and Moscow is good at selective revenge."

"And is Popov still the Russian we're looking for?" asked the defence secretary.

Trench coughed slightly. "We are following up a possible new suspect, although it's very tentative, and after Birmingham and the apparent image of bushy eyebrows, we remain focused on Maksim Popov."

The prime minister noticed the look between Trench and Harry Brooks.

"Am I missing something here?" Ford asked.

Gibson, at the end of the table, stared at Trench but said nothing.

"No, Prime Minister," Trench replied. "We are obviously investigating every possible intelligence lead. It's never good practice to put all our eggs in the same basket, so if there is even a hint that something or someone else might be playing a part here, we will follow it up until we're absolutely sure that we have the right suspect."

"You think we're searching for the wrong man?" Defence Secretary Blunt asked and blew out his cheeks.

"No, no indeed," Trench said quickly. "But we have received some additional intelligence which has generated some interest."

"Commissioner, Commander, you both know about this?" Ford asked.

Mary Abelard and Harry Brooks both nodded.

"And what is your view about this new intelligence?"

"Very tentative," Harry Brooks replied, choosing the same word Trench had used.

"What is this new intelligence?" Blunt demanded.

"I think at this stage," Trench said, "we will keep operational details close to our chest. But, of course, if it turns out to be both valid and credible, the Met and security service will bring it to COBRA for your general assessment."

"Dammit, all this secrecy nonsense," Blunt spluttered.

"Thank you, Jeremy," Ford intervened. "I think we can trust the DG to make the right decisions at the right time."

Blunt was about to speak but thought better of it.

Unbeknown to him and the rest of the cabinet, a new name had been added to the extensive file that had been built up by the Met and MI5 since the first shooting incident in London on 1st July. Lucas Meyer and an artist's impression of the man, considered by Geraldine to be a reasonable likeness, appeared in the Operation Buster file under the heading: "New lead to be investigated but not made public."

***

Geraldine had had a difficult conversation with both her boss and Harry Brooks after her visit from Rose and Tim. She had asked Grace, her deputy, to speak to the Met about providing a police artist for a Lucas Meyer sketch. She had made no reference to the tattoo. It was irrelevant in her view. But she sat with the artist for an hour and the result had been distributed to police forces around the country. Both Trench and Brooks had asked Geraldine why this information was only being made available now. Her reply had been only partially convincing. Like everyone, she said, her focus had been on the Russian intelligence officer identified by MI6 as the most likely suspect. It was only later when she went back in her mind over everything that had involved her both professionally and personally in the last twelve months that she had recalled the Lucas Meyer incident outside her house. She still didn't believe that Meyer was a Russian agent but thought it was necessary to introduce his name to the wider investigation.

The MI5 chief had thanked her but had added a warning to his director of counter-espionage.

"I know you have been through a lot," he said in a meeting in his sixth-floor office, "but I have to say your personal life is not something I want to have to worry about. This man came out of the blue. That should have sent alarm bells into your head."

Geraldine had stayed quiet.

"You say you checked him out, but that's not your job," her boss said sternly. "That's the job of our vetting system. You know that. You can't have a personal life, not in your position, until every aspect has been vetted, checked and double-checked. You let this man into your life, albeit briefly, and if he had an ulterior motive, and I'm talking espionage here, then it was a disastrous decision on your part."

Geraldine nodded.

"So, please, never again," Trench said. "Your safety is our safety. Harry Brooks has been very understanding, but I'm sure he is as disappointed as I am that you didn't bring this Lucas Meyer issue up from day one."

Geraldine had apologised and left the room feeling like she had been scolded by her head teacher.

She had one thought. *Please, God, don't let Lucas Meyer be the Russian assassin. Please let it be Maksim Popov.*

Then she immediately had another thought. *Please, God, don't let Lucas Meyer be Maksim Popov.*

***

Sandy was also in trouble. His report about Joseph Paine and the allegation that he had been abducted by a military or paramilitary or ex-military unit had not gone down well with his best contact at Counter-Terrorism Command.

He had a call early Monday morning.

"Rick, how are you?"

"Sandy, we'd like you to drop this stuff about Paine," the detective inspector said. "It's not helping. We've got the bastard and so far that's all we've got. The last thing we want is for his conviction to get screwed up over some wild allegation that has no substance. He was arrested by police outside a lock-up garage stuffed with incriminating evidence, and as far as we're concerned, that will put him away for the rest of his life. Do you get what I'm saying?"

"Yes, but..."

"No buts, Sandy. Otherwise, you can forget about ringing me in the future."

"Other reporters will be looking into this," Sandy said.

"Only because you raised it in the first place."

"But I can't stop them from investigating. Nor can I tell my news editor that it was all hogwash and we should drop it."

"That's up to you, but as far as we're concerned, it's not helpful. Got to go."

Sandy was mortified. He had known all along that he was treading a dangerous path by running the story, but the move by the prosecuting authorities to impose a secrecy blanket on Paine's upcoming trial had been a genuine news story. He had merely tried to put the decision into a speculative context. He had done that many times before in his career. It was legitimate interpretation. But now he faced losing his best contact if he continued to pursue the abduction line.

Sandy wrestled with his conscience and decided to take the middle road. He wouldn't make the Paine allegation an important part of his daily inquiries with the police and MI5. He would mention it only if it became an issue in any part of the trial held in open court. Hopefully, he could keep the news editor happy by producing more exclusive stories.

He didn't want his key contact to stop talking to him. Rick had already provided his best lines so far, and provided he kept away from the Paine abduction story, Sandy hoped his counter-terrorism detective inspector would continue to prove an invaluable contact.

***

Mikhail Gerasimov returned to the building which held safe deposit boxes in St James's Street. He went through the usual security procedures. The security man at the desk showed little interest, although he made one comment.

"Nice to see you again, Mr van Dijk."

Gerasimov ignored him.

He took his key from his jacket pocket and opened safe deposit box number 397. Inside was a white envelope and a two-foot-long rectangular metal container. He looked around. There were no cameras. This was supposed to be a private room for private business. That's what he paid for. He opened the container. Inside was a Russian-made PP-90-01 Kedr submachine gun with an integrated silencer. At fully automatic, it could fire 800 9x18mm Makarov rounds a minute.

He closed the case and placed it in the new holdall he had brought with him. He had dumped the other one in a waste bin near the railway station in Birmingham. He put the envelope inside his jacket.

Unopened. He then returned to the foyer and left the building. Again, he ignored the man on the desk, who looked up but decided against wishing the visitor a good day.

He waved to a taxi and told the driver to take him to Rebecca's address. But instead of entering the building, he walked round the corner to a café. He ordered a coffee and sat at the back, putting the holdall under the table. He took the envelope from his jacket and placed it in front of him. There was no name on the envelope. After the waitress had brought his coffee, he unsealed the envelope and drew out a single piece of paper.

There were three lines written in ink.

17SW1P3LD

Konets!

Vozvrashcheniye!

A postcode in Westminster he would need to check.

Finish!

Return!

Gerasimov shook his head. He looked up the postcode on a phone he took from the holdall. It was Lord North Street, Westminster. Moscow had been doing its homework. They had found or claimed to have found where Geraldine Hammer was now residing.

He checked out Lord North Street on Google and understood why she had moved there. It was a narrow street of five-storey eighteenth-century terraced townhouses, not far from Parliament Square, an area he knew would be packed with armed police. Targeting the director of MI5 counter-espionage in such a location was madness, he thought, unless Moscow's plan was to deliberately send him on a suicide mission. Judging by the note inside the envelope, perhaps that was what Moscow had in mind.

Then he thought again. If he was gunned down in the narrow confines of Lord North Street, the British police would have the perfect evidence of an official Russian plot. However many denials came from Moscow, his dead body and the Russian submachine gun would tell a different story. So he was expected to carry out the killing, escape and return to Moscow leaving no trace of Russian involvement.

The Russian agent shook his head again. He would check out the street. But he had already made up his mind.

He left the café and walked to Rebecca's flat. It was earlier than he planned, but he needed to put the holdall inside his leather suitcase.

***

Back at the safe deposit building in St James's Street, the security employee at the front desk rang a friend in the police force based at Lewisham in southeast London. He caught him on his lunch hour.

"Derek, it's Phil."

"Hi, Phil, what's doing?"

"Probably nothing. Just wanted your advice."

"Shoot."

"This guy, big bloke, not friendly. Seen him twice over a short period. Comes in here, says nothing, ignores me, does his business and leaves."

"So?"

"He came both times with a holdall. Carried it easy up to the desk. But when he left on each occasion, his right shoulder sloped down a bit."

"Good spot, Sherlock."

"As I said, probably nothing, but you know with all this Russian stuff going on and police descriptions of a large suspect, I just thought I might mention it."

"You told anyone else?"

"No, I didn't want to say anything officially because, well, it's my job, right? Safe deposit box holders here, it's all confidential. Like a bank. I'm not supposed to tell anyone what goes on."

"Ok, I get it. But tell me, if this big bloke comes in and removes something from his safe deposit box, did you ever see him go in and put something into the box? Like whatever he took out, he must have put in at some point?"

"Not on my watch, as far as I can remember."

"So no sloping shoulder when coming in, only when going out?"

The security officer thought about that for a moment.

"Ah, I see what you're getting at. No, just when going out."

"So could someone else have gone in to deposit whatever it was in the same deposit box? Is that possible?"

"Only with all the right security codes and passport."

"But it could be someone else, acting on the big guy's behalf?"

"Yes, but... if that was the case it would come up on the screen."

"And does it?"

"Let me check."

Three minutes went by.

"It's a company name with two directors. I've only ever seen one of them."

"So tell me."

"It's supposed to be totally confidential. So please don't hang me out to dry. I'd lose my job. The company's called IT Group Holdings based in Finsbury Park."

"And the two directors?"

"One of them's the guy who came in today. The big bloke. He's called Jean-Paul van Dijk."

"And the other one?"

"John Adams."

"So either of them could deposit something and then take it away?"

"Yeah."

"But you've never seen this John Adams?"

"No."

"Could anyone else deposit something other than these two?"

"Yeah, if we get a letter of authorisation."

"And did you?"

"Yeah, it says so here. Twice we got authorisation."

"And who delivered on those two occasions?"

"No name, just an official delivery service."

"Sounds dodgy."

"But it was all authorised. Says so here. I wasn't involved."

"How did they put it inside the box?"

"We have the keys for all the boxes. For when deliveries are made without the prime holders present."

"Sounds very dodgy."

"So, was I right to tell you?"

"Yes, leave it with me."

Chapter Twenty-Three
Maksim Popov Gets New Orders

Rebecca went to her wardrobe and picked up the leather suitcase. It was relatively light. She had noticed Jean-Paul leaving with the holdall. His country tweed suit was hanging up. She felt in all the pockets. There was nothing. Not at first. But then her fingers brushed against something tucked in at the far corner of the inside pocket of the jacket. She brought it out and stared. It looked like an eyebrow. A bushy, dark brown eyebrow. Just one. Slightly sticky.

Her heart jumped and she sat down on the bed. She recalled their conversation in bed when the TV news had mentioned the man with bushy eyebrows. The Russian assassin with bushy eyebrows. Was this a joke? Should she just laugh it off? It couldn't be true. Absolutely not.

In her mind, she went over everything she had learnt about Jean-Paul since he made his first appearance in front of her at the Côte brasserie in Kensington High Street.

Very little, was her conclusion. She was unconvinced by his claim to be half Dutch, a quarter Swiss and the rest Eastern European. The explanation for his French first name was also too easy. But at the time it seemed fun and there had been no reason to question him. Lunch at the Royal Garden Hotel had been somewhat overwhelming because of the anticipation of what might follow. His blunt request to move into her flat had taken her by surprise, but so far, she'd had no reason to regret her decision. He had never talked about the business he was setting up, and his absence for more than twenty-four hours remained a mystery. The most surprising thing, she thought, was the suit he'd been wearing when he arrived back from wherever he had been. What was all that about? He was definitely not a tweed suit sort of man. Did he want to look more British? Was that it? If so, why? What was behind it? And now the single bushy eyebrow. Sticky on the back.

Rebecca put the false eyebrow back in the inside jacket pocket and went through the suit again. Nothing else emerged. His new brown shoes had nothing hidden in the toecap. Rebecca realised she was behaving as if he really was a spy.

She then searched the flat. Every drawer, every shelf, under the bed, under the mattress, behind the umbrella stand in the hall, in the umbrella stand, in the small, mirrored cupboard on the wall in the bathroom and, finally, in and behind the toilet cistern. When she lifted the cistern lid, she couldn't believe what she saw. In the right-hand corner at the back, there was a plastic box, about six inches long by four inches wide, with sealing tape round it. She lifted it out and shook it. Whatever was inside didn't rattle or move around. The box wasn't heavy, but Rebecca thought it was full, which was why the contents didn't make a noise when she shook the box up and down. She was dying to open it. She was sure that what this box contained would tell her everything about Jean-Paul. Only spies and gangsters would think of hiding valuables in a sealed plastic box inside a toilet cistern.

She knew she shouldn't unseal the tape. Even if she managed it carefully, something would go wrong and Jean-Paul would know instantly. What then? She could laugh it off. But that would depend on what she found inside the box. On at least two occasions since meeting him, she had seen a look on his face when she had something that either confused or irritated him. Opening his plastic box could have consequences she did not wish to contemplate. But her curiosity overcame her. She wiped away the water drips and put her longest nail under the end of the tape. She began to peel it back slowly.

Then she heard a key slotting into the lock of her front door. With her heart thumping, she pressed the end of the tape back and replaced the box in the same corner. As the front door opened she put the lid back on the cistern and flushed it quickly.

Jean-Paul called out.

When she walked into the living room, her heart was still beating so fast she could've sworn he heard it. He looked at her strangely.

"I'm back early," he said. His holdall was on the floor.

"So I see," Rebecca said.

"You alright?"

"Yes, fine."

Rebecca's mind was in turmoil. The false eyebrow, the hidden plastic box, the holdall. What was in the holdall?

"What have you been doing?" he asked.

She blushed. She never blushed. But she could feel her cheeks reddening.

"Nothing," she managed.

Gerasimov stared at her.

"I wasn't accusing you of anything," he said. "I just wondered what you have been doing while I was out."

"Nothing," she repeated.

"No painting?"

"No."

"Just... nothing."

"Er, yeah."

Gerasimov picked up the holdall and took it into the bedroom. She didn't follow him. She heard him opening the wardrobe door, and there was the sound of a clasp snapping open. Then another noise, which she guessed was the holdall being placed inside the suitcase. He closed the wardrobe door and went into the bathroom. Rebecca stood transfixed in the middle of the living room. She heard the toilet flush. A minute later he stepped out of the bathroom and came towards her. She could hardly breathe.

He walked up close and put his arms around her.

"If you're doing nothing, I'm doing nothing," he said.

He picked her up and took her into the bedroom.

***

Derek, friend of the security officer at the safe deposit company in St James's Street, was Police Constable Derek Framer. He had been in the police force for eight years and had failed to fulfil his ambition of becoming a detective. He resented it. He especially resented his sergeant, who had never encouraged him to believe that he could ever be a detective. PC Framer looked set to remain a constable.

Having been given potentially significant information about a man who could theoretically be the Russian every one of his colleagues was hunting for, might have seemed a golden opportunity for PC Framer to change his luck and pass on the intelligence snippet to a superior officer.

But PC Framer did nothing.

First, he was worried that if he did tell someone of higher rank, he or she would demand to know where the information had come from. Then he would be forced to betray his friend. And his friend would lose his job.

However, the bigger reason was that PC Framer knew after eight years in the police force that he would be treated with disdain, even derision. How could someone as lowly as a police constable who would never make a detective be in the possession of such interesting information? He could hear his sergeant dismissing him and telling him to go back to his beat.

Also, to be fair to PC Framer, he was not apprised of all the latest details about the hunt for the Russian assassin. He had never heard of IT Group Holdings, based in Finsbury Park. Nor had anyone mentioned a John Adams to him. And certainly not a Jean-Paul van Dijk. That sounded Dutch to him. So how could he be a Russian? No Russian was called van Dijk.

PC Framer went over all these thoughts and came to the conclusion that if he passed his friend's suspicions on to his sergeant or higher up the command chain, he would get laughed out of court.

So he did nothing.

He decided that if his friend asked him if he had told anyone, he would just say he had discussed it confidentially and that no further inquiries were thought to be necessary.

***

Moscow

Major-General Maksim Popov was back in the bunker of the Aquarium. Less than sixteen hours after his appearance before the four three-star GRU generals, he had received a message that they wished to see him again. As soon as possible.

He wasn't greeted this time but was told to sit down.

"We have thought again about this situation in London," one of the generals said.

General Popov waited.

"It is our understanding," the same general continued, "that your trusted agent is currently residing with a woman. We believe that your confidence in his abilities is faulty. We know where he is living. We know he has picked up the latest package and he has taken it back to a flat where he is living with this woman. Are you aware of this?"

Popov looked astonished.

"General, I know he works in a somewhat irregular way with methods that perhaps you don't necessarily approve of," he said, "but I am sure he will get the job done. If he has moved into a flat with a woman, that would be in order to stay out of the limelight. I know he was initially booked into a hotel, but the logistics of his mission I left to him. He's the man on the ground and I felt it was right for him to make the decisions about where he should hide out. Perhaps being with a woman is not such a bad idea. Provides him with a cover story, don't you think?"

"My concern—our concern," the same general replied, "is that your man is resorting to unacceptable methods and that he is delaying what should have already been accomplished."

A second general interposed. "London is now alive with armed troops. Hiding in a flat with a woman might seem to be a prudent precaution, but the fact is, he has failed to achieve what he is supposed to have achieved and now he is enjoying himself with this woman and not focusing on what the president is demanding."

"Bluntly," a third general said, "we suspect that your agent is more concerned about carnal pleasures than he is about fulfilling the mission laid down by the president."

Popov was about to reassure the generals when the first general interrupted.

"So, our decision, approved higher up, is that you should go immediately to guarantee the mission is completed and then return with your agent in tow."

Popov once again looked astonished. "You want me to go to London?" he asked.

"Correct."

"But, as you know, my name is top of their list of suspects," Popov said.

"Of course, that was the plan. But now it's all going wrong. We need you to sort it out."

"General, I don't want to sound negative," Popov said, "but if they are looking for someone who looks like me, then every airport will be alerted, every policeman on the street will have my picture."

The four generals stared at Popov without saying anything.

The first general then spoke. "You seem to have forgotten that as far as the authorities in Britain are concerned, you are already in the UK. So you could hardly be arriving at an airport if you are supposed to be somewhere hiding out in London."

The other generals nodded their support.

The first general continued: "And as for your street policemen, the bobbies, they have shown in the past, have they not, that members of our esteemed organisation can go walkabout in their cities without anyone noticing and, by the way, return to Moscow without even so much as an 'Excuse me, sir, can you show me your papers?' So it may be more of a challenge for you, Major-General Popov, but we want you on a flight to London as soon as possible. Is that clear?"

"Yes, General, perfectly," Popov replied.

"Bring me back some of their raspberry jam," said the general who had, the day before, asked after Popov's wife.

Popov left the room without answering.

***

Rebecca lay awake and looked across at Jean-Paul asleep next to her. She moved her body away from him. He stayed asleep. As carefully as she could, she eased herself out of the bed and walked into the bathroom. She closed the door behind her.

Rebecca was curious about two things: whether the plastic box was still in the cistern and what was in the holdall inside the leather suitcase. She tentatively lifted up the lid of the cistern. The plastic box was still there, in the same place. She couldn't do anything about the holdall. Not right now.

She returned to the bedroom after flushing the toilet and found him with his eyes wide open.

Before climbing back into bed, as he watched her, Rebecca had a thought. She decided in that moment to do something she had never done before. But it would have to wait until tomorrow.

Chapter Twenty-Four

Rebecca Strong Becomes the Focus of COBRA

Tuesday 23rd July

Mikhail Gerasimov left the flat at 8 a.m., dressed in his country tweed suit. He explained that he was meeting with potential British business partners and wanted to look right. Rebecca tried to convince him that his blue suit would look even better, but she couldn't persuade him. He left empty-handed. No holdall.

She waited ten minutes before going to her wardrobe. The suitcase was there but nothing else. She reached in and grabbed the handle. It was heavy. She doubted it was full of business files and papers. If it was, why hadn't he taken it with him for his business meeting? The more she thought about it, the more she suspected he was lying about his business meeting. In fact, lying about setting up a business altogether. If he was such an avid entrepreneur, how come he could return to the flat in the middle of the day? She had never seen him doing anything that could be described as work, nor had he offered to take her out to a restaurant. Apart from one lunch at the Royal Garden Hotel, he had never suggested going out for a meal. They ate in the flat every evening. She cooked. She didn't mind but just thought it odd. A businessman, setting up a company. Why would he not want to take out his new girlfriend for a meal?

Rebecca lifted out the suitcase and put it on the floor. She could feel the holdall inside. But with no key, the contents had to remain a mystery. Likewise, the plastic box in the cistern. She decided it was too risky to peel off the tape. Whatever was inside the box was also something he clearly didn't need for his meetings. It was becoming more and more obvious that these meetings were just a smokescreen. For what, she had no idea. But she had begun to feel genuinely scared of the man who had walked into her life and revealed nothing about himself. Nothing, that is, that she could believe.

She went to her laptop and put "Sky News" into Google. She rang the number she found under the heading "Contact" and waited ten minutes for it to be answered.

"Hello, can I speak to Sandy Hall please?" she said.

"I can't just put you through, I'm afraid," said a woman with a slightly officious voice.

"I need to speak to him."

"As I said, I can't put you through. Is he expecting your call?"

"No."

"Would you like to leave a message?" the woman suggested.

"Yes," said Rebecca. "Tell him the Russian assassin is staying in my flat."

She gave her mobile number.

***

Sandy was out all morning, attending a briefing at the Met. He had a sandwich lunch with a contact at the Home Office and didn't return to Sky until after 3 p.m. He then had a series of reports to compile. The Met briefing had elicited no fresh information about the search for the Russian assassin, and Sandy got the impression the police were increasingly frustrated by the lack of progress. They now had a wealth of information, but none of it had pinpointed where the Russian might be hiding. Sandy had asked about the SAS and what they were doing, but the chief inspector who briefed the reporters said all such questions should be directed to the MoD. He rang the MoD press office without any hope of getting an answer and was duly given the predictable reply: *No comment.*

By the time he had finished for the day at around 5 p.m., he had still not checked his phone messages. He nearly didn't bother. It had been a long day and he had an early start, as usual, the following day. But the red light was flashing on his office phone. Without much enthusiasm, let alone expectation, he pressed the button for his messages. There was only one. It was the switchboard.

"Mr Hall, some woman rang with a message. She said to tell you that the Russian assassin was staying in her flat. I've got her phone number if you want to call her. She didn't sound crazy but probably is."

Sandy laughed. He did get a lot of crazies wanting to talk to him, which was why the switchboard acted as a barrier between him and them.

He wrote down the phone number in his notebook and sat back, wondering whether to ring or not. The switchboard was probably right. A nutter.

He also wanted to get away. But he dialled the number. The caller hadn't left her name.

The number rang five times before it was answered.

A woman's voice said hello.

"This is Sandy Hall here, I work for Sky News. I gather you rang me earlier. Sorry I haven't been back till now, but it's been a long day."

"Oh, yes, hello. I just wanted to confirm my order for new paintbrushes."

Sandy's face wrinkled up in surprise.

"My switchboard said something about the Russian assassin," he said.

"Ah, that's good," Rebecca replied. "Perhaps I can collect them tomorrow. If I ring first we can fix a time."

"I think we're at cross purposes here," Sandy said.

"No," Rebecca replied. "Absolutely not."

"Sorry, you're making no sense."

"So I'll ring tomorrow. Goodbye."

The phone went dead. Sandy sighed. A nutter after all.

Rebecca put her phone in her jeans pocket and smiled at Jean-Paul.

***

At GCHQ in Cheltenham, a team of six analysts sat in a white-painted room with no windows. In front of each of them was a computer more advanced and sophisticated than any other in the whole of the United Kingdom. The team was called simply D15. Created less than two weeks before, its sole mission was to examine, analyse and interpret any electronic communications within the Greater London area which might have relevance or interest for the investigation into the shootings in the capital and the Moscow connection.

Keywords such as *Russian assassin*, *MI5* and *terrorism* had been picked up on a regular basis. But none of the phone calls, texts, emails or multitude of social platforms had produced anything of interest or value so far that day. D15 had been told to pass on any intercepted communications from within London deemed to be significant or potentially significant to a single government customer, Jim Petherwick, Director-General Defence and Intelligence at the Foreign Office.

Anything sent from D15 had to be marked "Top Secret" and headed "Code Zero".

At 8 p.m., twenty minutes before he was due to go for dinner at the Reform Club in Pall Mall, Petherwick received an encrypted Code Zero email.

The communication from D15, copied to the GCHQ director, consisted of a transcript of three telephone calls.

The first was between a man called Phil Large, a security officer at a safe deposit company in St James's Street, W1, and Derek Framer, a police constable at Lewisham police station.

Petherwick read the transcript twice. He was astonished that such vital information appeared not to have been passed on to the Met. There had been no mention in the briefings he had received of a safe deposit company and two visits by a man who, theoretically, could be the Russian everyone was hunting for. The reference to IT Group Holdings and John Adams was dynamite. But who was Jean-Paul van Dijk?

Petherwick turned his attention to the second phone call. The Code Zero communication disclosed that a woman called Rebecca Strong had rung Sky News. He was taken aback by the extraordinary statement from the woman, claiming that the Russian assassin was living in her flat. It could be nonsense. But Petherwick thought otherwise. He concluded that she had said what she had said not to make a fool of herself or to make a fool of Sky's crime correspondent, but because it was her belief that she had a Russian in her flat. Petherwick was frustrated. He wanted to hear the phone calls, not just read the transcript. Especially the one from Rebecca Strong. How old was she?

He then read the third transcript. Sandy Hall ringing Rebecca Strong. Petherwick knew immediately why she had replied in such a bizarre way. Hall had phoned when she wasn't alone. She had company. The Russian, if it was indeed the Russian, must have been in earshot.

Petherwick read the transcript three or four times. Yes, he was convinced. If Hall had been listening properly and come to the same conclusion as him, Rebecca was telling Hall that she would phone back the following day when she could speak to him without anyone else listening.

He checked the date of the Hall/Strong phone call. Both had taken place that day, the first at 9:10 a.m., the second at 5:02 p.m., three hours ago.

Petherwick rang the foreign secretary on her mobile.

"Foreign Secretary, it's Jim Petherwick," he said. "We have a situation that needs a rapid decision."

He explained in general terms.

"Ring Number 10," Elizabeth Gantry said. "The PM needs to know."

"The police, MI5...?" Petherwick asked.

"Not yet," she replied. She was speaking from the back of her chauffeur-driven Jaguar. "Let the PM decide."

***

An hour later, an emergency COBRA meeting was chaired by Jonathan Ford, but with very restricted numbers around the table. Present were Elizabeth Gantry, Lawrence Fenwick, George Trench, Sir Edward Farthing and Colonel Rollie Gibson. No defence secretary and no Downing Street civil servant to take notes.

The prime minister had read the transcript of the three phone calls. Everyone present had been given copies.

"We have until tomorrow to make plans," he said.

"Excuse me, Prime Minister," Fenwick said, "but why don't we just inform the police and get them to raid this flat and grab the Russian?"

"First of all," Ford said, a little impatiently, "we don't know if this woman Rebecca Strong is a wild crazy or a genuine informant, or just getting her own back on a boyfriend she is fed up with. We can't have police armed with God knows what barging their way into a private flat and shooting at anything in sight. Therein lies disaster. Both for the Met and for the government. We can't afford for anything to go wrong, not after the shooting of the two police officers. This woman, if she is genuine, is courageous. Her life could be in danger if this Russian really is in her flat, but we still need to be absolutely sure."

"But I don't need to remind you, Prime Minister, that this Rebecca Strong woman has rung the crime correspondent of Sky News," Fenwick said. "Why didn't she go to the police? If she had, we wouldn't be in this position. This is not a political matter, it's a matter for the police, surely. We can't be seen to be involved in an operational situation. Let the police take over."

The prime minister was silent for a few seconds. He looked at Gibson, who, almost unnoticeably, shook his head. Once to the left, once to the right.

"No," Ford said. "There is too much at stake here. There are still unknowns. I want this handled in the most sensitive way possible. The police, of course, will be told, but not tonight. Not right now. Let's see what happens tomorrow. If Rebecca Strong rings the reporter and sets up a meeting, we will monitor it."

At that moment, he looked again at Gibson and continued. "If we are satisfied that she is genuine and there is every chance the Russian is the one we are after, then it must be dealt with carefully and appropriately. As I said from the beginning, I want this Moscow agent in our hands, whole and healthy, and standing in the dock at the Old Bailey. It's the only way we're going to win this one against Moscow. If we're all leaping to the wrong conclusion, we'll end up a laughing stock. DG, C, do either of you wish to say something?"

Trench was the first to nod. "Just to point out something none of us knew before. We have yet another name to conjure with. Jean-Paul van Dijk. If ever a name was made up, it's that one. Whether any of the names we have so far are Maksim Popov, I am beginning to have grave doubts. In fact, with all due respect to C, I wonder whether Maksim Popov exists at all. I know we have a photograph of a Maksim Popov when he was a colonel, but for all we know, this is all part of a Moscow scam to send us down the wrong trail."

Sir Edward Farthing looked furious. "We never said for sure that Popov was definitely the agent sent here," he said. "We gave our best assessment based on what Moscow station came up with."

"I'm sure DG wasn't implying anything," the prime minister intervened.

"And I would like to say something else," Farthing continued, ignoring Ford's remark. "As DG rightly said, we have several names in the frame, all of them probably false. But one of them is Lucas Meyer. I don't need to say any more about that and the circumstances in which his name cropped up. But I think, Prime Minister, if we are going to substantiate this woman's claim, it will be vital that Geraldine plays a part. If Lucas Meyer and John Adams and this Jean-Paul van Dijk are one and the same, she is in the unique position of being able to confirm it. Or she will be tomorrow, once we know what this woman Rebecca Strong is going to say."

Everyone round the table knew the MI6 chief was right. Geraldine Hammer might have escaped death by a miracle, and she had undoubtedly endured a traumatic experience in the bedroom of her house, but she knew what Lucas Meyer looked like. None of them said it, but everyone at the COBRA meeting had the same thought: Geraldine Hammer and Rebecca Strong had to compare notes.

Sir Edward had one more thing to say:

"This PC Derek Framer needs to be crucified."

The prime minister wrapped up the meeting.

"I'm going to ask Colonel Gibson to set up surveillance of the expected meeting between Rebecca Strong and Sandy Hall, with an outer perimeter of security service people," he said. "DG, are you happy with that?"

"Not the way I would normally do it," Trench replied, glancing at Gibson.

Fenwick nearly burst a blood vessel. "I really cannot see why this should not be handled in the appropriate way by a joint police/MI5 operation," he said. "We don't need..."

Gibson knew the home secretary was going to end the sentence with something like "some cowboy unit getting in the way".

But Ford had made up his mind.

"Let's meet again once this woman and the reporter get together, assuming they do at some point tomorrow," he said. "That will be the easy part. Once we know what she has to say, then I agree we should consider some form of meeting between her and Geraldine. I will leave the details on that matter for you, DG. Then and only then can we bring in the full works."

He added: "Until then, this has to remain totally secret. Is that clear?"

"Yes, Prime Minister," they all replied.

As they stood up, the home secretary asked, "What if Sandy Hall rushes straight to a camera and blurts out the news that the Russian has been found? He's a reporter, he won't care about the consequences."

To everyone's surprise, Trench replied, "We know Sandy Hall. I don't think he will do any such thing."

"And what if he rings the Press Bureau after meeting with this woman," Fenwick said. "Bang goes the secrecy you want, Prime Minister."

Ford frowned. It was the one thing he had neglected to consider.

Trench came to the rescue.

"Leave it with us," he said. "I have an idea."

They all looked at him. But he was already on his way out of the room.

***

In their routine daily log, the police protection team guarding 17 Lord North Street, safe house for Geraldine Hammer, reported no unusual incidents. The only line in the relatively brief summary for Tuesday 23rd July that provided a slightly different observation was the following:

"A large man in a brown suit was spotted at 10:15 a.m. walking slowly up Lord North Street in a westerly direction. He was carrying what looked like a map and appeared to be engrossed in reading it. Nothing suspicious indicated. It was concluded he was an out-of-town visitor and was looking at a map or tourist guide to check the historic significance of the street. No interception was considered necessary."

Chapter Twenty-Five
Rebecca and Geraldine Compare Notes

Wednesday 24th July

Rebecca rang Sky News at 9 a.m. She told Jean-Paul she was out all morning, collecting new paintbrushes. He planned to remain in the flat all day, working.

The same woman on the switchboard answered.

"Can you put me through to Sandy Hall, please," Rebecca said. She was standing outside Kensington High Street tube station.

Instead of getting the brush-off as she had the previous day, the woman was more amenable.

"Did you phone yesterday and ask for him?" the woman asked.

"Yes."

"He said to put you through if you rang again."

"Thank you."

"Sandy Hall," Sandy said when he picked up the phone.

"I rang yesterday and you rang me back," Rebecca said.

"Ah yes, I wondered if you would call again."

"You think I'm some crazy woman, right?"

"No, not at all."

"Liar."

"Well, it was kind of a strange message. And then I rang back and you sounded like you were talking to someone else."

"Half a brain would have told you I couldn't talk right then."

Sandy grinned. "Ok, well, sorry. So what's it about?"

"Can't talk on the phone. Can we meet?"

Sandy looked at his watch. He had to produce something by noon. Could he afford the time to meet this insistent woman?

"I need help," Rebecca said.

"Shouldn't you go to the police?"

"I thought you were a reporter. Don't you want a good story?"

"Ok, can we meet this morning, but later?"

"I'm in Kensington High Street, but we can't meet here," Rebecca said.

"So, where?"

"There's a Caffè Nero in King St, just up from Hammersmith Broadway," Rebecca said. "I could be there in thirty minutes."

"It'll take me longer," Sandy replied. "I have to come from Isleworth and I have stuff to do before then."

"So do I," said Rebecca. "Let's say eleven o'clock? I'll be inside."

Sandy looked at his watch again. The news editor would go spare if he disappeared for a couple of hours. Especially if the woman turned out to be a dud. But she didn't sound like a dud.

"Ok," he said. "What's your name, by the way?"

"Rebecca."

"Ok, Rebecca, I'll see you there."

***

The transcript of the call was sent to Petherwick in a Code Zero email and instantly forwarded by him to Trench's private office and to Gibson. It produced an instant response. MI5 already had a surveillance team waiting, and within two minutes, six men and two women from A Branch were on their way in two Range Rovers bound for Hammersmith.

The whole Shadow Force team left the flat in south London and piled into their Land Rover Discovery. Each knew what part they would be playing when they arrived in Hammersmith.

At 10:50 a.m., Rebecca walked round the corner from Broadway into King Street and entered Caffè Nero. She saw a couple talking animatedly at a table close to the window. All the tables were occupied, one of them by a single bloke. He was huge. His table was close to the one by the window where the couple was engaged in conversation.

Rebecca sighed. She needed a table. She queued for a coffee. She gave her name and waited. No sign of Sandy Hall. When she was given her coffee, she looked around but every table was still occupied. Then the big bloke got up and left the café. Rebecca walked quickly to sit down and looked without much interest at the couple while she waited nervously for the Sky crime correspondent to turn up.

She couldn't catch what the couple were talking about. Both in their late forties, she thought. The woman had an earpiece in one ear, the other dangling on her chest.

Rose was back with Seamus, her favourite comrade-in-arms. The former Royal Corps of Signals specialist was all set up to record every word spoken by the striking-looking woman at the next table. Gibson was sitting with Tim at the back of the café. George was manning the car parked off King Street, and Sam had just left to make room for Rebecca.

Sandy was five minutes late. He spotted a tall blonde woman sitting alone. Pretty gorgeous. He went over to her table.

"Rebecca, I presume?"

She smiled. They shook hands.

Sandy grabbed a plastic glass of water and sat down opposite her.

"So, tell me," he said, taking out his notebook.

"Are you going to take notes?" she asked, apprehensive.

"Just for reference."

Rebecca kept her voice down as she recounted what had happened since she met Jean-Paul van Dijk at the Côte brasserie. It took her ten minutes. When she mentioned the plastic box in the toilet cistern, the holdall and the heavy suitcase, and the bizarre tweed suit on Jean-Paul's return to the flat after his twenty-four-hour absence, Sandy looked suitably intrigued. She kept the sticky false eyebrow to the end.

"You're joking," Sandy said.

"No."

"Where is it now?"

"I put it back."

Sandy asked the obvious question. "What makes you think, apart from all these fascinating bits, that he might be the Russian assassin? Does he sound Russian?"

"Well, not as such. He hasn't said anything to me in Russian." She laughed.

"How would you describe him?"

"Big, I mean *big*. Squarish face. Muscles everywhere."

"Is he violent towards you?"

"No, but that's personal."

"Ok, sorry. I was really, you know, worried for you."

She smiled and looked into his eyes. He was quite sweet, she thought. In a shaggy sort of way.

Sandy changed tack. "You remember the incident in Birmingham? The explosion?"

"Yes."

"Was he with you on that day or over that period of time?"

"No, that was when he was away for twenty-four hours. When he returned wearing a tweed suit."

"My God! You realise you can't—I can't—keep this from the police?"

"I know, but I wanted your advice first. Also, I couldn't quite believe it. I needed to see someone else's reaction. You think it's him?"

"I don't know," Sandy replied. "But it could be. It sounds like it could be. You can't go back to the flat."

"I'll be fine," she said, unconvincingly.

"Do you know where he is today?"

"He said he was planning to stay in the flat."

Rebecca noticed that the couple at the table next to theirs had stopped talking. She briefly caught the eye of the woman.

"I think we should go," Rebecca said to Sandy. "Don't look now, but the couple behind you are listening, I think."

Sandy's phone rang.

"Hello," he said, glancing round at the couple.

"Sandy, it's David." Sandy's contact at MI5.

"David, hi," Sandy replied, surprised. MI5 rarely phoned him.

"We thought you might like a briefing on our latest assessment on the Russian issue," David said. "We're not offering it to anyone else."

"Er, yes, of course, great, thank you, that would be terrific. When exactly?"

"Well, the DG who will brief you can only spare half an hour or so. Today. Well, this morning, to be precise."

"Shall I come now then?" Sandy asked.

"If convenient, yes, that would be good."

"Ok, I'm in, er, Hammersmith right now," Sandy replied. "I'll get to you as quick as I can."

"Fine," David said. "I'll arrange a pass and will be there to meet you."

Sandy put the phone in his jacket pocket.

"Rebecca, I'm so sorry, I've got to rush," he said. "I really think you should stay away from your flat. I'll ring you later, is that all right?"

"Sure," she said and stood up. She was so tall. Sandy looked at her. He was about to shake her hand when she leaned forward and kissed him on his right cheek.

"Thank you for listening to me and, I hope, believing me," she said.

"I do," he replied, intoxicated by a gentle waft of perfume and blonde hair. "Definitely."

They parted outside the café and Sandy hailed a cab.

Rebecca noticed the couple were still there, and talking again. As she wandered off in the direction of Hammersmith tube station, Sam followed at a distance. Rose, Seamus, Gibson and Tim left the café at the same time and ran to the Land Rover round the corner.

Instead of going down into the Tube, Rebecca decided to walk back to the flat. She crossed The Broadway and walked to the left-hand pavement, heading for Olympia. She had only walked for about five minutes when a large car stopped ahead of her and a woman climbed out. Rebecca recognised her as the woman in the café and stopped. The woman didn't look menacing, but Rebecca took one step back.

"Rebecca," the woman said. "Please don't worry. I'm Rose, I was in the café. We need to talk."

Rebecca took another step back and looked around to see who could help.

Rose stood still.

"You probably recognise me, right? I'm sorry to startle you," Rose said. "I and my colleagues in the car are here to protect you. We know all about the

Russian. Let me introduce you to my colleagues. I promise you we're all on your side."

Rose smiled broadly. Rebecca looked confused and wary. But Rose turned round and went back to the car.

Rebecca glanced behind her, and her heart missed two beats. A huge man was approaching slowly. She recognised him too. The man stopped and smiled.

"What the fuck's going on?" she said.

"That's Sam," Rose said. She had turned back.

Sam came up closer.

"Rebecca, if I was you I'd run like hell," he said.

It was the first remark from these weird strangers that made her relax. A little bit.

"And if I do, will you chase after me?"

"Probably." He winked.

"Come on, Rebecca, meet the rest of the team," Rose said. "Call it the Rebecca Team, if you like."

Sam walked alongside Rebecca as she approached the car.

Gibson, Tim, Seamus and George all stepped out.

"Bloody hell, I need six of you to look after me?" Rebecca said.

"Six of the best," Sam said.

Gibson looked at his watch.

"Rebecca, we'll tell you everything you're dying to ask in the car," he said, "but we have to go. You're going to meet someone rather special, a woman, who needs to talk to you, and we're going to take you there. Is that ok?"

"Somewhat surreal," Rebecca said. "So I'm not being kidnapped?"

"Not this time," said Sam.

Rebecca decided she liked Sam. She sighed and climbed in the back.

"Sorry, a bit cramped, especially with Sam," Gibson said, "but we don't have far to go."

Rose sat on one side of Rebecca, Sam on the other. Sam grinned at her.

George looked in the mirror. "All set? Then off we go."

***

At Rebecca's flat, Mikhail Gerasimov was packing up. Soon after Rebecca had left, he had gone to the bathroom and lifted the lid of the cistern. He was about to remove the sealed plastic box, but he stopped. It was different. The box was in the right position; the tape looked secure, but he knew it was wrong. When he had last placed it in the right-hand corner, the two ends of the sealing tape had met at the front, at the bottom edge. The join was visible. Now there was no sign of the join. The box was facing the wrong way round. It had been removed and put back. Rebecca had found it.

He lifted the box out and examined it. The joins of the two ends of the tape were firmly in place. But there was a tiny speck of yellow on the join itself. Gerasimov knew immediately. Rebecca had begun to try and ease off one end of the tape with a yellow-painted fingernail. But she had changed her mind, or perhaps he had returned to the flat at the wrong moment. Had she found the box because she was looking for something suspicious? Looking everywhere?

He dried the box on Rebecca's pink towel and went into the bedroom. He searched the pockets of his tweed suit and found the single eyebrow. He frowned. Where was the other one?

The two discoveries were enough for him. It was time to leave. For whatever reason, or accumulation of reasons, Rebecca had become suspicious. Something had bothered her. Gerasimov cursed in Russian.

She had been gone for forty minutes. He removed the suitcase, unlocked it and pulled out the holdall. He checked inside, even though he knew Rebecca couldn't possibly have seen the contents. The submachine gun was there. He placed the plastic box with the passports and cash in the holdall and put it back in the suitcase. Then he took his tweed suit from the wardrobe, plus the shoes, and his limited number of shirts, boxers and socks from the drawers in the small cupboard next to the bed, and piled his clothes on top of the holdall. He tucked his toothbrush and razor into one corner.

He was dressed in his blue suit, a white shirt, no tie and black shoes.

He looked once round the living room. One of Rebecca's new paintings was half-finished.

Then he left, locking the door with the spare key she had given him. He put the key in his pocket.

***

Rebecca discovered little about her protection team, but she soon gathered that Gibson was in charge. She assumed they were some special police unit, but they gave nothing away. Rose and Sam did most of the chatting. She asked where they were going, and Gibson just said somewhere near Lambeth Bridge. She also asked whether they knew who she had been with in Caffè Nero, and did he know in advance that their meeting was being monitored and that she would be taken off somewhere? Rose said no.

Driving down Millbank alongside the Thames, George turned left just before Lambeth Bridge and then left again. He drew up next to a set of large garage doors and waited. The doors began to lift, and when they were halfway up, he drove in.

"We're here," Rose said.

"Hm, so I see," Rebecca said. "Where's here?"

They all climbed out. There was a woman standing a few feet away, waiting for them. It was Grace Redmayne.

She came forward, glanced quickly at the Shadow Force team, nodded to Gibson and smiled at Rebecca.

"Come with me, please," she said and walked off to the lift at the back of the garage.

"My name is Grace," she told Rebecca when they were going up in the lift. "You'll be meeting my boss. Sorry for the cloak and dagger, but it's the way it is."

"Where am I?" Rebecca asked for the second time.

"Thames House," Grace replied.

"Thames House?" Rebecca was none the wiser.

The doors opened and Grace led Rebecca down a corridor on the sixth floor. Everyone who went past them seemed to be young, Rebecca noticed. None of them greeted Grace or looked at Rebecca with curiosity. Grace stopped at a door on the right and knocked.

The door was opened by Geraldine Hammer.

"Rebecca, very good to meet you. Please do come in," she said. "Grace, could you get Amelia to bring in some coffee? Coffee alright?"

"Fine, thank you. Black, no sugar," Rebecca replied.

"I apologise for the somewhat unusual morning you have had," Geraldine said.

"Cloak and dagger," Rebecca replied.

"Yes, quite. Please sit."

Rebecca sat in front of the desk.

"Let me explain what's going on. My name is Geraldine. As you probably realise, this is the headquarters of the security service, MI5."

"Ah. Am I being recruited?"

Geraldine smiled. "We always need good new people."

"I paint."

"So I understand."

Rebecca gave Geraldine her quizzical look.

"Actually, Rebecca, we have brought you here for a specific reason, and there's a certain amount of urgency about what I'm going to ask you," Geraldine said.

"Ok."

"I'm afraid I can't go into any detail, for what I hope are obvious reasons. But it came to our notice that you were in a highly unusual and potentially risky situation. To be frank, you had, or thought you had, a Russian living with you who worried you."

"How long have you been bugging me?" Rebecca asked.

"Rebecca, as I said, I can't go into any details, but I'm right, aren't I?"

"Yes, but you know that from your friends in the café, listening to me talking to... well, talking to someone."

"The point is, Rebecca," Geraldine continued, "we are now in a highly volatile situation. We have a Russian agent who has already been responsible one way or another for several shootings. We believe there could be more incidents. The police have a number of suspects. It's our job here to provide the intelligence to pinpoint which of these suspects might be the one we want. It could be more than one."

"You think the bloke in my flat is one of the suspects?" Rebecca asked.

"Clearly, you do, Rebecca, which is why you're here."

"Ok, so what do you want to know?"

"Rebecca, this is very personal. I don't know how to put it any other way. But we have one particular suspect in mind, and we want to be sure we have it right before we act. It's possible that I have met someone in the past who is the same person now in your flat."

"You knew Jean-Paul?"

"Not exactly."

Amelia Prendergast, Geraldine's thirty-four-year-old personal assistant, came into the room at that point and placed two cups of coffee on the desk. She looked at Rebecca with interest but said nothing and then left.

"I know that sounded odd," Geraldine said. "What I'm trying to tell you is that I believe the man I met some time ago may be the Russian currently causing this crisis. And he may be your Jean-Paul."

"So you do know him?"

"With a different name."

"What name?"

"I can't tell you that."

Rebecca shook her head. "I'm not normally slow," she said, "but perhaps you should ask the question you really brought me here to ask."

"You'd make a good intelligence officer," Geraldine said. "Ok, here it is."

Geraldine sipped her coffee.

"I had a very brief relationship with this man and am aware of a few things about him which I imagine you will have noticed if this man is the same one living with you now."

"Oh my God," said Rebecca. "You actually want some personal stuff? You want to compare notes. Just to make sure?"

"Yes. I'm sorry."

"Ok, fire away."

Rebecca looked at Geraldine, who appeared to blush. She was an attractive woman. Nice hair, Rebecca thought. Had they shared the same intimacies with the same man? Was confirmation of this shared intimacy really all they needed to be sure the Russian agent was currently her lover?

"Like, woman to woman, is that ok with you?" Geraldine asked. She had warmed to this tall, sexy woman. She felt for some reason that she could trust her.

Rebecca raised her eyebrows in anticipation.

"When we met, this man was charming," Geraldine said. "We went to the opera and then back to his apartment. He never said what his nationality was, but I assumed European. Maybe Dutch or Danish."

"Half Dutch," Rebecca said.

Geraldine shrugged. "I don't know. But as you can probably guess, and I apologise for this..."

"For heaven's sake," Rebecca interrupted. "Don't mind me. Let's compare notes, if that's going to do it for you. He's not the love of my life."

"Ok, thank you," Geraldine said, looking relieved. "Well, the fact is it wasn't an experience I enjoyed. I was, you know, totally in the mood, as it were. But I felt smothered. He wasn't charming anymore. He was pretty rough, and he hurt me."

"Oh my God, your guy sounds like my guy."

"Are you sure?"

"Well, as good as, although I have to say I didn't let him take charge, if you'll forgive me for saying so. Yes, big as hell, but it was ok."

"Was there anything else you might have noticed?"

"Yes, he has a tattoo on his left leg. A dagger."

Geraldine's breath caught. "Do you know where he is now?"

"He said he was going to be in the flat all day, working on his so-called business," Rebecca replied.

Geraldine picked up her phone and dialled a single digit. "Grace, go, go, go. Now."

"What's going on?" Rebecca asked.

"Rebecca, it's the same man. Beyond doubt. I'm sorry. I shouldn't be telling you this. But right now, armed police will be preparing to break into your flat to arrest your Jean-Paul van Dijk."

"I could have given you a key," Rebecca said. "And he's not my Jean-Paul, not anymore."

"Thank you, Rebecca, you've been brilliant. Your door will be repaired. It's the way the police do it, I'm afraid."

"So what happens in the meantime? Where do I go? I'm not staying in the flat with a dodgy front door."

"The team that brought you here will look after you until this Russian is under lock and key and your flat is safe."

Rebecca suddenly thought of something. "I suppose—as you know everything, it seems—you know that I found a sealed plastic box in the toilet cistern in my bathroom. What do you think is in it?"

"I shouldn't really say, but probably passports," Geraldine replied. "Lots of them."

"How many does he need?"

"At least three and possibly more."

"Three?"

"Apart from Jean-Paul van Dijk and the name he used with me, this Russian has used one more name that we know of."

"Which is?"

"It's part of the investigation, I'm afraid."

"Come on, Geraldine, if I can call you that. I think I deserve to know. If it wasn't for me, you'd still be looking for him."

Geraldine smiled. "Ok, but I have to trust you to be totally discreet. None of the names have been revealed to the public. I'll tell you one of them. It's John Adams. When you were having lunch with Jean-Paul van Dijk at the Royal Garden Hotel, he was registered there under the name John Adams."

"Bloody hell," Rebecca said. "And who was John Adams supposed to be?"

"Like your Jean-Paul, a businessman. Both their names were down as directors of a company. But they are false names and belong to the same person."

"How the hell is it possible for a Russian to go waltzing around London, bedding two women under different names and getting away with it, never mind the murders of two police officers and the attack on that poor woman?" Rebecca asked.

Geraldine said nothing.

"Oh my God. Was that you?" It had suddenly dawned on Rebecca. "Was that first shooting on you?"

"It was a lucky escape," was all Geraldine said.

Rebecca reached forward and put her hand on Geraldine's arm resting on the desk.

"I'm so sorry. I'm wittering on about this bloody Russian, and all the time you're sitting there knowing that this same bastard tried to kill you," Rebecca said. She sat back again.

"Well, it's a bit more complicated than that," Geraldine said. "But thank you for being sympathetic. Actually, I'm glad you put two and two together. I wouldn't have told you. In my job I can talk to no one except my colleagues. It's nice to be able to talk to an outsider, if you don't mind me putting it like that."

"Same goes for me," said Rebecca. "You and I have one thing in common. For ever. What's his real name, by the way?"

"We thought we knew and then we weren't so sure, although some of my colleagues are more convinced than others that we do know who it is," Geraldine replied.

"Blimey, that sounds kind of all over the place. So what is our Russian called, as far as some of you lot believe?"

"It's classified."

"Geraldine, we're friends, right? I'm just curious. I have spent the last two weeks with a bloke called Jean-Paul van Dijk who is, or was, also John Adams and whatever he called himself with you. I'd quite like to know what he's really called, even if you personally no longer believe it's the right name. God, I'm sounding like you now."

"Sorry, Rebecca, I can't," Geraldine said.

"Ok. But I told Sandy Hall all about the guy in my flat. What are we going to do about that?"

"Don't worry," Geraldine replied. "We'll sort that out."

"But he might do something on Sky."

"Leave it with us."

"But you don't want me to repeat this conversation or anything about being brought here, right?"

"No, please no. I can't prevent you from telling the world, but my instinct is I can trust you to be totally discreet. That would certainly help me, particularly with the job I do.

"Yeah, that's cool," Rebecca said. "Your job's cool too. Oh, and by the way, thanks."

"For what?"

"For rescuing me from a Russian assassin."

Geraldine grinned. "You're welcome," she said.

Chapter Twenty-Six
Mikhail Gerasimov Evades the Police

Twenty armed police officers in full raid gear searched Rebecca's flat for an hour but found nothing. No suitcase, no holdall, no plastic box in the cistern, no tweed suit. Nothing. The front door was hanging on a single hinge. Number 10 was informed. The raid had drawn a blank. The Russian agent had flown.

News of the raid in the street spread rapidly. But Sandy learned of the drama only after he had left Thames House, and from his news editor. In fact, his news editor was astonished that his crime correspondent had been inside MI5 headquarters interviewing the head of the security service and yet had learned nothing of the drama happening down the road in Notting Hill. It was not an argument Sandy was going to win, so he said he would go straight to Notting Hill and do a live report as soon as he could.

He had spent thirty minutes at MI5, sitting in Trench's office, with David, his contact, also present. Although the briefing from the MI5 chief himself was a scoop for Sandy, it was made clear from the start that everything was to be off the record. Nothing to be attributed to Trench. Just "security sources". That would have been acceptable if Trench had come up with something genuinely newsworthy. But for half an hour he spoke in general, sometimes ambiguous, terms about the Russian threat and the investigation underway to find the chief suspect. Sandy began by taking notes, but after five minutes his biro remained poised but without adding anything to his notebook. He couldn't understand why he had been given an exclusive interview. What was it for? Several times he glanced at David, sitting beside him, raising his eyebrows in an attempt to show that the answers being provided by the director general were producing nothing quotable. David pretended not to notice. Not for one moment did Trench hint that at that very moment something dramatic and unprecedented was going on elsewhere on the sixth floor. Sandy didn't raise the Rebecca issue with the MI5 chief initially, not wanting to put her in a difficult situation, but with such potentially vital information in his possession, he had to reveal it at some point.

With the allotted thirty minutes completed, Trench thanked Sandy for coming in and asked if there was anything else he would like to raise. Sandy looked at David.

"Well, there is one more thing," he said.

"Please," Trench said.

"It's my understanding that the Russian agent, or perhaps I should say, a likely suspect, might be hiding out in a flat in London," Sandy said cautiously. "In west London."

"From one of your reliable sources?" Trench asked with a hint of sarcasm.

"Very reliable."

"Are you planning to make this public?" Trench asked.

Sandy thought that was an odd question.

"Not right now, but perhaps when there are other developments," Sandy replied, looking again at David.

"Well, there will be other developments, I'm sure," Trench said in his enigmatic way. "You can always check with David here."

Something was up. Sandy knew it. Had Rebecca gone to the police after seeing him in the café? Was there some police action going on while he was trapped in Thames House, unable to be phoned by his news desk? He had handed over his mobile phone at the security desk when he entered Thames House.

David stood up and ushered Sandy out of the room.

"I hope that was useful," he said.

"What's happening, David?" Sandy asked. "Something's happening."

"I'm afraid there's nothing I can talk about right now," David said. "Perhaps later. Give me a call."

Rebecca was still inside the same building, also on the sixth floor, when Sandy was taken to the lift and waved out of the front entrance of Thames House after retrieving his phone.

When the taxi dropped him at St Lukes Road, Notting Hill, the whole street had been cordoned off. He hadn't been given the exact address of Rebecca's flat but it was obvious from the toing and froing of detectives and forensic teams in white bodysuits where the police raid had taken place. Sandy had phoned Rebecca as soon as he left Thames House but there had been no reply. He left a message.

He rang the Press Bureau and received an anodyne comment. Police officers were investigating a house in west London after receiving information from a member of the public. No further comment could be made at this time.

"Am I right in saying that the member of the public was a woman and that she was living in the flat that was raided?" he asked.

"Nothing further can be said while the investigation is ongoing," the Press Bureau spokesman said.

Sandy was getting angry. He had had the best scoop possible from Rebecca; he'd had a briefing from the head of MI5. Yet he had nothing to show for it. He couldn't reveal Rebecca's identity, nor any of the amazing information she had given him. Suddenly, Sandy realised he hadn't asked the most important question.

"Is the woman in the flat alright?"

The Press Bureau spokesman didn't reply immediately.

"All I can say, Sandy, is that during the investigation at this particular location, no member of the police force, or member of the public, suffered any injury."

"And is any member of the public, as you put it, currently in the protection of the police?" Sandy asked.

"I really can't say, I'm sorry. It's early stages," the spokesman replied.

"But no Russian found in the flat?"

"No one has been arrested at this time."

"One more thing," Sandy tried. "Can you confirm that the raid was specifically linked to the hunt for the Russian assassin?"

"Multiple leads are being followed," the spokesman replied. "That's all I can say."

Sandy was exasperated. But he was used to the Press Bureau's bland responses and statements. The press officer had as good as confirmed that the raid was part of the investigation into the shootings. It had been hard work but he had got something. Now he had to decide how much he could hint at from the wealth of information he had in his notebook from the time he had spent with Rebecca. He tried his contact at Counter-Terrorism Command but there was no reply.

He rang Rebecca again but she still didn't answer. He was disappointed for two reasons. First, he needed to find out who she had contacted after their meeting in the café and where she was now. Second, he still had her perfume and blonde hair in his mind. And the kiss on his cheek.

***

Mikhail Gerasimov didn't have a plan B. Plan A was to find a woman to live with temporarily while he completed his mission. Nothing like having an attractive blonde on your arm when trying to avoid the curious stares of passing policemen. Ninety-nine times out of a hundred, they would focus their eyes on the woman and start talking about her as soon as they walked past. Even female police officers. And none of them would be looking for a Russian agent with a tall blonde in tow.

Now he was on his own. And with a heavy suitcase. Walking the streets of London. He was wearing the hat he had bought in Birmingham and kept it low over his eyes. He waved at a taxi and told the driver to go to Victoria Station.

He sat back and looked out of the window. He saw no sign of troops on the street but there were plenty of police officers. Occasionally a mobile police van went by with sirens sounding. Otherwise, people were walking around normally. It was a sunny day. London looked welcoming and vibrant. But he knew the whole city, in one way or another, was on alert, and he was the reason. He didn't mind. He was used to high-risk combat environments, and being a wanted man didn't faze him.

However, he had failed to keep Rebecca loyal and on side. She had grown suspicious of him, and that was a weakness on his part. Strangely, he also regretted having to leave her. She had played her part perfectly, providing him with a relatively safe sanctuary. But he liked her. Her surname had proved singularly appropriate.

He had to admit to himself that he had also liked Geraldine Hammer. Each woman, in her own way, had been a challenge. Now, here he was, the mission still unfinished, and Moscow was getting angry. The Birmingham operation had been unscripted, and he knew the higher command would be seething at his incompetence. Even perhaps plotting his downfall. Moscow never accepted failure. There were always repercussions. Often fatal. So if he wanted to return to his country in one piece and not concealed in a coffin in a diplomatic bag, he had little choice but to continue with his mission. Meanwhile, he had to find accommodation.

The taxi dropped him off at the station and he walked quickly through the crowds to the left luggage office. There were armed police at regular intervals. None of them gave him more than a glancing look—there were plenty of other people walking around with suitcases—but he kept his head down and his face averted. He removed the holdall from the suitcase and told a monosyllabic left luggage worker that he wanted to pay for it to be held for a week. He started to say that he would return for it while he toured London but he only got halfway through the sentence. The uniformed employee had turned away with the holdall to place it on a rack. He asked for Gerasimov's name and gave him a receipt for £50. Gerasimov said his name was Hammer. The employee's expression remained unchanged.

Gerasimov was approaching the main exit of Victoria Station when he heard a voice behind him. "Excuse me, sir."

He turned. Two police officers with semi-automatic machine guns held across their chests were walking towards him. He stood absolutely still. Running was not an option.

"We noticed you enter the station with that suitcase and now you're leaving with the suitcase. In the current security situation, we are carrying out random checks," the taller of the two officers said.

"Of course," Gerasimov said.

"Can you open your case please, sir?" the officer asked. The other officer tightened the grip on his machine gun.

Gerasimov lay the suitcase down, opened it and stood back. They both peered inside and one of them rifled through the clothes with one hand.

"No wife to fold your clothes, sir?" the officer asked.

"Er, no, you're right—it is a bit of a mess."

"Thank you, sir. Sorry to bother you, sir. Have a nice day."

Gerasimov closed his suitcase and left the station.

Sometimes, even a Russian assassin has a lucky day.

***

Like Sandy, Rebecca also discovered the Russian had vanished from her flat only after she left Thames House. Grace took her down to the garage, where she met up with Gibson and the team. Once they had driven out onto the road at the back of MI5 headquarters, Gibson told her he had some news. Bad news for the police, but maybe good news for her.

She had an odd reaction to what Gibson then told her. She was amazed that Jean-Paul had exited before the police arrived. How could he have known? She had left the plastic sealed box exactly as she had found it, and the tweed suit was still hanging in the wardrobe. Yet, somehow, he'd known she suspected something. And that she might tell someone else.

What she found surprising was that she was relieved he had made his escape. She didn't want to be the one who handed him on a plate to the police, even though, after her chat with Geraldine, she now knew for certain what sort of man he was. It was also frustrating. She wanted to know what was in the plastic box. Geraldine may have been right about the passports, but now she would never know for sure. And the holdall? What was in it, and where was it now? Where was Jean-Paul? Would he come back to the flat to take revenge on her? Rebecca wished she had known about the unsuccessful raid on her flat before she had said goodbye to Geraldine. She would have peppered her with these questions. Was she now in more danger than before?

"Where are you going to take me?" she asked as George drove the Land Rover across Lambeth Bridge.

Gibson swivelled round from the front seat.

"Your flat is a crime scene," he said, "so, I'm afraid that's off limits for you at the moment. We'll find you somewhere safe, near where we are, and protect you until this Russian is under lock and key."

"All my stuff's at the flat," she said.

"Don't worry, tell us what you need and we'll get it from the flat in due course," Rose replied. "Your Russian flatmate won't be coming back."

"He has a key," said Rebecca.

"We'll change the locks," Rose said. "And your door, by the way."

Rebecca was deflated. She liked Rose and Sam, but being hidden away under some protection arrangement was the last thing she needed. She heard Rose booking a room for her in a hotel and decided that as soon as she was on her own, she would ring Sandy Hall.

***

At 4:30 p.m., Maksim Popov, his wife, Natalia, and eighteen-year-old son, Dima, stood in the queue at passport control, Heathrow Terminal 2. They had flown in from Moscow by Aeroflot. They had arrived as Russians, but with a different surname. Maksim Popov's hair was short, shaved above the ears. His eyebrows were no longer bushy.

The general at the meeting in the Aquarium was right. Popov and his family were only questioned briefly about the length of their planned visit to the UK, where they would be staying and what the purpose of their trip was. Popov replied: just a week, at the Rubens Hotel in Buckingham Palace Road, Victoria, and solely for the education of their son, who was studying the role of monarchies in European history. The passport officer, a woman, looked at Dima for a moment but asked no further questions. She checked their passports on the computer system but nothing materialised to worry her. As he was a Russian, she looked closely at the tall man in front of her. Even peered at his eyebrows.

"The Rubens, you say?" she said.

"Yes," Popov replied.

"Have a nice stay," she said, and beckoned the next passenger in the queue to come forward.

Major-General Maksim Popov, career GRU Spetsnaz officer, entered the United Kingdom with shaved eyebrows under the name of Sergei Preobrazhensky.

Chapter Twenty-Seven
An Invitation to a Picnic Sets off Alarm Bells

Gerasimov took a room in the Travelodge at 3 Bondway, Vauxhall, SW8. No irritating questions were asked. He said he would pay with cash and booked the room for a week. He had no intention of staying that long. He went upstairs to the third floor. Room number 312. He placed the suitcase in the corner by the window overlooking the street. In the distance he could see a large building. The Oval cricket ground. He sat on the bed and removed a passport from his jacket, plus the key for the safe deposit box in St James's Street, an emergency mobile phone and five hundred twenty-pound notes. The three passports in the names of Lucas Meyer, John Adams and Jean-Paul van Dijk were still in the plastic box inside the holdall at the left luggage office in Victoria Station. The passport now in his hands would, he hoped, be his ticket out of the UK. It was in the name of Dragomir Chudov, a Bulgarian national.

The hotel had no room service. He hadn't eaten all day. He rang reception and asked for the number of the nearest pizza restaurant. After he put in his order and had been promised delivery in forty minutes, he lay back on the bed and closed his eyes. He had not worked out what he would do the following day. He had checked out Lord North Street and had spotted the car with the two police officers. He had no wish nor motivation to assassinate Geraldine Hammer, but even if he did, trying to carry out a hit on the narrow street would be suicidal.

There was no chance he would get away with it. Being so close to Parliament and Downing Street, any incident at whatever time of day or night would provoke an immediate response. Geraldine Hammer was significantly safer at 17 Lord North Street than she had been at her home in Gladstone Street.

There was also the small matter of the holdall. Both the Kedr submachine gun and the 9mm GSh-18 pistol he had used at the Gladstone Street shooting were in the holdall at Victoria Station left luggage office. He knew it had been a risk to leave the weapons in the care of the bored railway employee, but without the safe haven he had enjoyed while living with Rebecca, he had had no alternative. Sometimes, he knew from experience, doing something blatantly obvious could pay off. A left luggage office was too easy, too simple. Would a Russian on the Most Wanted list casually walk into Victoria Station and leave the weapons he needed for his next assignment sitting in a holdall on a rack? Sometimes, the obvious worked. The two police officers had spotted him walking into the station with his leather suitcase and had seen him leaving with it. But they hadn't bothered to watch him as he walked to the left luggage office or seen him remove a heavy holdall from inside the case and hand it over for safekeeping. Luck had been on his side. But how was he to retrieve the holdall without being stopped?

Lying on his bed in the hotel, he made two decisions. He couldn't risk returning to Victoria Station. And there was nothing he could do against Geraldine Hammer while she remained in her safe house in Lord North Street. He had just two options: lie low for as long as possible until circumstances changed, or get out of the UK fast, using his Bulgarian passport.

Suddenly, his emergency phone pinged.

The text message read: *"Ya zdes. S sem'yey. Kak naschet piknika, chas zavtra, Dulwich Park severnyy konets."*

The Russian agent read it twice and frowned. A complication. His plans were now in disarray. He switched off the phone and removed the battery.

***

Forty minutes later, the D15 team at GCHQ were still pondering over the Russian text. Did it need a Code Zero warning or was it as harmless as it sounded?

"I'm here with the family. How about a picnic at one o'clock tomorrow at Dulwich Park north end."

The team of six analysts decided it needed to be seen and interpreted higher up the chain. They sent a Code Zero email to Jim Petherwick at the Foreign Office, with a copy to the GCHQ director.

As soon as it arrived, Petherwick copied it to Number 10, George Trench's private office and Gibson. The prime minister had been adamant. The distribution of Code Zero communications was to be strictly limited. Unless or until he called a COBRA meeting, the police were, provisionally, to be kept out of the loop.

Trench summoned Geraldine, Grace and Jasper Cornfield.

"We have a development," he said as they all sat down. He showed them the translated text. "Geraldine, what do you think?"

"Back-up or replacement?" she wondered.

"Or nothing to do with anything?" Trench asked.

"Two or more Russians meeting in a park in Dulwich? Definitely our man being paid a visit," she replied.

"Look at it from Moscow's eyes," Grace said. "It has basically all gone wrong. Geraldine's alive and well–thank God. Mission not accomplished. The bad guys in the Kremlin want results. So they send in the cavalry."

"More than one?" Trench asked.

"Yes, probably."

"Jasper?" Geraldine turned to him.

"The text says family. It could just be code for one, two, three agents arriving," Jasper said, "but that would be too risky. Three Russians arriving in the UK? We'd spot that. No, I think family means family. The perfect cover. Whoever it is has managed to enter the UK with members of his family. Wife, or someone representing his wife. A child, even."

"So, we need to check all passengers coming in over the last day or so," Geraldine said. "Probably not direct from Moscow, too obvious, more likely from Europe. Jasper, can you go and get that sorted?"

Jasper left the room.

"Meanwhile," Trench said, "we need a plan. The prime minister is still playing his high-stakes game; the police have yet to be informed of this development. Why, I've no idea. Basically, we need Dulwich Park surrounded so they can't escape. This is our best chance."

Geraldine shook her head. "Normally, I would agree. But I think the reason why Number 10 is so twitchy about this is that they don't want a swarm of armed police descending on a public park, with cameras flashing as two Russian agents are arrested in broad daylight. But do we have the evidence to put before a court? Lots of circumstantial stuff but no forensics, no definitive CCTV images, no one actually caught in the act. I can see the Crown Prosecution Service dithering and then deciding there's no case. Two, three, four Russian agents, however many it is, get deported. And we get nothing. The PM wants them in a dock with copper-bottomed evidence. So, in my view, if we're to do the PM's bidding, this has to be dealt with differently and low-profile."

"That was the PM's very argument thirty minutes ago," Trench said.

"We can send in a surveillance team, obviously," Grace said. "But then what?"

"The PM has turned to Gibson as usual," Trench said with a sigh. "We'll have to put up with it, but I would have thought the Hereford team would be better and more appropriately suited to this job. When Lockridge finds out he's going to go ballistic."

SAS chief Major-General Thomas Lockridge was, like the police, out of the loop for the moment.

Geraldine was having second thoughts. "DG, it's really not the job of Downing Street to mastermind our operations," she said. "Grace is right, we should send a surveillance team to mount a twenty-four-hour watch on the two Russians, assuming, that is, there are only two and the others, as Jasper said, are wife and child. Ok, let Gibson and co do their stuff, but there's no way his team of six can follow two targets."

Grace was nodding energetically.

Trench said, "The PM basically ordered me this morning to leave it to Gibson."

"In my view, it's out of the question, DG," Geraldine said. "Sorry, but this is a coup for GCHQ. If we don't make maximum use of this intelligence, we will never be forgiven and we will never forgive ourselves.

"I'll speak to Gibson," she went on. "For all his special relationship with Downing Street, he's a professional, not a prima donna. If he loses these targets, his team will be blamed. They can start it off, do whatever they have to do to monitor what happens in Dulwich Park, and then leave us to follow up. Hopefully, Jasper will come back with details of the new arrivals. If we know where they are staying, that's half the battle. The other guy, Popov or whatever he is called, is hiding out somewhere, and our lads can follow him wherever he goes."

Trench said simply: "Approved."

***

Sandy had had a frustrating day. He had followed the news, not broken it. His news editor was being less than understanding. Where were his contacts? he was being asked constantly. His main one, Rick, had vanished, or at least he wasn't answering his phone. Sandy had sent him a text but so far he hadn't heard back. MI5 seemed to be playing a similar game. Not returning calls. But worst of all, Rebecca had also disappeared. Her flat had been raided, the Russian—if it was the Russian—had bolted, and the search for him was continuing. Sandy had been told no one was hurt, so he assumed Rebecca was alright. But where was she?

London was now a locked-down city. Hundreds of extra police had been drafted in from the Thames Valley region and from even further afield. Troops were guarding Thames House, the Houses of Parliament, Downing Street, the Ministry of Defence and the Foreign Office. Sandy's last report on Sky News referred to an unprecedented crisis. He had also found a Tory MP who expressed amazement that with all the police and troops on the streets, the Russian intelligence agent at the heart of the drama appeared to have carte blanche to wander wherever he wanted. Most of the national newspapers were following the same line: "Russian assassin slips through net" was *The Mirror*'s headline. "Are the police winning? NYET" said the *Daily Express*. "Agent Houdini," was *The Sun's* offering. Even *The Times* couldn't hold back its sense of dismay at the lack of progress in tracking down the Russian: "Police face questions over hunt for Russian agent."

Sandy was about to try his contact at Counter-Terrorism Command when his mobile rang. It was Rebecca.

"Rebecca, where have you been? Are you alright, what's happening?" Sandy blurted out.

"Slow down, Mr Crime Reporter. That's three questions before you've even said hello," she said.

"Sorry, but I've been trying to get hold of you."

"How sweet."

"Haha, what can you tell me?"

"Nothing, really. I'm fine. Not at the flat, obviously."

"Where are you?"

"Can't say."

"This is going to be one of these conversations, isn't it? I ask, you don't answer."

"Don't be cross, Sandy. It's just the way it is for the moment."

"Ok, I understand, or I think I do. But tell me one thing. When I left the café, did you go back to the flat?"

Rebecca didn't answer immediately.

"No," she said finally.

"So, you weren't there when the police raided your flat?"

"No."

"And you haven't been back since, obviously?"

"No."

"Did you know about the raid beforehand?"

"No."

"So, it was just luck you didn't go back to your flat after I left?"

"No, something happened that stopped me from going back."

"What happened?"

"I can't tell you."

"Rebecca, I'm not going to write a story about why you didn't go back to your flat. I'm just curious."

"Ok, I was sort of picked up."

"Who by?"

"Can't tell you. Actually, I don't know. Not for sure."

"And you're still with them?"

"Kind of."

"And you're ok?"

"Yes."

"Can we meet at some point?"

"Like on a date?"

"I meant, you know, to do with the Russian stuff."

"So, you don't want a date?"

"Well, yes, but..."

"So, yes."

"When?"

"You're very eager."

"Sorry, this is a bit confusing. We're sort of going round in circles."

"Ring me. But not for a bit. If I can, I'll ring you. Ok?"

"Yes. Good."

"You're quite cute really."

Sandy laughed.

She rang off before he could respond.

Sandy stared at his phone. The conversation with Rebecca had taken an unexpected turn. He began to imagine things he hadn't thought about for quite some time. But then his phone rang again. He grabbed it, hoping it was Rebecca, but it was Ed Claridge, wanting an update on Joseph Paine's kidnappers. Sandy had nothing to tell him. With all the drama about the escaped assassin, the allegations by Paine had slipped well down the list of priorities. He also remained wary of reporting on a subject he knew would do him no favours at the Met. No national newspaper had taken up his initial speculative story with any real interest, although a couple of the tabloids hinted at unlikely sources who suggested the SAS may have been involved in abducting Paine. The MoD had dismissed the stories, and the Paine allegations were quickly forgotten. However, a pre-trial hearing at the Old Bailey had been set. So even though it would be largely held in camera, Sandy knew the issue would return. He promised Paine's solicitor that he would keep pressing.

Sandy tried his contact at Counter-Terrorism Command once more. This time, he answered.

"Rick, how are you? It's Sandy."

"Can't talk, Sandy, too much going on," the detective inspector replied.

"Anything you can share?"

"No, sorry."

"Any developments?"

"Can't say."

"Anything?" Sandy pleaded.

"I suppose I could tell you one thing, but be careful with it."

"Ok."

"You might pay a visit to a safe deposit company in St James's Street," the detective said. He gave the address. "A big cock-up. Russian came and went. That's all I can say."

He rang off.

Sandy checked the address on Google. He told the news editor and left the building with a cameraman.

When they reached the address, Sandy asked his cameraman to stay out of sight for the time being. He buzzed the door and it opened.

"Can I help you?" It was the same security man who had greeted Jean-Paul van Dijk.

"Yes, I'm sorry to bother you but I work for Sky News, Sandy Hall, and am following up about the visit you had here by the Russian," Sandy said in as casual a way as he could.

"Did the police tell you?" The man looked shocked.

"No, it's just sort of leaked out, but it's... Well, it's sort of old news, really, so I just wondered if you could chat about it briefly."

"I don't think I'm allowed to," the man replied.

"Oh, you don't have to worry. There's nothing secret about it, and as I say, it's all a bit late now. It's just a question of tying up loose ends, if you like."

"Well, the police said I should keep it to myself."

"Yes, but that was then. It doesn't matter now. They're going to catch this guy soon."

The security man looked confused.

"So, when did he turn up, and what was he picking up?" Sandy asked.

"I don't know. It's all confidential. I've no idea what he took out."

"Did he give his name?"

"I'm not allowed to say names."

"But did you give the name to the police?"

"Yeah, I gave the names."

"Names plural? There were more than one?"

"Well, I only saw one but there was another one."

It was Sandy's turn to look confused.

"Sorry, so there were two?"

"Two names on the list."

"List?"

"On the account."

"You mean two names of people who could open this particular safe deposit?"

"Yes, I told the police."

"But you only ever saw one of them?"

"Yeah."

"What was he like?"

"Unfriendly."

"No, I mean, what did he look like? Was he big, tall?"

"Yeah, big bloke."

"Did he have bushy eyebrows?"

"What?"

"Bushy eyebrows. Did you notice if he had bushy eyebrows?"

The security man thought for a moment. Frowned.

"No, not that I remember."

"And he came once and took something away?"

"Twice."

"He came twice?"

"Yeah, I told the police."

"What was he carrying?"

"A holdall. Heavy job."

"What do you mean?"

"Like it had something heavy in it. As I told my friend, his right shoulder sloped down."

"You told a friend?"

The man look startled. "How do you know that?"

"You just said. You told a friend."

"I can't talk about that."

Sandy wasn't getting anywhere. He was about to ask if the security guy could talk briefly to camera but then remembered something. Rick, his contact, had said there had been a cock-up.

"When did the police question you?" he asked.

"It was yesterday."

"And when did you speak to your friend?"

"That was the day before."

"So, Monday. Why didn't you ring the police?"

"I did," the security man said, looking indignant.

"But you said they didn't come and see you till yesterday?"

The security man looked uncomfortable.

"My friend's a policeman," he said.

Sandy got it. The cock-up. The man's friend hadn't passed it on.

"What's your name?" he asked.

"Phil Large, but you can't use that. I'd lose my job. Please."

"I've got a camera guy outside; we could do a quick recording," Sandy tried, without much hope.

Large stood up. "No way," he said. "I'm not going on the telly. You've got to leave."

"Ok," Sandy said. "Don't worry, relax, I won't use your name. Thanks for your help."

Sandy left and told his cameraman there was no deal. But it was a good story.

Two hours later, Sandy was on Sky with what the broadcasting station claimed was breaking news.

"The police hunting for the missing Russian assassin believe he is carrying a holdall which could contain a potentially dangerous weapon or device. He is known to have taken the holdall to a safe deposit company in west London. Whatever he put inside the holdall was taken from a safe deposit box The Russian and one other man, assumed also to be Russian, were listed on the company's register of clients. They were the only ones authorised to open the safety box. I understand that this information was known to the police for twenty-four hours before any action was taken. There has been no sign of the Russian agent or the holdall. The Metropolitan Police declined to make any comment. But in a new statement, the police warned members of the public not to approach the suspect, who is described as armed and dangerous."

***

The railway employee at Victoria Station left luggage office never saw the Sky News report. He didn't watch Sky. In fact, he rarely watched the news on television. He started to read the *London Evening Standard* on his way home from work but only glanced at the front page before turning to the sports pages.

Chapter Twenty-Eight
Russian Agents Rendezvous for a Picnic

Thursday 25ᵗʰ July

Just to confuse everyone, a CX report arrived on the desks of the prime minister, selected cabinet ministers and the heads of the intelligence services around 8 a.m. The report from MI6 head of station in Moscow said:

"Major-General Maksim Popov, believed to be in London as head of the Unit Zero assassination unit, was spotted by a trusted source in a limousine heading out of Moscow. Covert surveillance of GRU headquarters later picked up Popov entering the Aquarium. He stayed for ten minutes before returning to his limousine.

"Another prime source reported that Popov was at Moscow's Sheremetyevo international airport yesterday morning at 12 noon local time. He was accompanied by a woman, believed to be his wife, and a young man. Every attempt was made to discover where Popov was flying to but without success. However, there was an Aeroflot flight 2592 leaving at 1340 due at Heathrow at 1600. The wife and young man, presumed to be his only son, did not emerge again, indicating that all three had left on the same flight.

"The presence of Popov in Moscow makes less certain the previous intelligence that he has been in London for the last three weeks."

When the foreign secretary, Elizabeth Gantry, read the last sentence, she assumed the MI6 head of station in Moscow was being tongue-in-cheek.

Then she thought, probably not. Intelligence was not an amusing business.

Geraldine read the CX with a sense of foreboding. She had been convinced for some time that Maksim Popov was a red herring. She didn't blame MI6, especially not the head of station in Moscow. Acquiring actionable intelligence in a place like Moscow had become increasingly challenging. The Russian internal security service, the FSB, had grown in size by a factor of ten in the last five years. All foreign diplomats from the West were followed everywhere by teams of agents. Intelligence officers plying their trade under diplomatic cover faced near-insurmountable obstacles daily. Running secret agents in Russia had never been a job for the fainthearted, but now it was even more risky because of the vow of instant revenge by the Kremlin on any Russian national suspected or caught in the act of espionage. Moscow station's discovery of Unit Zero and its probable leader Major-General Maksim Popov had been a fine piece of work, Geraldine thought, but then it had all begun to fall apart. They had all become too obsessed with a Russian with bushy eyebrows, to the extent that CCTV images of suspects without bushy eyebrows had been given less rigorous analysis than they should have been. The earlier CX report which had revealed two of the suspected members of Unit Zero were in Syria and that another had died had further weakened MI6's case. The only other name on the original list supplied by the Moscow station, Lieutenant-Colonel Mikhail Gerasimov, had largely been forgotten.

Geraldine had been frustrated by her sister agency's devotion to the Popov scenario. But she could hardly criticise her MI6 colleagues when she herself had committed a gross error of judgement by failing to raise her concerns about Lucas Meyer earlier in the investigation. Valuable time had been lost. More than three weeks after the first attempt to assassinate her, she hadn't been able to answer one particular question with absolute certainty. If the Russian agent still at large in London was using the names Lucas Meyer, John Adams and Jean-Paul van Dijk, what was his real name? Could he actually be Maksim Popov himself? She had become increasingly sceptical.

Now that question was at last answered. She still had no idea what Lucas Meyer's Russian name was. But it wasn't Maksim Popov.

The mysterious Popov was, she was sure, the writer of the text message telling Lucas Meyer to meet him "and his family" at the north end of Dulwich Park at 1 p.m. today. So where was Popov at this moment? And had he really brought his wife and son?

Suddenly her door opened and Jasper Cornfield burst in.

"We know where he is and who he is," he nearly shouted. He looked excited.

"Tell me," Geraldine replied in as calm a voice as possible.

"The CX was right. He caught the Aeroflot flight from Moscow which arrived at Heathrow at four o'clock yesterday. Him and his wife and son."

"But not as the Popov family, right?"

"No. There's another name to add to our growing list of Russians. Preobrazhensky. Sergei Preobrazhensky. Wife, Natalia; son, Dima. Eighteen."

"And?"

"They're staying at the Rubens Hotel, Victoria. A Branch has been alerted."

"Gibson. We have to tell Gibson."

"Yes, but his team is strictly reserved for Dulwich Park. It'll all be set up by now. Do you want me to check with him?"

"Yes, and let me know."

Jasper was about to leave the room when he stopped.

"By the way, Popov, or Preobrazhensky, doesn't have bushy eyebrows. Not anymore, anyway. Just normal eyebrows now."

"Did he ever have bushy eyebrows, I wonder," Geraldine said without smiling. It was beyond a joke.

Jasper closed the door behind him.

Geraldine looked at her watch. It was 9:30 a.m. Three and a half hours to go before the Dulwich Park rendezvous. Planning and more planning had been underway for hours, with the DG's office, the A Branch surveillance team and Shadow Force. And the police. She had insisted that the Met be brought into the loop. It was absolutely out of the question in her view for the police not to be informed of the most dramatic development since the assassination attempt on her on 1st July and the shooting of the two police officers outside her house. Downing Street's wishes had been ignored. Again, with George Trench's approval.

Geraldine had rung Commander Harry Brooks herself. She explained that new intelligence had just emerged. Although the police had primacy over MI5 in all operations where an arrest was expected, Geraldine had told Brooks that while it was vital for the police to be in the know, the initial and possibly later stages of the day's proceedings should be left in the hands of MI5. Her service would be in overall charge of all those involved, and that included Shadow Force. The key to success at this stage was not action and arrest but intelligence-gathering, she told Brooks. There was a good chance, she said, that enough intelligence could be gleaned from the meeting in Dulwich Park for an arrest to be made by the end of the day. The success of the surveillance operation would depend on a minimal presence in the area. Both Russian agents would be on maximum alert. There was also the wife and son to worry about. They were innocent bystanders, or relatively innocent. There would also be other people in the park, especially at lunchtime.

Shadow Force would be unarmed. So, too, the A Branch team, filling an outer perimeter surveillance role. Police action would be required later, provided everything went according to plan. Geraldine knew that if the Russians were going to be charged, they had to be caught in the act of committing a criminal offence. Chatting in a park, even if the subject matter contained threats or plots, wasn't going to be enough. Rushing to arrest two picnickers without concrete evidence of a crime would be a gift to Moscow.

General Lockridge, Director Special Forces, was also informed about the Dulwich Park meeting. The general already had a chip on his shoulder from the priority given by the prime minister to Gibson and his team. Geraldine had warned George Trench that if Lockridge wasn't told about the upcoming drama, it could cause irreparable damage, especially since the prime minister had authorised the presence of an SAS squadron in the capital. Trench had agreed to speak to Lockridge, which was in itself unusual. The Director Special Forces had personal access to Downing Street at all times and didn't need or expect any sort of intervention by the head of MI5. But the call had been made and it had paid off. Lockridge promised his squadron would be on two-minute alert status for the whole day.

Everything that could be planned and anticipated had been considered. Jasper Cornfield and Major John Fisk from the MoD had been particularly astute about raising potential problems, especially when it came to likely moves by the two Russian agents. Major Fisk stated the obvious, but sometimes the obvious was worth stating. He said at no stage should anyone take anything for granted; these were two highly trained intelligence and special forces officers. He could make no predictions about their behaviour. One thing, however, he was certain about: they would say nothing in the park which could ever be viewed as prima facie incriminating evidence that could be used in a future trial.

***

Mikhail Gerasimov arrived in Dulwich Village an hour and a half before his 1 p.m. rendezvous. He was dressed in a dark blue light windcheater, a white T-shirt, blue jeans and white trainers. He was carrying nothing. The day was sunny but not that warm. Not perfect for a picnic, but he didn't imagine the meeting would last long.

The arrival of Maksim Popov in the UK meant only one thing. Gerasimov, the chosen agent to take revenge on the British security service, was regarded in Moscow as unreliable at best and a failure at worst. He had failed to kill Geraldine Hammer, and he, and only he, knew that he had no other plan to target her.

Meeting Popov in a public park with other people walking around seemed unnecessarily risky. He hoped that at no stage would he be expected to actually sit on the grass or a bench and share a picnic with Popov and his family. That would be truly bizarre.

He looked around and started walking south towards the north end of Dulwich Park, heading down Lordship Lane. He turned left down Friern Road and walked casually along the street, but his eyes were alert for anything that seemed not quite right. There were plenty of parked cars but no one sitting in them. No closed vans. He went back to Lordship Lane and followed the same procedure when he turned up the next street, Upland Road.

One vehicle stood out amongst the parked cars. It was a large grey van with no markings. No one was sitting in either the driver or passenger seat. Under the windscreen wiper was a parking ticket. He merely

282

glanced at the van and walked on to the end of the street.

He walked back down into Lordship Lane and turned into Overhill Road. Nothing caught his eye. He then checked out Belvoir Road and Melford Road. Again, nothing to worry him. He returned to Lordship Lane and crossed over into the park. As he walked around East Lawns in the north end of the park, he examined everyone he came across as discreetly as possible. Half a dozen dog walkers. Three families sitting on blankets and doing nothing in particular. A couple, the man smartly dressed, the woman in jeans and a sweatshirt, with a large carrier bag next to her, were engrossed in conversation. Gerasimov thought of Rebecca. He imagined the man had popped out for lunch in the park to meet his girlfriend. An illicit rendezvous. Like the one he was about to participate in but for different reasons.

The big grey van and the parking ticket worried him. He knew it was wrong.

He still had forty minutes to go before he was due to meet Popov and his family, so he wandered off southwards to check out the rest of the park. By the time he had finished, he had two things on his mind: the parking ticket on the van and the couple, who never seemed to stop talking. But they never kissed. If the man was having an illicit meeting with his girlfriend, they would have kissed. She would have brought food. Perhaps it was in the carrier bag. But Gerasimov hadn't seen her reach into the bag once since he arrived. So, two things to worry about.

One minute past 1 p.m., Popov, with his wife Natalia and son Dima, walked across Lordship Lane and entered Dulwich Park at the same entrance his fellow agent had used earlier.

At that moment, the couple stopped talking. Rose and Seamus, who was looking considerably smarter than usual, suddenly began to kiss. But she pulled away and put her left hand into the carrier bag. She took out a sandwich wrapped in a plastic cover. Underneath was a miniature electronic eavesdropping device with a directional microphone. Gerasimov could only guess what was inside the bag, but his suspicions about the couple were confirmed.

Inside the grey van with the parking ticket in Upland Road, four men and one woman, employees of MI5's technical branch, sat in front of laptops, each with headphones on, and waited.

Chapter Twenty-Nine
Mikhail Gerasimov Escapes

Gerasimov took out a pen and a pad of paper from his windcheater jacket and scribbled something down. As Popov and his family got closer, he dropped the piece of paper on the grass, turned away and walked off in the opposite direction. Popov looked surprised and gestured to his wife to lay a blanket down on the spot where the paper was lying. He picked it up as she flung a tartan blanket on the grass and put a picnic hamper on one corner.

The scrawled writing said: *"Za nami nablyudayut."*

They were being watched.

Popov immediately looked up and saw a couple sixty yards away. They looked as if they were about to go but then changed their mind. Popov decided to go ahead with the picnic, if only to cause more confusion for the watchers. His fellow Russian was already in the distance, walking southwards. He didn't turn around. Popov shook his head at his wife and frowned before she could ask what was going on. He then told her to lay out the picnic and to behave normally. His son seemed unaffected and sat down on the blanket.

The couple, who were sixty yards away, appeared to have decided to stay in the park. Popov noted the man was wearing a smart suit and the woman, jeans and a sweatshirt. He knew they were the watchers. There would be others. Popov thought his best option was to stay put. At least it might allow his comrade to make his escape without too many watchers on his tail.

Gerasimov walked quickly to the other end of the park. He knew he was being watched and followed, but he made a calculation. If they had wanted to arrest him, they would have done so already. He knew why they hadn't. They needed more. They needed evidence. They needed an observable crime. They needed proof that he was the one they had been hunting for three weeks. They had caught the contract killer, Joseph Paine, but they needed the Russian at the heart of it. They needed him. All wrapped up and presentable to a court. These thoughts went through his mind as he reached the edge of the park and began an elaborate ritual to evade his watchers.

He hailed a taxi and told the driver to take him to City Airport in the Royal Docks, east London. There were cars following all the way. At least three, he guessed, would contain members of the surveillance teams deployed to watch his every move. When the taxi arrived at the airport twenty-five minutes later, he paid and ran into the terminal. He was lucky it was crowded. He went straight to the toilets. Only one man was standing in front of a urinal. He was wearing a long tan-coloured raincoat and a small peaked cap. He was carrying a satchel over his shoulder. Gerasimov pushed him hard against the urinal and smashed his head on the wall. The man slumped to the floor. His satchel fell off his shoulder.

Gerasimov picked up the satchel, dragged the unconscious body into one of the six closets and closed the door. He removed the man's raincoat and cap and put them on. He listened. No one else had come in. He closed the door behind him. As soon as he was out of the toilets, he joined a crowd of businessmen heading for the exit. The queue for the taxis was too long, but he spotted a coach with its left indicators flicking. It was about to leave. He ran and banged on the door. The driver pressed a button to open the door.

"You with the National Pharmaceuticals?" the driver asked.

"Yes, sorry for being late," Gerasimov said.

The driver said nothing. Gerasimov climbed in. The coach was half full. They all looked at him but soon lost interest. The coach drew away from the curb. Gerasimov didn't look back. He would have seen four men exiting the terminal waving their arms. They were joined by two others, looking equally bewildered. Gerasimov had no idea where he was going. But he relaxed for the first time that day.

The coach was going to Cambridge, he discovered. He heard the city mentioned several times. Sitting further back from the other passengers, who were all grouped together in the first eight rows, he closed his eyes and pretended to be asleep.

The coach arrived at a large hotel outside Cambridge just over an hour later. Gerasimov waited until everyone was off and started sorting out their luggage. He then left the coach and walked into the hotel. At the concierge desk, he asked them to phone for a taxi to take him to Cambridge railway station. Ninety minutes later, he was on a train to Liverpool Street station in London. A taxi to the Travelodge in Vauxhall, and he was back in his room by 8 p.m. He was confident that none of his watchers had followed him once he had left the City Airport terminal and boarded the coach to Cambridge. It had been a seven-hour detour, but it had worked.

***

Unaware of the drama following the Dulwich Park rendezvous, Sandy Hall rang his contact at

Counter-Terrorism Command and asked if anything was happening.

"MI5 screwed up," the detective inspector said.

"How?"

"They let him go."

"Rick, what are you telling me?"

"We're all furious. They had him in their sights and they let him go and then lost him."

"Who are you talking about? The Russian?"

"Yes, the Russian. The bastard Russian. We could have got him but the security service scouts and girl guides thought they knew better."

"Can you tell me more?"

"Not really. I shouldn't have told you anything, but we're mad here."

"So, you say you had the Russian or knew where he was?"

"Yeah. Right there, he was being watched."

"Where?"

"I better not say. But in a public place. South London. He skipped, they followed and lost him."

"Police not involved?"

"No, strictly Thames House operation."

"Bloody hell. What's happening now?"

"Nothing. He vanished and we're expected to charge around London like numpties with blindfolds trying to find him."

"Can I report any of this?"

"Don't see why not. It'll teach them a lesson. But no police sources. Keep it general. It's a nightmare. Got to go."

Sandy's breaking story caused a sensation. He had rung his MI5 contact, who declined to make any comment. He wouldn't confirm or deny the claim that the Russian assassin had been tracked down, watched and then allowed to slip away. Sandy had pushed harder, asking, if it was true, why had MI5 allowed the Russian to escape? Was there a good reason for it? And why weren't the police involved?

The last question gave the game away, at least in the mind of his MI5 contact. He knew Sandy had been given the story by the Met. But he still refused to make any comment.

Sandy felt he had no choice but to report what he had been told by his Counter-Terrorism contact, who had never previously let him down.

For the six o'clock news, Sandy reported:

"In a dramatic development in the hunt for the Russian assassin, Sky News understands that the suspect was tracked to a public area in south London this morning. For reasons that have not been explained, the Metropolitan Police was not involved in either tracking the suspect or mounting a surveillance operation. That had been left to the security service, MI5. Few details have emerged, but sources have told Sky News that the failure to ensure the suspect remained under close surveillance has led to an angry reaction within the Metropolitan Police.

"After three weeks of largely frustrating police and MI5 investigations, the pinpointing of the main suspect should have been the breakthrough all Londoners have been waiting for. The security threat level has been critical for several days because of the assessment carried out by MI5, which indicated another attack was imminent.

"Why the suspect was not immediately arrested is a question that now has to be asked. Ministers will come under pressure to explain to the public and to parliament why a suspected dangerous Russian agent is now not behind bars, and why only MI5 was involved in today's operation. MI5 does not have arresting powers. This is why the police would normally have been involved in a joint operation with the security service.

"Meanwhile, as these vital questions are asked, the suspect has vanished."

Sandy made his report while standing outside New Scotland Yard. The six o'clock news presenter in the Sky office in Isleworth then came on and asked Sandy what explanation there could be for MI5 to be acting on its own without the police.

Sandy replied, "It is possible that there is not yet sufficient evidence to charge the suspect with specific crimes. We have had one attempted assassination of MI5's counter-espionage director, for which a former army corporal is to stand trial. Then there was the fatal shooting of two police officers guarding the MI5 director's house in south London, and the explosion at MI5's regional office in Birmingham. If the police had absolute proof of the identity of the suspect involved in the second two incidents, with forensic evidence to back it up, I would have thought this morning's operation would have been joint MI5 and police. All I can speculate is that more intelligence as well as hard police evidence is still needed."

"But how could the Russian suspect have evaded the surveillance operation?" the news presenter asked.

Sandy answered, "Clearly that is a massive setback. It can take a couple of dozen MI5 watchers to carry out round-the-clock surveillance of a single target. With such a high-profile case and with London on critical threat alert status, it is inconceivable that MI5 would not have deployed the maximum number of watchers to ensure the suspect remained in sight at all times."

"So, now no one knows where he is?" the news presenter asked.

A somewhat unnecessary question, but the presenter was about to wrap up the story and move on to the next item on the news schedule.

"That's correct. He could be anywhere," Sandy replied, a little melodramatically.

***

As Gerasimov was travelling by train from Cambridge to Liverpool Street, the MI5 watchers designated to follow Maksim Popov and his family had no problem keeping them in sight. Popov, his wife and son enjoyed a picnic in Dulwich Park, staying for more than an hour. Rose and Seamus had also remained in their position. And the team in the grey van, now with two parking tickets on the windscreen, was still in Upland Road and waiting. Waiting for any transmission that would provide additional intelligence about the main suspect and whatever future plot they might have in mind.

The hour was a waste of everyone's time. Popov and family hardly spoke at all. When they did, it was mundane chat. The food, the weather, London in summer, tourism plans for later in the week. Everything was in Russian and instantly translated, and instantly dismissed as inconsequential.

When they finally stood up, gathered their picnic paraphernalia and walked off, twenty men and women from MI5 got ready for the next phase of the surveillance operation. But it was to prove relatively straightforward. The Popovs caught a taxi after waiting for ten minutes in Lordship Lane. Two unmarked cars and the grey van followed at discreet distances. The taxi set them down in Piccadilly Circus.

Popov took his wife and son down Piccadilly. They stopped at Fortnum & Mason and waited for the famous exterior clock to sound the hour before entering the store. They browsed for forty minutes and then moved to the Diamond Jubilee Tea Salon for afternoon tea. Their MI5 watchers also browsed but stayed outside the salon.

The Popovs later walked down Piccadilly to Hyde Park and made their way to the Rubens Hotel in Buckingham Palace Road. The MI5 watchers noted they entered their room in the hotel at 5:45 p.m. No orders had been given to question Popov. For the moment, it was watch and wait.

**

Like the Met Police, Geraldine was furious that MI5's watchers had lost Lucas Meyer. She still thought of the Russian as Lucas Meyer, just as Rebecca referred to him only as Jean-Paul van Dijk. Now he would be hiding out somewhere under another name altogether.

The whole investigation was turning into a farce. The MI5 watchers were normally brilliant at their job. They spent most of their working hours following Islamic terrorist suspects and had developed surveillance techniques that had proven to be effective and productive. But the Russian had been a match for them.

Geraldine called in Grace and Jasper. When they arrived, she posed the obvious question. Where was the Russian now?

Jasper gave a recap of what was known.

"What we know so far," he said. "He took a taxi from Dulwich Park to the City Airport. Everyone assumed he was going to catch a flight out, and the airport was put on maximum alert once it was realised where the taxi was heading. But he was smart. He went into the terminal, straight to the toilets, we assume, although he wasn't actually seen entering them. That was the first mistake. The guy he knocked out wasn't discovered for five minutes.

By the time the alarm was raised, there was no sign of the Russian. He had left wearing the guy's raincoat and cap and carrying a shoulder bag. He wasn't spotted. Checks were made everywhere but to no avail. The queue for taxis was too long, so the obvious exit route was by Docklands Light Railway. He could have gone to Canning Town, Canary Wharf or Bank and then left to get another taxi. But we got the police to check all stations. Nothing."

"Buses, coaches, shuttle buses, he must have left in something?" Geraldine queried.

"Agreed, but National Express coaches don't go from City Airport. You have to pick them up from down the DLR line. Canning Town is the first one," Jasper said.

"So, could he have just run off, done it by foot?"

"Out of the question. We had more than a dozen people on him. If he had run off, he would have been spotted and followed."

"And yet, he left the terminal, albeit in someone else's coat and hat, and somehow managed to find a means of transport to get away," Grace said.

"Were there not other coaches waiting to pick up passengers—private ones, for example?" Geraldine asked.

"Yes, but they were all checked out," Jasper replied.

"How many were there and where were they going?" Geraldine asked.

Jasper said the airport transport desk had produced a list. There had been three waiting outside the terminal when the Russian arrived by taxi. But two left as he ran in and the third one pulled out around three minutes later.

"At that stage it's believed the Russian was still in the terminal because the surveillance team never saw him come out," Jasper said.

"And where was that coach going to?" Geraldine asked.

"Some pharmaceutical conference in Cambridge."

"Did the police check it out?"

"I don't think so," Jasper said. "He couldn't have been inside the terminal and on that coach before it left. But I think everyone was focusing on transport going back into London."

"So the other private coaches had destinations in London?" asked Geraldine.

"Yes, Olympia and the O2 arena."

"If he was on that coach to Cambridge, he won't be there any longer," Grace said.

"What we need," Jasper said, "is a lucky break."

***

While Gerasimov was making his escape from his MI5 watchers, Rebecca had been stuck in the room of her hideaway hotel that the Shadow Force team had found for her. Although in constant touch with her protectors, she was bored and frustrated. Rollie Gibson made sure she had a regular supply of takeaway food delivered to her whenever she wanted it. But she longed to return to her flat. Her painting commissions were on hold.

She watched the news and saw her new friend Sandy reporting about the missing Russian and the apparent bungle by MI5 surveillance teams. It made her feel unsafe, despite knowing that Gibson, Rose and the others were not far away and ready to spring to her aid if she was in trouble.

For the moment, she was resigned to staying like a prisoner in Room 260.

Rebecca was at the Travelodge in Vauxhall, within sight of the Oval cricket stadium.

Chapter Thirty

Mikhail Gerasimov Makes an Extraordinary Decision

At 8 p.m., Rebecca had had enough. She had to get out of her room. A quick walk, she thought. She brushed her hair and dabbed some pink on her lips. She opened the door for the first time in hours and walked to the lift. When it reached the ground floor, she stepped out and then shot back in again.

Jean-Paul van Dijk was at the reception desk and had stared straight at her.

Rebecca pressed the button for her floor. Her heart was pumping like an overheated boiler. She reached the second floor, fully expecting to see Jean-Paul standing there, but when the doors opened, the corridor was empty. She ran to her room and locked the door. For the first time in her life, she was terrified. She sat on the bed taking deep breaths. At any moment, she thought, he would be pounding on the door.

But minutes ticked by, and all was quiet. She went to the window and peered out cautiously. Traffic was going by as usual. There was no sign of him. She went back to her bed and phoned Rose. She had mobile numbers for all of Shadow Force, but she chose Rose.

"Christ, what's wrong?" Rose asked after hearing Rebecca's breathless voice.

"You won't believe this, but I've just seen him," Rebecca said.

"What!"

"Here, at the hotel. Just standing there."

"Did he see you?"

"Yes."

"Lock your room. We're coming now. Don't move an inch!"

It took the Shadow Force team four minutes to reach the hotel. George stayed with the Land Rover while the rest of the team rushed past the reception desk and took to the stairs. Both Rose and Gibson banged on Rebecca's door.

She opened it tentatively and they piled in like a rugby scrum. Rebecca couldn't stop herself. She laughed.

"Goodness, guys, I'm ok, there's no one hiding in the cupboard," she said.

Gibson calmed everyone down.

"Rebecca, tell us. What happened?" he asked.

Rebecca explained. Seeing the expressions on all their faces, she put her hands on her hips and reassured them that she wasn't mistaken. She said she'd sat in her room expecting him to hammer on her door just as they had a minute ago. They wanted to know what he was wearing and whether he was carrying anything. Like a holdall. Rebecca said she was pretty sure he wasn't carrying anything, and in the two seconds between coming out of the lift and jumping back in, she thought she'd seen him wearing some sort of windcheater and possibly jeans. No hat or cap. No sunglasses.

Gibson played the commanding officer. "Rose, you stay here, get more detail from Rebecca. Sam, Seamus, go out and hunt around. Talk to people, see if anyone saw a man of this description rushing out of the hotel. Tim, you and me, let's talk to reception. Find out whether he is staying here too, although that would be a helluva coincidence. Let's move it."

Almost as an afterthought, he turned back to Rose. "Ring the police and get them to put a helicopter up to search for him."

Gibson and Tim went downstairs to the reception. Gibson knew he should leave it to the police, but he flashed his old army ID and demanded to see the register of guests. The receptionist, a girl who looked about sixteen, responded to his authoritative voice by instantly swinging the computer round to face him. Many of the rooms were empty. He and Tim peered at the screen. They looked for Meyer, Van Dijk or Adams, but nothing came up. So they went back to the beginning and went down the list more slowly. There was a Mr and Mrs Ilinksi in Room 11, a Mr Baruska in Room 290, a Mr Deng in Room 300, a Mr and Mrs Yahontov in Room 53, a family called Varga in Room 17 and a Mr Chudov in Room 312.

Gibson asked the girl, "Do you have any idea what Mr Baruska in Room 290 looks like?"

"No," the girl replied.

"Mr Deng in Room 300?"

"Very small."

"Mr Chudov in Room 312?"

"No, sorry."

Tim had a sudden thought.

"One of your guests was at reception like seven or eight minutes ago and then left. A big man, wearing a windcheater. Do you know who that was?"

The girl looked confused for a moment.

"Yeah, he said he was checking out but then didn't."

"And?" Gibson asked.

She looked down.

"I think he said Room 312."

"A big man?" Gibson asked.

"I guess so."

"So, Mr Chudov, Mr Dragomir Chudov."

She hesitated, then, "Yes, Room 312."

Gibson's phone rang. It was Harry Brooks.

"What's going on?!" the Met commander shouted.

"We're at the Travelodge in Vauxhall. We think he was staying here," Gibson replied.

Brooks shouted an expletive. "Colonel, this is police work. For fuck's sake, leave us to do our job."

Gibson didn't back down. "We're here because we're protecting a witness, as you well know. She rang for help. We tipped you off straightaway."

Brooks was still angry. "It's a farce. Too many bloody people falling over each other. This guy is going to get away. Again. I'm on my way. Be there in ten minutes."

"He's now called Dragomir Chudov," Gibson said.

"It's like Walt Disney!" the Met commander shouted down the phone and rang off.

Gibson turned to Tim. "Prepare for fireworks," he said. "We better leave the room search to the police."

Just then Sam and Seamus returned.

"This guy has a habit of disappearing," Seamus said.

"Tell me about it. Harry Brooks is going ballistic," Gibson said.

"By the way, there's a helicopter up," Sam said. "They were quick with that. If he's skulking somewhere, hopefully, he'll be spotted."

Sam stayed at reception to try and be helpful to the police when they arrived. Gibson and Seamus used the lift to the second floor and went to Rebecca's room.

Rose opened the door.

"Anything?" she asked.

"Nul," Seamus replied.

"Very funny."

Gibson's phone rang.

"You-know-who is here and he wants you downstairs," Sam said.

Gibson shrugged. This was not the time for a stand-up fight with the police. Shadow Force wasn't called Shadow Force for nothing. It wasn't supposed to exist, and the last thing Gibson wanted were witnesses to a row with the commander of the Metropolitan Police Counter-Terrorism Command. He left the room.

Seamus sat on the bed next to Rebecca.

"Well, Ms Strong, now look what you've done," he said, grinning.

"So, it's all my fault, right?" Rebecca said with her usual quizzical look.

Rose interrupted. "Ignore Seamus," she said. "If it wasn't for you, this guy would probably have committed another atrocity and be back in Moscow with his wife and kids."

"He has a wife and kids?" Rebecca asked, startled.

"No, I was talking, you know... To be honest we haven't a clue who he is, let alone whether he's married."

"You like him, this Russian bastard?" Seamus suddenly asked.

Rebecca thought for a moment, refusing to be riled by the scruffiest member of Shadow Force.

"No. But maybe a little, before I discovered who he was," she said.

Seamus exchanged looks with Rose.

"But you've no regrets about turning him in?" he asked.

"I didn't turn him in, as you put it," Rebecca replied. "I was being spied on in that café and you picked me up, remember?"

Seamus was about to reply when there was a loud banging on her door. Rose went to open it. Harry Brooks marched in.

"Ms Strong? Can you come with us please," he said, ignoring Rose and Seamus.

Rebecca looked at Rose with her eyebrows raised. Rose nodded.

"Before we go," Harry Brooks said, "had you been to Room 312 where our suspect was staying?"

"Of course not," Rebecca answered indignantly. "I had no idea he was here."

"And why didn't you ring the police?" Brooks was still angry and suspected this tall blonde standing in front of him was part of a Shadow Force conspiracy.

"Because I needed instant help," she replied. "I was scared as hell and thought he was going to come and get me. I rang this lot because I knew they were just down the road and they're supposed to be protecting me."

"Supposed to be," Brooks said and glared at Seamus and Rose. "Now, please, come with me."

Rebecca grabbed her handbag, smiled at Rose and followed the police officer.

The police found nothing incriminating in Room 312. The suitcase with an assortment of clothing, but nothing else. No holdall. The suitcase was removed in plastic sheeting, and a forensic team spent two hours scooping up every speck of dust from the carpet and bedding. But Room 312 drew a blank.

**

At 9:20 p.m., Mikhail Gerasimov sent a text in English from his emergency mobile phone to Maksim Popov. Since exiting the Travelodge, he had left the area as quickly as possible but without running. After walking fast south-east for about twenty minutes, he came across a black bin bag outside a charity shop. He ripped it open and took out a torn brown overcoat, a pair of blue tracksuit bottoms and a red sweater. Colour coordination was the least of his problems. He left the bin bag where he had found it and ran round the corner into an alleyway lined with dustbins. He put the discarded clothes on. None of them fitted his large physique. The coat was particularly tight over his windcheater. The red sweater was superfluous, so he threw it into one of the bins.

He emerged from the alleyway looking like a homeless street sleeper. To add authenticity, he smeared dirt on his face. As soon as he heard the police helicopter, he dived into a shop doorway and lay curled up. People passed him in the street but paid little attention to the scruffy-looking man asleep in the doorway. It was a warm evening and most of the people who walked by were wearing light clothes, but the heavy brown coat didn't look out of place. Not on a man who had fallen on hard times and had nowhere else to sleep.

As soon as the helicopter moved on, he got up and walked slowly down the street, hunching his shoulders, with his head bowed, continuing south. Then he stopped and turned round and headed for the only place he was sure would be empty where he might be able to sleep for the night. He knew it was a risk: going north, returning to the area where the police would be focusing their search efforts. The sudden idea that had come into his head was also fraught with danger. But it was so outrageous it just might work.

It took him half an hour on a roundabout route, keeping his head down. The coat stretched across his chest made him look awkward. But he arrived at his destination. He climbed over the fence, walked quickly to the back door and saw in the dark, as he had gambled it would be, that it was a temporary, makeshift construction, plain wood, unpainted, with a basic padlock. He bent his steel comb to force one of the teeth into the lock and twisted it. Picking the lock took him less than a minute.

Mikhail Gerasimov, now with the alias Dragomir Chudov, was back inside Geraldine Hammer's house in Gladstone Street.

Chapter Thirty-One

The Night-Duty GCHQ D15 Analyst Sets a Ball Rolling

Since closing the door of their room in the Rubens Hotel, Maksim Popov had gone over in his mind all the options he now faced. His comrade's warning had narrowed the choices, but Popov never panicked. He had spent so many years in the military intelligence community and as a special forces Spetsnaz officer that he was confident he could meet every challenge. There was always a solution. He told his wife and son to go down to the hotel dining room to eat. He needed to be alone to work out his next move.

He couldn't get out of his mind the four generals in the Aquarium. All of them were old-style Soviet-era types, rigid in their views, implacably unwilling to accept defeat and mostly lacking any sense of humour until they had imbibed at least five glasses of vodka. Apart, perhaps, from the one who requested a jar of English raspberry jam. He clearly had enjoyed Popov's discomfort at having to fly to London to sort out the mess caused by his colleague and comrade. The raspberry jam parting shot was no friendly gesture but a reminder that Popov would be welcomed back only if his mission was successfully completed. The raspberry jam would then be gratefully received. If he failed, a jar of English raspberry jam would be viewed as an insult and as a symbol of Popov's incompetence.

Popov was a proud man. He had seldom failed during his career. But there were too many unknowns complicating his decision-making. The whereabouts of his fellow agent was the biggest. Gerasimov had warned him that he was being watched in the park, so Popov assumed that his family was now the subject of a full surveillance operation. They would be in the hotel and outside waiting for him to leave. His room would be bugged. He was effectively trapped.

But Popov knew he had one positive thing going for him. Apart from entering the UK with a false passport, he had committed no crime. Unlike his comrade, he was not on the run. They knew he was at the Rubens Hotel. They could pick him up whenever they wanted. But so far they had held back. The reason was obvious: they expected and hoped that he would lead them to the agent currently eluding the police. If the wishes of the four generals back in Moscow were to be fulfilled, Popov had to meet up with or at least be in contact with his fellow Russian. Wherever he was. There had to be a way without handing both of them on a plate to the British police.

Unit Zero had been set up because of the perceived failings and weaknesses of Unit 29155. The other unit's failure to eliminate Sergei Skripal, even when supplied with what should have been a deadly nerve agent, and the ridiculous bravado of the two GRU agents commissioned to carry out the assassination, had caused a furore at the highest level in the Kremlin. Popov had been selected to lead a new unit to ensure that future assassination and sabotage missions succeeded as planned. It was felt that a major-general was required to instil a greater degree of discipline and professionalism. But Popov, as leader of Unit Zero, was not expected to operate in the field himself. He was to be the master tactician, the man the Kremlin could trust to deliver.

So far the mission had failed. The four generals blamed him and now expected him to clear up the mess.

But there was one secret which only he, Popov, knew about. And that secret could play a big role in whether the mission would succeed or not.

There was a mole inside MI5.

The four generals in Moscow had not been apprised of this intelligence nugget. Popov's contacts were far-reaching. Some of them he would trust with his life. One of his longstanding contacts worked for Russia's foreign intelligence service, the SVR. His contact was listed by a codename in his phone. Venedict. A former Spetsnaz major turned SVR officer, he had been serving undercover at the Russian embassy in London for two years and had built up a small but highly productive network of agents.

One of them worked for MI5.

All the information about Geraldine Hammer had come from this source. Venedict had passed it on to Popov while he was in Moscow planning Unit Zero's first operation overseas.

Geraldine's safe house address in Lord North Street had been picked up by Venedict from a dead drop in Hyde Park. His MI5 mole had a number of favourite dead drops, the classic tradecraft method for passing secret messages between agent and controller which had remained largely unchanged since the Cold War espionage period. The Hyde Park drop was under a rock at one end of a row of rhododendrons. Geraldine's address in Gladstone Street had been secreted inside a hollow oak tree root in a graveyard in Muswell Hill and had been included in Popov's planning blueprint for nearly a year. Mikhail Gerasimov, alias Lucas Meyer, had been given the address as part of his research in London.

The mole, codenamed Svekla, Russian for beetroot, had never passed on details of secret MI5 operations. To that extent, the mole's usefulness had been limited. But the mole had been particularly helpful in providing information about individual members of the security service: their names, addresses, marital status and families. The mole knew everything about Geraldine Hammer: what coffee she liked, her favourite holiday location and where her two children went to school.

Popov's phone pinged. The briefest of text messages, in English, read: *"Love to meet up. Back in town."*

So his fellow conspirator was still at large. Popov texted back, in English: *"Nice to hear from you. Where, when?"*

His phone pinged back immediately: *"Glad to see you any time, Bill."*

Popov looked at the message with astonishment. He repeated it over and over again. There was a meaning somewhere. He thought back to what Venedict had told him, but nothing came to mind. Not at first. Then, after ten minutes, he suddenly smiled. Glad and Bill. Bill and Glad. William Gladstone. Gladstone Street. He was in Gladstone Street. 16 Gladstone Street. Brilliant, but extraordinary. Why there, and how could he be at Geraldine Hammer's home? Popov shook his head in admiration. It would be the one place no one would ever imagine checking. Provided he had got inside the house without being spotted.

Now, somehow Popov had to do the same.

He texted back. *"Look forward to it."*

Popov removed the battery from his phone.

The texts in English were lost in the wash of millions of communications. No keywords had been included. The Code Zero team at GCHQ missed the significance of the exchange between the most wanted suspect in the country and Popov.

***

After an hour of questioning by two police officers from the Met's counter-terrorism command, Rebecca was handed back into the care of the

Shadow Force team. Reluctantly, as far as Harry Brooks was concerned. He only agreed to release her to Gibson after receiving a phone call from Geraldine.

Geraldine trusted Gibson to look after Rebecca. After their honest admissions to each other at the meeting in Thames House, Geraldine had warmed to Rebecca. She had smiled when Rebecca had said they were now friends. She felt protective towards her, and she knew Gibson and his team felt the same. She particularly wanted Sam to keep Rebecca safe. He had already saved her own life at her home in Gladstone Street, and she had no doubt he would be the one to protect Rebecca. Not for the first time, Geraldine realised she liked Sam. Big Sam. So, she had made the call to Harry Brooks, and Rebecca was back in Gibson's care.

At first, Shadow Force took Rebecca to their cramped over-the-shop rented flat to discuss where she might safely stay for a few days until her own apartment was ready for her return. She was desperate to get home and told Gibson she was sure Jean-Paul would never go back to the flat. Why would he risk it, and for what purpose?

Sam was the only one to come up with a possible reason. "He must like you, surely?"

Rebecca grinned but shook her head. She was never going to see Jean-Paul van Dijk again.

***

At midnight, Popov closed the door of his bedroom and went into his son's room, which faced the back of the hotel. Popov was dressed in dark, casual clothes and a woollen hat stretched low over his forehead. His son was asleep.

He started to lift the window. There was no moon visible, but even in the dark, there was enough ambient light for him to see the way down to the ground, which he had checked earlier in the evening. There was a small garden area surrounded by buildings. He would need to climb down the nearest drainpipe to the bottom, slip across the garden and climb to the roof of the next building before descending once again. He gambled that his watchers would be in cars at the front of the hotel and possibly down the side road, but not lurking in the garden below.

Popov was a tall man but not as big as his fellow agent waiting for him at 16 Gladstone Street. He eased his body out over the window frame head first and grabbed the drainpipe to his left. It looked old but solid, like the hotel itself. With both hands gripping the drainpipe, he slowly muscled his body over the ledge and swung down. It was the riskiest moment. The weight of his body crashing against the metal pipe could have brought the whole lot down. But the large, black-painted, slightly rusted brackets with screws buried in the masonry held firm. It took him a minute to reach the ground after slipping down the length of the pipe. Bent double, he moved through the rose bushes and small hedges to the other side. He stopped for a minute. But apart from the normal sound of late-night traffic, he heard and saw nothing to alarm him.

He began a slow and awkward climb up a drainpipe the other side of the garden. While he had trained for this sort of escapade, drainpipes were notoriously unknowable structures for someone wishing to climb up or down. This drainpipe had little paint left on the metal, which suggested the maintenance department of this particular section of the building was less attentive to repairs. But Popov managed to reach the top and climb over onto the flat roof. He lay full length and worked his way forward like a lizard with short irregular snatches of movement. He peered over the side and saw a drainpipe to his right. At the bottom was a road with parked cars. There were no pedestrians. Now it would be a matter of luck.

It was just after midnight. He scrambled to where the drainpipe head was sticking up and was about to clamber over when he received a text in Russian.

"Nash drug zavtra vozyrashchayetsy domoi."

It was from Venedict. The mole, Svekla, had revealed that Geraldine Hammer was due to leave her temporary safe house in Lord North Street and return to her house in Gladstone Street. No timings were mentioned. Popov could hardly believe it. The target was returning home. Straight into a trap. This time, his fellow Russian would complete the mission.

Popov climbed over the edge. He glanced down once more. Still nobody in the street. And most importantly, no one jumping out of a car to grab him when he landed. He reached the pavement and walked quickly down the street, turning right at the bottom. He glanced once behind him, but no one was following. He stopped a London taxi and asked to be taken to Garden Row SE1, two roads down from Gladstone Street.

There were few people around. He didn't see a single police car. He got out at the top end of Garden Row and walked up the main St George's Road towards Waterloo station, before turning right into Gladstone Street.

The road was dark. There were street lights, but most of them were buried within the spreading leafy branches of lime trees. The darkness made him feel less apprehensive. Every house he passed had drawn curtains. There were no lights on, not even upstairs in the bedrooms. He climbed the three steps leading up to number 16 and knocked gently. The door was opened almost immediately, and a hand beckoned him in.

***

Only one of the six analysts in the special section D15 at GCHQ was on duty for the late shift. Her role was to continue to monitor all potentially suspect or curious or unusual electronic communications within the Greater London area. The day-shift analysts had uncovered nothing that needed urgent attention. But it had become a routine for the day-shift team to leave anything even remotely interesting for the night analyst to ponder on during the late evening and night when the number of texts, emails and phone calls diminished. The woman, in her mid-twenties, spent time on one text from a phone in north London which called for an urgent meeting the following morning to discuss an emergency, but there were no responding texts. She continued examining about fifty communications, most of them texts.

At 11:23 p.m., she became fascinated by four texts: a conversation between two people involving an exchange of twenty-five words.

The first text read: *"Love to meet up. Back in town."*

The second read: *"Nice to hear from you. Where, when?"*

The third: *"Glad to see you any time, Bill."*

The fourth: *"Look forward to it."*

Twenty-five harmless words. Had D15 not been set up specifically to cover the Greater London area during the emergency in the capital, the electronic conversation would have passed through the airwaves without any government snooping. And on the face of it, there was nothing in the twenty-five words to make even the brightest intelligence analyst sit up and take notice. But these were unprecedented times. Every text in the London area could have a hidden meaning, a suspect choice of words or a coded message.

The analyst read the four texts six times before she realised what was nagging her. It was the name, Bill. And the comma before it. Was the text sender referring to himself, signing off as Bill? Or was he calling his friend Bill? It could be either. Was it worth spending more time considering whether the texts had potential for further examination?

There was one thing which did make the twenty-five words more worthy of investigation than anything else she had read so far in her night shift. The original text sender only mentioned the name Bill in his second message. If there had been any doubt about who he was, he would have written Bill in the first text, signing himself off. And the same if he was addressing his friend, although it would have been more normal for him to have started the first text with "Hi, Bill".

The young analyst knew that people texted in different ways. A large percentage used abbreviated words to save time. If these were two longstanding friends, there wouldn't be a reason to mention names at all. The texts in front of her were between two people who appeared to know each other well, and yet one of them felt the need to mention the name Bill. She knew there had to be something in the third text which other experts in the intelligence community might grasp. She couldn't see it and was annoyed with herself that she wasn't able to decode what she felt sure was a hidden message. Without wasting any more time, she sent the four texts direct to MI5 and MI6, and included her ponderings on Bill. She bypassed Petherwick at the Foreign Office because of the late hour, even though she and the other members of D15 were ordered to deal directly and only with him as the initial receiver of all Code Zero intelligence. But she wondered whether

Petherwick, even if he was awake and reading his emails from GCHQ, would react immediately.

***

At Thames House on the third floor, it was the turn of Jasper Cornfield to be on late duty. He normally hated the night shift. He didn't mind being on his own, but he preferred the camaraderie of Thames House at its busiest during the day. Regular night shifts didn't help his social life, although he seldom went out during the week. He had a number of close friends, both male and female, but he had never broken the rule on answering their questions about his job. He hadn't even told his parents, who believed his story that he worked at the MoD. They understood that such a job entailed sensitive work and never liked to pry.

On this night, however, Jasper was fully alert, working the late shift without regrets. The security crisis and the hunt for the Russian intelligence agent had been going on for too long. There had to be another breakthrough. The last one, the Dulwich Park rendezvous, had ended in a fiasco. Everyone involved was to blame, but MI5 had come out the worst. Poor Geraldine had been mortified and was still struggling to regain the reputation she'd had before the near-fatal shooting incident on 1st July.

He was surprised to see the email from D15 at GCHQ, sent direct, not through the normal channel at the Foreign Office. He read the four texts and the note attached.

He agreed immediately with the analyst. There was something odd about the language. The choice of Bill in the third text was bizarre. He read the third text slowly and then fast. Then he got it. It was like suddenly seeing the answer to a crossword clue.

Trying to keep calm, he rang his boss. It was after midnight, and Geraldine was asleep in her safe house in Lord North Street, but Jasper's voice made her instantly alert.

"Jasper, what's up?" she asked.

"I've just had a communication from D15. It's not conclusive, but I believe I know where at least one and maybe the two Russians are at this moment. Or soon will be," he said breathlessly.

Geraldine waited.

"I think they're in your house. In Gladstone Street."

Geraldine leapt out of bed and nearly dropped the phone. "Explain."

Jasper quickly described the contents of the third text and pointed out the first and last words. Glad and Bill.

"Bill. William Gladstone."

"I got it. Unbelievable," Geraldine said as she threw her nightie onto the bed and started scrambling into a trouser suit.

Jasper was going to tell her that the analyst at D15 had made all the running with her astute reading of the texts, but Geraldine told him she would be in the office in ten minutes. She planned to run the short distance between Lord North Street and Thames House. She also said she would ring Gibson to get him to check out her house and report back before alerting the police, George Trench and Number 10.

"Well done, Jasper," she said.

***

The Russian text between Venedict and Popov was highlighted and sent urgently as a Code Zero communication. This time, the analyst in D15 sent it to Petherwick with a copy to her boss at GCHQ, and to cover herself, also to MI5 and MI6.

The Code Zero email wasn't given the attention it merited because by the time it arrived, there was a full-scale operation underway to lay siege to 16 Gladstone Street. Shadow Force was in the vicinity and had reported back that Geraldine Hammer's home had visitors. Plural.

Chapter Thirty-Two
Settling in at Number 16 Gladstone Street

The two Russian military intelligence officers sat in the dark at each end of the yellow-flowered sofa in the first-floor sitting room of Britain's director of counter-espionage. Major-General Maksim Alexei Popov, leader of Unit Zero, and Lieutenant-Colonel Mikhail Nikolayev Gerasimov, the most experienced and formerly most trusted member of his sabotage and assassination team.

Gerasimov, now shorn of all of his aliases, offered tea.

Popov peered at him with his right eyebrow raised. The eyebrows were beginning to grow back.

"Tea? No," Popov said.

"Not sure what else I can offer," Gerasimov said. "I could look."

"Mikhail Nikolayev, you are jesting," said Popov. "We have perhaps an hour before I must head back."

Gerasimov was more relaxed than his superior. "I am not clear, Maksim Alexei, why you have been sent. I have things in hand. Am I to be recalled?"

"Only once the mission is complete," Popov replied.

"So, you are my babysitter?" Gerasimov asked.

"There is no reason to be impertinent," Popov said. "I am here because you are perceived in Moscow to have gone off on a limb. You have strayed from the mission path. I have been asked to tell you, order you, to carry out some sort of spectacular event that will finally send the message to the British. So far, nothing has gone according to plan, and I, as well as those higher up the chain of command, want answers."

"Such as?" Gerasimov was not giving an inch.

"Why is MI5's director of counter-espionage, who is unwittingly hosting our little chat, still alive? This is the second time you have broken into her house—proof that you haven't forgotten everything we taught you. Yet here we are and there she is, the other side of the Thames, presumably asleep in her MI5 house. You have to admit to the irony."

"The first time I tried I was pounced on by a bear of a man—"

"But you didn't shoot."

"I had no time."

"Mikhail Nikolayev, you always have time. That's what the training taught you. Mission first, bouncing bear, or whatever you have to deal with, second. Did you have sex with her?"

The question took Gerasimov by surprise. His hesitation was enough for Popov.

"So, you failed because she was a woman?"

Gerasimov didn't reply.

"And the two packages we sent you, what went wrong there?" Popov asked. "Where is the second one, do you have it here?"

"No," Gerasimov said. "But it's safe."

"Safe how?"

"I can pick it up when I want. It's safe."

Popov looked unconvinced.

"I'm here but you're on your own," he said. "Thanks to the farce in the park, my every move is watched."

"Except for now, right?"

"Yes. But then it's going to be even tighter when I return to the hotel. Through the front door."

"So, you'll leave it to me," Gerasimov said.

"Not quite. Whatever you were planning, everything has now changed."

"How?"

"Your target is moving."

"Moving from Lord North Street?"

"Tomorrow."

"Where?"

"Here."

"Here?"

"She's coming home."

Gerasimov felt a cold shudder going through his body. He knew Popov had a special source. It was why, as Lucas Meyer, he had known where the woman from MI5 lived when he first came to London to plan for the Kremlin-ordered revenge mission.

"There'll be no escape this time," Gerasimov said.

"No, not this time," Popov replied. "You have to finish what you failed to do last time."

"No, I meant no escape for me."

"That's for you to sort out," Popov told him. "The last thing she will expect is you sitting on her sofa. Surprise is your best asset. Make it work. Then leave the country. I shall leave with my wife and son in the normal way and there will be nothing they can do. As for you, they're looking for a Russian with a European name, not a Russian with a Russian name. I shall expect to see you back in Moscow."

***

Shadow Force had one extra passenger in the Land Rover en route to Gladstone Street. Rebecca had insisted, then demanded, she be taken along. Despite unanimous opposition from the team, she presented two arguments. First, she didn't want to be left alone in the flat, which she described as almost uninhabitable. And second, if Jean-Paul van Dijk needed to be cajoled into leaving Geraldine's house calmly and without causing a punch-up, perhaps she could be the one to appeal to his better nature. If he had one.

She had turned to Sam for support. "As you said, Sam, he kind of liked me, so seeing me outside might help."

The rest of them left it to Gibson to make the decision. He didn't look happy, but he agreed. As they got ready to go, Rebecca went to the bathroom and took her phone out of her back jeans pocket. She quickly texted Sandy Hall.

"Get to 16 Gladstone St fast. Biggest scoop of your life. R x."

She then turned her phone off.

***

Sandy was awake and dressed in his flat. He texted her back, but it wasn't acknowledged. He grabbed a jacket, notebook, biro and tape recorder and threw them into his shoulder bag as he booked an Uber. When he left the apartment block, the car was already waiting for him.

***

They parked the Land Rover two roads down from Gladstone Street and split up into pairs, Gibson with Sam, Seamus with Rose, Tim with George. None of them was armed. Rebecca tagged along behind Rose. Gibson, Sam, Seamus, Rose and Rebecca walked hunched low, using the cars parked bumper to bumper in Gladstone Street as cover. Tim and George took the next road and worked their way round to the back of number 16, following in reverse the route that had been used by Gerasimov when escaping from the house days before. Gibson and Sam both had high-powered binoculars. Rose had fitted all of them with two-way tactical radio systems.

When Tim and George were in position up close to the back door of Geraldine's house, Tim whispered into his mic, "Padlock on the ground. Forced entry. No one in the kitchen."

From the front, the house looked empty. There were no curtains drawn. No lights. The street also looked normal. The police had removed the tape. It was no longer a crime scene. Peering through the binoculars, Gibson at first saw nothing to indicate anyone was inside. But as his eyes adjusted to the dark, he thought he could see two shapes. He handed the binoculars to Rose. She looked for a few minutes and nodded.

"Definitely two people in there," she said. Sam agreed.

Gibson had been told by Geraldine to check but do nothing. No heroics. Just call her back. Gibson rang Geraldine and reported the unpadlocked back door and the appearance of shapes in her front room on the first floor.

"Any doubts?" she asked.

"No."

"More than one shape?"

"More than one."

"Wait for the cavalry."

***

In the sitting room, Popov stood up.

"I've got to leave," he said.

He went to the window and peered out into the semi-darkness. Not all the street lights were functioning. Something worried him. A movement? Behind one of the parked cars? There it was again. Someone was there. He moved away from the window.

"It may be too late," he told his Russian comrade.

Gerasimov jumped up from the sofa and went to the window. The first sirens broke through the silence.

***

By the time Sandy arrived in his Uber, Gladstone Street was under siege. The sight that met his eyes set his heart racing. A multitude of police cars and other vehicles. Two ambulances. And behind a windowless van, a group of half a dozen men, all in black with balaclavas and assault weapons. Large floodlights were being connected up to a generator, and all the way down the street, police were ushering residents from their homes.

He texted Rebecca: *"I'm here, where are you?"*

Much to his surprise, he received an instant response.

"Me too."

The reply so shocked him that he thought she must be joking. Under what possible circumstances could Rebecca Strong be in or near Gladstone Street?

He texted back: *"Really? Where?"*

"Can't say," she replied.

"Are you all right?"

"Bless. Yes."

Sandy was the only reporter there. The police had put tape across the road, but no one was on tape duty. He bent under it and walked towards the melee, keeping well to the right. He was within grasping distance of the black-attired group of serious-looking dudes behind the van when a police officer spotted him and shouted.

The van group glanced round and at least three of them raised their weapons in his direction.

The police officer hurried towards him.

"Who the hell are you? This area is cordoned off," he said and made ready to grab Sandy.

"Sandy Hall, Sky," he said. "I'll keep back and just watch. Ok?"

Then an amazing thing happened. One of the dudes by the van said to the police officer, "Don't worry, mate. He's with us, we'll look after him."

The police officer hesitated and then turned round and walked away.

Sandy grinned at the group of men.

"Hey, thanks. In case you didn't hear me, I'm Sandy Hall, Sky News crime correspondent," he said.

"Yeah, we heard, and we know who you are," the tallest of the men said. "You were the first one to report about us, right?"

Sandy grinned again. "Yeah, sorry about that," he said. "I was in Millbank and saw you getting out of a van."

The six SAS soldiers grinned back. "No harm," the tall one said.

"Skip, we might be needed."

A soldier with a bull neck and wide chest pointed down the street. A huge man with three police officers behind him was moving to take up a position halfway across the road behind a high steel barricade.

Skip, a captain and leader of the group, put his right hand up. "Wait," he said.

Sandy began taking notes. He was in the equivalent of a ringside seat.

The huge man was Sam Cook. In the rush to get to Gladstone Street, neither the police nor MI5 nor the SAS had brought with them a Russian speaker. When the error was discovered, Gibson stepped in. He was standing back from the massed array of armed police officers, along with the rest of Shadow Force and Rebecca. He'd offered Sam. The senior police officer in charge, a uniformed chief superintendent of average height, looked astonished when Sam emerged. First, he had no idea who he was, and second, he had no idea why he was there at all. But he was such an impressive size that he just gaped and nodded.

"You speak Russian?" he asked.

"Yes," Sam replied.

The police officer passed him a flak jacket and phone and told him to ring Geraldine's home number, which he provided. It rang ten times before it was picked up. The chief superintendent gave Sam a list of questions. Sam stared at the police officer with a look of disdain. He didn't need to be force-fed. The police officer didn't seem to notice.

The first question seemed to Sam to somewhat state the obvious. The two Russians inside Geraldine's house were fully aware of what was assembled outside and didn't need to be told. But Sam thought he'd better play along, although he did start by introducing himself, which was not in the script. He spoke loudly and slowly. There was no other sound in the street.

"Menya zovut Sem, zdes' vooruzhennaya politsiya. Vy znayete ob etam?" Did the Russians know what they were confronting?

"Konechno," the voice came back. Of course.

At the first sound of Russian from the huge man standing behind the steel barrier, every police sniper instinctively flinched. Rebecca, standing behind Rose, desperately wanted to know whether Sam was talking to Jean-Paul or the other one. Although it was a warm July night, she shivered and reached her hand across to touch Rose. She swivelled round and understood immediately.

"Don't think of him as Jean-Paul, Rebecca," she said.

Rebecca wished Sandy was next to her. She couldn't text him again because Gibson had told her to switch off her phone.

"Pozhaluysta predstav'tes'," Sam said, asking the Russian to identify himself.

"Sergei Preobrazhensky."

"Spasibo. Pozhaluysta ukazhite drugovo cheloveka." Sam asked for the name of the second person in the house.

"Dragomir Chudov."

"Spasibo."

The chief superintendent standing next to Sam nudged him.

"Anything?" he asked.

"Getting there," Sam said, covering the phone with his hand.

"Net vykhoda," he told the Russian. "Tak chto vykhodi pozhaluysta. S vysoko podnyatymi rukami. Vy ponimayete?"

"Da."

The chief superintendent was nudging him again.

"Tell them to come out with their hands up," he whispered loudly.

"I just did. Please leave me to do this," Sam replied with obvious irritation.

"Did he agree?" the police officer persisted.

Sam stepped away from the chief superintendent.

"He understands the situation and what I was telling him to do, but he has not agreed to come down. Not yet."

At that point the SAS captain approached from behind the van.

Sam told the Russian to stay on the line.

"What gives?" the captain asked.

"No movement yet," Sam replied.

The captain addressed the chief superintendent. "When you're ready, I'll send two of my team round the back. I want to deploy three to the roof. Then we'll be in position to move fast on your order."

The chief superintendent looked impressed and worried at the same time. He agreed to both wishes but said he wanted Sam to continue phone contact for the moment.

"Weapons?" the captain asked.

"Not sure yet," Sam replied. "I intend to ask."

The captain nodded and returned to his men.

"Eto Sem," Sam told the Russian with the complicated name.

Silence.

"Net vykhoda. Tak chto vykhodi pozhaluysta s vysoko podnyatymi rukami," Sam said, ordering them both to come out with their hands raised in the air.

Still silence at the other end.

"Vy ponimayete?" Sam asked.

"What are you asking?" the chief superintendent queried. He had moved closer to Sam.

Sam once again covered the phone with his hand. "I asked him if he understood what I'm saying."

"Why, is your Russian not good enough?" the police officer asked.

Sam ignored him. He repeated the question to the Russian.

After a few seconds, Popov replied: "Da."

"Tak chto vykhodi seychas. Medlenno," Sam said, telling him to come out slowly.

"Nyet."

"Yesli vy ne pridyote' eto plokho konchitsya dlya vas," Sam warned.

He had diverged from the prepared script for some of his questions, but this warning he picked from the list provided by the chief superintendent. Sam thought it was melodramatic and a touch of Hollywood, but he felt obliged to stick to the script on this occasion, knowing the police officer nudging him every few seconds would want to know. Coming sixth on the chief superintendent's list, it read: "If you don't come out, it will end badly for you."

Popov replied, "Ya ne veryu vam."

The police officer nudged Sam.

"He doesn't trust us," Sam said.

"Vy mozhete doveryat' mne." He tried to reassure the Russian that he could be trusted.

"Vy nas zastrelite," Popov replied.

Before the police officer could nudge him again, Sam turned to him and told him the Russian was concerned they would be shot as soon as they left the building.

"Tell him they will be shot if they don't come out now," the chief superintendent said, glancing at the row of police snipers and the sudden appearance of three black-clad SAS soldiers on the roof of number 16.

"Nyet," Sam replied to the Russian. "Ostav' svoye oruzhiya."

"You said no. Even I know that word in Russian," the chief superintendent said. He gave Sam an angry look.

"I told him to leave their weapons," Sam said. "There's no point deliberately provoking him. Not if we want this to end peacefully."

"I just want it to end. I don't care if it's peaceful or not. They killed two of my officers."

Sam shook his head in amazement.

The Russian had not responded.

Sam repeated his request.

"U nas net oruzhiya." Popov denied they had any weapons.

"Tak chto ukhodi seychas," Sam said, inviting them to leave immediately.

"Nyet," was the response, and the phone went dead.

Chapter Thirty-Three
Decision Time for the Two Russians

Commander Harry Brooks and Geraldine Hammer arrived at almost the same time in chauffeur-driven cars. The police officer now guarding the taped-off end of Gladstone Street lifted it up for them to bow under.

As they walked together towards the assembly of police officers, Geraldine saw someone she thought looked familiar standing close to a van, next to a tall man in black. Sandy Hall stared back, wondering who she was. He recognised Harry Brooks, but the head of the Met's Counter-Terrorism Command didn't glance in his direction.

"Who's that woman?" Sandy asked the SAS captain.

"Not for you to know," he replied.

Sandy was perplexed. Then he had a flash of inspiration. She could be the owner of number 16 Gladstone Street. If so, he had, almost, come face to face with MI5's director of counter-espionage. An attractive woman, Sandy thought. He kept his inspirational deduction to himself.

The SAS captain, who had remained by the van while the five other members of the unit had deployed to their allotted positions behind the house and on the roof, cocked his head to the right as a message came through his earpiece. The captain replied "roger" and turned to Sandy.

"Wait here and have fun watching," he said. He then left.

Sandy quickly made a call to the Sky News night desk.

"It's Sandy. I'm at Gladstone Street, SE1. I need a cameraman now! Massive story. Russians under siege. But put nothing out. No one else is here."

He then tried texting Rebecca again but got no reply.

***

Sam saw Geraldine approaching, although she stayed a few yards away. He smiled at her. She smiled back and raised a hand briefly.

Rebecca also saw Geraldine and waved to attract her attention. Geraldine didn't spot her at first, but then saw the hand waving and a head of blonde hair. She walked quickly to where four of the Shadow Force team were standing.

"What on earth are you doing here?" she asked Rebecca and looked at Gibson for an explanation. He shrugged.

"I didn't want to miss out," said Rebecca.

Geraldine looked surprised. "I'm sorry but you need to go. This is a police matter, not Shad..." Her voice tailed off. No one had told Rebecca about Shadow Force.

"Shad?" asked Rebecca.

"Not my lot," Geraldine replied quickly.

"But this is all about you and your lot. And me, right? I want to be here. See him come out," Rebecca said, tossing her hair back.

Geraldine said nothing.

"Your Lucas, my Jean-Paul," Rebecca said very quietly.

Geraldine looked at Gibson. "Keep her back and safe. If anything happens to her..." she said before going over to where Harry Brooks was talking to the police officer in charge.

Brooks, Geraldine and the chief superintendent were joined by Sam.

"Hello, Sam," Geraldine said.

"Geraldine."

"So, no joy so far?"

"No, but he's talking. Or was. He gave his Rubens Hotel name, Sergei Preobrazhensky, but it's Popov of course. The other guy he named as Dragomir Chudov."

"So, Lucas Meyer," Geraldine said.

"Yes. Sorry."

Geraldine's heart melted, which took her by surprise.

Harry Brooks interrupted. "With the greatest respect, Geraldine, how the hell did this guy Popov get here from the Rubens Hotel? It's supposed to be surrounded by your boys."

"We'll deal with that later, Harry. Let's get these two out and away. Ok?" Geraldine replied.

The chief superintendent, who'd looked confused when Sam and Geraldine were talking to each other, cleared his throat. "I ordered the military to get in position," he said self-importantly. "If they're not coming out, we'll need to grab them before any shooting starts."

Harry Brooks gave a frowning look at Geraldine.

"All in good time," he told the chief superintendent. "Let's look at other options before we send in the Hereford lot."

***

It was frustrating for Sandy. He could see everything but hear nothing. But as soon as the cameraman arrived, he could start shooting the drama as it unfolded. He would be the only reporter giving a live account of what he hoped was going to be the most exciting end to a siege in London since the Iranian embassy siege in 1980. When he'd seen reruns of that during his journalist training course, he had envied and admired the immaculate reporting of the BBC's Kate Adie who delivered her lines live as similarly black-attired SAS soldiers swung into action to rescue hostages held inside the embassy by six Iranian gunmen.

Sandy looked anxiously at his watch. It was 1:20 a.m. He knew that it only needed one evacuated Gladstone Street resident to ring the papers or the BBC or ITV and within a short time hordes of camera crews would descend on the area. He would still have the advantage because he was inside the taped-off part of the road. But without a cameraman next to him, that advantage would vanish. Somehow, when he did arrive, Sandy would need to come up with a credible reason to persuade the police officer standing guard at the end of the road to let his colleague with the camera join him behind the SAS vehicle.

Suddenly, he saw a figure waving from behind the tape. Sandy walked quickly to the police officer, who was pushing back his colleague.

"Officer, sorry to bother you," Sandy began.

The police officer turned round and looked shocked.

"Who are you?" he demanded.

"Sandy Hall, I'm with Sky News, we're embedded with the military, special assignment. This is my colleague."

The police officer laughed. But the word "embedded" struck a chord. Even though he was a relatively inexperienced police constable, he had heard of the MoD's Green Book policy under which selected reporters could be deployed with military units on operations.

"Are you with the MoD?" he asked.

"Yes, kind of," Sandy replied. His colleague couldn't help smiling.

"Do you have special IDs?" The police officer was determined to stop the man with the camera entering the forbidden area if he could.

Sandy glanced back down the street and saw a lot of movement.

"Officer, I think we're needed. We have to get down there," he said, beckoning to his colleague.

They both showed their Sky News passes, and before the police officer could stop them, they were heading to the van and then on further because no one seemed to notice them. Apart from the police officer, who started to gesticulate but then gave up and continued looking outwards in case any other reporters claiming to be on embedded assignments turned up.

***

At the back door of number 16, Tim and George had been apprised of Sam's phone conversation with Maksim Popov. Both of them doubted Popov's claim that he and the other Russian were unarmed. The gunman Sam had tackled in Geraldine's bedroom had been carrying a 9mm pistol and had shot two police officers without hesitation. There was no way he and Popov were now in Geraldine's sitting room without a weapon between them.

The two Shadow Force members were joined by two SAS soldiers who had just climbed over the fence.

"Major!" one of them whispered loudly.

Tim was part of the SAS community even though he hadn't served in the regiment for several years, and he kept in touch with many of the older members of the elite unit.

"Sergeant Rob O'Brien," the soldier said.

"Ha, Rob! I didn't recognise you in your fancy gear," Tim whispered back.

They both grinned and shook hands. Tim introduced the soldiers to George. They nodded.

"Any sign?" Sergeant O'Brien asked, peering through the kitchen window.

"Nothing," Tim said.

The sergeant muttered into his mic.

"We're going in soon. Waiting for the order," he told Tim.

**

Downing Street had been adamant. There was to be no long siege. The timing of any military action was left to the police officer in charge of the operation, but the prime minister wanted it all wrapped up as quickly as possible. Well before dawn, when London would start to rumble into life. "No daytime spectacle" were his last words to Police Commissioner Mary Abelard.

Jonathan Ford's phone call to his press secretary at 12:30 a.m. had put it another way. He wanted the public to wake up to the news of the government's spectacular success at tracking down the suspected Russian assassins and their capture in a brilliantly executed military operation. SAS to the rescue, courtesy of the prime minister.

**

Maksim Popov and Mikhail Gerasimov were sitting in an isolated world of their own. They had never before experienced a situation of such hopelessness. And yet neither of them wanted to acquiesce to the demands of the big man down in the street.

Gerasimov had known who he was immediately. Even in the dim light of Gladstone Street, he had recognised the man who had burst into Geraldine Hammer's bedroom and tumbled him down onto the bed. Gerasimov had more respect for the big man than the rows of armed police waiting to shoot them. The big man's Russian was good.

Popov and Gerasimov didn't go near the window for fear of being targeted by snipers. They were trapped. They knew they couldn't try and escape via the back door. They had only one card to play. It was clear from what the big man had asked that their opponents in the street believed them to be armed. They didn't have a weapon between them, but it might give them an advantage. Or at least something to bargain with to give them time to think of a plan.

They were still on the sofa.

"We need an intermediary," Popov said.

"The embassy?" Gerasimov suggested.

"We can't ask the embassy to help," Popov said. "We're not exactly here on official business."

"But how else are we going to get out of here?"

"I have a man who could help."

"So ring him, Maksim Alexei."

Popov stood up and took two steps towards the window. The curtains were still drawn back. He kept to one side, the curtain covering most of his body. Before moving away, he saw that the big man was no longer standing by the steel barrier. There was a group of people on the other side of the road, standing close together as if in deep discussion. The big man was there. He couldn't be missed. Popov also caught sight of a tall woman with long blonde hair. She was also in the group.

He spotted one more thing. A police officer with a peaked cap, standing slightly away from the group, was on the phone and looking up. Not towards the window where Popov was trying to conceal himself in the curtain but higher up. Towards the roof.

"They're on the roof," Popov told Gerasimov.

Gerasimov jumped up.

"Make your call," he said.

As he spoke, Gerasimov raised his eyes to the ceiling and cocked his head to one side. He heard nothing.

Then the phone rang. Popov and Gerasimov stared at it but neither made a move to pick it up. It rang about fifteen times before Popov decided to answer it.

"Da," he said.

But it wasn't a voice in Russian the other end of the line. It was an English voice. A woman's voice.

"Is Jean-Paul there?"

It was Rebecca.

"Jean-Paul?" Popov swivelled round to look at Gerasimov.

"Please tell him it's Rebecca."

Popov held the phone down and covered it with his other hand.

"Rebecca?"

Gerasimov shook his head vigorously.

"You should speak to her."

"Nyet nyet nyet."

Popov held out the phone.

"Answer it," he ordered.

Gerasimov was angry. But he took the phone and slowly put it to his ear. "Eto kto?"

"Jean-Paul, is that you?" Rebecca asked.

"Eto kto?" Gerasimov repeated, asking who was speaking.

"It's Rebecca."

"Ukhodi!" Gerasimov told her to go away.

Popov interrupted.

"Radi Boga! Pogovorit s ney."

Now it was Popov who was angry. He swore at his colleague and ordered him to speak to her.

Rebecca was talking as Gerasimov returned the phone to his ear.

"What do you want, Rebecca?" he asked.

"So, Mr Dutchman, not even half-Dutch after all," Rebecca said.

"What do you want?" he asked again.

"Look, I don't care if you come down or not or what happens to you. But these people here are getting edgy, so use your common sense and get the hell out of the house and we can all go home."

"Home?"

"Well, not you, obviously."

"Rebecca, are you talking to me on your behalf or your new friends?"

"You were my friend not that long ago. What was that all about?"

The chief superintendent was looking so exasperated he moved in to try and seize the phone from Rebecca's hand. But Sam's mighty forearm came down between them.

"Leave her," he said.

"But this will just antagonise them," the police officer whispered. "It's totally contrary to police negotiation methods."

"Maybe, but it could work," Sam said.

He told Rebecca to continue.

"Well?" she asked her former flatmate.

"We *were* friends," Gerasimov said.

"So, for old friends' sake, you and your buddy should come down. I'll wait here."

Gerasimov said, "I'll talk to my colleague. Goodbye, Rebecca."

Sam nodded his head in approval. The chief superintendent raised his eyebrows as high as they could go. He then walked away to consult Harry Brooks.

"This is getting nowhere," he said to the commander. "I want to send in the military. They're ready at the back and ready on the roof."

Sandy and his cameraman filmed the whole sequence. A tall blonde in tight jeans talking to the two dangerous Russians. A great piece of drama. Sandy didn't tell his colleague he knew who the tall blonde was. But he was mesmerised by her courage. They'd picked up the odd word, but she spoke quietly, except for her opening question. "Jean-Paul, is that you?" Sandy felt a twinge of jealousy.

Rebecca, her role over, retreated.

"Well done, Rebecca," Gibson said.

Rose reached forward and gripped her elbow.

Seamus grinned his approval. "You told him," he said.

Rebecca caught a glimpse to her right of a raised TV camera pointing in her direction. She saw Sandy waving, and waved back. When this was all over, she thought to herself, she was going to forget all about Jean-Paul van Dijk and find out a lot more about the Sky News crime correspondent. It made her smile, although she realised how tense she was after her brief entry into the Gladstone Street drama.

Sam was now part of the small group whose views were being taken into account when deciding the next steps to be taken to bring the siege to an end swiftly. The key players were the chief superintendent and Harry Brooks because it was strictly police jurisdiction, but Geraldine, the SAS captain, Sam and Gibson were there to object, persuade or agree. Harry Brooks was now tending towards military action sooner rather than later. But Geraldine emphasised how important it was that both Russians came out from her house alive and remained alive. The message that had come down from Number 10 was that they were to be arrested, not killed. The prime minister wanted a trial. The SAS captain warned that nice tidy ends to sieges were rare. If the Russians were armed, the chances were that once his boys had crash-entered the house, someone was going to fire a gun. Survival of the

Russians could never be guaranteed. Sam urged a postponement of the military option to see if Rebecca's appeal bore fruit. But he agreed with the SAS captain. Once you employ specialised troops, he argued, you can't expect them to ask first and shoot later.

They all looked at Gibson.

"In my view," he said, "we should give the Russians twenty minutes to debate their options. It's already nearly three o'clock. They'll be tired and hungry—unless your fridge is packed with goodies, Geraldine?"

Geraldine shook her head.

"So," Gibson continued, "if we synchronise our watches, the captain's men should go in simultaneously from the back and roof at three fifteen. I have two of mine at the back door. They can be used as a blocking force in the event of something going wrong."

The chief superintendent, who was beginning to feel left out of the decision-making, commented, "So far they have made no attempt to phone anyone for help or advice or orders. But if they do, we're well set up to eavesdrop."

He looked at the SAS captain, who said, "My guys on the roof have fixed up a parabolic microphone dangling down near the window. We'll hear loud and clear. We've also had a camera peering into the front room. They are just sitting on the sofa. No sign of weapons but..."

"They must be armed," the chief superintendent said.

"Geraldine, what do you think?" Harry Brooks asked.

"Under normal circumstances, I would agree," she said. "But one of the Russians was on the run before he settled down on my sofa and the other was staying in a hotel before he arrived here. It's possible that neither brought weapons with them for their rendezvous.

"I doubt this was intended to be their moment for some sort of spectacular attack," she went on. "This was, as I said, a rendezvous point, one they clearly thought was going to be safe ground. Any further action planned would surely have been elsewhere. So, it's possible, but no guarantee, that we have two desperate Russian military intelligence officers sitting in my front room with not a gun between them."

Gibson had a thought. "It might be just a rendezvous. But why did they choose Geraldine's house? Perhaps they intended to wait for Geraldine to come home and have another go at her. In which case, one or both might well be armed."

"Either way," Harry Brooks said, "why don't we send in the captain's men now and get it all over and done with? If they're unarmed, it'll be a straightforward arrest."

"With the greatest respect," the captain chipped in, "in a perfect world that might be right. But what if they do have weapons or act in a way which makes my men believe they have weapons? That's when your nice, easy arrest situation gets muddy."

"Right. Three fifteen then, sixteen minutes to go," Harry Brooks said before the chief superintendent could say anything.

Everyone looked at their watches.

Chapter Thirty-Four

The Siege of Gladstone Street Comes to a Climax

Popov rang his special contact codenamed Venedict. It was after 3 a.m. but the phone was answered immediately.

"Eto Maksim. Izvini. Ty nuzhen mne zdes. Pryamo seychas."

"Kakovo chorta! Gde? Chto proiskhodit?"

"Gladstone Street, SE1. Nam nuzhen normalny posrednik."

"Nam?"

"Nas dvoye."

"Mne nuzhno vremya."

"Net vremeni. Seychas ili budet pozdno."

"Budu cherez tridtsat' minut."

"Ya popropuyu zaderzhat."

"Gde na ulitse?"

"Ty uvidish'."

The conversation was recorded by the three SAS soldiers on the roof, and by the night-duty analyst with D15 at GCHQ. The D15 analyst sent a Code Zero translated version to Petherwick at the Foreign Office and to the director of GCHQ.

"It's Maksim, I apologise. I need you here. Now."

"For God's sake. Where? What's happening?"

"Gladstone Street, SE1. We need a friendly intermediary."

"We?"

"Two of us."

"I'll need time."

"No time. It's now or too late."

"Thirty minutes. I'll be there."

"I'll try and delay till then."

"Where in the street?"

"You'll see."

The content of the phone call between the two Russians, Maksim Popov and an unknown person, was soon available to those who needed to know. Sam Cook in his capacity as sole Russian speaker in Gladstone Street told the gathering around him of the new development. Popov had rung someone he clearly knew well.

The chief superintendent was adamant that there should be no delay.

"We should stick to our timetable," he told everyone. "We don't need some bloody Russian official coming to tell us what to do."

"Wait a minute," Geraldine said. "Whoever this person is, he will be of interest to us."

"Meaning?" an exasperated chief superintendent asked.

"Meaning he will probably be a senior Russian intelligence official," Geraldine replied. "Someone we may not know about. I'd like to see who he is."

Harry Brooks was worried. "If we wait for him to arrive and then it all drags on for hours, we'll lose control. It'll end up a Russian publicity stunt."

Gibson agreed. So did the SAS captain. But Geraldine stuck to her guns.

"If he's here in thirty minutes it won't delay us for long," she said. "We'll allow him one phone call to persuade them to give up. If he fails we push him back to the other end of the road and the captain can get on with it. Then Moscow can't say we didn't try all diplomatic options, and I'll find out who this Russian is. If he persuades them to come down, we get our arrest without drama."

Harry Brooks nodded, looking at the chief superintendent, who was shaking his head vigorously.

"Ok," Brooks said. "I can't say I like it, Geraldine. But let's wait until he gets here. We'll give him ten minutes. That's it. Then he can see for himself what we do to get justice in this country. I don't really care what Moscow thinks."

Sam looked admiringly at Geraldine. She had won her argument. She was a feisty lady and Sam liked her. More than he was prepared to think about right then. But he feared she was way out of his league. He then realised Geraldine was looking at him and smiling. He smiled but looked away quickly.

Before he could contemplate what was going on in his head, the phone in Sam's hand rang. Sam had given the number to Popov with instructions to call as soon as he and his fellow Russian had decided what to do.

Popov spoke in English for the first time. Sam thought this was a positive move, possibly indicating a potential willingness to bring the siege to an end.

"We need more time. A mediator is coming from the embassy."

Sam told Harry Brooks, the chief superintendent, the SAS captain and Geraldine, who were all standing close to him, what Popov had just said.

"Play hardball," Geraldine said. "Tell him we don't need a mediator."

Sam looked surprised, especially after what had been discussed only two minutes earlier. Brooks nodded his agreement.

"It's too late for mediation," Sam told Popov. "This is not some diplomatic cocktail party. You need to come down now. You have five minutes."

The chief superintendent, who had stepped forward, appeared delighted. He glanced at the SAS captain, whose face was expressionless although his eyes narrowed and he spoke quickly into his mic.

"Get ready for the go," he whispered.

Popov was taken aback by Sam's brusque tone.

"The mediator will be here in twenty minutes," he said to Sam. "I thought the British justice system was all about fair play."

"You'll get your fair play if you come out, both of you, with your hands up," Sam replied.

"You have men on the roof, is this part of your little game?" Popov asked.

"There is no game," Sam said. "Just a simple equation. You come out, you live."

Popov laughed. "I've seen too many Hollywood movies," he said. "I have no wish to do a Butch Cassidy and Sundance Kid."

Sam looked at Geraldine and the two police officers.

"What?" Geraldine asked.

"He said he doesn't want to end up like Paul Newman and Robert Redford in Butch Cassidy."

The chief superintendent had had enough. "He's taking the piss, sorry for my French," he said, turning to Geraldine.

"It's actually a good sign," she said. "Russians do have a sense of humour. Now you can tell him we will wait for the mediator."

Sam looked surprised for the second time. The chief superintendent exploded, blowing out his cheeks and glaring at Geraldine.

Brooks was about to say something when Sam lifted the phone to his ear.

"That can all be avoided if you do as I say," he told Popov. "But to demonstrate the fair play you seem so interested in, we will allow you your mediator but on a strictly limited timetable."

"Spasibo," Popov replied. The line went dead.

The previously agreed 3:15 a.m. time for action had come and gone. Thirty-five police officers, half of them armed, four paramedics in two ambulances and six members of the SAS could do nothing but wait.

Sandy had no knowledge of the Russian mediator on his way and no inkling of what the group of people had been talking so earnestly about. But his cameraman had been taking shots of the three soldiers on the roof who had been fixing what looked like an abseiling rope round a chimney pot. Basic Tarzan stuff, he thought, and then realised that would be a great intro to his story once the SAS went in to end the siege. At least, he hoped the SAS would be going in.

He and his cameraman had stayed well back in the shadows. Everyone else in the street was so focused on the house and the anticipation of dramatic action at any moment that, by a sheer miracle, the Sky News team was left alone. Only Rebecca had noticed Sandy and his colleague coming forward from the end of the street, and Geraldine had forgotten about the man with the familiar face she had seen behind the SAS van.

Popov and Gerasimov also had nothing to do but wait. Popov was sure, Gerasimov less so, that the British would keep to their side of the deal and hold off on any form of offensive action until after their intermediary had arrived. Popov had no great expectation that Venedict would come up with a solution different from the one outlined by the big man down below. Neither he nor Gerasimov had any illusions about the way it was all going to end. However astute and cunning Venedict might be, the chances of them sitting comfortably on a flight back to Moscow by the end of the new day were zero. Or nul, as they would say.

The Russian intermediary arrived at the taped-off end of Gladstone Street at 3:48 a.m. He introduced himself to the police officer, who was still looking out for a media avalanche. The police officer, who for some inexplicable reason had not been informed of the impending arrival of a third Russian, folded his arms and barred the way. Harry Brooks hurried down the street towards them.

"It's ok," he told the indignant policeman. "Let him through."

The Russian stepped under the tape raised reluctantly by the policeman. Venedict was quite short, no more than five foot five. He was bald and barrel-chested and was wearing a smart suit with a white shirt but no tie. Very Putin, Brooks thought.

"You are?" he asked.

"I am political counsellor at the embassy," the Russian replied.

"Name?"

"Kostya Oblonsky."

"Come this way, Mr Oblonsky," Brooks said.

They approached the key players in the drama. Brooks introduced the Russian visitor but didn't identify any of them to him. Oblonsky put his hand forward, but no one moved to shake it. He was a whole foot and three inches shorter than Sam Cook and looked up at him like a child to an adult.

Geraldine tried not to show her interest in the short, barrel-chested Russian. She recognised him immediately. He had been on her list of Russian intelligence officer suspects but somehow he had evaded all MI5's attempts to pin him down as an SVR or GRU member working undercover. She was delighted that her instincts about the Russian "diplomat" had been correct. Kostya Oblonsky, she thought, your time here in London is up.

Sam dialled Geraldine's home number and handed the phone to Oblonsky, who immediately moved away from the group. He spoke quietly for five minutes and then walked back, handing the phone to Sam.

They all waited for him to speak. Oblonsky gave the air of being a man who knew his business. He hunched his shoulders and held his head as high as he could, stretching his neck. It was both arrogant and an implicit acceptance that as a short man he needed to make up for it by adopting a threatening, imposing physical presence. Yet, he seemed nervous at the same time. He knew who the attractive woman with auburn hair was. He didn't know anyone else in the group.

Oblonsky spoke English but with a jarring, heavy accent. His word selection seemed to have come from an outdated teach-yourself-English textbook.

"The two gentlemen are being avoidably oppressed by this exhibition of British aggression," he said.

"The two gentlemen, as you call them, are Russian military intelligence officers wanted for outrageous criminal acts on our streets," Geraldine told him.

Oblonsky shrugged. "I know not a thing about who they are, but I can tell you they are not who you say they are," he replied.

The chief superintendent muttered under his breath but loud enough for all to hear, including Oblonsky, "This is a waste of time."

Oblonsky ignored him. "If you would extricate all these policemen," he said, pulling his shoulders back, "I will go in and speak to them and be escorting them to a safe place. This is agreed."

"Nothing's agreed," the chief superintendent muttered as loudly as before.

"I am an intermediator," Oblonsky continued.

"You're from the Russian embassy, right?" Brooks asked.

"I am here in a private capability," Oblonsky said. "The embassy is closed at this dark hour."

"Mr Oblonsky, as far as we're concerned you are here as a representative of the Russian embassy and the Russian government," Geraldine said. "It sounds like your two gentlemen are refusing to come out as we requested. In which case, your role is over."

"There is no question of you going into the house," Brooks added. "We wouldn't want to put you in any danger."

Oblonsky chortled, his shoulders shaking. "Why would I be in danger?" he asked. "The two gentlemen are just sitting as innocents in this house, are they not?"

Oblonsky seemed to be enjoying himself. He thought he was getting the upper hand.

"This house, Mr Oblonsky, does not belong to them, as you well know," Geraldine said. "They are trespassing."

"Ah, madam," the Russian said pompously, "trespassing is of course a serious criminal activity. In Moscow too."

The chief superintendent had had enough.

"Sir, this is not about trespassing," he said to Oblonsky, glancing at Geraldine as he emphasised the word. "It's obvious to me at least that you are just delaying things. If your two colleagues are not prepared to come out, then your presence is no longer helpful."

The police officer raised his eyebrows at Harry Brooks, who nodded his approval.

However, Oblonsky had one more try.

"I do not wishing to be dogmatic but under the Vienna Convention the two gentlemen who are, yes, Russian nationalities, are enjoying diplomatic immunity and therefore you have no right to interfere with their liberties."

"Thank you, Mr Oblonsky," Brooks said. "We have taken your interesting version of events into account and would appreciate it if you would please leave the area. I will get a police officer to escort you back to your car."

Oblonsky looked genuinely astonished and shot the harshest glare he could summon in the direction of Geraldine Hammer, the bane of his life and the life of all Russian spies left in the UK after her purge.

He stood his ground but two police officers, one armed with a Heckler & Koch submachine gun, took him by the elbows and guided him away down the street. The group watched him climb into the car and waited until it had moved off.

The group then retreated behind the armed police officers, and the chief superintendent gave two orders into his mic. The SAS captain put his thumbs up and whispered into his own mic.

"This is Sierra Echo, go!" he said.

At the same time, the floodlights, which had sat dormant in position for an hour were switched on, illuminating the house like it had been hit by a massive explosion.

The three black-clad SAS soldiers on the roof swung out and down like bungee jumpers. But instead of hurtling to the ground, their bodies jerked for the briefest of seconds as the separated ropes stopped in mid-air and they crashed backwards through the glass of Geraldine's first-floor front room. Smoke poured through the broken window as each soldier hurled stun grenades into the room, setting off blinding flashes of light.

Unseen by Sandy and his colleague, who was so excited he nearly dropped his camera, the two SAS soldiers at the back simultaneously burst through the back door and ran up the stairs. No shots were fired. The two Russians were unharmed but were lying like corpses on the sofa, semi-conscious from the stun-grenade blasts. Geraldine's expensively decorated sitting room was filled with smoke. Her mother's mirror with the dragons and serpents was still on the wall and appeared to be unscathed.

Popov and Gerasimov began to stir after a few minutes. Gerasimov rubbed his head and tried to get up. But the five SAS soldiers all moved at the same time, pointing their semi-automatic machine guns at his chest. Popov opened his eyes, turned his head towards Gerasimov and gave the slightest of shrugs in his direction. The combination of glaring light from outside and the lingering white smoke from the stun grenades had created an eerie atmosphere.

Two of the SAS soldiers searched for guns while the other three kept Popov and Gerasimov covered. Nothing was found.

Sergeant Rob O'Brien, former colleague of Major Tim Plews, was the first SAS soldier to speak.

"Gentlemen, stand up and put your hands behind your head," he said.

Popov and Gerasimov did as they were ordered, albeit unsteadily.

O'Brien and one other SAS soldier snapped plastic handcuffs round their wrists. They were told to move forward slowly.

At that moment, Tim and George appeared, took one look at the scene in front of them and both gave a thumbs-up before returning downstairs and out of the back door.

Popov and Gerasimov, surrounded by the five SAS soldiers, made their way slowly down the stairs.

Sergeant O'Brien spoke into his mic. "Coming out. All good."

Outside, the SAS captain turned to Harry Brooks. "They're coming out. No problems."

The pure theatre could not have been more dramatic. The appearance of five SAS men in the front doorway, holding up the two Russians as they stumbled down the steps with their hands tied behind their heads, smoke billowing from the smashed windows on the first floor, became the enduring image that appeared on the front pages of every newspaper, courtesy of Sandy's cameraman.

It was Sandy's greatest scoop.

Chapter Thirty-Five
The Case against the Two Russians

The Met Police were in a panic. The prime minister had personally thanked Dame Mary Abelard, the Commissioner, for the successful end to Operation Buster. Home Secretary Lawrence Fenwick appeared on every TV news bulletin praising the work of the Met Police, MI5 and the army. He said it was a fine example of a joint operation. The hunt for the suspected Russian agents was over. The two Russian nationals had been medically assessed and were now being held in police custody. Fenwick announced that the threat level had been lowered. Every newspaper headline was positive.

For the SAS, it was another glory day as far as opinion writers and editorials were concerned. There was no mention of an organisation called Shadow Force. Sandy Hall was the only reporter who gave an account of a very large man who had been used as a Russian speaker to talk to the suspects inside the house in Gladstone Street, but he had no reason to suggest or speculate that he might have been part of some unknown group. He referred to him as a police interpreter.

It was all good news. There was a sense of relief everywhere.

However, there was one ingredient missing from the national euphoria. Evidence. The prosecutable criminal case against the two Russians was alarmingly thin. There was no forensic evidence to tie either of them to the fatal shootings of the police officers in Gladstone Street. The CCTV images, which had been gathered from at least a dozen locations, from the moment when the main suspect jumped out of the fresh food van he had hijacked after the shootings to the hooded figure seen in the area outside MI5's regional office in Birmingham, were so obscured no prosecutor could rely on them. Above all, there were no weapons. No gun to link to the shootings in Gladstone Street, nothing in Geraldine's house or Rebecca's flat that could be presented as prima facie evidence against one or both of the Russian military intelligence officers.

Harry Brooks had spent an hour questioning Rebecca. He had found her helpful and full of interesting personal information about the man she called Jean-Paul van Dijk. She had spoken of the heavy holdall, the bizarre brown and green tweed suit and pipe, the plastic box hidden in the toilet cistern and his supposed business meetings. But no holdall had been found. There was no brown and green tweed suit hanging in his cupboard in the Travelodge, and no sign of a pipe. The security guard at the safe deposit company in St James's Street had been questioned on numerous occasions. But, for reasons that were obvious even to the frustrated police officers who spoke to him, he had no idea what the mysterious holdall had contained. He repeated on each occasion he was questioned that it was his professional conclusion at the time that the holdall was heavy because of the way the man's right shoulder had sloped downwards. The police were sick of hearing about his Sherlock Holmes theories.

Neither Russian gave his real name. Maksim Popov insisted he was called Sergei Preobrazhensky. A search of his hotel room at the Rubens uncovered his passport in that name. His wife and son were taken into custody and questioned but were released after twenty-four hours and ordered to leave the country. Rebecca's Jean-Paul van Dijk and Geraldine's Lucas Meyer stuck to his story that he was called Dragomir Chudov. His passport in that name was taken from his jacket, along with £2,000 in twenty-pound notes. There was nothing to indicate his real name.

When all the material the police had collected was put together in a file and passed to the Crown Prosecution Service, Harry Brooks knew that it would fail the basic requirements for a trial on any charge that related to murder, attempted murder, conspiracy to murder, espionage or threat to life. On the face of it, Preobrazhensky and Chudov, suspected of being, respectively, the commander and senior member of the Russian sabotage and assassination group Unit Zero, were guilty of breaking and entering, damage to property, trespassing and travelling on false passports. There was no link of any kind between either of them and former Corporal Joseph Paine, now awaiting trial at the Old Bailey on charges of attempted murder, grievous bodily harm and possession of a Glock pistol.

Separately, MI5 began an internal investigation that covered a number of key questions arising from the failure to pinpoint the Russian responsible for shooting the two police officers and confronting Geraldine Hammer in her bedroom; the circumstances that led to Maksim Popov leaving the Rubens Hotel without being spotted by the eight-man surveillance team; and the confusion about the identity of the Unit Zero suspect roaming the streets of London. Clearly, MI6's conclusion that it was Major-General Maksim Popov, selected to carry out what was seen as a revenge mission against MI5, had diverted attention away from other possible suspects. Too much of the early stages of the joint police/MI5 investigation had been taken up with hunting for a man with bushy eyebrows.

There was one other worrying aspect of the internal inquiry. How did the Russians know the identity of MI5's director of counter-espionage, and how did they acquire her address?

Joseph Paine had known where and when to wait for Geraldine's car on that fateful morning on 1st July. How was he so sure that she would be arriving at that particular time? Was there any possibility there could be a mole? If so, was the mole working inside MI5 itself? It was a stunning question that had to be answered. Quickly.

***

Two weeks after the siege of Gladstone Street, two couples, unbeknown to each other, were sitting on separate floors of a French restaurant, Mon Plaisir in Monmouth Street, central London. Both couples were engaged in exactly the same ritual. Getting to know each other, a little nervously. Plenty of laughter and embarrassed looks. On the first floor near the front window, Rebecca and Sandy were grinning at each other, sharing the dramatic experience of Gladstone Street. Occasionally, Sandy or Rebecca would reach across the table and touch the other's hand to emphasise a point as they recalled the long night together.

Arriving later for lunch, Geraldine and Sam were shown to a table at the back of the restaurant on the ground floor. To reach the table, Sam had to bend almost double to avoid slamming his head against the low ceiling of the archway leading into the area at the back. Geraldine turned at that moment and laughed. He grinned as he slowly returned himself to his full height. He held the chair for her to sit down.

Geraldine looked immaculate. She was wearing a tailored, figure-hugging dark blue jacket and matching knee-length skirt, a simple but expensive white blouse and an opal and moonstone necklace. Her auburn hair, recently cut, was set in waves and looked soft around her face. Sam was wearing a navy blue suit with a grey polo-neck woollen jumper. He sat down in front of her, and even though he tried to hunch down, he still towered above her at the small table. The back of his head hit a painting on the wall behind him.

"Sorry," he said without any reason. He was more nervous than she was.

Geraldine gave him a reassuring smile.

"You don't need to apologise about your size, Sam," she laughed. "I was very grateful for it in my house."

She nearly said bedroom, but suddenly that word seemed full of possibilities which neither she nor Sam were anywhere near ready to contemplate.

An hour and a half later, Rebecca, as ever in jeans with smart red high-heels, and Sandy, in a slightly creased charcoal grey suit, came down the stairs and spotted the couple laughing at a table in the back room. Rebecca walked towards them and pulled Sandy along with her.

"Hey, you guys," she said.

Geraldine, who had her back to them, looked round and immediately smiled. Sam looked instantly embarrassed.

"Don't get up," Rebecca joked. "Great to see you. Together."

Rebecca held Sandy's arm.

"Sandy, this is, er, Geraldine and Sam. Friends of mine. Geraldine and Sam, this is Sandy." She grinned broadly.

Sandy was astonished. He recognised them both. And they both recognised him.

"Nice to meet you, Sandy," Geraldine said. Sam just nodded and smiled.

"I'll leave you two lovebirds to it," said Rebecca, flicking her long blonde hair off her face. "Have fun. Geraldine, we must meet up again. Soon?"

"Sure," Geraldine replied.

Rebecca giggled and, still holding Sandy's arm, walked off to the front of the restaurant. Both she and Sandy also had to bend down in the archway. Geraldine was the only one who had sailed through without having to duck.

After they left Mon Plaisir and turned down Monmouth Street, Sandy took Rebecca's hand and looked at her to gauge her approval. She smiled at him and swung their joined hands in the air.

***

The same day, at 4:30 p.m., the prime minister received a phone call from the attorney general. The news he imparted was bleak. The Crown Prosecution Service had examined all the evidence that the police and MI5 had collated and had concluded that there were insufficient grounds for charging either of the Russians with serious offences. They could be charged with breaking and entering, but travelling on a false passport would require extensive police investigation and would depend to a certain extent on the cooperation of the Russian authorities, the likelihood of which was judged to be remote. The director of public prosecutions said a charge of breaking and entering would undoubtedly lead to a conviction. But the attorney general told Jonathan Ford it was his advice, both as the government's top lawyer and as a member of the cabinet, that to charge the two Russians with such a lowly offence as breaking and entering when one of them was suspected of being responsible for two fatal shootings and the bomb explosion in Birmingham would be embarrassing for the government.

It was his recommendation, after consultation with Elizabeth Gantry, the foreign secretary, and Lawrence Fenwick, home secretary, that the two Russians be deported forthwith.

The prime minister rarely swore. But after putting the phone down, he said "bugger" so loudly that his private secretary came rushing into the room, fearing some dire emergency. He waved her away.

His grand plan had failed. He had wanted above all else to teach Moscow a lesson. To put the Kremlin under the spotlight by holding a trial at the world's most famous criminal court and demonstrating through brilliant legal argument and a mass of incriminating evidence that the United Kingdom had caught two of their assassins red-handed and sent them to prison for the rest of their lives. He didn't know whether the Kremlin establishment would care about the fate of these two particular individuals, but a high-profile trial reported on by the world's media, detailing how the British authorities had outsmarted Moscow's secret agents? That, surely, would not be welcomed by the Russian leadership and might just make them think twice before authorising another hit squad to target Moscow's perceived enemies overseas.

The prime minister called in the cabinet secretary and asked him to arrange for Sir Edward Farthing and George Trench to come and see him at 6 p.m. As an afterthought, he said he would also like Geraldine Hammer to attend.

All three arrived outside the black front door of Number 10 at five minutes before the hour and were ushered into the hall with its chequered floor. The cabinet secretary greeted them and led the way into the White Drawing Room, an elegant room where Ford normally met world leaders. He wasn't trying to impress his visitors; he just wanted them to appreciate that despite the failure to prosecute the two arrested Russian agents, he, as prime minister, would not be bowed by the Kremlin's malevolence. The White Drawing Room always made him feel proud of his country and its history and traditions. Two Russian agents escaping the justice they deserved wasn't going to change that.

Ford was gazing at a picture by J.M.W. Turner above the fireplace when his visitors entered.

He shook their hands and they sat down.

"This is not the day of celebration I had hoped for," the prime minister said.

Farthing, Trench and Geraldine, sitting in a semi-circle in front of him, looked uncomfortable.

"However, I am satisfied we did everything possible to stop these Russian suspects from carrying out further atrocities," Ford said. "It is unfortunate to say the least, especially for you, Dr Hammer, that we are now in a position where all we can do is send them home. You understand, of course, that it would be humiliating for us to charge them with some minor offence."

All three nodded their heads.

"I have to say that it seems extraordinary to me that neither of these Russians had any weapons or any other form of military or espionage equipment when they were detained," he went on. "It's as if they were enjoying a quiet time together in Dr Hammer's sitting room without a care in the world. Absolutely bizarre. As a result we have nothing to throw at them. The holdall, if it ever existed, has vanished into thin air."

No one interrupted. The prime minister was in a contemplative mood.

"But I haven't called you in to discuss what went wrong," he said. "That's a matter that will have to be dealt with at the appropriate time by the appropriate authorities. No, my reason for asking you here is this. How do you think Moscow will react when we deport these two agents? Will they laugh at us? Will they ignore it? Or will they take lessons from it?"

The chief of the secret intelligence service was the first to speak.

"Personally, prime minister, I think Moscow will condemn the action we take," Sir Edward Farthing said. "Russia's state media have already run official denials of any connection between the two agents and the Russian government. But at the same time, the careers of Maksim Popov and the other agent, whose identity we are still trying to confirm, will be over. They will be viewed as failures and could face punishment. We are, by the way, pretty sure that the other agent is Lieutenant-Colonel Mikhail Gerasimov, whom you will remember we named as a possible member of Unit Zero from the very beginning."

Geraldine waited for her boss to make his contribution.

"Prime minister, it's difficult to know these days how Moscow will respond," the head of MI5 said. "But hopefully, deportation of two of their top agents will be seen as a slap in the face. If I'm right, I think it unlikely that they will, as it were, try again to mount some sort of revenge mission in the UK. At least not in the foreseeable future."

"Thank you, C, thank you, DG. Dr Hammer, do you have anything you wish to add?" the prime minister asked, turning his attention to the only person in the room who had been directly targeted by the Russians.

"Returning them both to their mother country without a scratch on them might be seen as a victory in Moscow," Geraldine said. "But as DG said, there's no way of knowing for sure. Either way, I doubt we will be seeing a return to these shores of Maksim Popov or Mikhail Gerasimov, if that's his name."

She then added, "Or Kostya Oblonsky, come to that. The foreign secretary's decision to expel him back to Moscow was definitely the right one in my view. Despite his bonhomie outside my house on the night of the siege, he is a nasty piece of work."

"Well, thank you for your thoughts," the prime minister said. "Hopefully we can all get back to some sort of normality. And Dr Hammer, I hope you have recovered totally from your horrible experience. At least we can expect a conviction in your case. Joseph Paine will surely go down for life. The attorney general seems confident of the result."

"Thank you, Prime Minister, I am well," Geraldine said.

Sir Edward Farthing coughed.

"C?"

Ford was familiar with Sir Edward's coughing routine. He had something unwelcome to add.

"I fear the result of the trial of Joseph Paine may run into difficulties," he said, folding his hands in his lap. "The Shadow Force issue could be an obstacle."

"Nonsense," Ford said. "That may well come up. His lawyer has indicated as much. But anything like that will be dealt with in camera. The attorney general says the judge for the trial is a stubborn individual with a reputation for dismissing fanciful claims by defendants, especially those who are facing long imprisonment."

"Fanciful, Prime Minister?" Sir Edward said, raising his eyebrows.

Jonathan Ford stared at the chief of the secret intelligence service and made a decision. It was time for a new C.

Chapter Thirty-Six

Popov and Gerasimov Return to Moscow to an Uncertain Future

The two Russian military intelligence agents were escorted by armed police across the tarmac to the aircraft steps for their one-way flight to Moscow on Aeroflot. Gerasimov was carrying his smart leather suitcase. At the gangway, they were handed over to an official from the Russian embassy who just gestured them into the plane and watched as they climbed the steps. The official said nothing to the two police officers. The officers stood for a few minutes looking up at the plane for no particular reason and then headed back to the terminal.

Popov and Gerasimov sat in the front seats of business class. Neither spoke.

***

The following morning, at 7 a.m., a railway employee at Victoria Station arrived for his day shift at the left luggage office. After dealing with two early customers, he went through the register of unclaimed luggage and noticed that one bag had been held in storage for nearly a month. According to the register, the customer had paid for a week. It wasn't unusual for people to return well after their allotted time, but a month seemed out of the ordinary. He stood up and walked slowly to the racks behind him. The bag, numbered 354, was on the top rack.

The top rack was full. Every kind of bag was slotted in tight, one against another. Three rows. He knew the abandoned bag would be at the back, and he cursed. He went to get a step ladder. Once up on the top rung, he lifted a couple of the bags in the front row and placed them on the floor. He did the same with the row behind. The bag in front of him in the back row was a pink suitcase. But it wasn't the right number. He moved more bags from the front and second rows until finally, he spotted the bag with the number 354 on a label tied to the handles. It was a holdall.

He tried to move it, but it was heavy. He needed to get another four bags out of the way before he could get sufficient leverage to pull the holdall towards him and off the top shelf. He nearly fell backwards off the step ladder when he eased it from the rack. He swore again. He gingerly climbed down, struggling to keep his balance with the holdall in his right hand. He put the bag down on the floor and got his breath back. He put the step ladder away and heaved up the holdall onto the reception desk.

He was not the staff member who had signed in the holdall, and no one had mentioned anything to him about a long-forgotten piece of luggage. The employee was not trained in how to deal with suspicious bags, but he felt instinctively that the holdall fell into that category. The station was no longer filled with armed police officers, but two Transport Police officers whom he knew reasonably well were standing together about fifty yards away, watching the early commuters coming through the gates. He waved at them. At first they didn't see him. But then one of them noticed and nudged his companion. They came over.

"What's up, mate?" one of them asked.

"Maybe nothing," the employee said, "but this holdall has been here for about a month and it's quite heavy."

The Transport Police officers looked at the holdall but didn't touch it.

"Any idea who left it?" one asked.

"No, sorry, it was signed in for a week," the employee said.

One of the police officers spoke into his mic.

"You touched it?" the other officer asked.

"Er, well, yeah. I had to get it down, didn't I?"

Within fifteen minutes, a black police van came to a halt outside the station and half a dozen police officers walked smartly into the concourse and straight to the left luggage office. They told the railway employee, somewhat melodramatically, to stand back as they examined the lock on the holdall. One of the police officers put protective gloves on and lifted the holdall off the front desk. They didn't attempt to open it. The employee was asked a mass of questions, none of which he could answer, other than to confirm that the holdall had been at the back on the top rack for about a month and that for reasons he couldn't explain it hadn't been noticed until now. And no, he had no idea who had left it in the care of the left luggage office for so long.

The half dozen police officers looked at each other in astonishment. Unlike the railway employee, they all knew that a holdall connected to the Russian affair was missing. They also all knew that what the holdall contained might produce crucial evidence to incriminate the two Russians.

The name on the label was Hammer. It meant nothing to the police officers.

The holdall was taken from the left luggage office and driven with siren blaring to Scotland Yard, where it was handed over to the Met's Counter-Terrorism Command. Harry Brooks called the army bomb squad, and within half an hour the holdall was carried back out of Scotland Yard and placed gently inside an armoured vehicle which was then driven off to Chelsea Barracks.

The holdall was sitting in the middle of the large parade ground at the barracks when a team of bomb disposal experts arrived in full protective gear.

Under normal circumstances, a controlled explosion would have taken place, irreparably damaging the holdall and its contents. But under instructions from Commander Brooks, that wouldn't be happening today. The contents of the holdall were of vital interest and had to be preserved at all costs. A robot bomb sniffer produced negative results. There was something metallic inside but nothing to suggest wiring or explosive material.

Two army bomb disposal specialists approached the holdall. They examined the lock. It was nothing fancy. They inserted a thin screwdriver device and the lock sprung up. They pulled back the sides of the holdall and bent in to look. One of the bomb disposal soldiers went on one knee and, with his protective glove, felt around the inside, pushing various clothing items to one side to reveal the heaviest objects at the bottom. The soldier stood up and looked across the parade ground at a group of police officers waiting nervously under an archway. He attempted to do a thumbs-up, but with the heavy glove enfolding his whole hand like a boxing glove it looked more like a wave.

When Harry Brooks was told of the contents on the phone, he exploded in frustration and anger. Later he received an email listing everything that had been found:

- One brown and green tweed suit, trousers and jacket.
- Two crumpled shirts, white.
- Three pairs of blue socks, not fresh.
- Four boxer shorts, not fresh.

- One pipe. No tobacco smell.
- One broad-brimmed hat.
- One balaclava, black.
- Four passports in the names of Lucas Meyer, Jean-Paul van Dijk, John Adams and Mikhail Gerasimov.
- One Russian PP-90-01 Kedr submachine gun with single box magazine, all rounds intact.
- One MP-443 Grach pistol with two rounds missing.
- Three business cards in the name of IT Group Holdings.

***

Moscow

Dressed in freshly laundered army uniforms and polished shoes, Major-General Maksim Popov and Lieutenant-Colonel Mikhail Gerasimov arrived at the front entrance of the GRU Aquarium headquarters at Khodynka airfield and showed their identity passes. Their arrival was spotted and noted by the MI6 agent on watch duty.

The two men had been allowed a night's sleep before confronting their fate at the hands of the four generals. As they walked down the corridor towards the room where the generals were waiting for them, Gerasimov turned to Popov.

"I'm thinking of resigning. Finishing with this business," he said.

"Don't be hasty," Popov advised. "See what they have to say first."

"Can't be good. For either of us."

They knocked on the door and entered the room. The same four generals who had sent Popov on his ill-fated mission to London were sitting in their usual places. Their Russian army hats were, as before, perched neatly in a row on brass hooks.

Popov and Gerasimov stayed where they were. They stood by the door waiting to be called forward. For a few seconds nothing happened. Then all four generals, as if they had been counting under their breath, stood up and started to clap. Slowly at first and then more rapidly and with increasing enthusiasm. One of the generals beckoned to Popov and Gerasimov to approach. They sat down once the generals had stopped clapping. The generals sat down in unison. Popov and Gerasimov tried not to show either surprise or relief.

"Well, Maksim Alexei and Mikhail Nikolayev," the oldest of the generals said with a smile, "you have returned in triumph. The British have been humiliated. Your work is done. We have been authorised to congratulate you. You gave us a spectacle of your own making. This is in the finest traditions of Glavnoje Razvedyvatel'noje Upravlenije." He was referring to GRU.

"Generals, thank you," Popov replied formally.

"You will want time, of course, with your families," the same general went on. "But then we have a new mission for you."

Popov quickly glanced at Gerasimov and slightly raised his regrowing bushy eyebrows. Gerasimov kept quiet.

"Yes, General, thank you," Popov replied.

The meeting appeared to be at an end. But two of the other generals started speaking at the same time. One waved the other on to go first.

"Mikhail Nikolayev," the general said. "I have one question for you."

"Yes, General?" Gerasimov said.

"You seem to have a propensity for women," the general said. "Can I assume that this propensity is born of a desire to fulfil your mission at all costs, whatever the sacrifice?"

"Yes, General, indeed, General," Gerasimov replied with not a hint of a smile.

"I am relieved to hear it, Mikhail Nikolayev," the general said, and sat back.

The other general who had wanted to speak leaned forward.

"Maksim Alexei," he said. "I wonder if you had time to purchase the jar of raspberry jam?"

Popov looked concerned.

"General, many apologies," he replied. "It was an aspect of my mission to London which I am afraid I failed to carry out. I hope you will understand and forgive me this one lapse."

"Oh yes, Maksim Alexei," the general replied, with a chortle. "On this occasion I think I can forgive you."

"Thank you, General," Popov said.

"Perhaps next time," the general said.

Chapter Thirty-Seven
Shadow Force Survives. So Does the Mole

Former Corporal Joseph Paine of the Royal Logistic Corps was found guilty at the Old Bailey of attempted murder, possession of a Glock pistol and grievous bodily harm. He was sentenced to life imprisonment. The first and final days of the eight-day trial were open to the press and public. The intervening six days were held in camera after the judge agreed with the prosecution's argument that the case involved national security and the lives of key witnesses were at stake.

Sandy was at the court for the final day. From the press box, he saw Edward Claridge sitting behind Paine's barrister.

After the judge had sentenced Paine, Claridge looked in the direction of the press box and caught Sandy's eye. He indicated with a jerk of his head that he wanted to see him outside the courtroom. Sandy was in a rush—he had to do a live report in twenty minutes—but perhaps Claridge might have something he could use in the report, provided it didn't break the restrictive legal rules laid down by the court. He couldn't report anything which might be viewed by the judge as contempt of court.

Sandy left the Old Bailey's Court Number One and looked for the lawyer. He was standing by the lifts.

"Ed, hi," Sandy said. "I've only got a few minutes."

"You may have only a few minutes but my client has got at least fifteen years," Claridge said pompously.

"Ed, I'm sorry but I am limited in what I can say, as you know," Sandy replied. "What we were talking about before I assume came up while the court was in camera and so I can't report on it."

"The Crown denied everything," Claridge said. "No secret organisation involved in the grabbing of my client off the streets, no huge man nearly suffocating him in the back of a Land Rover, no secret interrogation in a farmhouse in Oxfordshire with the same huge man threatening his life, no deliberate tipping off of the police when they had finished with him and let him escape. All lies, they said."

Sandy had heard it all before. Or nearly all of it. There was one word that stood out. One word which the lawyer hadn't used before, and it made Sandy look at him with new interest.

"Did you say huge man?" he asked.

"Yeah, I told you before, a big bloke was the one who grabbed my client and put his arm around his neck till he nearly died."

"But now you're saying huge. Which was it?"

Claridge looked confused.

"Big, huge, what does it matter? He was really big, my client said."

"How big?"

Claridge looked exasperated. "I don't know, I don't remember. Actually, yes I do. He said at one point the bloke looked like he was seven feet tall. So not just big but enormous. That's why he nearly suffocated in the back of the car and later at the farm under interrogation."

Sandy was staring at him as if he had said something new and extraordinary.

"What?" Claridge asked.

"I just thought of something," Sandy replied. "But, Ed, I'm sorry I have to dash or I'm going to miss my deadline."

He shook the lawyer's hand and turned away towards the stairs. He was about to run down when he stopped and went back to the lawyer, still standing by the lifts.

"Paine didn't say what they were called did he?" he asked.

"What, who, you mean the people who grabbed him?"

"Yeah."

"No, they never used any names."

"Not the huge man?"

"No, none of them."

"And they never said they were police or military or anything else?"

"No."

"Ok, thanks. Bye."

Now he knew for certain who the huge man was, Sandy ran back to the stairs and took the steps two at a time.

Later, he had plans to meet Rebecca. He was fairly sure he was going to ask her to move in with him but he had a feeling she would turn him down. Not because they didn't like each other a lot. More than a lot. But because she was fiercely independent and she loved her flat, despite the police invasion and the memories she would always have of sharing it briefly with a muscular Russian who'd killed two police officers and intimidated her new friend, Geraldine Hammer.

Sandy was also used to his independence. He thought he could live with Rebecca and imagined it, especially when he lay alone in his bed. But on the other hand, he could see their relationship faltering if his work and her independence clashed. Perhaps, after all, he would delay asking her to move in. Just bide his time and wait for the moment. If it ever came.

***

Shadow Force had dispersed. Each member had a week off, although they had to remain on standby at all times. Seamus and Rose went to their respective flats and spent most of the week catching up on sleep, but texting each other every day. George returned to his family and pretended he had been away on exercise. Tim hired an MGB sports roadster and drove down to Dorset for the week.

Sam now had something extra in his life and he was coming to terms with it, with increasing excitement. He and Geraldine had been on four dates. For the first time in his life, he was no longer over-conscious of his size. She had disarmed him by flirting with him outrageously. After the third date, he knew instinctively that she was stronger than him. It was difficult to define. He was twice her weight and more than a foot taller, but she was a Queen Boadicea. He didn't mind. On the contrary.

Gibson had work to do. He had been asked by the prime minister to write up a full report on everything Shadow Force had been involved in over the previous few weeks. It was not for general circulation. It was a personal report for the prime minister alone. Not even the foreign secretary was to get a copy.

When Jonathan Ford read the twenty-four-page report, he was satisfied that Shadow Force still had merit and value. The trial of Joseph Paine had come close to exposing the secret group, but neither Paine nor his lawyers referred to Shadow Force by name. Why would they? No such organisation officially existed. Even the judge in the Old Bailey trial had no inkling of Shadow Force. The two words had never passed the lips of anyone in the courtroom. And most importantly, the words had never appeared in the media. Not even on Sky News, which had led the way throughout the crisis.

The prime minister smiled. It was a good feeling.

***

The MI5 Russian mole, codename Svekla, finished up for the day. The mole's boss, Geraldine Hammer, had been in a particularly amicable mood. She smiled more than usual and had been spotted on more than one occasion looking dreamy. At least that was the description that went around the office.

The mole wasn't smiling and looked tense. But it was 7 p.m. Time to leave.

Outside on the steps of Thames House overlooking the river, Svekla saw Geraldine Hammer talking to someone from another branch of MI5.

Geraldine waved.

"Bye, Amelia, see you tomorrow," she shouted.

Amelia Prendergast, Geraldine's secretary, personal assistant and Russian spy, waved back and walked off towards Parliament Square.

With her Russian controller codenamed Venedict expelled, she wondered when his replacement would get in touch.

Author Profile

After sixteen years as a reporter with the Daily Express, Michael Evans moved to The Times in 1986, where he became Defence Correspondent and then Defence Editor. He developed a reputation for having some of the best contacts in the defence, military and intelligence world. He covered six wars in the field including Bosnia, Kosovo, Iraq and Afghanistan. From 2010 to 2013, he was The Times' first Pentagon Correspondent based in Washington DC.

Back in London, he still writes extensively on defence and intelligence issues for The Times. The author of four fiction books, one of them for children, and four non-fiction, including a memoir, First With the News, he is married with three sons and writes a daily blog on world issues called michaelevansbook.blogspot.com and also tweets every day, @MikeEvansTimes

www.michaelevansauthor.co.uk

What did you think of
Shadow Lives?

If you enjoyed this book and would like to share your reaction, please post a review on Amazon, however brief.

<u>Publisher Information</u>

Rowanvale Books provides publishing services to independent authors, writers and poets all over the globe. We deliver a personal, honest and efficient service that allows authors to see their work published, while remaining in control of the process and retaining their creativity. By making publishing services available to authors in a cost-effective and ethical way, we at Rowanvale Books hope to ensure that the local, national and international community benefits from a steady stream of good quality literature.

For more information about us, our authors or our publications, please get in touch.

www.rowanvalebooks.com
info@rowanvalebooks.com

CPSIA information can be obtained
at www.ICGtesting.com
Printed in the USA
BVHW072020251122
652783BV00005B/81

9 781914 422089